P9-EJT-771

WITHDRAWN

THE
POETRY
OF
SECRETS

THE
POETRY
OF
SECRETS

Cambria Gordon

SCHOLASTIC PRESS / NEW YORK

Copyright © 2021 by Cambria Gordon

Peacock photo ©: Morphart Creation/Shutterstock.

All rights reserved. Published by Scholastic Press, an imprint of Scholastic Inc., *Publishers since 1920*. SCHOLASTIC, SCHOLASTIC PRESS, and associated logos are trademarks and/or registered trademarks of Scholastic Inc.

The publisher does not have any control over and does not assume any responsibility for author or third-party websites or their content.

No part of this publication may be reproduced, stored in a retrieval system, or transmitted in any form or by any means, electronic, mechanical, photocopying, recording, or otherwise, without written permission of the publisher. For information regarding permission, write to Scholastic Inc., Attention: Permissions Department, 557 Broadway, New York, NY 10012.

This book is a work of fiction. Names, characters, places, and incidents are either the product of the author's imagination or are used fictitiously, and any resemblance to actual persons, living or dead, business establishments, events, or locales is entirely coincidental.

Library of Congress Cataloging-in-Publication Data available

ISBN 978-1-338-63418-1

1 2020

Printed in the U.S.A.   23
First edition, February 2021

Book design by Baily Crawford

For Howard

OCTOBER 1481

Trujillo, Kingdom of Castile, Spain

1

The day Isabel followed a handsome stranger into an alleyway, her grandmother's words echoed in her head: *Your impulsivity will be the death of you.* But Isabel could not help herself. In these moments, it was as if an unseen physical force took over her body, compelling her to act and ignore the consequences. She had been sitting on her favorite writing bench in the plaza mayor, the main town square, working on a poem, when an older couple strolled by her bench.

"Whatever could you be scribbling, my dear girl?" remarked the woman, nostrils swollen.

Isabel was glad she had dabbed rose water on her neck this morning, as the woman was very close and, unlike Isabel, she smelled foul. The woman leaned over to get a better view of Isabel's notebook, her giant linen headdress jutting in two points, looking like a horned animal ready to charge. "Why, those are words! Shouldn't you be at home, learning a new stitch?"

Isabel ground her top and bottom teeth together.

"What's our world coming to," said the woman's male companion, the corners of his lips dipping down, "when young ladies can read and write like grandees?"

This was not the first time someone had rudely commented on what Isabel was doing on that bench, but she could tolerate it no longer. "Well, *this* young lady thinks there's more to life than embroidery, gossiping, and chewing búcaro," Isabel blurted.

The handsome stranger darted past right then. Isabel threw her writing materials into her leather satchel and ran, leaving the couple standing there, mouths agape.

He looked older than her, perhaps eighteen or twenty. She had not seen him before, which was unusual, their village being so small. His shoulder-length dark hair was tied in a cord, and he wore hose and black leather boots under a belted green doublet.

She began a made-up conversation between them, based on the poem she had just penned.

Her: A lifetime without love is of no account.

Him: Love is the water of life.

Her: Drink it down with heart and soul.

She knew people didn't speak in that way. She simply liked imagining having someone in her life who was as passionate about love as she was. At sixteen, she was still unbetrothed, and despite her romantic notions, she relished her freedom. Dios help her if she were married to a proper Spanish gentleman. He'd never allow her to write. Maybe she wouldn't wed at all and would become a famous poet instead. Later this evening, a public poetry reading was being held in the Moorish quarter, and for the first time, Isabel thought she might be brave enough to stand up and actually recite one of her own works.

Just inside a narrow alley, the striking young man paused and turned halfway around. She caught a glimpse of his profile. Long lashes, skin smooth and uncovered by beard. He darted into a tannery and she thought about walking right into the store to get a good view of him. But she did not. Practicality outweighed impulsivity. She needed to get back. It was Friday evening and the sun was almost setting. Sighing, she gathered up the layers of her skirt and reversed direction over the cobblestones.

A religious processional approached from the west, blocking her way. Though these were common in Trujillo, Isabel never got used to them. She waited for the macabre scene to pass her by, her eyes on the ground so she wouldn't have to watch the leather scourges break the flesh on the backs of the penitents. The ends of the cords held wax balls laced with filings of tin and splinters of colored glass. It was all so barbaric.

When she could finally cross the street, she hurried to where the paved road changed to dirt just outside town. She purposely let her dress drag in the dust. The dirtier the better. Another five minutes' walk and she'd be home.

At the mouth of a narrow, winding alley, Diego smelled the scent of roses behind him. He paused, wanting to see where it came from, but his father's voice buzzed in his brain like a trapped fly. "It's time you learned the family business!"

Family business, mi culo, he thought. My arse. As the son of Count Altamirano, Diego must learn how to recognize the proper forks for fish and meat, play the lute, and become adept at courtly flirtations.

There was no part of that life he wanted to lead.

His father had sent word to Diego at University of Coimbra in Portugal, where he was in his second year. Enough frivolous pursuits in art and philosophy. It was time to do his duty for the Crown and act the part of the noble title he was to inherit. Diego supposed he should be grateful for the education he had been afforded so far. Unlike other sons of aristocrats, he did not have to become a page and train in a royal household. His parents enrolled him in grammar school to learn Latin, and then later, when he asked, allowed him to attend college. But there was an urgency in his father's latest letter, and Diego had been unable to refuse him. When the family horse and carriage had shown up to fetch him at his leased house near campus, he was resigned.

Upon arriving home, he and his father had argued.

"Why now?" Diego asked.

"Our family is part of the Order of Chivalry. Whether you desire it or not, you will inherit my title."

"But I want to be a painter, you know that."

"Stop with that nonsense," said the count. "If you

must have art in your life, then become a patron and buy some devotionals to adorn your walls."

"I want to be of use to society, Father."

"Then help me with tax and rent collection."

Diego had acquiesced, as he always did.

Thus he found himself today, trudging through the streets and alleyways of Trujillo, meeting all the tenants on the Altamirano estate. He stood at the entrance to a tannery, the putrid smell of grimy animal skins soaking in urine nearly making him back out. At this very moment, his own classmates, dressed in short cassocks and square caps, were probably reading philosophy. Or perhaps even studying the techniques of the painter Verrocchio and his young apprentice Leonardo da Vinci. Diego's favorite professor was likely gesticulating in that comical way he had, with one elbow in the air. He had recommended Diego for an artist guild in Lisbon earlier this year, but Diego had not even bothered asking his father. Sons of highborns didn't join guilds.

A customer buying a horse saddle exited and the tanner turned his attention to Diego. Just in time. Thinking about philosophy and famous paintings had made Diego want to toss his dagger at something and shout obscenities. He needed to act the part of a count-in-training. Let the cursed tax collection begin.

Seville, region of Andalucía, Spain

Fray Tomás Torquemada blew out the candle and lay down on his wooden board. His coarse pants and tunic irritated his skin, but this was how he preferred it. Pain was purification. The only way to salvation. Sleep would not come easy to him this evening. Tomorrow was the first day of the Order of the Inquisition and he would be riding from the capital to spread the gospel to those Godforsaken, uncivilized villages all over the country. A vein in his neck pulsed with anticipation. Maybe he should wash, a ritual cleansing, to calm down? No, that's what the dirty Jews did before the Sabbath. A lot of good it did them. They could never wash off the impurities. The filth was under their skin. Even worse than the Jews were the conversos, heretics the lot of them.

He rolled onto his side, the hard surface digging into his shoulder. Torquemada had not always been his surname. But it was apt. It meant twist and burn. How fitting that he would be the one making the converso sinners writhe in the flames of the stake. Who better to ferret out the false Christians than someone who descended from Jews himself? He must point his finger the hardest so it would never be turned on him. He sat up and spat for good measure into his chamber pot. Those once-Jewish converso swine belonged where he voided his own waters each morning.

Finally, his queen had understood! All those years of listening to her foolish childhood confessions had paid off. She and that weak husband of hers, King Ferdinand, had seen the light of reason. He, Tomás, would get to fulfill his lifelong dream of uniting Spain under one Christian God. Sin was the only reason his country had been divided. The sin of tainted blood running through the veins of conversos, sullying good Christians by inter-marrying and breeding with them. These impostors were liars, converting and being baptized in public, but Judaizing in private, lighting candles on Fridays and eating all that horrid food fried in oil. Not to mention cutting off a piece of skin on the male sex organ. It was unholy, altering the body God chose for you. Eliminating them once and for all was the key to redemption. He would lead the charge of the limpieza, the cleaning of the coun-try, and personally see that the punishment equaled the crime. He whispered the words of Saint Vicente Ferrer. Per quae peccat quis, per haec et torquetur. We are tortured for our sins.

He had never felt this assured. He was a hunter. And he would not quit until all his prey was annihilated.

2

Entering the house, Isabel set her satchel down on a small oak table. Beatriz, her younger sister by just a year, stood at the door to the cellar, tying a ribbon on her linen dress. Isabel scooted in front of her. Beatriz swatted her on the behind, but Isabel grinned. She had made it down first.

The sudden shift from warm to cold always made Isabel shiver as she descended the stone steps to the lower level of the house.

"How I hate eating dinner down here in this dank, frigid prison of a room," complained Beatriz behind her.

"And you never miss an opportunity to remind us how you feel," Isabel hissed back.

"Hurry, girls," called Abuela, who was already there with Mamá and Papá, putting the finishing touches on the table.

Mamá eyed the bottom of Isabel's gown. "Nice and dirty. A fine job. No one will think you put on your Friday best."

The fruity aroma of grapes mixed with the scent of freshly baked bread. Isabel loved it down here, under the arched ceilings, away from the dust and horse manure of the streets of Trujillo. Even though the ground was not paved in their cellar, the dirt floor stayed compact. The white lace cloth lay perfectly crisp across the table. Isabel had taken the linen smoother herself this morning, dampening the material as she pressed out the wrinkles.

Sitting on top was a pair of tall silver candlestick holders, standing at attention like sentries, wearing soldier's hats of small white candles. Papá covered his thinning hair with his good skullcap, the one with the garnet and gold thread. Mamá used a flint and fire steel to light the taper, then used the taper to light the candles. She covered her eyes and recited the women's prayer in Aljamiado, a mix of Hebrew and Spanish. *"Kun estas kandelas, arrogamos al Dio, el Dio de muestros padres, Avram, Isak, i Yakov, ke muz de vida saludoza."* With these candles, we pray to God, the God of our fathers, Abraham, Isaac, and Jacob, to grant us good life and health.

The timbre of Mamá's voice was confident, knowing she was safe, hidden away from the prying eyes of nosy neighbors and Church officials.

Most people in Trujillo assumed their cellar was only for the pressing, fermentation, and bottling of wine. Papá's vino tinto, made from grapes he imported from a nearby farm, was known throughout the region, and his distinct green bottle could be found in the homes of many nobles and important people in local government. But the cellar also held another purpose. Their hidden weekly Shabbat dinners.

The Perez family were conversos. Throughout the four kingdoms of Spain, there were thousands of people just like them, both Muslims and Jews, known as the converted ones. Though Isabel and her family were Christian on the outside, attending church diligently every Sunday, and even displaying Jesús on his cross in their sala so no one would question their devotion, they were part of a small minority who still maintained their original traditions in private.

By now Isabel was used to her family's strange rituals

belowground; she didn't even think twice about it. But this wasn't always the case. Her earliest memory was of being a small, frightened girl, sitting at the cellar table in the eerie glow of candlelight. Papá had looked at Isabel and Beatriz, then ages five and four, and declared, "It's time you learned the truth." He paused dramatically. "We are Crypto-Jews."

"Are we mummies?" Isabel had asked, thinking of corpses lying in underground caves.

"No, cariña, we're secret Jews," Papá clarified, slightly amused.

Mamá's face became dark and serious. "Listen to me very carefully, girls. You must never tell anyone what we do down here."

"But I can tell the Cohens?" Isabel asked, thinking of their dear Jewish friends and the new twins Señora Cohen had just birthed.

Papá shook his head. "Not even them. Someone might overhear."

That didn't seem fair! "The Cohens have Friday night dinners aboveground, out in the open," Isabel whined. "Why should we have to hide?"

"There are laws against conversos Judaizing," explained Mamá, "which means participating in Jewish traditions. You would not be safe if the wrong person learned of our weekly ceremony." She took hold of the girls' hands. "From now on, ensure that you have dirt under your nails and your dresses are sullied every Friday. That way no one will think we are preparing for Shabbat. Keep our secret deep in your heart and not on your lips." Then she made them swear and vow in the king's name never to reveal the truth.

Over the years, Isabel had found it easy to keep the promise, to follow along with her parents' traditions and accept their double life.

With the candle blessing complete, everyone took their seats except Isabel, who was lost in thought. Not about the memory of her first cellar dinner, but about the reading this evening. She had already memorized the poem she'd written, so that wasn't what concerned her. How was she going to slip out of the house unnoticed and get to the Moorish quarter?

"Isabel, we're waiting!" said Mamá.

"Sorry," she mumbled, pulling out her chair.

With no son to bless since Isabel and Beatriz's baby brother, Rodrigo, or Ruy as they called him, had died last winter, Papá turned to his daughters, resting his hands on each of their heads. Beatriz flinched, moving away from Papá's touch. Isabel leaned in to give him this small pleasure.

"May you be like Sarah, Rebecca, Leah, and Rachel," said Papá. "May God bless you and guard you. May God show you kindness and grant you peace."

Abuela then recited the blessing over the bread. "Take some challah, Eva." Abuela always addressed Isabel by her Hebrew name down in the cellar, never the name she received at the baptismal font. Isabel actually preferred Eva. It was prettier. She did not appreciate being named after Queen Isabella. The woman was a fickle ruler, and ugly to boot.

Abuela passed the bread plate to Beatriz. "You too, Malka."

"That's not my name."

"It wouldn't hurt you to acknowledge it every once in a while," Isabel snapped at her sister.

"There was talk today in the taberna," said Papá. "Someone thought they saw an Inquisition spy standing in the corner by the bar."

"Here in Trujillo?" said Mamá.

Papá nodded. "They were watching who was eating pork and who was not. Luckily, I had not ordered any food, even though someone nearby called me out as a Marrano."

"He called you a pig?" asked Isabel.

"To Spaniards, *Marrano* is just another word for a Jewish converso," explained Papá. "Like *Morisco* is another word for a Muslim converso."

"That's hardly the same thing," said Isabel, not appreciating being equated with swine. "At least *Morisco* sounds like the word *Moor*."

"I prefer the term *New Christian*," said Beatriz.

Papá's eyebrows joined together in distress. "Make no mistake. The authorities are waiting for conversos like us to backslide into Judaism. And not just in tabernas. In carnicerías, keeping track of who buys meat during Lent and who doesn't. In church, noticing who snickers at the mention of Madre Mary, and who is solemn."

"I never smile at Santa Madre's name," said Beatriz.

"Yes, you're the perfect Christian," said Isabel.

Beatriz tossed back her head, her hair nearly whipping Isabel in the face.

Isabel was well aware of the tenuous ground the conversos walked on. The Jews judged them for rolling over, for converting too easily and turning their backs on God. The Christians accused them of tainting the blood of their children by intermarrying with Old Christian nobility. But Inquisition spies in their midst? This was new.

Papá swirled the wine in his glass, checking for sediment. "We must all be vigilant. A knock on the door at night might not mean a friendly visitor."

"Who, then?" Isabel asked.

"A story was told today of someone's cousin in Seville denounced for heresy."

"Heretics are the devil," said Beatriz.

Papá shook his head at her. "Heretics are anyone who does not believe what the majority believes." He then looked at the rest of them. "They took this cousin away in the black of night. He was asked to name other heretics. He thought quickly and named a dead aunt. The inquisitors dug up the aunt's bones and burned them."

"Manolo, por favor," said Mamá. "Not at the table."

Isabel's hands grew cold and she tucked them under her thighs. "That could never happen here in quiet Trujillo."

"Let us hope not," said Papá.

Beatriz set down her glass too hard and some water spilled out onto Isabel's well-ironed cover. "If you were clear in your own mind, Papá, these little trips to the taberna wouldn't be a problem for you."

"What are you referring to?"

"Are you Christian or Jewish?" demanded Beatriz.

"I am in between," answered Papá.

Was this why Isabel didn't feel connected to the religious fervor around her and worshipped Rumi, Ibn Arabi, and the other Muslim poets of Spain instead? Because she lived in the "in between"?

"The Cohens are Jewish. Señora Herrera is Old Christian. Even Zahra knew who she was," said Beatriz, her voice escalating. "They are black and white, and we live in the gray."

"I hope you weren't discussing religion with our servant," admonished Mamá, who had relieved Zahra, a Muslim, from her duties last month. It was becoming too great a risk to employ a worker who might gossip in town about their weekly rituals.

"Look around you, Papá," said Beatriz, ignoring Mamá. "This whole country is Christian! When are you going to accept it?"

"When they accept us," he growled.

Did he mean as Jews or conversos? Isabel wondered. She thought about Don Abraham Senior, the trusted tax-farmer-in-chief to King Ferdinand and Queen Isabella. He kept his Jewish religion and did not convert, yet he had achieved great power and access to the crown. But she remained quiet. She did not want to defy her father.

"Plenty of New Christians hold high positions," continued Beatriz. "Constanza's father sits in the government council."

"I'm speaking about anti-Jewish laws spanning hundreds of years, frenzied mobs attacking innocents," said Papá, his voice strident. "The Jews have been forced to leave every country we have ever lived in. We are blamed for plagues, floods, economic hardship. Old Christians would say it's our fault their hair turned gray if they could."

"You're being ridiculous," argued Beatriz. "Old Christians simply want to live among others who are like them."

Abuela cleared her throat. With a trembling finger, she pointed at Beatriz. "And God said, you shall not wrong a stranger or oppress him. For you were strangers in the land of Egypt." She lowered her hand. "Now eat some bread."

Beatriz pulled off a chunk of the braided loaf and slid down in her chair. Silent, for the moment. But Isabel knew it would only be a matter of time until she started up again.

Where Papá held on to his Jewish history for politically defiant reasons, Mamá for nostalgia and comfort with what was familiar, Abuela was a true believer. Isabel felt guilty that she did not believe in Abuela's God with the same passion, for Isabel loved her grandmother the deepest. The one gift she was able to give Abuela, however, was that unlike most privileged young Spanish women, Isabel was lettered. Abuela had taught Isabel to read and write years ago, down in this very cellar. Abuela's own father had taught his daughter to read in the same way, by candlelight in their room belowground.

"Let's not argue on the Sabbath anymore," said Mamá, ladling out portions of adefina, a stew of lamb, aubergine, and bulgur wheat flavored with garlic and pepper. It was the same each Friday. The hot dish would lie covered over a low fire all night so Mamá would not have to cook on the Jewish day of rest. It would still be warm for lunch tomorrow.

The conversation turned to lighter matters. Specifically, new dress fabric the girls would need for the christening of Señora Herrera's granddaughter.

Beatriz turned to Mamá eagerly. "Can we pay a visit to Señor Cohen's studio tomorrow?"

Yuçe and Rachel's father sold the most beautiful cloth in all of Trujillo. Isabel and her sister had a closetful of dresses sewn from his fabrics. Taffetas for Christmas and Easter, threaded with reds and yellows and golds; velvet and woolens in violet and emerald for when they went calling. Yuçe, now just eleven years old, would take over the business one day.

"Tomorrow is the Sabbath," said Mamá. "David doesn't work on Saturday, you know that. But it also happens to be the Feast of the Booths, Sucot. After sundown, we will go to the Cohens' for dinner."

"We shouldn't be celebrating Jewish holidays out in the open," said Beatriz.

"It's hardly out in the open. It's in the judería," said Mamá, referring to the neighborhood where all the Jews had been forced to move last spring. It was a chaotic time, Isabel remembered. The Cohens had to sell their lovely home and work studio to a Christian family and purchase a smaller house in the Jewish quarter. Mamá had told her they lost maravedis on the sale.

Beatriz scowled. "As long as I can buy some new fabric."

"We won't be able to exchange money," clarified Papá. "But you can shop and choose fabric to be picked up later."

Isabel was looking forward to the evening. It felt like ages since she had seen the twins.

Papá turned to Isabel. "In the meantime, tomorrow after sunup will be ledger day."

"Tomorrow?" she groaned.

Papá's lips folded inward. "I'm behind as it is."

Isabel was devoted to her father and knew the freedom he granted her was conditional on her fulfilling certain family duties. She was the eldest child and would one day inherit the vineyards (only to have to relinquish them to some blaffard husband as part of a dowry), but that also meant that more was required of her. Papá's accounts of bottles sold and money owed would take hours to transcribe, hours she preferred to fill composing poems. With the extra work, there were advantages, though. Namely, that her parents viewed her differently from other girls her age and gave her more leeway. They used to make Zahra travel everywhere with her as a duenna or companion. But since the servant girl was no longer in the Perez employ, and Abuela could not keep up with Isabel's pace, they allowed Isabel to walk through town unaccompanied. Like today, when she briefly followed that young man. "Of course, I'll find the time."

The clock tower on the Iglesia de Santiago chimed ten. The

poetry reading would be starting at half past the hour. Isabel had an idea. "I think I'll start on those ledgers tonight," she announced, rising to clear the dishes. If they thought she had stayed down here in the cellar working, they would not look for her. And her nosy sister wouldn't wonder why she was not abed in their shared room.

A rumbling noise came from upstairs. Isabel nearly dropped the stack of plates in her hand. Someone was banging on the door, insistent as a barking dog.

3

"I have nothing to hide," said Beatriz, sliding her chair back calmly. "I'll get the door."

Isabel's heart was thrumming too fast to think of a clever comeback to her sister's superiority. The rest of the family followed Beatriz upstairs, but not before Mamá had blown out the Shabbat candles, and Abuela shut the cellar door behind them.

"Everyone, take your place in the sala," whispered Papá.

Isabel took up her sewing kit and tried not to stare at the cellar door. If the wrong person went down there before the dishes were cleared, they would be doomed. Abuela found the silver polish and began working on a chalice. Papá busied himself stuffing his pipe.

When Beatriz swept open the front door, there stood the alguacil, the town constable. Don Sancho del Aguila was at least twenty-five years older than Isabel, maybe even older than Papá. In his black cape lined with fox fur and his plumed hat, he would have looked distinguished if not for the yellowing teeth and webs of red veins on both his cheeks.

"Don Sancho," said Papá. "Please come in."

What could his presence mean? Could this be the roundup Papá had heard so much talk about? Yet the alguacil was alone.

Perhaps that was a good sign? How many people did it take to drag away a heretic?

Beatriz moved to open the shutters on their balcony window, on the street side. Madre mía! The wooden cross hanging on the opposite wall was crooked. It could be viewed as a sign of disrespect toward the Holy One, causing suspicion. Isabel tried to signal to her, but her sister wasn't looking. There was no time to straighten it. If it came to that, Isabel would say they had only just used it to pray with.

"I've come to order some vino tinto," Don Sancho said.

"Wonderful news!" said Papá, smiling. "I mean," he continued more soberly, "I'd be happy to oblige you."

Mamá audibly let out her breath. "Please, let me take your cloak and hat. Make yourself comfortable." Then she fluttered about as a bird, bringing Don Sancho brandy, olives, and nuts.

"It's my Patron Saint's Day next week," said Don Sancho, lowering himself onto a divan. "Sanctius. The brave soul was impaled by the Moors in Córdoba."

Between his yellowing teeth and the vision of impalement, Isabel felt like she might vomit up her stew.

"And you plan to have a feast with wine to go with it," guessed Papá.

Don Sancho regarded Isabel, who remained on the settee. "My mother"—he made the sign of the cross in her memory—"used to prepare the traditional saint's feast every year. I need a wife to do it for me now." He licked his lips, as if he were considering Isabel for a meal.

Papá and Mamá exchanged a glance. They seemed to be on her side, offended at the way he looked at Isabel, too. Papá leaned forward. "The Tempranillo grapes are tasting especially rich. The farm in Plasencia from which I import them had a good crop this season."

"And from all appearances," said Don Sancho, cracking open a pistachio nut, "you've had a successful selling season, too. This home has, what, five rooms?"

"Does it?" said Papá, obviously uncomfortable with this talk of status. Old Christians of such impeccable lineage as Don Sancho did not appreciate seeing New Christians doing as well financially as the Perezes. Isabel learned long ago not to arouse the envy of the other girls by wearing too fancy a dress. Beatriz was the opposite. The more ornate the better.

"Perhaps you'd like to do a wine tasting, to choose something appropriate for your party?" continued Papá. "I have some opened bottles in the kitchen. Or better yet, I can bring you a sampling of the different grapes. Tempranillo, Garnacha Tintorera, Merlot . . ."

"What I'd prefer to see is your wine press," said Don Sancho, standing up. "I've heard rumors that the iron screw and capstan were soldered back when the Reconquista began."

Isabel leapt from her settee. "Forgive us, Don Sancho. But it's a mess down in the wine cellar. Baskets of grapes everywhere. You can't even open the door more than a sliver. Another time?" She didn't wait for an answer. "I'll just slip downstairs and bring you some grapes to sample."

Don Sancho looked pleased to be attended by Isabel. He nodded and sat back down, his thumbs in his armpits. "Very well."

When she returned, the men were discussing the latest criminal activity in the community. Beatriz had seated herself on a floor cushion and taken up Isabel's sewing. Mamá held a handful of empty pistachio shells, still as a statue. It seemed to Isabel that her mother might never leave her spot lest Don Sancho crack open another nut. Isabel gave Don Sancho the grapes and his hand touched hers briefly. Clammy. It was all she could do not to recoil.

"Nine hundred head of sheep stolen, coin clipping, and a wealthy Jewish widow had adulterous relations with a married Christian man. And that was just this week," Don Sancho said.

"Did they recover the sheep?" asked Papá.

"Not yet. But how far can nine hundred sheep roam?" Don Sancho's belly rose up and down as he chuckled.

Papá twiddled his thumbs. "And the widow. What sort of fine will she receive?" Papá's tone seemed cavalier, as if he didn't really care what the answer to his question was, but Isabel knew there was more to it. He always circled his thumbs when he was nervous.

Don Sancho huffed. "Six thousand maravedis. But that won't be sufficient. She will ride through town on a donkey so everyone will know her crimes. Then the Christian, poor soul, must be questioned to see if he came under the influence of any evil thoughts from the Jewess." As warden for Trujillo, it was Don Sancho's job to keep the peace, and mete out proper punishment. Even if what he considered appropriate might seem too harsh to Isabel's ears. Owing more money than Papá made in a year, plus public shaming, simply for loving the wrong person? Honestly.

Don Sancho tasted the grapes and smacked his lips loudly. "Juicy," he said, looking directly at Isabel. "I'll take five cases of the Tempranillo." He stood up.

Beatriz retrieved his cape and hat and curtsied to him before she handed them over. Isabel wanted to yank the coat from her hands and thrust it at Don Sancho. Why was everyone in the family being so deferential?

"We must enjoy these frivolities while we can," said Don

Sancho at the door. "The war in Granada is coming. Soon all extra funds will be needed for the effort."

"Indeed," said Papá.

Don Sancho raised his plumed hat. "May this be the final battle in the long Reconquista! A una España unida!" To a united Spain.

Isabel saw her grandmother shift uncomfortably. Isabel knew what Abuela was thinking. As a Jew deep in her heart, Abuela would never salute, *To the Reconquista!* Because a united Spain meant one united in Church and Crown. One religion for all. Which left no room for people like the Cohens and all practicing Jews on God's green earth. Isabel put her finger to her lips for Abuela to keep quiet.

Papá hesitated for a moment, then lifted his pipe. "To the Reconquista."

4

Everyone was in a state of agitation once Don Sancho left. Or so Isabel thought.

"What a serendipitous visit that turned out to be," said Mamá happily as she and the girls went down to clear the table in the cellar. The oil lamps burning in the sala and kitchen cast a beacon of light into the darkness below.

"He couldn't leave quickly enough, as far as I'm concerned," said Isabel.

"I thought he was impressive," said Beatriz, "with that sparkly ring and his fine clothes."

"Appearances aren't everything," Isabel retorted.

"I expected someone in his position to be greedy with power, but he was quite friendly," said Beatriz.

Isabel curled her upper lip in scorn.

"You wore that same sour expression his entire visit," said Beatriz. "Maybe if you'd wiped it off your face, your eyes would have seen who he truly is."

"The true Don Sancho is a salivating hunchbacked toad," declared Isabel.

Beatriz piled glasses on a tray. "How nice it must be to go through life so blithely that you can just discount a person because of the way they look."

"It wasn't the way he looked," corrected Isabel. "It was the way he looked at *me*."

Beatriz colored. "Again, how nice for you."

"Enough of this age-old argument," piped in Mamá. "You both have your gifts."

Beatriz stopped in the middle of the cellar steps. "Don't patronize me, Mother. You may live to regret it."

Mamá waved her hand at Beatriz. "Take those glasses upstairs before you drop them."

The bells of the church tower rang out faintly, though Isabel could still hear them from her spot belowground. She counted the tolls. God's boils! It was half past the hour, the time of the poetry reading. If she didn't leave now, she'd miss it entirely. "Mamá, why don't you and Beatriz go to bed," suggested Isabel. "Let me finish clearing the table. I want to get a head start on those ledgers this evening anyway."

Mamá looked surprised, but acquiesced. And Beatriz was more than happy to get out of cleaning up.

With everyone retired to their rooms, Isabel donned her cloak, took her leather satchel, and quietly left the house. She'd have a load of cleaning up to do later, but she didn't care.

The first time she'd stumbled into a reading, she had been wandering through the Moorish quarter looking for a poetry book by Rumi, when a notice tacked to a stone wall caught her eye. In the top corner was a charming drawing of a hummingbird drinking nectar from a flower. It was written in Arabic, but she asked a turbaned man nearby to translate it for her. The gentleman used the Castilian words recital de poesía, recitation of poetry. It was to take place that very night, in the upper plaza on the hill. She paid a page one coin to get a message to Mamá that she would be home late, and went. As the sky shifted from purple to slate, and the sweet scent of jasmine filled the air, the event began. Isabel assumed someone would read aloud from a well-known book of poems. But that was not what happened. They were original works! A few poets held parchment paper, while others performed from memory. It had been the most thrilling evening she had ever experienced.

As she hurried along the quiet streets tonight, it dawned on Isabel that the threat Papá spoke about, being carted off in the middle of the night by the Inquisition, applied to Moriscos, too. Many Muslim converts to Christianity secretly practiced their former religion, like the Perezes did, and they largely made up the audience at these readings. They were also the enemy of the Crown, as the Moors still held Granada, the last Muslim stronghold that prevented a united Christian Spain. Not all of the poems at these readings were about love. Some were about the Jewish God or Allah, which might offend an Old Christian within earshot. The innocent poetry readings could now be fraught with unintended blasphemy. What if Don Sancho and his foot soldiers raided tonight?

But when she arrived, she tossed the idea out of her head. Everything was so beautiful it seemed impossible anything bad could happen here. Colored blankets were strewn across the benches, and lanterns flickered everywhere, making the atmosphere warm and inviting. Isabel found one of the last seats on a sandstone bench, one of many rows carved into the hill like an amphitheater. Next to each seat were goblets. A servant boy scurried in and out, pouring wine. Someone plucked strings on a lute. She couldn't tell if the reading hadn't yet begun, or if they were between sets, but at the moment, the large crowd buzzed with conversation. The men and women seemed to be from all classes of Muslim society. Some had bright turbans on their heads, and wore fancy, billowing pants, covered by tunics tied at the waist in different fabric. Others looked like they had rolled in from their sleeping corner on the street.

The crowd hushed as a veiled girl began to recite in Spanish.

> *"O young buck, adrift in the brush, take heed of the*
> > *rustling sound*
> *It is not the hunter, but I, your doe, who will bring*
> > *you to the Heavens."*

Then a second person, a young man, stood up and improvised a concluding verse in the same rhyme and meter the girl had used.

> *"O young doe, I see you there, drinking from the*
> > *brook*
> *I don't fear the hunter's bow, for it is I, with sharp*
> > *arrow to thrust."*

The crowd cheered, approving of the wit and flirtation of both readers. It went on like this for a long time, with people randomly reciting and others taking the parlay. A girl sitting near Isabel, who looked to be about the same age as her, stood up. She had long black hair and eyes the color of clear blue sky. In accented Castilian, she began.

> *"Her lover blows the flute,*
> *tempting snakes upward from his basket*

but though she wants to succumb to his charms, she
cannot
for under her veil flows royal blood
Her father, the king, will smite him down, driving a
sword through his chest, the blood blossoming
on his working-class shirt
So she remains watching, undulating inside his
oasis."

No one stood up to add to her poem. It spoke for itself.

Finally, the moderator, a deep-voiced Moor, asked if there were any more poets in the audience. They had time for one more. Isabel's heart pounded against her ribs. Slowly, she lifted herself off the bench, but then a man in front stood and beat her to it. She sat back down, both relieved and angry, though which emotion was dominant she couldn't say.

Afterward, she approached the dark-haired poetess. "I enjoyed your poem." Up close, Isabel could see that the girl fell more into the street urchin category of attendees, her face smudged with dirt.

"Gracias." The girl stuck out her hand, her blue eyes twinkling. "My name is Atika. I live over in the Gypsy camp."

So she was a Romani, thought Isabel, preferring the more proper description. Atika had used the common term, Isabel assumed for her benefit, but she knew it wasn't really the correct term. Because of their dark skin, Spaniards wrongly assumed the Romani were from North Africa and started calling them Gypsies, from the word *Egypt*. Like the name Marrano, it didn't feel right. "We live at the base of the vineyards on the edge of town. My father is a wine producer."

"Yet you're lettered."

"How could you know that?"

"Most people recite from memory," said Atika. "You stood out tonight."

Isabel said nothing, aware of her higher status in both dress and leather notebook.

"Are you Jewish?" asked Atika. "Everyone knows they are the bookish ones."

Isabel laughed. "They are, but not the women, unfortunately. Actually, I am New Christian." She felt the need to categorize herself, even though Atika probably didn't think twice about the distinctions between conversos and practicing Jews. In fact, Atika's life was likely much more interesting than Isabel's own provincial one. "Tell me about your family."

"My father, Vano, came from a long line of Italians who came to Spain over one hundred years ago," explained Atika. "My mother was Muslim, originally from India, but was sold into slavery when she arrived in Gibraltar at the age of thirteen."

"Were you raised as the daughter of a slave?"

"Not exactly. My father saw her, this beautiful woman in a head scarf, disembark from a ship. He stood at the slave market, watching as a rich man who owned a gambling den purchased her. For months, my father followed him in secret. Then, one day, when the rich man was at the marketplace, my father began to dance around him, shaking a tambourine. The distraction was enough to pick his pocket. Guess what was inside?"

Isabel could not imagine.

"The key to the man's home! That night, my father entered with the stolen key, kidnapped the beautiful woman, and freed her. The rich gambler's body washed up on the riverbank a few nights later."

"Did Vano kill him?"

She shook her head. "It was never proven." Atika's eyes grew wet. "But he and my mother only had a short time of happiness together. She died giving birth to me."

Isabel was in awe. Here was a girl her age who had suffered so much already. Yet Atika wrote of snake charmers and oases, of sword-wielding heroes and veiled princesses—a magical world that belied the harsh reality from which she came.

They talked long after the crowd had dispersed until finally Isabel pulled herself away. The dinner dishes awaited. Isabel and Atika made plans to see each other again. Isabel knew her parents would say she should choose more appropriate girls to spend time with. But her Old and New Christian acquaintances were dull, hiding behind their tapestried walls, only going out on Sundays. In Atika, Isabel suspected she had made a like-minded friend for life.

Finished for the night, Diego found his horse where he'd left him tied earlier, by the fountain on Calle Pavo.

The animal whinnied, pleased to see him after so many hours.

Diego held out a carrot, which the horse promptly chomped entirely. "I'm sorry, old friend. Tax collecting took longer than I planned." Somewhere to his left, deep in the Arab quarter, applause and laughter pierced the quiet night. Something was going on there tonight, and for a moment, Diego thought about venturing over. But his mother liked to eat late-night supper with him when the count was traveling, and Diego knew better than to keep the countess waiting.

As he trotted home, he pictured dinner tables all over the Iberian Peninsula. And even farther away. South to the Kingdom of Fez, where the Mohammedans lived and dined on tables inlaid with mother-of-pearl. East to the Republic of Genoa, where his friend from school, Andrea Grimaldi, ate on long mahogany mesas with over twenty guests each night. And farther east to Constantinople, where Ottoman sultan Mehmed sat with his generals. Diego heard the Ottomans had built a mosque over the site of the Church of the Holy Apostles. Imagine that. Minarets and Iznik tiles replacing reliquaries containing bones of saints. The audaciousness! At each of those tables, he could almost hear their long-winded arguments, taste the flowing wine, and see the views from their windows. Views he wanted to paint.

There was a world beyond Trujillo that he longed to see. This tiny village was not his destiny. He was sure of it.

5

In the morning, the Perez family gathered in the kitchen as Mamá poured hot water into cups of fresh mint leaves. During Shabbat, she always kept a smaller container of water over the low fire, next to the bigger stew pot. Everyone stood holding their tea, except Abuela, who sat on a stool. Isabel tried not to yawn and give away the reason she hadn't slept very much, though she was pleased at how clean the kitchen looked.

"Five cases is a decent order," said Papá, blowing on his warm drink. "Though I confess, I thought Don Sancho would order more."

"It must not be a very grand party," said Beatriz. "Constanza's family and friends drank one hundred bottles for her confirmación."

"The man seems lonely," said Mamá. "He needs a wife." She turned to Isabel. "You don't actually think he's a toad, do you, cariña?"

Isabel chewed the inside of her cheek and said nothing. Perhaps that description had been a bit too harsh.

"I didn't think so," said Mamá, satisfied. "All he needs is a proper woman to take care of him."

Isabel scoffed. "Some poor, unlucky woman."

Mamá raised one eyebrow. "I'm talking about you."

Isabel took too big of a sip of tea, scalding her tongue. "What did you just say?"

"I'm saying that it's time to think of your future. You're sixteen."

"But . . . but I'm not ready!" she sputtered.

"In Abuela's day, girls became betrothed at fourteen," said Mamá.

Isabel shot her grandmother a pleading look. Why wasn't she protesting? Abuela clasped her fingers behind her back as if she was holding not only her own hands but her tongue as well.

"No one I know is even betrothed yet," said Isabel.

Mamá sipped her tea. "You can postpone the actual marriage ceremony until you're eighteen. But having a betrothal in hand brings peace of mind."

"In that case, let him wait three years until Beatriz will be eighteen," offered Isabel.

"Sadly, I'm not the firstborn," said Beatriz with no trace of sadness at all.

Isabel glared at her sister. "Yet yesterday you claimed to want him."

"You mistake admiration for desire, dear sister."

Papá cleared his throat. "Don Sancho asked for you specifically, Isabel."

Isabel was horrified. "Impossible!"

"He said as much to me, privately, while you were retrieving the grapes last night," added Papá.

"Then I refuse to accept."

"You're being ungrateful," said Mamá, looking at Beatriz.

Isabel's hands tightened into fists.

"Go fetch some water from the well," Mamá said to Beatriz. "And let us speak with Isabel alone."

Beatriz crossed her arms. "Oh, but the conversation is just getting interesting."

"You'll know all the details soon enough," said Papá. "Go on."

When Beatriz stormed out of the kitchen, Isabel did not hold her tongue. "You can't be serious!"

"Shhh," said Mamá. "We don't want the neighbors to hear."

"What, that we fight?"

"No. That you would refuse such a prestigious match as Don Sancho," said Papá.

"Forgive me. For a moment, I forgot the rules of society. Let me recite them again in case you need reminding, too. Spanish ladies of marrying age must acquiesce to the attentions of any interested male," Isabel began, "the more prestigious, the better. We must act demure and bow down in their presence. Serve them wine and meat and . . . pistachios. We must dress modestly and speak only when we are spoken to. We dare not express ourselves. We dare not have hobbies of our own. And we certainly dare not show anyone we can read or write, for we ladies might take over the world one day. And where would the prestigious bachelors be then?"

Where had all this venom inside her come from?

"It's unequal and immoral!" she yelled. "Why do the men get to decide all the rules?"

Mamá moved to close the windows. "Quiet now."

Isabel glared at her parents. "Why must you always be so worried about what other people think?" Her life, her plans were being ruined and all they cared about was the neighbors.

"As conversos, it goes with the territory," admitted Mamá.

"Well, I'm sick of the territory. Every step I take is a lie." Isabel had no idea she felt this way until now.

"I know our double life has been hard," said Papá. "And you've been exemplary at keeping the secret. It's not fair that we're asking you for even more sacrifice." He paused. "But truth be told, this isn't about being fair. That sentiment buys us nothing. This is a matter of survival. And our currency happens to be you."

Isabel released a bitter chuckling sound. "If that was supposed to cheer me, you failed."

"The fact remains that Don Sancho is one of the most powerful municipal officers in Trujillo. He was appointed by the king himself. No one would dare accuse us of Judaizing when our eldest daughter holds the title of Doña del Aguila. Your marriage will guarantee our safety."

"So it's up to me to save the entire family from persecution? I didn't choose this religion. You did! I did your bidding for sixteen years. Now it's my turn."

Mamá slapped Isabel's cheek. She had never raised a hand to her before.

Smarting, but not backing down, Isabel said coolly, "Well, that's it, then. I hope your insistence on identifying with Judaism was worth it."

"It *is* worth—" Abuela started.

"Not now, Abuela." Papá turned to Isabel. With a firm voice, he said, "This discussion is over. Do not challenge my decisions again, do you understand?"

Isabel wouldn't nod.

"You will obey me!" he yelled. "And you will become Doña del Aguila."

Isabel flinched. Papá rarely raised his voice. He let the girls whine, complain, rage at him, but he never yelled back.

Doña del Aguila. The name was ugly, sharp with serrated edges. It cut into her resolve, slicing the fight right out of her.

"Surely there have been other suitors who've inquired about me? Someone younger?" Her voice was quieter now, begging.

Mamá shook her head. "None so far, I'm afraid. Obviously, your countenance pleases and your talents abound. But not everyone can abide the uncertainty of marrying a converso, someone with"—she frowned—"impure blood. Thankfully, Don Sancho doesn't seem to mind."

"But what about love?" Isabel's voice was practically a whisper.

Mamá took Papá's hand. "You will grow to love him."

Isabel's eyes pricked. Her breath came in shallow bursts. She threw her teacup across the kitchen. Then she ran through the sala and out the door.

6

Trembling, she leaned against the shed in the back of their house. The chickens nested quietly in their pen, under a cloudless sky. How could the morning be this tranquil when her heart was in shards like that teacup?

A flicker of color bobbed in the foreground. A slow, shuffling sound. "Isabel?"

It was Abuela, her red scarf wrapped around her ears.

"Over here," Isabel managed to exhale.

When Abuela reached her, she took Isabel in her pudgy arms and said nothing. Just held her until the sobbing subsided.

Eventually, Isabel pulled away, pressing the heels of her palms into her eyes to stem the tears. "Are Mamá and Papá right behind you?"

"No. They sent me out alone."

"To try and talk sense into me?"

"They think I'm a better messenger."

Isabel gave a hollow laugh and the chickens began to cluck. "Better how? You approve of this match, too. I can't understand. Don't you want me to marry a Crypto-Jew? Or a converso at least?"

"I wish that were possible, mi nieta. With all my heart. But these times require us to make sacrifices."

Her words brought Isabel no comfort.

"It wasn't always this way, you know," said Abuela.

"You mean girls were not required to wed gluttonous, yellow-teethed mobards back when you were young?"

Abuela chuckled. "Long before that." She untied her scarf and held it in her hands. "Centuries ago, in the land of Al-Andalus, when Spain was ruled by the Arabs, the Jewish people could practice their religion freely and marry whom they wanted within their own faith. Some even had more than one wife!"

Isabel's hand flew to her mouth in shock.

"Polygamy was frowned upon, believe me. But the point is, not all marriages were arranged. It was a time of great communication outside of religious practices as well. Muslims, Jews, and Christians exchanged ideas about Greek philosophy, mathematics, astronomy, medicine, botany," continued Abuela. "Artists, scholars, and writers could gather together and argue or converse openly."

"Sounds like paradise," said Isabel, softening. They both leaned against the shed. She rested her head on Abuela's shoulder, feeling like she had as a child, when Abuela would stroke her forehead and lull her to sleep.

"While we were never in the majority," continued Abuela, "Jews did rise to positions of power. You could find us everywhere, from royal secretaries to administrators of buildings belonging to the Church. If a Jew felt they were being treated unjustly, they could register an official complaint to the king and queen and receive protection. But underneath all that intellectualism, the highest authorities of all three religions felt threatened. Rabbis, caliphs, priests. It frightened them when people said science was just as true as the word of God."

"And what's wrong with science?"

"It draws upon facts and reason. It doesn't rely on faith. Science brings knowledge, and with that comes a sense of control in the universe. People began to think that God did not dictate everything, that they had free will to act."

"Do you believe that?"

Abuela seemed surprised at being asked. "Certainly not. I feel safer with God in charge of my life. But don't look to me for answers. Look at Maimonides, one of the greatest Jewish thinkers in the world, from just nearby in Córdoba, believe it or not. Even he was influenced by science and philosophy. He said that both religion *and* rational thinking came from God. And that God decided humans should have free will."

What a radical way of thinking! Goose pimples appeared up and down Isabel's arms, yet there was no breeze. "I can't believe people dared to doubt the ways of the Church. It must have been a terrible controversy."

Abuela nodded, the bun she always wore pinned at her neck bobbing.

"The clerics pushed back. Persuasive Dominican and Franciscan friars wrote papers comparing the minority religions to the devil, preached hatred in town squares, and worked common folks into a fever. There was even a public debate on heresy in Barcelona between the Christians and the Jews. Actually, just one Jew, Nachmanides."

"Who won?"

"No one, I'm afraid. But it caused problems for us. The argument was over the Messiah. The Christians said that Jesús was already here. Nachmanides argued that our Messiah had not yet come. Nevertheless, after days of testimony, the Christians stopped the debate and decided the Jewish religion was invalid."

"All this fighting over ideology," said Isabel. "I had no idea."

Abuela nodded. "At the same time, the Christian kings and queens were waging wars against the Moors, reconquering cities that had been taken from them."

This Isabel did know about. Everyone did. When the Moors crossed over from Morocco seven hundred years ago and took the capital of Toledo, their leader, Tariq, became the face of evil in every Christian child's bedtime story told thereafter. The Spanish queens and kings, determined to reunite their country under a Christian banner, took back city after city from the Moors. It all made sense to her now. The Church, with their fears about Jewish and Muslim teachings, emboldened the Crown.

Abuela continued. "By the end of the twelfth century, the golden age of Al-Andalus was over. Spain became a land once again ruled by religion, where belief was a matter of life or death." She paused. "I also think there was jealousy."

"Over what?" asked Isabel.

"The power, wealth, and influence of the Jews."

"How ridiculous that sounds today," said Isabel, imagining someone like little Yuçe holding all the power when he grew up.

"It is hard to believe. But there has always been fear of the outsider. Many Jews and Muslims willingly converted during this time, desiring to be on the inside, part of the majority. They thought erasing the past would make their lives easier. My family remained Jewish. But everything changed for us on June sixth."

The air weighed heavy with silence. Even the chickens seemed to quiet down to listen to Abuela.

"The year was 1391. My grandfather, Rabbi Crescas, was head of one of the twenty-three sinagogas in Valencia. He was well respected by Jews and non-Jews, despite the incendiary rhetoric that had spread throughout the city for months. Nearby in the town of Seville, a Christian monk named Ferrán Martínez had been giving public sermons, calling on good Christians to destroy sinagogas, lock Jews in their ghettos, and force them to accept Christianity. He said the Jews were unbelievers and that pillaging their homes was not a crime.

"It was a blazing Thursday afternoon. In the judería, the summer heat made everyone lazy. Grandpa Crescas and my grandmother, my father, and his four sisters were sitting at the table, finishing their midday meal. Abuelo rose to return to sinagoga for evening prayers. My father heard shouting from the street. When he looked out the window, he saw rabble-rousers chanting, 'Lock them in! Lock them in!' My papá and abuelo ran to the east gate of the judería but it had already been locked. Angry rioters circled around it, daring my father and grandfather to defy them. They turned back, running to the west gate, but someone called out, 'Don't bother. The other gate is blocked, too.' As they arrived back home, black smoke billowed from the roof. Their house was on fire. My grandmother and the children were standing outside, handkerchiefs covering their faces. Other neighbors, whose homes and shops were also burning, stood near. 'The sinagoga!' yelled my grandfather. A large group, including the men in my family, rushed to the sinagoga, but that, too, was aflame, including the Torah." Her voice broke.

"It's all right," said Isabel gently. "You don't have to continue."

"I need to. It has to be told."

Isabel put her arm around her grandmother's shoulders.

When Abuela had composed herself, she continued. "A mob encircled my grandfather and their neighbors. 'It's the rabbi,' yelled a youth. I remember my father telling me how the young man bared his teeth at Abuelo, so ugly and cruel. My grandfather, in his black gown, beard, and skullcap, was tackled to the dirt. 'Become baptized or die,' screamed a second rioter.

"My abuelo struggled to stand up. He wouldn't kneel. He would not give them what they asked. As he recited the Shema prayer, they dragged him through the streets. A week later, he took his own life in prison rather than convert to Christianity."

"Madre mía! What happened to everyone else?"

"My grandmother had a cousin in Hervas. When the chaos died down and the gates were finally unlocked, the family left Valencia permanently. That's how I was born here, on the other side of the country, in Extremadura."

Isabel was consumed by the story, but now that Abuela was finished, the sense of her own hopeless future fell down upon her, heavier this time. There were no fires or vengeful mobs in Trujillo. She felt as if she was being forced to marry someone she despised for the sake of a sacrifice that happened nearly one hundred years ago. "I'm sad for Grandpa Crescas. For your father and the whole family. But I don't understand why Judaism, or any religion for that matter, was worth dying for."

"Do you know the story of Adam, the first human?"

"Claro." Of course.

"Then you know that God created a single man and then a woman and all of humanity descended from them."

Isabel nodded. She felt like a child again, being tested by a stern Fray Francisco as he watched her dutifully recite her Latin benedictions in church. But she relayed the story as she knew it. "God created Eve out of Adam's rib and they ate an apple from the forbidden tree and saw their nakedness and were expelled from the Garden of Eden. Then Cain and Abel were born, and so on."

"Your details are correct, but you're missing the deeper meaning. God did not create two men at once, he simply created Adam. To ensure that no one could say, 'My ancestry is better than yours.'"

Isabel traced circles in the dirt with the toe of her shoe. "But the Old Christians do feel superior in lineage to the Jews."

Abuela nodded. "It's strange. The Jews call themselves the chosen people, but we have never felt better than anyone else. On the contrary, being chosen means we have more responsibility: to both God and our fellow human beings. Yes, we are physically closer to God since He chose us, but the closer you are to God, the more you sense your insignificance. It is the opposite of feeling superior to someone. God is infinite. All our feelings of self-importance fall away when we stand before infinity." She paused. "I think that's a concept worth dying for."

Isabel still had questions. "If being Jewish is so important, why did your grandmother and all her children convert?"

Abuela's head dipped down in shame. "They were afraid. My abuela was a widow. She had children to feed. Her family in Hervas had already converted. They didn't imagine that being baptized had any significance. Not the way it did for Grandpa Crescas. It was merely a means of survival so they could keep Judaism alive in secret."

"Then you and Papá were born Christian?"

"Officially, yes. Your mother, too. Her parents were Crypto-Jews as we were."

Even though Isabel had been living the same duality, she had questions, ones she'd never considered before. "Does it not make people go mad, living a double life?"

"One adapts. But I prefer to think of it another way. That we are simply in a period of waiting before we can go back to being openly Jewish."

"Like the Cohens," said Isabel.

"I'm not sure they're so safe right now either, mi nieta. But yes, like the Cohens."

Isabel thought about how many generations had converted before her. "What if the waiting lasts too long and people forget the traditions and prayers and Judaism disappears altogether?"

"That could happen," admitted Abuela. "It already has in some converso families. They believe in the divinity of Jesús. They will never return to Judaism. I don't judge them. That's their choice."

Isabel crossed her arms. "Well, *I* don't have a choice. At least when it comes to marriage."

Abuela clucked her tongue in the direction of the coop. Isabel didn't know if it was meant for her or the chickens. "Sometimes you are as immovable as a fence post."

Isabel didn't deny it. A breeze came up, rustling leaves in a nearby tree. She wished she hadn't hurried out of the house without her mantle.

"I remember my father talking to me about the Talmud," said Abuela. "Other than the Torah, it's the most important book for the Jewish people. Grandpa Crescas and he used to study it together at the sinagoga before all the troubles in Valencia. My father's eyes would light up like stars when he described how the text turned in circles and went sideways over the page in all different sizes. I remember feeling jealous because I knew I would never see a Talmud in real life. Imagine being envious of your own father!"

"Why did you think you'd never see one?"

She sighed. "I was a girl. Women didn't study sacred Jewish texts."

"But your father taught you to read."

She raised one finger in the air. "In Castilian. Jewish books were forbidden in converso homes." Abuela gave me a wink. "But I managed to learn Hebrew anyway. I pestered my father every day until he finally relented and wrote down the aleph-bet from his memory. After that, I practiced putting letters together to make words and he had no choice but to correct me."

"And I thought I was stubborn," Isabel teased.

"There's a lesson from the Talmud on uniqueness that I've always liked," said Abuela. "Coins are minted by the king, made from one mold. Each one looks the same. But God is more powerful than a king. God mints each human being to be different. Yes, we are created in His image, but it's a spiritual image. Like Adam, humans have two legs, two arms, one head. But no two people look the same. Skin can be dark or fair like yours. Even within the same family. Take how different you and Beatriz look. You have your mother's wide-set eyes and long, wavy brown hair. Beatriz has your father's high forehead and prominent nose."

That was true. Isabel often felt guilty that she had the prettier features.

"God puts His unique stamp on everyone so they can be different on the outside *and* on the inside," explained Abuela.

"It was intentional!" exclaimed Isabel. "That means our differences are good because everything that comes from God is good!"

The rising sun illuminated Abuela's smile. "Celebrating our

differences is one of the best parts of Judaism. We embrace the stranger, the one who doesn't belong."

Isabel sighed. "I wish I lived during the golden age of Al-Andalus. I would be a poetess."

"I believe we can return to that time again," said Abuela. "Not in my lifetime. But maybe your children will live to see that day, and their children's children and all those who come after."

The thought of Abuela not being alive to see paradise disturbed Isabel so greatly she wrapped her arms around her middle to hold in the pain. Maybe she connected to Abuelo Crescas's story after all. "It's just so melancholy, isn't it?"

"Your betrothal?"

"That, and the future. The past. Everything."

"Listen carefully. Your task right now is to make the best of your present situation. You have been given an opportunity to protect your family. A sacrifice we are all grateful for, believe me. But you will lead a comfortable life with Don Sancho. You can clean him up. Get him to use a woolen cloth soaked in lemon on those teeth. Follow Maimonides's advice and feed your husband only when he is hungry. The alguacil clearly does not know when to stop. And know that his age is his deficit. He will make you a rich widow in no time. And your dowry and our land will be returned to you."

How strange to be discussing someone's death who had been very much alive in their sala last night.

"Every New Christian will be envious of your parents," added Abuela.

Then why did it still feel so much like a punishment? "I don't want envy. I want—" Her voice broke like Abuela's had.

There would be no poetry in her life. Isabel wished she could run as far away from Trujillo as her legs would carry her. Her eyes welled up again.

Abuela took her hand. "There's something I want to show you. I've been saving it for your wedding day, but I think you need to see it now."

7

Retying her scarf around her head, Abuela led Isabel to a spot close to where they dumped their latrine. She looked around. "Has Beatriz returned from the well yet?"

"She must have," said Isabel. "I don't see her."

Abuela brushed off some dirt to reveal a hole and pulled out a milk tin.

"You're storing milk from our cows out here?"

Abuela shook her head. "It's the only place I could think of safe enough for a Jewish text. No one would think to look out here, next to the contents of our chamber pots."

Isabel giggled. "You've hidden a book inside that milk can?"

"Of sorts." She lifted off the top of the canister and removed a roll of thin parchment. Carefully, she spread it on her knee. Isabel could not read the writing.

"Are you sure it's a Jewish text? It looks Moorish."

"The writer was Jewish but wrote this poem in Arabic. My grandmother was able to rescue a few belongings from the house in Valencia before the fire consumed it. She passed this down to me. It belonged to an ancestor of hers. A young girl, I think. I can't remember anything else. And I don't know how to translate it."

"May I hold it?"

"Be careful."

Isabel gently touched the parchment, her hand quivering slightly. The ink felt alive on the page before her. All these years she'd thought she was the odd one, because no one in her family read as voraciously as she did, let alone recorded their thoughts on paper. This discovery was nothing short of a miracle. "I wonder what the poem says. I wonder who she was," she murmured.

"I've been meaning to take it to Isaac the bookbinder," said her grandmother. "But these eyes are old. You be my vision and ask him to have it translated for you." She gave Isabel a kiss on each cheek. "And tell me everything!"

8

The Jewish bookbinder did not work on Saturday. His shop would be closed on Sunday as well, in deference to the Christian day of rest. Therefore, as she added up Papá's ledgers, Isabel could only count the minutes until Monday. She sat at the table in the cool cellar, surrounded by large cone-shaped baskets piled high with grapes. There had been a delivery this morning and the aroma was especially sweet, even without sugar added. Tomorrow, Papá and his trusted helper, Pedro, would dump the heavy baskets into the press.

Each basket had two leather straps, so the grape pickers could wear the carriers on their backs. It was laborious work, to hand-pick the grapes off the vines, then carry their load three kilometers to the market. Luckily, Papá owned a mule, so for his share, the workers only had to strap the baskets onto the beast and lead the animal directly to the cellar. Once, Isabel had tried to lift a full basket, and she had tumbled backward, landing on her bottom. She had not been able to raise it more than a few centimeters off the floor.

Isabel heard the creak of the cellar door. "How is it coming?" Papá was always impatient, anxious to see the profits each month.

"Slowly, to be honest." She had been working all morning, but something didn't add up. The total was off. In the wrong direction. "I keep finding an inconsistency. I think it's my math."

She heard the heavy thud of Papá's feet on the stairs. "Let me take a look."

His eyebrows joined together as he scanned the columns of accounts received. "Unfortunately, your numbers are perfect. A few of my best innkeeper customers have stopped ordering as much wine as they used to. They say it's because business is slow, but I think there's another reason."

Isabel put down her turkey quill. "Surely it can't be the quality of your vino tinto?"

He frowned. "No. Simply Old Christians trying to show their loyalty to the Crown by not buying from conversos."

"Then we'll just have to find new customers," said Isabel with more conviction than she felt.

An hour before sundown, the Perez family left for Sucot dinner at the Cohen house. Abuela stayed home, not feeling well. Abuela had preferred the family wait until after three stars appeared in the sky, signaling the official end of Shabbat. But Mamá wanted to leave earlier. Isabel glanced back to wave goodbye to Abuela, and thought she saw a curtain flick closed in the window of their neighbors' house, the Herreras. Or maybe it was simply her imagination.

The low sun cast a pink glow near the granite-rock mountains as the family passed through the muralla, Trujillo's defensive walls. Just outside the city loomed the iron gates of the Jewish quarter, dark and imposing. It seemed to Isabel as if no light could ever seep through those bars.

Beatriz stopped a few meters from the gates. "I'm not going in there." Her voice quivered.

"Don't be foolish. The judería is nothing to be afraid of," said Papá.

Beatriz's feet were firmly planted in the dirt as if she had grown roots.

"I guess you don't want new dress fabric, then," said Mamá, wisely.

Beatriz shifted her weight. "I just wish there were another way."

"Well, there isn't. This is where the Cohens live now," said Mamá. "With the rest of the Jewish community. And we're not going to make them feel uncomfortable about it either."

Isabel wished Abuela were here so she could ask her if Grandpa Crescas liked living in the judería. Perhaps it was different back then and Jews chose to live all together in one tight community instead of being forced to move there.

"Besides, we've been celebrating Sucot with the Cohens every year since you were born," added Mamá. "It's tradition."

Beatriz's knuckles turned hard and white at her sides. "We aren't supposed to go calling on Jews anymore. Constanza said so."

Papá looked exasperated. "Some towns are adhering to those ridiculous laws, but no one is enforcing them in Trujillo." He took Beatriz by the arm, dragging her behind him. "Come. Let's not draw more attention to ourselves than needed."

As they entered through the gates, Beatriz covered her nose with a gloved hand.

The streets were dirtier here, not like those in Isabel's neighborhood, which were swept by brown-shirted peasants once a week for a coin. The smells were different inside the quarter, too—not bad, just unfamiliar. Roasted meats and cinnamon and a strong citrus scent.

"I smell pomegranate," said Mamá, smiling.

Street signs in painted Hebrew letters hovered above merchants' shops. Abuela would know their meaning. Some had crudely drawn pictures next to the foreign words: a shoe, a ring with a jewel inside, a spinning wheel. A woman on a corner sold geraniums, their pink and red petals standing out as strongly as a dash of lip paint on a powdered face. Young men scurried by, heading home for the holiday, wearing the traditional cone-shaped hats Jewish males wore outside the judería. When Isabel was small, she thought the hats looked like upside-down cooking funnels.

A group of older men stood a few feet from the wall, a coffin on the ground in front of them.

Beatriz pointed to the wooden box. "The stench is coming from over there."

"Don't point," said Papá. "They're guarding the body, may he or she rest in peace."

"Why aren't they putting the corpse in the ground?" asked Isabel.

"They're waiting until sundown. So as not to be easily seen and draw attention to their burial customs. The Crown isn't happy about ceding good land to Jews for a cemetery."

Mamá looked up at the sky. "Thanks be to God that we were able to bury Ruy in the Christian cemetery the morning he died." Every Saturday, Mamá put a rock on little Rodrigo's grave, returning home with red eyes. Isabel did not know if her mother was more distraught about his passing or the fact that he could not be buried with a Star of David on his marker.

One of the men guarding the coffin tipped his head to them. *"Hag Sameach."* Happy holiday.

"Hag Sameach," returned Papá.

Despite the dirty streets and sense of darkness from the tall iron gates, there was a freedom in here, the happy-holiday greetings escaping off the tongue like a bird in flight.

"How long do you think this dinner will last?" asked Beatriz. "Constanza invited me to play todas tablas."

"You just want to see her brother, Juan Carlos," teased Isabel.

"I do not!" Beatriz's neck flushed and she reflexively scratched her scalp.

"Don't tell me you have lice," said Mamá, stopping to examine Beatriz's hair.

She pulled away. "Stop. It's just a scab."

The area she scratched, to the left of her middle part, was familiar. Once, Isabel caught her sister staring into the looking glass, sticking a peineta into her head so hard it drew blood. Isabel was astonished, but didn't say anything, thinking she had poked herself accidentally. A week later, while braiding Beatriz's hair, Isabel spotted the scab. But that was last spring. How could the skin still be caked in that same spot after all this time? Unless Beatriz kept picking at it?

"Señora Herrera peeked out her curtain when we left the house," said Beatriz, directing the attention away from herself.

So Isabel had been right about the movement in the window.

"She might tell someone," warned Beatriz.

"She has no idea where we're going," said Mamá. "And the fact that we left before sundown takes away all suspicion. Observant Jews would not be walking out of the house this close to the end of Sabbath."

"Let this be our last visit, then," said Beatriz. "We can't be friends with the Cohens anymore."

"Have you no loyalty at all, Beatriz?" admonished Isabel. "You took care of the twins when they were born! Even taught Rachel to stitch a sampler! Or have you erased that from your stingy memory?"

Beatriz fell silent.

"This must be it," said Mamá, looking up at a narrow wooden building. Some of the wood slats stuck out, uneven with the rest of the facade. The whole house, in fact the entire block of houses, tilted to the left, like dominoes stacked against one another ready to fall. Remembering the Cohens' old house, a few streets away from their own, Isabel felt sad and shocked at the sight in front of her. Their previous home was built of river stone on the lower half, and strong wood on the upper half. Inside, there had been a sala bigger than the Perezes', with the most beautiful ultramarine damask drapes covering the front window openings.

Mamá knocked on the unpainted wooden door and Beatriz's lips began to move. Isabel recognized the Latin of the Paternoster, as if there were some evil influence she needed protection from.

A smiling Señora Cohen opened the door. "*Hag Sameach.*" She wore a gown of plain beige sackcloth, with a red badge sewn on the upper left corner, identifying her as a Jew.

Isabel knew Jews were now required to don the gowns, but she had not yet seen someone so dear to her wearing one. What a terrible irony that the tailor's wife could not even put on her husband's fine cloth.

Beatriz whispered to Isabel. "She looks wretched in that dress."

"Is that all you can say about their situation?" hissed Isabel. "Have some compassion."

Beatriz dug her elbow into Isabel's stomach. It didn't hurt but made Isabel want to jab her back. Isabel withheld her ire and did nothing.

David Cohen stood next to his wife, a pince-nez tilted on his nose, his mouth in a thin, grim line. Though he was one of the leading textile sellers in the Kingdom of Castile and León, today he looked distraught.

Mamá assessed the main room of the apartment. Three cots in the corner, a table in the center, and a hearth against the wall. "It's not so very different from your old place, Hannah," she lied.

"Minus two rooms." Señora Cohen smiled wearily. "But David works directly downstairs and the butcher is only a three-minute walk." She brushed off some dust from a royal-blue enameled vase. Isabel remembered it from their old sala, the way it sat so prominently on a polished cedar pedestal, its color matching the drapes perfectly.

Mamá handed Señora Cohen the cake she had baked. "It's honey, the way you like it."

"The children are outside. Come."

On the Cohens' balcony, a makeshift booth, or suca, had been erected. The roof tiles that ordinarily would extend over the balcony had been temporarily removed so that only the skeleton of rough wooden beams remained. Leafy tree branches lay across the beams, covering the top just enough so everyone sitting under it could still see the stars. Straw mats suspended from the roof on three sides enclosed them in the cozy space. The fresh smell of myrtle and willow, mixed with the hanging apples, grapes, and pomegranates, made Isabel feel like she was in the middle of a fruity forest. The only furniture inside the suca was a chestnut-wood table. A long bench ran along one side and five chairs sat opposite.

Rachel, eleven years old, was devouring a plate of sweet baked *biscochos* all by herself at one end of the table.

"I'm eating dessert before dinner even begins!" said Rachel.

"That's enough of that." Señora Cohen grabbed the plate of cookies from the table and headed into the house.

Isabel looked around. "Where's Yuçe?"

Rachel rolled her eyes. "In the workroom, as always."

"Let's go see the new fabrics," said Beatriz, yanking her sister's hand.

They walked through the apartment, past the adults, who were standing, drinking glasses of the vino tinto Papá brought.

"The girls want to choose some new fabric," Isabel heard Mamá say.

"Of course," said Señor Cohen. "But you'll have to come back tomorrow to pay for them."

"Monday is better for us," said Papá. "I'll send Isabel over."

Señor Cohen leaned back on his heels. "That's right. I nearly forgot. Sunday is church day for you people."

Mamá and Señora Cohen smiled uncomfortably at each other.

"How do you stomach it?" continued Señor Cohen. "Reciting those Latin words under the watchful eye of some golden statue of Jesús? Reminds me of the time our idolater ancestors worshipped the golden calf in the Sinai desert, do you not agree?"

Isabel hurried Beatriz out of the room before her sister could show off her Latin skills. They certainly did not need to incite Señor Cohen any further. He seemed like a different person tonight. She had never heard him so aggressive.

Downstairs, Isabel and Beatriz found themselves in a small open-air courtyard. Dead weeds poked their heads through faded tiles on the ground. From the open window spaces of the apartment above, dishes clanked and Papá's and Señor Cohen's voices escalated. Hearing the two fathers argue gave Isabel an uneasy feeling.

Beatriz pointed to an open door on their right. "That must be it."

Inside the small room, Yuçe, Rachel's twin brother, stood with his back to them, pulling down a bolt of green silk damask. Bolts of fabric lay askew on shelves that threatened to collapse from the weight.

"Hola," said Isabel.

He turned, his face lighting up, and promptly dropped the roll of fabric on his foot.

Beatriz laughed.

Yuçe stared down at the floor, then bent to pick up the material. When he stood, Isabel scrutinized him. "Have you grown since we last saw you?"

"He's become a giraffe, all spindly legs and arms," said Beatriz.

Isabel glared at her sister. "How would you know? You've never seen one."

"Pope Pious II had a menagerie greet him in Florence; among them was a giraffe. I heard it described in church."

Her sister missed no detail at Mass. "Well, I think you grew two centimeters at least, Yuçe," said Isabel.

He flushed wildly, fingering his left ear, which stuck out farther than the right. "I probably look taller in this tiny space. I miss our old workroom. Everything is so crowded together in the judería." He replaced the fallen fabric bolt. "How long have you been here?"

"A few minutes. The grown-ups are drinking wine and your sister is eating all the dessert, of course."

Beatriz went to the shelves to get a closer look at the fabrics.

Yuçe cleared a corner of the crowded area and sat down on the floor, folding a cloth remnant for Isabel to sit on.

Something black and furry scurried across the floor.

"Madre mía!" exclaimed Isabel.

Yuçe sprang up, striding over to a wooden box in the opposite corner. He lifted the top to reveal a stick propped up with a morsel of bread in the center. "Spiteful rat. Hopefully, he'll find his way into this trap. I brought in some stray cats from the river thinking that would solve the problem. But they scratched all the silk with their claws. Now I'm trying this."

"Did those stains ever come out?" asked Isabel, a little calmer now that she knew there were actual traps in the room. Yuçe had come to their house a few months ago asking for unripe grapes.

Yuçe grinned. "The verjuice worked like a sorcerer's charm! Who would think something as simple as that would take out stains from rat droppings?"

Beatriz grunted from her position by the shelves. She did not like discussing anything dirty that came from the body of an animal or human. "Any new patterns from Turkey or India?"

"I wouldn't know," said Yuçe, turning sour. "Father hasn't taken me to the port in Cádiz in a long time."

"There must be a logical reason," said Isabel.

"His third apprentice, Samuel, has left us. Now all I do is add padding to suits and sew linings and pockets."

"That doesn't sound too bad."

"It's much more exciting to be greeting the ships. But Papá's eyes are going and, with Samuel gone, he can't see the small stitches."

"Did Samuel fall ill?" asked Isabel.

Yuçe shook his head. "Papá says it's because of the anti-Jewish statutes. Samuel feared he'd be arrested if he worked for a Jew who engaged in, what was the word? Oh yes, handicraft."

"Honestly, if Jews are legally forbidden from hand-making anything, what are they supposed to do instead?" said Isabel. Since Papá bottled wine and affixed his own label, one could argue they manufactured something, too. But being conversos protected them. For now. It was confusing trying to figure out which restrictive laws were being enforced and which weren't. If you took the anti-Jewish laws at their word, no Jew would be allowed to practice medicine, be a butcher, glassblower, candle-maker, or even cut his own hair for that matter. Yet there were scant aristocratic households in Castile and Aragon, including the royal family's, who did *not* have a Jewish physician visit them when someone fell ill. Everyone knew this truth. "It's plain hypocrisy if you ask me."

"Perhaps your new friend the alguacil can protect Samuel and convince him to return to work," said Beatriz.

Isabel exhaled impatiently. "He's not my new friend."

"That's not what I heard Mamá and Papá discussing."

"What are you two speaking about?" asked Yuçe, eyes wide. "Let me in on the secret!"

Beatriz answered for her. "Isabel and Don Sancho, the alguacil, are betrothed."

"It is not an hecho consumado," snapped Isabel. "He hasn't asked officially yet."

"But *I* want to marry you!" proclaimed Yuçe.

Isabel scrubbed the top of his curly hair, laughing. "That's sweet. But you'll find a more suitable girl who's your own age . . . in about seven years." His mouth curved down in a pout.

She turned to the shelves where her sister was still examining every thread. "Have you found anything you like yet?"

Beatriz carried four bolts of cloth over to them.

"Lovely," said Isabel. "Yuçe can cut them after dinner. Let's head back upstairs, shall we?"

"Business is booming," Señora Cohen was saying as the girls and Yuçe entered the suca.

The adults sat on one side of the table, the children on the other.

"The countess keeps him so busy. All those dresses for so many occasions," continued Señora Cohen. "The Altamiranos lead a very social life."

At least they were off the earlier topic of golden calves, Isabel thought, relieved. The battle of converso versus true Jew seemed to be over.

Señor Cohen recited the blessing over the bread and everyone joined in. Except Beatriz, of course. She never spoke Hebrew. Every time Mamá tried to teach the girls a blessing, Beatriz complained it felt foreign on her tongue, like a hot chili pepper.

"And thank you, God, for commanding us to dwell in the suca," concluded Señor Cohen.

"Can we sleep out here tonight?" begged Rachel, her smile pure and delighted.

"We'll see," said her mother.

They dipped apples in honey and ate chicken roasted with prunes.

"Our ancestors built these cabañas so they could gather their bountiful crops and not have to walk the long distance home each night during harvest season," said Señor Cohen.

Papá chuckled. "You act as though we don't know the purpose of this festival."

Señor Cohen demurred. "Of course you do. Forgive me. Speaking of harvest, how is your grape season coming?"

"We've had a good year I'm not ashamed to say," answered Papá.

"No. Shame never enters your mind, does it?"

Isabel begged silently for Papá to let the insult slide. Mercifully, he did.

"Everything is delicious, Hannah," said Mamá.

"You sleep easily at night, do you not?" baited Señor Cohen. "Knowing your wine-bottling business is safe?"

"I don't follow," said Papá.

"Let me enlighten you. Every morning we wake up, not knowing if our trade, the one we've worked at all our lives, become experts in, will be taken away from us by the whim of some Christian cleric's statute."

"My business is feeling the strain as well," admitted Papá. "Believe me."

Señor Cohen scowled.

Isabel tried to ameliorate the situation. "Rachel, Yuçe, let's play a game. How about truc? Where are your cards?"

Rachel went to go find them inside, but Señor Cohen continued. "Have you lost any workers yet?"

"I just have Pedro," answered Papá. "He's been with me for fifteen years."

Señor Cohen removed his pince-nez and rubbed the corners of his eyes. "My third apprentice has quit. And the second is about to walk out as well. Those anti-Jewish laws have put the fear of God in them."

"Perhaps I could give him temporary work until it's safe for him to return."

"Oh yes. The big hero, Manolo Perez, to the rescue." Señor Cohen replaced his pince-nez and looked coldly at Papá. "We won't be needing your charity. Samuel would never work for a converso anyway. He'd choose an Old Christian over someone who abandoned his own God any day of the week."

"I have never abandoned God," seethed Papá. "We are *anusim*, forced to convert under duress."

"Then why has He punished you?"

Papá's head tilted in question.

Señor Cohen laughed. "Whose fault do you think it is that Soli died?"

At the mention of Rodrigo's Hebrew name, Mamá gave a startled cry and turned as white as the tablecloth.

Isabel wanted to reach out her hand to comfort her, but Rachel returned just then with the playing cards. Isabel dealt quickly, concentrating on the images drawn on them—cups, batons, coins, swords—hoping Señor Cohen would stop.

"Rodrigo had the tremors," said Papá through clenched teeth, clearly furious that he had to explain anything at all yet doing it anyway. "His body was wracked with fever. Who understands why these things happen?"

"No," corrected Señor Cohen. "Your son died for your sins. Just like your new Lord, Jesúcristo, did." He raised one finger in the air. "Soli's death is your punishment for rejecting God!"

Papá stood abruptly, nearly tilting the bench backward. "Benita, let's go." He gestured at the girls. "Isabel, Beatriz, now."

"But I haven't cut the honey cake," protested Señora Cohen.

"We'll eat our dessert at home. Benita made two," said Papá.

Yuçe, Rachel, Beatriz, and Isabel exchanged sympathetic looks. But they were powerless to change anything.

Out on the street, Isabel was shaking. She wanted to cry for the way her innocent baby brother's name was used for adult gain.

For Señor Cohen's preposterous superstitions. For how someone could hurt another human being in such a way.

And yet as they walked back in silence to their comfortable house in their clean neighborhood, a small voice inside her whispered questions she had no answers for. Did Mamá and Papá truly want to go back to being openly Jewish like the Cohens? Or did her parents enjoy the status of living as conversos so much that they preferred to have it both ways?

On Monday, the sun had not yet risen to its apex as Diego began another tedious day of tax collecting. Already, his memories of university were disappearing. He could not remember the exact shade of the leaves on the trees in the quadrangle. Was the green more like silver coins or fresh grass?

Abraham ben Mordohay, the Jewish bottle-maker, stepped out from the back of the store, wiping his hands on his apron. Soot and dust covered so much of his face that only the whites of his eyes stood out. "Buenas, your most excellent lord."

Diego flinched at the title. He was no lord. But the formality could not be helped. The lower classes always addressed the titled nobility as lord.

"How is your family?" asked Diego.

"Bien, gracias. My daughter is going to be married."

"Enhorabuena. And business, it is good?"

"Sí," said ben Mordohay. "I'm finishing up a large order for the Perez vino tinto."

"I know it well. Quite delicious."

Ben Mordohay fidgeted with his hands. "Em . . . I . . . already paid my rent this month, your lordship."

"Of course." Diego berated himself for not bringing it up earlier. He'd gone and made the man uncomfortable. "I'm actually here for the alcabala tax. The special levy for the war with Granada."

"In that case," began ben Mordohay, "let me gather the money. It's in the back."

"The amount is one thousand," called Diego.

Ben Mordohay returned, handing Diego the paper

currency. Diego counted it. There was just nine hundred maravedis. He was short.

Ben Mordohay averted his eyes.

Diego's father would not have hesitated. He'd have this poor man killed right here and now. But what good would that do? Who would take over this business? Ben Mordohay's new son-in-law, who probably knew nothing about making bottles?

Diego patted the bottle-maker on his hand. "Thank you. The count will be pleased." Later, Diego would take the balance out of his own purse, using the allowance his mother had slipped to him before he left for school.

"Don't tell your father," she had said. "He doesn't need to know."

And the count certainly didn't need to know that part of the Jewish bottle-maker's taxes included money that came from his very own household.

It was just a small act of rebellion against his father. But it was something.

Diego exited the shop to a litany of bows and thank-yous from ben Mordohay, and went next door to the bookbinder. His was one of the last Jewish shops, other than the bottle-maker's and a few others, that still remained outside the Jewish quarter. This was not a business visit. It was a diversion. The binder owned the land where his shop stood, passed down through his family for generations, so there was no rent to be collected, just the alcabala tax for the war effort, which Diego had collected last Friday. Diego wanted to inquire if any illuminated manuscripts had arrived from the docks over the weekend. Ships from as far as Tripoli, Ceylon, and Quanzhou arrived daily in the port of Cádiz, containing spices, fabrics, books, silver. But lately, it seemed all the treasures were going the opposite way, leaving the country, as if these objects of art and literature—like their Jewish and Moorish owners—no longer felt safe in their homes.

"Buenas tardes, Isaac," said Diego upon entering.

Isaac lifted his head from a document, then lowered his looking glass. "Back so soon?"

"I was just next door, and wondered if there was anything new I might look at."

"I'm going to have to start calling you Señor Curioso."

Diego grinned, wishing his own father would call him by a term of endearment.

"I've got something you might find interesting," said Isaac.

"Don't keep me in suspense."

Isaac's eyes narrowed. "But we mustn't view it here."

Diego followed Isaac downstairs into a storeroom carved out of the floor. He thought he saw an exit, or at least another pathway dug into the back of the room, but he couldn't be sure. Books lined the walls from floor to ceiling. Strewn on the long center worktable were half-bound covers in silver and leather, sheets in groups of four folded into quires. A sheep's skin hung drying near the wall, the first stage of making paper. Pumice stones for rubbing parchment thin and smooth were piled in the corner. The air felt stifling in the dim light. Isaac pulled down a makeshift trapdoor, loosely covering the opening above them. Dust rained down and Diego sneezed.

"Jesús," said Isaac.

"*Salud* is fine," mumbled Diego. Isaac was trying to adhere to Christian customs out of respect for Diego, but Isaac was a Jew, not a converso. There was no reason for him to have to say the name of the Lord. Christians believed a little piece of your soul left the body from a sneeze and needed an extra blessing for safety. But Jesús was not Isaac's Lord.

The binder lit an oil lamp, holding it up to a book that lay open on the table. Diego gasped. There were bright peacocks and waterfalls on one side of the page, while the other side depicted four men in red robes and triangle hats, playing some sort of game. In between the illustrations were strange letters in black script.

"It's absolutely exquisite," said Diego.

"It's a megillah. It contains the Jewish story of Purim. This edition is over one thousand years old, at least. I'm about to wrap it up and send it to the docks. If all goes according to plan, this book will set sail, safely nestled in a crate bound for Salonica."

Diego gently ran his finger down the gilded edges. "What are those men playing?"

"Dice. In truth, it's dreidel, a Jewish game, but they don't want the king's men to realize this or they will be arrested."

Diego stared at Isaac. "It's always been like this for the Jews, hasn't it? Living two existences in order to survive?"

Isaac's eyes were downcast. "I'm afraid so."

Diego shook his head. "It sickens me." He looked at the book with longing. "Shame I can't borrow it for a day. I'd like to copy those peacocks."

"Your father would burn it," said Isaac. "And possibly do worse to you."

It wasn't just the books that were in danger. It was the people who read them, and who dealt in them. Sadly, Diego knew from his father that it was only a matter of time until all Jews would have to give up their trades and people like Isaac and the bottle-maker next door would have to find other ways to feed their families.

Diego tried to imprint the colors onto his memory, the malachite green and orpiment yellow of the peacock feathers, the vermillion of the robes, the azurite of the water. "Thank you, Isaac, for showing—"

"Hello?" came a female voice from the front of the shop.

Isaac quickly closed the megillah and threw a tattered tapestry on top of it. "I'll be out in a moment," he called.

Again, the dust tickled Diego's nose. *"Achoo!"*

"Jesús," said the female voice.

Did he smell roses?

Diego and Isaac made their way upstairs to the main counter of the shop. A girl stood before them. Her auburn hair was tucked into a knitted cap, but there was so much of it, it threatened to tumble out around her shoulders like the waterfall he'd just seen in the book. Her marigold-colored dress was simple yet elegant.

Though a partlet covered her low neckline, he could see a glimpse of skin just below that, as pale as the moon. He kept his gaze straight ahead, though he wanted to look lower.

Her eyes blinked once. "It's you."

"Me?" said Diego.

"Rather, I thought you looked like someone. From the other day."

"I *am* someone," he said, amused.

Her accent was atypical. Not nobility, but not commoner either. She tucked a hair back into place. He wanted to be her fingers. To know what her hair felt like between them.

"Are you apprenticing here?" she asked him.

Diego gave a deep laugh. He wished.

The girl turned her face away.

Perhaps she thought he was being haughty? "You misunderstand," he began.

"Master Diego was just leaving," said the bookbinder, all business now.

Did Diego see her eyebrow go up at the mention of his name? Now that she knew who he was, he felt at a disadvantage.

"Until next week, Isaac," said Diego. He tipped his hat to the girl. "Señorita . . . ?"

"Perez," said the girl. "Isabel Perez."

9

"What an arrogant young man," said Isabel when he left the shop. He was the same person she had followed the other day. She was sure of it. And this fact flustered her, so that she could do nothing else but act insulted. His green eyes, now that she could see them straight on, were so penetrating, it had felt as if they might sear her.

The binder said nothing. "How can I help you?"

With great care, Isabel removed the scroll from her satchel and handed it to Isaac. "It's my grandmother's. Well, not exactly hers. It belonged to her grandmother, and quite honestly, I don't know how far back it goes. Can you tell me what it says?" Now that she had the precious manuscript in front of her, she felt calmer. She blinked and the effect of the boy's arresting eyes floated away. She was eager to hear any details this man might give her about what her grandmother had kept hidden all these years.

Isaac put on gloves of beige kid leather that looked soft enough to eat. Then he unrolled the parchment, placing small weights on all four corners of the paper.

"It's Arabic. Perhaps twelfth century or earlier. I would venture to say the scribe could be from Andalucía. See that decoration in the upper right corner?"

Isabel peered closer.

"It's a rudimentary pomegranate, the symbol of Granada."

How beautiful. She could almost smell the lushness of the south. It made her recall a line she'd heard at the poetry reading:

"The perfumed fountains of Granada exploded in
*   fragrance of citrus,*
filling bedrooms at night with dreams of
*   orange suns."*

She had transcribed it into her notebook because it was so evocative.

"Is it a love poem?" That very same poem had taken a turn to the sensuous, with the second speaker comparing a woman to a blossom on an orange tree.

"I'll need more time to find out, I'm afraid," said the binder. "I have a Moorish colleague who might be of help." He paused. "If I get it translated, do you have someone to read it to you?"

She ground her teeth together. "That won't be necessary."

It never ceased to infuriate her, the way people presumed she was not lettered. She recalled the day she and Abuela first began their lessons. Papá had brought home a world map a few weeks prior, given to him by one of his wine customers who had just returned from a sea voyage. The shapes of the landmasses with their fancy, calligraphed locales enthralled Isabel. Everything seemed so exotic, made more so because she could not read the names on any of the continents. She sneaked down to the cellar every day to pore over the map. Until one afternoon Abuela followed her.

Abuela had leaned over Isabel, smelling of milled wheat and honey. She pointed to some tiny dots on the map. "Do you know what that is, mi nieta?"

Isabel shook her head.

"Those are the Faroe Islands," Abuela explained. "And that's the Empire of Tamerlane." A sprinkle of flour from Abuela's hand fell onto a big country in the lower right section of the map.

Isabel turned around. "Will you teach me how to read the words?"

"I was waiting for one of you girls to ask! I fear the only way to get your sister to read is if there were words printed on the fabric of her new dresses." They both had laughed.

During their learning sessions, the letters of the alphabet seemed to float above the parchment like tendrils of smoke, arranging themselves into rich meaning. From then on, the dank cellar ceased to frighten Isabel. It always reminded her of that moment when she finally cracked the code. After she mastered the maps, she demanded books, though the only ones they were allowed to have in the house by law were religious in nature and rather dull. One day, when she was thirteen, Isabel was walking with Abuela through the Moorish quarter. While Abuela bargained with a spice merchant, Isabel picked up a book of poems in a tiny stall next door. One page and she was hooked. It was the language of love. Romance and secret trysts. Oh, to be cherished like that by a man someday! Forget religious rapture. That was the bliss Isabel longed for.

Back in the bookbinder's shop, Isabel looked at Isaac, with his ink-stained hands, surrounded by books and old manuscripts, as well as pearly white paper, pumiced smooth to receive new ink from a scribe. He did not know how lucky he was. "Do you, by chance, have something to write with?"

Isaac reached below his front counter, placing a turkey quill and small glass vial of dark ink in front of her. He tore off a scrap of used parchment, handing that to her as well. She dipped the white feather into the black liquid and, in proud, unmistakable script, wrote down her street address.

"Please send word when you have something for me."

To take a coffee or not? Diego had one more tax collection out in Plasencia, a two-hour horse ride northwest. It was getting dark. Brigands would be in the hills waiting for anyone riding by with something to steal. He had fought off his share of thieves. Even used his dagger once on a man who had reached his grubby hands into Diego's purse in Lisbon. The bandit was no match for Diego's height and powerful arms. Protecting his coins did not worry him as much as not seeing that exquisite woman again. Isabel Perez. Standing at the edge of the plaza mayor in front of a café, Diego pondered what to do. The alley that led to the bookbinder's shop had no exit. She would have to walk through the plaza. Perhaps he'd linger just a few more minutes.

He could have any girl he wanted. In Lisbon, he'd certainly had his share. Women he paid for, and some who gave of themselves for free. Then why could he not rid himself of the contours of Isabel's cheekbones? Her face was new and familiar at the same time. And that smell, roses. He sensed it everywhere, taunting him.

Shouting came from behind him. He turned to find a brawl starting in the middle of the plaza. Two men— one bearded and in rags, the other upper-class by the look of his slatted sleeve—circled around each other, like a toreador and his bull, kicking up dirt. The man in rags grabbed a bottle from a nearby table in the plaza and swung at the well-dressed man. The rich man drew his sword. Diego pushed through the small crowd, hoping to stop someone from becoming seriously injured. But before he could get to the center, the bottle made contact and the aristocrat fell, blood beginning to form a sticky circle on the back of his head. He struggled to get up, but the ragged man struck again.

"Halt!" came a booming voice. "Halt, I say!"

A heavyset gentleman, clearly the alguacil from the officer's uniform he wore, huffed over to the brawling men and pulled them apart.

Diego offered his assistance, but the warden seemed to have control over the situation. "It's not the first time this beggar has caused us problems," he told Diego. He held the raggedy man in a choke hold while motioning for the owner of the café to bring some wet towels for the man on the ground, who was moaning. The alguacil whistled for his horse, which was standing nearby, then he easily threw the man in rags sideways over the saddle, tying his feet together. The beggar grunted in protest.

Seeing no need to remain in the middle of the plaza, Diego returned to the café. Suddenly, he smelled roses and looked up. The girl, Isabel, was making her way straight to the ruckus. His feet vibrated. He set about to move toward her, to protect her from the blood and this unsightly scene. It would be the perfect excuse to speak to her again.

But the alguacil had the same idea. He got to her first. They exchanged words. She tried to peer around him to see the fallen man, but the alguacil gripped her arm and prevented her from doing so in a way that seemed, to Diego, too harsh. Then he put his hand on the small of her back and led her away, out of the plaza, with the possessiveness of one who owns another.

Diego could do nothing but stand in the dust and watch them disappear around a corner.

10

Days later, after an early breakfast of biscuits and sheep's cheese, Isabel found herself with a few moments alone in her room to compose. Beatriz had gone to fetch cookies from the sisters at Convent San Clemente, her regular chore before church on Sundays. Serving the recognizable pastries if guests came calling was just one more way to show they were a good Christian family.

Her leather notebook lay on a slightly slanted narrow desk, two small metal weights on either side to hold it open. There was a pot of gall ink beside it. For his ledgers, Papá and Isabel mixed their own ink from gallnuts, white wine, and green vitriol, which they gathered from the ground after a hard rain. Add to that some dried-up sap of the acacia tree, and it thickened to a nice black substance, perfect for writing.

Isabel had had a dream earlier in the week in which something was burning—perhaps the Torah in Great-Grandpa Crescas's sinagoga? It would make a powerful poem. But the young man's face, the one from the bookbindery, kept appearing in her mind's eye, so that when she dipped her quill in the ink, the words came out jumbled on the parchment.

O breath of fire, consuming eyes of green.

She hadn't meant to say that at all. She meant to say:

O breath of fire, consuming the word of God.

Her bedroom door was ajar, and Isabel could hear Beatriz, who had just returned home, in the kitchen. "I left the coin as always and took the bundle of cookies from the niche."

"I wonder what they look like," said Mamá.

"We'll never know. Tight wimples and eyes bright with the love of Santa Madre, I imagine," described Beatriz, quite poetically, Isabel thought.

Isabel put away her writing just as Beatriz entered their bedroom.

"You're wearing *that* to church?!" cried Beatriz.

Isabel looked down at herself. She wore a long-sleeved beige cote-hardie-style gown. The collar was scoop-necked, and buttons extended down the center in a straight line. "What's wrong with it?"

"The color is drab. And the bodice is much too revealing. What if Don Sancho sees you? What will he think?"

"I don't give a raccoon's tail what he thinks." She fumed, remembering the way he had pushed her out of the plaza mayor the other day. As if she were a mule and he her owner.

Beatriz wore a high-collared fuchsia silk dress with birds and trees stitched on it and a veil to match. She always dressed modestly, choosing to wear the more traditional face-covering veil, while Isabel preferred a snood on the back of her hair. The girls were forever arguing over which headpiece was the most appropriate.

"How can you breathe under there?" said Isabel, lifting up her sister's veil.

"There are holes, you know. The air circulates just fine."

"Unfortunately, Beatriz, you'll never be an upper-class girl, no matter how hard you wish it. With Papá's small plot of land, we are firmly tethered to the middle."

Beatriz sniffed. "I'd rather look like an honorable Christian middle-class girl than a bar maiden."

Isabel laughed. "You're just jealous of my décolletage. Be patient. Mine grew last year. Yours will, too."

"You need to take more care with your appearance on Sundays. It's an insult to our Savior."

Isabel adjusted Beatriz's peineta, tempted to move it to the spot where the scab was, though she did not. "Would you rather I wear sharp combs in my hair like you?"

Beatriz flinched anyway. "Ouch!"

"I hardly touched you."

Beatriz would not meet her eye.

Isabel was suddenly filled with a mixture of love and great pity for her younger sister. "What are you doing to yourself?" she whispered.

"Nothing." Beatriz flushed, her cheeks as rosy as her dress.

If only she would confide in her. Weren't sisters supposed to share those kinds of details? They were practically twins; their mother had become pregnant again when Isabel was just five months old.

"Next time you sneak out to one of those foolish poetry readings of yours, I'll tell Papá," Beatriz said instead, glowering. "Mark my words."

Foolish Isabel. Sisters didn't share confidences. They lay in wait for you to make a mistake.

The second time Isabel had slipped out to attend a reading, she felt like she was being followed and had turned to see her sister, half a block behind. She could not think of a reason to be out and had told Beatriz the truth.

"Poetry? That sounds like an excuse for blaspheming," Beatriz had remarked. "And many false prophets will arise and lead many astray. Matthew 24."

Rather than try to decode Beatriz's cryptic quoting of scripture, Isabel pulled off the sapphire brooch that she always wore pinned to her left breast. "Keep it. But promise me you won't tell Mamá and Papá where I'm going. They'll just worry for no reason."

Beatriz had nodded, and thus far had not told. But she was acting so sanctimonious lately, Isabel couldn't be sure of anything.

Now, in their shared bedroom, Isabel made one last attempt to have a rapport with her sister. She looked deep into Beatriz's eyes, trying to discern what on earth would make her feel guilty enough to poke herself in the scalp like that. There was nothing there but pools of darkness.

Isabel did not change her dress.

Though Trujillo was not a large enough city to warrant its own cathedral, it did have five churches, and Isabel had to admit that the one the Perez family attended, Iglesia de Santiago, was the most impressive. Ceilings towered above, high enough to fit twenty horses stacked. There was real gold trim on the main altar. In the center chapel, a scalloped shell decorated the vault, and

Isabel sometimes traced circles in the air, mimicking the lines inside, imagining the seaside.

The family grew solemn as they approached. Churchgoing was serious. Everyone watched everyone else, and each member of the Perez family had learned to master the scrutiny. Except Abuela. Betraying her innermost beliefs had begun to take a toll. She had become more brazen in her advancing years so that Isabel and Mamá had to keep an eye on her, lest she say something incriminating. Papá and Beatriz led the family into the nave. Mamá and Isabel flanked Abuela, each taking an arm.

"I can't imagine anything in this earthly world that compares to the beauty and splendor of our house of worship," Beatriz said, turning her face to the ceiling.

"Sinagogas don't need to adorn themselves to be close to God," said Abuela behind her.

"Shhh, Abuela," said Isabel gently, knowing the word *sinagoga* should not be uttered here.

While Papá looked for an empty pew, Mamá took five vouchers from the cleric at the door. This proved that the Perezes attended church. People were stopped randomly on the street and asked to show their vouchers.

"Look at Señor Osorto," whispered a woman behind Isabel, clucking her tongue.

"His limp is new," said the woman next to her.

"Spending a night in jail will destroy anyone's hip," said the first woman. "I don't care how old he is. You can be sure he won't forget his voucher again."

Mamá, Isabel, and Abuela waited patiently next to Papá and Beatriz for another family to make their way to the end of a half-empty pew.

Beatriz took Papá's hand. "I lied when I said there was nothing more beautiful than Iglesia Santiago. The cathedral in Burgos is supposed to be grandest of all—like a palace. You promised we could see it one day. How about before the winter season?"

Papá frowned. "The journey takes three days in each direction. I can't leave the grapevines for that long."

"And who would tend to Ruy's grave?" added Mamá.

"Such pathetic excuses," said Beatriz, dropping her hand.

The beige fabric on Isabel's dress may not have been fancy, but it was heavy. And hot. She opened her fan to dry the perspiration on her face just as she heard a familiar voice.

"Buenos días, Señora and Señor Perez," said Don Sancho.

Isabel turned to receive a bow and a hat tip from Don Sancho. "Señorita Isabel. May I say that you have brought the sunshine indoors with that dress?"

Though Beatriz was completely veiled, Isabel could see the shock on her sister's face. Isabel felt vindicated, although she knew Don Sancho's taste in clothes was blinded by something else. Lust, no doubt. Perhaps it *was* cut too low. She crossed her arms over her bodice.

"Gracias, Don Sancho," replied Isabel politely.

Mamá, Abuela, and Beatriz took their seats. Isabel moved to follow Beatriz into the pew, but Don Sancho seemed to want to speak to her. Papá lingered so Isabel would not be standing alone with the older gentleman, which would have been improper.

Don Sancho leaned in close, conspiratorially. "We did not get a chance to speak after the scuffle in the plaza. I trust your parents have relayed my offer?" His breath smelled of garlic and raw meat.

"Not in great detail," Isabel replied. "But they did mention it, yes." Isabel wore just a sheer piece of silk pinned to the top of her head, so she could not hide behind a veil. But she kept her fan over her face, hoping he wouldn't catch her disgusted expression.

He clasped his sausage fingers together. "Splendid!"

"You do know I'm only sixteen," pressed Isabel. "I wouldn't want to act too hastily. Eighteen is a perfect age for marriage, don't you think?" At this, she dropped her fan and gave him a seductive smile. If she was going to wear a dress like this, she may as well act the part.

His eyelid twitched. "I'm—I'm not sure . . ." He paused, clearing his throat. "I will speak to your father about it."

Papá and Isabel finally took their seats, and to Isabel's dismay, Don Sancho went around the other side of the pew and squeezed in, to the right of Mamá. He acts as if he's part of the family, thought Isabel. Though a group of Old Christian women nodded at them approvingly.

A pair of stately nobles, a husband and wife, walked down the center aisle. Isabel recognized the silk fabric, an artichoke pattern in vermillion and gold. One of David Cohen's. And behind them, that young man! The one from the bookbindery. The one who kept creeping into her poem.

Who were they?

She turned to the group of Old Christian ladies sitting behind them. "Perdón. That family who just passed us. I forgot the señora's name. I delivered some vino to them and I just want to ask how she enjoyed it." One could not expect to be a good member of Christian society and not know the names of every important family. It needed delicacy.

"Count Alfonso and Countess Graciela Altamirano," said

one of the women. Her voice sounded weak and raspy beneath her veil.

Altamirano. That was the name the Cohens had mentioned the other night. The ones who kept Señor Cohen busy with all those dresses. "Of course. Foolish me. And the young man behind them?" Isabel's voice rose up at the end, as if it were an afterthought to inquire about him.

"Their son, Diego. He's just returned from University of Coimbra," the raspy-voiced woman replied.

This was the reason she had not seen him before in town. He had been away at school.

"Normally they worship in their private chapel at home," the woman continued. "But I guess they want to show him off today. Handsome, is he not?" she added, her smile sly beneath the lace.

Nothing got past a group of gossipy old ladies. Isabel supposed they were all the same, no matter which religion they came from. Everyone wanted to play matchmaker. Anyway, Isabel knew it was impossible. She was a converso with tainted blood. And the Altamiranos were from the oldest, purest Christian lineage one could find in Spain.

"He's all they have," added another woman, in a lavender veil. "Her other two babies died in childbirth."

Isabel watched as the count and countess, along with their son, took the entire front pew. She shifted closer to her sister to keep him in view. Isabel could see his brown hair was not tied in a cord as it had been the other day but hung just below his shoulders.

"What are you staring at?" asked Beatriz.

"The statue of the Lord Jesúcristo standing next to the burro. It looks more real today, don't you think?"

Beatriz's eyes darted to the front. "Is Juan Carlos up there?"

"I have no idea," said Isabel.

Beatriz touched her scalp, on the scab no doubt. "Then move down. It's too hot in here for our arms to be touching."

Isabel took one last look at the back of Diego's head. Diego! What a fine, strong name. She then slid to the right, where a tall man promptly blocked her view.

Fray Francisco de San Martin approached the pulpit in his rich vestments: a long-sleeved white gown with a black velvet cape around the shoulders, cowled at the neck. His head was styled in a tonsure, shaved in a circle, leaving his hair in a ring from ear to ear and his pate bald. Four altar boys, in white gowns and red sashes, helped prepare the candles and the incense.

"Before we begin," said Fray Francisco, "I have an announcement. Next Sunday, a special guest will be delivering the sermon. Someone of high authority in the Church. I trust you to make every effort to arrive early. Carry your infirm neighbors if you have to. And those too old to come each week." He paused, his eyes sweeping the entire room. "Do not miss this. Or you may live to regret it."

Murmurs went through the crowd.

Isabel heard the name Torquemada spoken by the ladies in the pew behind. A shiver went through her. Would the private confessor to Queen Isabella truly visit their small village?

"Buenas noticias!" said Beatriz.

"On the contrary," whispered Isabel. "That does not sound like good news." If it were indeed to be Torquemada, that could only mean bad omens for conversos. The Dominican monk had been with the queen since she was a young princess and was rumored to be of converso origin himself. It was also common knowledge that he made no secret of his hatred for anyone, Jew or Moor, who did not accept the Lord Jesús as their savior.

"Nonsense," argued Beatriz. "We need inspiration from someone closer to el Dios. Scripture can be limited with these small-town friars." She clasped her hands together in supplication.

"There's no need to pray for a new sermon. It's going to happen."

"I'm just grateful that my wishes were heard."

"Be careful what you wish for."

"Don't be so narrow-minded that you close yourself off to new ideas," said Beatriz.

Trying to reason with Beatriz was a losing proposition. Isabel directed her attention to the front. The service was beginning.

After Mass, it was time to approach the altar to take the Host. Maybe she would have a chance to see Diego again. But it was not to be. Because of his advantageous position in the front pew, he was one of the first to receive communion. As he left through a front exit, she was able to catch only a quick glimpse of his shoulders before he disappeared.

Since her family was seated so far back, it took nearly fifteen minutes before they reached the front. Isabel smelled the soapy scent of the friar's hand, unsuccessfully masking the odor of onions. He inserted the wafer and she distractedly let it dissolve in her mouth. Her sister, however, looked positively beatific, tipping her head back in pleasure like a kitten being petted behind the ears.

Since Diego was a boy, the primary meal of the day had consisted of no fewer than three kinds of animals. Today, they were dining on pork, goat, and peacock.

"The sauce on this peacock is divine," commented the countess. "Cook informed me it has bacon, onion, chicken broth, minced almonds, lemon juice, bitter oranges, honey, walnuts, and cloves."

Diego smiled indulgently at his mother. He had more pressing things on his mind than the ingredients of sauces. "Father, what is the name of the alguacil?"

The count was working on a particularly gristly piece of pork in his cocido and didn't answer immediately.

The countess filled in her husband's silences, as she usually did. "Why do you ask, m'hijo?"

"I saw a brawl earlier this week in the plaza mayor."

"Nothing serious, I trust?" said the countess.

"On the contrary, the alguacil had the situation under control in a matter of minutes."

While Diego waited for an answer from his father, he looked around for Martín, their kitchen servant, to light a fire at the hearth. The alcazarejo de los Altamiranos sat atop a high rocky slope, boasting a view of the Tagus River and surrounding townships rivaled only by the royal castle. Built in the thirteenth century out of granite, it was a defensive home given to some distant Altamirano relative who led military troops to victory in Castile. With its fortresslike exterior design, it could, if need be, protect those inside from attack. But it was also constantly frigid.

Unfortunately, Martín was nowhere to be found.

The count swallowed dramatically, then dabbed a

napkin at the corners of his mouth. "Don Sancho del Aguila. Came up through the army. Quite formidable."

Diego rested his fork, trying to remain unaffected, though jealousy spiked in his veins. "Is he married?"

The count scoffed. "Why concern yourself with such things? Tell me how the tax collections are going. Have you calculated the numbers for this week?"

"Perhaps the alguacil has a daughter of marrying age?" inquired the countess. She never liked to speak of business at the table.

"He has no offspring," said the count, always eager to correct anyone in the room. "I hear he's planning a betrothal to a converso girl. Though how long that will last is anyone's guess."

"What do you mean?" asked Diego. At the mention of the girl, his heart thumped beneath his doublet.

"The situation with the New Christians is precarious at best."

"Is that your opinion or are you speaking from fact?"

"Fact, without a doubt. I've just been made a Familiar." He smiled proudly.

So that was it. The reason his father wanted him to leave school in such a hurry. The Altamiranos were now even more beholden to the monarchy.

The countess raised a wineglass to her husband. "A great honor."

"As a lay official, I'll be reporting directly to the Inquisitors," continued the count.

You mean spying, thought Diego. A collaborator.

"They are going to police Judaizers with a firm hand.

By this time next year, we will have had so many autos de fe it will be a commonplace occurrence."

Acts of faith. Diego had heard about one in Seville earlier this year. A classmate of his at university had attended. It was a trial of sorts, but it sounded like a complete farce. After being put to the question, which was really an excuse to apply torture, the very public spectacle consisted of announcing the crime, followed by a dramatic processional to hear the sentencing. Six people were eventually burned alive at the stake, also publicly. His classmate had described the screams of the victims and the ghastly stench as nothing short of bestial.

Diego felt ill. "Con permiso, Mother. If you'll excuse me." He turned to his father. "I'll have those numbers to you later this evening."

He stumbled into his bedroom and promptly threw up the fancy peacock sauce into his chamber pot. He didn't even know Isabel, and already he was sick with worry for her. Yes, he had hoped to court her himself, but that was out of the question now that he had learned she was a converso. His father would forbid it, as her bloodline was tainted. Perhaps he could simply warn her to be careful.

After he cleaned himself up, he moved to his desk. He composed a letter, sealing it with burgundy wax and his personal stamp.

He went searching for Martín, finally locating him in the cellar, salting bacalao. The fish fillets hung on hooks down below, drying out for weeks. In the winter months, when fish ran scarce, they would soak one in water to bring it back to its original form and eat it. Usually, Diego might view a scene such as this—dead fish hanging on hooks, with a single source of light coming in from the tiny window, reanimating them so they almost danced— as a subject for a still-life painting. Some painters were starting to move away from devotionals and depict secular moments of life. But now all he could see was Isabel tied to a post, the waves of her luxurious hair going up in flames.

"Martín, please get this message to Isabel Perez. Isaac the bookbinder will have her address."

11

On Wednesday afternoon, Abuela rushed breathlessly into the kitchen, where Isabel was peeling off the outer layers of chick-peas. Next to her lay a bowl filled with tiny opaque skins, still holding their spherical shape.

"He's here," announced Abuela. "The bookbinder. He translated the poem!"

"Where is everyone else?" asked Isabel.

"Your father took Beatriz out on a wine delivery. Your mother is airing out all of our dresses behind the house. The moths have begun to settle into them. We should hurry, nonetheless."

Isabel quickly removed her apron and went into the sala. "Señor Isaac, so nice to see you again."

He wore the same plain gown as David and Hannah Cohen, with the red badge indicating he was a Jew, and the funnel-shaped hat. Abuela served tea while they exchanged pleasantries. Finally, she could wait no longer. "Did you bring the poem?"

Isaac emptied the contents of his pockets: two coins, a small looking glass, a pamphlet printed from a press, and a note, sealed with wax.

Isabel frowned. "You lost it?"

"Isabel!" admonished her grandmother. "You must exercise more patience."

"No matter," laughed Isaac. "I know she is eager. It's here somewhere," he added, patting his gown.

Abuela pointed to the pamphlet. "What is that? It doesn't look handwritten."

"It's from a printing press!" exclaimed Isaac. "My colleague, Sa'id, gave me a sample from his own machine while he translated the poem. I was very excited to see it. Now we can print so much more than just the Bible." He took a sip of tea.

"Qué maravilloso!" said Abuela, reading the pamphlet. "Wonderful."

Isabel did not need a lesson on the wonders of Gutenberg right now. She knew all about him. They used his version of the Bible in church. "Señor. The translation?"

"Of course." Finally, he found a small piece of parchment in a hidden place inside his tunic. "Ah. Here it is," said Isaac. "I left your original at the shop, not wanting to risk losing it on the way."

"Wise choice," said Isabel, snatching the handwritten paper from his hand, impatient as a small child in front of a plate of Christmas turrón.

Isabel read aloud in Castilian.

"O gazelle, you who graze constantly in the
   meadows,
I resemble you in wildness and in blackness of the eye.
Both of us are alone, without a friend, and we heap
   blame
always on the decree of fate."

Isabel's throat caught on the last word and she found herself unable to speak.

"What does it mean, this word *gazelle*?" asked Abuela.

"The translation is not exact. *Zabyatan* is the Arabic word for gazelle," clarified Isaac. "But we don't have those here in Spain. Perhaps the author means a roe deer?"

Isabel remained quiet. Abuela looked at her, concerned. "Are you all right?"

"Es que . . . it's just that . . . the writer longs for companionship," Isabel finally replied. "And her fate, even though she may be betrothed, leaves her still feeling alone." Her eyes filled with tears.

"I didn't hear it say anything about being betrothed," said her grandmother.

Isaac cleared his throat. "If I may. Do you know what the poet is referring to when she says the 'blackness of the eye'?"

Isabel used her lace handkerchief to dab her own eye. "The girl and the deer both have black eyes, I suppose," said Isabel. "Kohl, perhaps, lining the girl's rims."

"I don't think so," said Isaac. "The old Arab poets admired *hawar* and wrote of it often."

"*Hawar?*" asked Isabel.

"The intense contrast between the black iris and the white cornea. *Hawar* is a feature of beauty. By mentioning the blackness of the eye, the poet thinks of herself as beautiful, but her destiny is sentencing her to a life of solitude. Where no one will appreciate that beauty."

Isabel broke out into full sobs.

"I-I had no idea this poem would move you so," stammered Isaac. "If you'd like, I can try and find out more about the poetess. Ibn Sa'id thinks he knows who her father is. It is rumored he was a well-known poet as well."

"Gracias, Isaac," said Abuela, comforting Isabel, who was suddenly terribly afraid of a life of solitude, even with a husband by her side.

Beatriz entered through the front door. Isabel feigned a smile, hoping Beatriz wouldn't notice she'd been crying.

"Is there a party occurring? Because I didn't receive an invitation," she said, lifting her veil and removing her gloves.

Isaac stood abruptly, spilling his tea in the process.

"Señor Isaac was putting in an order for wine," said Abuela, dabbing the wet table with the bottom of her apron.

Isabel covered the parchment with her kerchief. "Is Papá with you?" She was not necessarily trying to hide the poem from him, she just didn't want to cause concern. Other than Papá's book of daily Hebrew blessings he kept hidden in the deep recesses of the cellar, this was now a second form of contraband on their property. In addition, she and Abuela had confided in a stranger to consult on it. The more people who knew about it, the riskier it was. Papá would put a stop to it, saying it wasn't safe. As far as Beatriz was concerned? She was an unknown. Isabel didn't know whether she could be trusted or not.

"He went straight to the vineyard," answered Beatriz, staring at Señor Isaac. Isabel could sense her sister wanting more information.

"We're finished now," said Abuela. She turned to the bookbinder. "We'll get back to you about your order."

He looked confused. When no explanation was forthcoming, he shrugged and headed for the door. "I almost forgot," he uttered, turning back. He handed Isabel the sealed note from the contents of his pockets. "This is for you. A messenger came by my shop asking for your address. I told him I was coming here and would deliver it personally."

Curious, Isabel took the note and slipped it into her own pocket.

Beatriz eyed Isaac's back as he left. When the door closed behind him, she said, "Isaac. Isn't that a Jewish name?"

"Your father does business with Jews all the time," answered Abuela. "Come, Isabel. Let's finish those chickpeas. Beatriz, we need your help in the kitchen."

"Oh, all right. Let me put my gloves away and hang up my veil first," said Beatriz, heading toward their shared bedroom.

Isabel wanted to read the note alone, without the presence of her nosy sister. "I'll take your things."

Beatriz narrowed her eyes at Isabel for this unexpected kindness but handed over her belongings.

Isabel hung up the veil in the armario, next to all the other perfectly pressed ones her sister wore daily. Then she pulled out the note. The red wax seal lay fixed and unbroken. It held the initials DAM. Don Sancho's surname was Aguila. Was there a third family name she didn't know about, one that began with an *M*? What if Don Sancho refused to wait until she was eighteen? What if he was proposing marriage formally, through this very paper? But when she read the message, it was not at all what she expected.

Meet me in front of the public baths in the Moorish quarter, at the ninth hour this evening.

It was signed, *The bookbinder's apprentice.*

12

DAM. Diego Altamirano. Since spotting him in church, she had known he was no apprentice. But when she had met him at the bookbinder's, her question seemed innocent enough. Now, seeing his handwriting on the paper, she felt ashamed at her ignorance, wishing she could take back what she said.

Diego Altamirano was sending *her* a message? Why did he want to meet? Was he attempting to court her? Certainly, he would have heard about Don Sancho's interest or her own converso lineage at the very least. It was hard to believe he lived in the alcazarejo—such an austere-looking place. He didn't seem cold, though. The opposite. The note and the man were shrouded in mystery and she was determined to find out more.

Abuela and Beatriz were in the kitchen. She would go and help them, act like nothing had changed, while she figured out yet another cover story so she could leave the house tonight. She knew she was playing with fire. One of these days, someone in her family was going to catch her.

Abruptly, an original poetic verse popped into her head, though strangely, it was from Diego's point of view.

> *By God, I am suited to great things*
> *And I walk with haughty step*

But I dare you to look 'neath
O poetess of Trujillo

What would her ancestor, the Jewish poetess, think of that? Did the girl ever write as if she were a man?

There was no time for such indulgences. She rushed back into the kitchen to help Abuela and Beatriz prepare the meal.

"No primer plato?" remarked Beatriz as the family sat together at the small table in the sala later that evening. "I thought we were starting with the lentil soup, then following with the garbanzo beans and red pepper rice and veal cutlets."

"I was so hungry, I wanted to eat it all together," said Isabel.

Beatriz huffed. "And whatever Queen Isabel wants, she gets."

"Don't use the queen's name in vain," said Papá sternly.

"I think it's a nice change to eat all the courses together," said Abuela, giving Isabel a small smile, for her eyes only. How Isabel adored her grandmother—every crease in her face, the crisscross pattern on her right cheek and the smattering of thin lines near her eyes.

"This plate is chipped in case you hadn't noticed," said Beatriz. "Most of them are." She was certainly in a dark mood this evening.

Mamá looked down, embarrassed. "We're saving for Isabel's dowry. Unfortunately, we can't afford to replace our dishes right now. They'll have to do." She was getting older, Isabel noticed. The crown of her head was threaded with gray at the roots. It wasn't so long ago that her mother played escondido with her and Beatriz, hiding under the table, giggling like a young girl. Even though the thought of her dowry, and possibly the grapevines, going to that wretched Don Sancho made her cringe, Isabel smiled warmly at her mother.

"You'd better not complain, Beatriz," said Papá. "Or there won't be anything left for your dowry."

Beatriz moved the red peppers and rice around on her plate. "I don't know if I want to get married."

"Don't be silly, hija," said Mamá.

"I'm thinking about taking the veil and vows when I'm of age."

Abuela gasped and slipped a hand through the top of her dress. Isabel knew she was touching the hand-shaped charm she kept sewn on her undergarments to ward off the evil eye. "*No dizirlo ankora,*" she said in Judeo-Spanish. "Don't say that again."

"Why not?" said Beatriz defiantly.

"You are dishonoring the family, that's why," said Papá.

"Dishonor, verdad? Really? Your hypocrisy is amusing."

Isabel braced herself for another dinner-table fight.

"Your taking the veil is out of the question," said Papá.

"But you led me here." Beatriz's smile cloyed in its insincerity. "I owe it all to you."

She had a point. The Perezes were conversos because of a decision made by Papá's and Mamá's families. Maybe he shouldn't complain that she had become too good at her job.

"You want to be cloistered, never showing your face to the world?" asked Mamá.

"Surely you realize there are other orders, Mamá. Nuns who grow vegetables and administer good deeds out in the community. I can tend to the poor or help take in children whose parents have been captured by the Inquisition."

"How charitable of you," said Papá icily. "Those helpless

Jewish and converso children would not be in a convent at all if there were no Inquisition to begin with."

"Constanza says there is a special place in Heaven carved out for charitable girls who do the Lord's work," said Beatriz.

The silence at the table was thick like a slab of meat.

Beatriz looked around and laughed. "Don't have a billy goat, everyone. I merely said I was *thinking* about it."

Papá, Mamá, and Abuela remained scowling. Isabel took advantage of the enmity toward Beatriz to guide the conversation to her own agenda. Clearing her throat, she said, "There's an added benefit of eating tonight's meal all at once. We left in such haste from the Cohens', we forgot to have Yuçe cut our cloth. I thought I might go over there tonight and pick it up." She glanced at Papá, gauging his reaction. They had not spoken about Sucot since their abrupt departure. His face remained impassive.

"It's true," agreed Beatriz. "We won't have enough time to sew new dresses if we don't get that material. The christening is in two weeks."

Isabel was grateful but confused. Beatriz helped Isabel's cause by her desire for a new dress, but did her sister not just profess her desire to join a convent and eschew all worldly goods? The girl was more erratic than the acidity of grapes.

Mamá looked alarmed. "You'll never make it out of the judería before curfew, Isabel. The gates are locked by half past nine."

"Then I'll bed with Rachel."

Papá threw down his napkin. "You will not go out this evening, Isabel. Nor will you go back to their house. Ever. That ingrate David Cohen is no better than the Inquisitors."

"Who will we buy fabric from, then?" complained Beatriz.

Mamá glanced imploringly at Papá. "Manolo . . ." But she did not go further than saying his name. She would not contradict him in front of the family.

"You heard my answer."

Isabel would have to think of another plan for a rendezvous with Diego.

The only sound for the rest of dinner was their forks scraping the plates. As Mamá stood up to clear the dishes, Isabel dabbed her brow with her napkin. "I don't feel so well. If you'll excuse me."

Mamá, her lips white, did not question this. Clearly, she was still furious at both Beatriz and Papá. With Beatriz and Abuela helping to clean up, Isabel knew she only had a few moments to slip away. She would figure out something later to tell her sister when she returned to their shared bedroom.

Isabel unlatched the iron grill that covered the small window opening in the bedroom. Though she'd jumped from the second floor many times before, it still hurt upon landing. Shame she wasn't as agile as housebreakers, men who could climb ropes to upper floors with the ease of a monkey, stealing a family's silver in no time, then drop down without injury. In her haste to escape, her dress caught on the sharp point of one of the iron bars. She did not glance back. He would be there in less than fifteen minutes. There was not a moment to lose.

13

Isabel made her way down the dirt road, damp from the current cloudburst. Rain occurred so rarely in the region of Extremadura that a part of her wanted to run along the riverbank with her mouth open, catching drops on her tongue. But her curiosity about Diego trumped everything else. She drew her cape over her head and quickened her step.

She saw two Jewish boys, scurrying under an arch, their identifying badges flashing on their beige tunics, rushing to make it into the judería before the gates were shut. Isabel shuddered to think of innocent children locked out, sleeping in the excrement-filled streets, prey to prostitutes, pickpockets, or cardsharps. Mamá was always trying to frighten her and Beatriz with tales of pícaros, the ne'er-do-wells of Trujillo.

The bricked dome of the mezquita rose above the sleepy buildings. She was nearly there. Isabel knew the Moorish quarter well, from her wanderings in its narrow warrens, searching for artisans' shops that might sell books of poetry.

The church bell rang nine times just as Isabel turned the corner. The Moorish baths were directly in front of her. And there he was, standing under an eave, lit by the moon. His eyes widened when he spotted her and she found herself smiling broadly as she approached him.

But then his expression became serious. "Forgive me. You must think I'm mad sending you a note like that, asking to meet me here."

"I wouldn't commit you to an asylum, but I am curious. I sneaked out of my home, in fact."

Up close, his jaw seemed unshaven, but it was too dark to tell for certain. His nearness warmed her, though she could not imagine why. There was at least an arm's distance between them.

"I'm sorry if I've made things difficult for you in regard to your parents," he said.

"I've done it before. Please don't concern yourself."

"I imagine you have Don Sancho to do that now. Concern himself with you, I mean."

Isabel's eyebrows went up. "You know of Don Sancho?"

He nodded sheepishly. "Recently, I discovered his name linked to yours, yes."

So he *had* been asking around about her. She waited for more explanation, but he was quiet.

"You still have not revealed the purpose of our meeting," said Isabel.

Diego glanced around them. Everyone seemed to be indoors, waiting out the rain even though the usual hour for shopping was still at hand. Most people in Trujillo did not sit down for dinner until the tenth hour after high noon.

"Shall we walk a bit?" he said.

Maybe the answer to her question would be forthcoming. He seemed preoccupied, but there was a gentleness about him that she found charming. She nodded, walking alongside him.

The rain eased into a drizzle. No horse and wagons were yet about, so that a hush fell over the whole quarter. The only sound was the crunching of their feet over the flint chips strewn on top of the dirt. Isabel wished she had not worn chopines. The clogs kept the mud off the bottom of her dress, but they were noisy. As they walked, Diego began to tell her about his studies at the University of Coimbra in Portugal.

She did not want him to know she had been asking about him, too, so she feigned surprise at hearing of his education. "So that's why I had not seen you in town before. You've been away at school."

He seemed amused. "You were wondering about me, then?"

She flushed, realizing she had revealed her cards anyway. "No, I just mean, when I saw you on the calle—I mean, at the bindery—you did not look familiar."

"I was born here in Trujillo, but I've been gone for quite a while. I'm in my second year." He frowned. "I don't know if I'll be returning to school, however."

"And why is that?"

"I don't want to bore you with my family obligations. I'd rather speak about the great artists of the world."

"I don't know much about art," admitted Isabel. "Do you have a favorite painting?" she asked.

"All the best oil painters are coming out of Italy. Masaccio, Michelangelo. There is quite literally a rebirth occurring there. My favorite is Verrocchio's *Baptism of Christ*, without question. Mainly because of his young apprentice, Leonardo da Vinci. Da Vinci painted one of the angels in the lower left corner and Verrocchio did the second one." Diego moved his hands enthusiastically when he spoke. "Verrocchio's angel looks like a typical boy you'd see on the street. The face isn't unique, the body is flat and posed simply. But da Vinci's angel has no earthly model at all. He gave her weight and dimension, turned her body in a complex way to give her a sense of movement, and made the light shine on each individual strand of hair. Because she is beautiful, the viewer knows she is divine. It is an ideal beauty. The angel is unified in both substance and soul." He paused, infectious excitement in his eyes. "You must go to Florence and see it. It's at the Church of San Salvi."

Diego made her feel dizzy with possibility. He spoke about the future as if it were nothing. And everything.

"This massive rebirth in Italy is not just in the arts," he continued. "It's also about new ideas in sciences and astrology. There have been writings by Muslims, Jews, and even Catholic philosophers that are turning the world upside down."

"Like the time of Al-Andalus."

He stopped walking to regard her. "I'm impressed."

She felt proud she could contribute something to the conversation. "And have you read all these written works?" she ventured.

"Hardly. I only know Castilian and Latin fluently. But they hired a Jew to teach Hebrew at my university. Of course, he is not allowed to hold a professorship title, but I managed to get a good start on it before I had to leave."

"The language of the Jews?"

He nodded. "There is a movement called the School of Christian Hebraists."

Incredible. Wouldn't Abuela be surprised to know that Christians were studying Hebrew. "I'd like to learn Arabic," said Isabel, thinking of her ancestor's poem.

"I feel that one must be a philologist, a language scholar, to understand not just painting, but all forms of the arts and sciences. When translating ancient philosophy, one wrong word can change the entire meaning."

"It's the same with poems," said Isabel. "Each word is placed in a verse for a reason."

"You read poetry?" he asked.

She nodded. "And write. Or at least I try to."

"I'd like to hear one of your poems."

She flushed, remembering her attempt to write about the burning sinagoga when all she could think of were Diego's green eyes. "Maybe later. Tell me," she said, changing the topic. "What is the most scandalous philosophy being discussed at the moment?"

"Oh, there are many." They walked for a few seconds while he thought. "Take the struggle between divine providence and human choice. If we believe that God is all-powerful and all-knowing, we must believe He has the ability to predict the future as well. If God knows all our actions before we make them, then everything is predetermined. He has His hand in all things."

Isabel pondered this. "You mean all our actions would be decided before we make them?"

Diego nodded.

"What if a man kills another?" she said. "Can he simply blame it on God, claiming he had no choice in the matter?"

"I don't accept that excuse. I believe the opposite theory. That God created man to have choice, to live by his own moral conduct. It's up to each one of us to behave virtuously or become evil. We must balance this within ourselves."

"So God does not punish?"

"No. Otherwise the vicious man would not be allowed to live a happy life. I'm sure you know plenty of cruel people who live a full life and die at peace, so this is not the case. By the same token, tragedy befalls the good, pious person who has never hurt anyone in their life."

Like her brother, Ruy. It didn't make sense that he died so young. Was that predetermined? If so, for what reason? He was the most innocent boy she had ever seen. Why was Torquemada's body not lying in a grave instead of her brother's? "Who can we blame, then, for tragedy if not God?"

"Laws of Nature," he explained. "We do not know why a boulder falls on a good person and kills him instead of the evil person standing next to him. Nature is without morality. But God gave *man* the power to learn right from wrong. To learn from his mistakes."

"Do you believe a vicious person can change?" she asked.

"I do. If he truly feels guilt and asks the person he wronged for forgiveness, that is the first step. So, if he is in the same situation again and doesn't commit the same crime, then he has truly repented, and he can be forgiven."

"But only Jesús has the power to forgive," she said, recalling her years of church lessons. "You're speaking heresy." She did not hold back her surprise.

From Diego's unruffled expression, it was obvious he had no fear of being accused of a crime such as this. His family was too powerful.

"I'm not saying God does not exist," began Diego. "I'm saying that perhaps the natural next step in theological thinking is some sort of duality between God and man where man has the power to shape his own character and influence his own future."

"He has free will, then." Isabel had never been so grateful for a lesson from Abuela in her entire life.

Again, he turned to face her. "Where on earth did you come from, Isabel Perez?"

A small smile escaped her lips, but then she became

self-conscious at his attention. She watched a tunic-clad gentle-man crossing the street while she tried to sort out her emotions. Signs of life began to stir in the quiet neighborhood. A couple passed them but paid them no mind. Candles were lit in windows. Sounds of laughter came from a nearby taberna.

Despite how impressed he was with her, she needed to guard her tongue. She did not know this man at all. He could even be a spy. Though from the earnest way he looked at her, this seemed doubtful. He was smiling at her right now, in fact, a grin so daz-zling that she struggled to keep the stroll businesslike. "But is free will an absolute?" she ventured. "Surely, there are circumstances beyond our control." She was thinking of the four prisoners accused of Judaizing, but it was too dangerous to discuss that. She introduced a safer example instead. "Take the rule of curfew. On my walk over here, I saw two boys rushing to reach the judería before the ninth hour. If they had been late, they would have been locked out, stripped of their clothes, and given a fine. That does not sound like freedom to me."

"Well, I was referring to free will of man versus God. But let's expand on your idea, free will of man versus man. I would argue that one has free will when they are guided by reason. The logi-cal Jew knows what time the gates close and chooses to return home safely, before the ninth hour. With this choice, he has achieved freedom from the tyranny of his impulse, the desire to stay out late."

"And the ones whose job it is to lock the gate? Do they have free will *not* to lock it?"

"Absolutely. Though I doubt they would exercise that choice. They'd face certain termination from their job."

Or death by beating from their superiors in the Holy Office, she thought. She wondered: Was Diego a person who was actually sympathetic to the Jews? Or was he merely a thinker who loved philosophy, with all its morasses, and could argue just as easily for the Inquisition as well?

"Tell me about the poetry you enjoy," he suggested.

She described the readings she had attended and the battles, all in artistic fun, to finish someone else's poem.

"Give me an example."

She grinned. "Well, the first person might say, *The wind has made a coat of mail, from the water.* And the next person listens to that rhyme pattern and says, *What a coat of armor—Suitable for battle only if it were frozen.*" She paused. "Did you catch what they're talking about?"

"I have absolutely no idea."

"It's a metaphor, for chain mail—only it's river water!"

"Delightful. Did you write that?"

"Oh no. But a relative of mine—" She stopped herself. Best not to mention she was related to a Jewish poet.

They continued walking and talking. He accidentally brushed her forearm, then retrieved his hand quickly. Her skin tingled where his hand made contact.

Shouts came from another street to their left. Diego looked alarmed. "Wait here."

Isabel was not about to stay put. She promptly ran after him.

Some young boys, no older than ten, had a small pyre kindling in the middle of the street. They were hooting and laughing as they threw sticks into the center of the logs.

"They're just some harmless ruffians," said Isabel when she caught up to Diego. The light drizzle would probably put out the fire soon anyway.

"Don't speak so fast," said Diego, his grim expression illuminated by the orange flames. "Look at what they're burning."

Isabel took a step closer. Those weren't logs—they were books! "Are they mad? Destroying the written word like that?"

But Diego wasn't listening. He rushed at the boys, yanking them by their arms, tossing them aside like sacks of sand. Next thing she knew, he had pulled off his cloak and, using the damp side of the wool, quenched the fire. Smoke escaped from the sides of his coat, but the fire was extinguished.

"Get out of here before I call the bailiff!" he shouted at the boys.

The boys dispersed, but not before throwing some stones at a shuttered Moorish stall. "Moriscos!" they shouted.

Isabel knelt down, taking Diego's damaged cloak into her hands. Though it smelled like singed animal hair, there was something intimate in holding a garment that had just draped his body. She turned it around, checking inside the sleeves. "I'm afraid it's beyond repair."

"No matter," he said, rummaging through the ashes. Bits of white parchment floated in the sky like moths. Isabel recognized foreign letters written on the paper, markings on wings. Arabic. Hebrew.

Diego picked up a square of leather wrapping, but it was charred beyond recognition. "This might even have been the Qur'an. I can't be sure. It appears there were some Jewish texts in the fire as well." He looked toward the direction the boys ran. "The little cagadas."

Now it was Isabel's turn to regard Diego. *Cagada*, or excrement, was not a nice word. He was as upset as she was. She *could* trust him.

"I would not have believed something like this could happen

in Trujillo if I didn't see it with my own eyes," admitted Isabel, returning his cloak. "How can people destroy something so precious?"

Diego strode to a peasant begging nearby and threw the man his coat. The beggar bowed and muttered his thanks.

"There's a bench over there," said Diego, pointing to a tile artisan's shop. As she followed, Isabel was aware that her heart was beating too fast. Being with him, she felt as if she were a bird in a cage, content to perch and be fed yet yearning to flap her wings and break free. She had no word, no previous experience, to describe it.

Diego swept the water off the tiled seat with his gloved hand so she could sit down without wetting her cape and dress. He remained standing, rearranging the dagger on his belt. "I owe you an explanation for why I asked you to meet me."

He abruptly sat down beside her.

Was he going to grab her and kiss her? Would she enjoy it or scream for help?

"I sent you that note to warn you," said Diego. "And now with this book burning, I'm afraid it's confirmed. You're in danger."

"From whom?"

"From the Inquisition. From the civil authorities. From people like my father. And, perhaps most worrisome of all, your future husband."

Bile rose within her. Who was he to lure her out of her house at night just to frighten her? "This is nothing new. We've heard whispers for years." She pulled back her shoulders. "I'm Christian."

"You're New Christian, are you not?"

"Yes. There are many families like ours."

"You are now the target, I'm afraid. More than the Jews. More than the Muslims. Conversos are the official enemy, according to the new papal bull. They say you are the ones who are scheming to destroy Christian Spain from the inside. My father was just in Toledo and heard it from the queen herself. There will be auto de fe tribunals. It's hard to know how many people will be saved and merely reconciled to the Church, or how many will be—" He didn't finish. His pained eyes shone in the moonlight.

"Burned? Here in Trujillo?"

Diego nodded. "You can't afford to make a mistake. Especially in front of Don Sancho."

"Why are you telling me this?"

Diego paused. "Because I . . . I thought you should know." His eyes turned away.

So he did fancy her! She was at once both thrilled and panicked. The information he relayed went beyond Papá's hunches. They felt more real, more horrifying. She thought that if she could only bury herself in his chest as if he were her human armor, her own chain mail, everything would turn out all right. She clasped her hands in her lap to prevent herself from reaching out to him. "Thank you for your candor. I promise to be careful."

The church bell chimed eleven times in the distance. Had they been talking for two whole hours? That was a long time, yet it did not seem nearly enough.

He sprang up from the bench. "I've kept you out too late. May I walk you home?"

"I would like that." She would be able to have at least another quarter hour with him. If they walked slowly, even longer.

14

Tiptoeing, Isabel slipped into her bedroom. Her sister's sleeping figure lay peacefully under the linen, her breath slow and even. Isabel quietly removed her cloak, still damp from the rain, and hung it on a hook.

"Missing something?" trilled Beatriz's voice behind her.

"Oh!" Isabel exclaimed in surprise. "You're awake."

Beatriz sat up on her pallet, holding a small torn piece of orange cloth. "Of course I'm awake. It's almost midnight, the hour of matins."

"You've been rising in the darkness to say prayers?"

Her sister nodded. "There's something mystical about being the only one up in the house, don't you think? Knowing that elsewhere in Spain the monks and the nuns are doing the same thing at the same time?" Beatriz spread the slip of orange fabric on her bed, smoothing out the wrinkles. She calmly lit a candle.

God's earwax. Isabel's dress *had* torn. Was Beatriz going to taunt her with the evidence of her escape all night?

"Psalm 118 said: *media nocte surgebam ad confitendum tibi.* In the middle of the night, I will rise to give thanks unto thee. What a simple and beautiful sentiment. I do believe my body has become used to the routine. Now I wake up just before the bells chime, all on my own."

"How lucky for you," said Isabel dully. Still her sister said nothing about the torn fabric. Isabel could not take the suspense and forced the subject. "Where did you find that?"

"On the iron grate of our window."

Isabel thought fast. "I crawled out to get Señor Cohen's fabric after all. I knew Papá wouldn't approve. Please don't tell."

"Then where is our new dress material?" demanded Beatriz.

"Still at the studio, if you can believe it. Yuçe hadn't had time to cut it. He was at sinagoga, actually. Both he and his father. I told Señora Cohen that Papá wouldn't let us return to their house, so she said she'd ask Yuçe to deliver it this week. She feels simply awful about what happened the other night."

Beatriz's expression did not seem to care whether Hannah Cohen felt guilty or not. "And the color?"

"Perdón?"

"The dress fabric? Which color did you choose?"

"Oh. Periwinkle. The one you preferred the night of Sucot."

"How did you get past the gates of the judería?"

"Since it was such a short visit, I was able to slip out, just before the hour."

"But it's nearly midnight. What have you been doing all night, then?"

"Sitting in the center courtyard, writing by the moonlight. I didn't want to disturb Mamá and Papá and I thought it best if I waited until they bedded down." Isabel removed her gloves. "Come now, Beatriz. Are you quite through interrogating me?"

Beatriz snorted. "I'm not sure."

Isabel rustled around in a drawer. "Here. Take my fan. You always liked the jewels on the handle."

Beatriz snatched it from Isabel, squinting up at her sister. "I think I believe you. But let's just hope you have not sneaked out to meet a paramour. Don Sancho wouldn't take kindly to that."

Isabel's stomach dropped. "Whatever gave you that idea?"

"You're flushed."

"If you must know, it was a very romantic poem I was writing." Isabel hoped that was the end of it.

"Well, next time Don Sancho comes calling, best not to mention this little writing hobby of yours."

"I don't plan to. He wouldn't understand."

"Though I do wonder what he'd say if he knew his betrothed attended readings of illicit Moorish poetry."

"You wouldn't dare say anything!"

"While I think it would behoove you to suffer, I will not say a word. For now."

Isabel sat down on her sister's pallet, confused. "I don't understand. You *want* me to suffer?"

In the flickering light of the candle, Beatriz's face looked contorted, evil almost. "You live in the clouds, dear sister, with your poetry and your romantic notions."

"You think it's only me who wants beauty and rainbows? You're the one who can't abide basic human bodily functions. I saw how you reacted in the judería."

Beatriz rolled her eyes. "That's not what I'm talking about. You have the gaze of any male you want. Perfect hair, perfect nose, perfect décolletage. You have no idea what real pain is." She paused, raising her face to the ceiling. "We glory in our sufferings because we know that suffering produces perseverance. Romans 5:3–5."

Isabel stood abruptly. "I've heard enough."

"There's still hope, though," said Beatriz. "Your soul can be saved." She touched the scab on her head. "Through pain."

And all at once, Isabel knew what Beatriz was doing with that peineta. "You are like one of those horrible self-flagellants, aren't you?"

Beatriz didn't meet her sister's eye.

"A penitent, hurting herself to show remorse. What sin have you committed?"

"Being born."

Isabel shook her head. Who was this impostor who lived in their house? Were her friends following the same path? "Does Constanza know you do this?"

Beatriz did not answer.

Isabel persisted. "What about Juan Carlos?"

Something shifted in Beatriz's eyes. Or maybe it was just the flicker of the candlelight. "He has nothing to do with this."

Could it be that Beatriz's internal conflict was too much to bear? That her attraction to Juan Carlos did not reconcile with her hope for a future as a chaste nun? Did imagining the pleasures of the flesh make her feel too guilty, so she drew blood from her scalp? Perhaps. Whatever the explanation, at this moment, Isabel chose not to exploit her sister's weakness, but rather file it away for the future.

Beatriz thrust her shoulders back. "It isn't me you should be concerned about. Look to your own backyard. Time is running out for you to pay for your sins."

"I will keep your words in mind. Thank you for setting me straight." Isabel gently took the orange remnant out of Beatriz's hand. "Dear sister, what would I do without you?"

Thursday, the day after his evening stroll with Isabel, Diego stopped at an inn outside the walls of Trujillo. All morning and afternoon had been spent riding up and down the region of Extremadura, checking on various Altamirano tenant farmers. The paths were narrow and rocky, and it was slow going in places. His throat was parched and his bota bag had long run out of wine. He tied up his horse, took a swig of water from the well out front, washed his face and hands, then entered.

The inn was bustling. Underneath a low ceiling, groups of men, both young and old, sat on long tables, eating mutton, their voices loud from drink. The air was pungent with the smell of sweat and meat.

"Diego! Mi caballero."

Diego turned to his left, following the voice. "Lord Varjas! What a surprise."

His old friend waved him over. "Join me for a mug of wine."

Diego took a seat, removing his hat. Though they were both nineteen years of age, the other man now had a small belly that protruded over his sash. "How long has it been?"

"Since before you left for University, no?" replied Varjas. "We used to spend quite a bit of time in places like this, didn't we?"

"Indeed," said Diego. "Any news from Madrid?"

"More of the same. The queen is talking about moving the capital to Madrid since the water supply is so plentiful. The Toledanos aren't on her side, as you might imagine. Two autos de fe this week. Nasty business. But those deceitful conversos need to be put in their place."

Though it was difficult for him, Diego nodded in agreement. How could it be that such enlightenment was happening in other parts of Europe, but Spain was stuck in the twelfth century?

"How are they ever going to extricate all the conversos from their spouses and children and punish the correct people?" Diego wondered aloud. "Marriages go back to after the mass conversions of 1391. It's a mess of intermarriage and Jewish great-grandparents."

"Then they'll dig up the graves of the New Christians and burn their bones posthumously."

Diego cleared his throat, unnerved. "And what are they saying about this Portuguese treasurer, Isaac Abravanel?"

Varjas laughed. "It's true Her Majesty trusts only the Jews to handle the royal treasury. Plus, all his funnel-capped brethren are constantly filling the royal coffers to remain in her good stead. I have no doubt the king and queen will grab him for their own. He never took the baptism oath, so he is safe." Varjas waved over a maid. "Bring another bottle of rioja for my friend here."

The girl smiled devilishly at Diego, leaning over him to clear the dirty glasses. She was uncorseted, so her breasts practically fell out in front of his face. "My room is upstairs, second door on the left," she whispered into his ear. Diego did not take the bait. He gave her no second glance.

Varjas stared at his friend with incredulity. "Since when do you pass up a chance at the pleasure of the flesh?"

Diego hesitated.

"Excuse me," said a gentleman sitting at the table behind them. "I couldn't help but overhear." He turned to face Varjas. "Are you from Madrid?"

"What concern is it of yours?" said Varjas, resting his fingers on his pistol.

The man had a round, open face. His eyes were heavily lidded, and his blond hair spread out around his face like a furry dog. To Diego, he seemed harmless.

"I didn't mean to alarm," said the man. "I'm heading there myself. I've just returned to Spain, having been abroad." His Castilian accent was flawless.

Diego's attention piqued. "Abroad?"

The man nodded. "I was born in Paredes de Nava, but I've been in Italy the past four years."

"May I ask where in Italy?" said Diego, leaning in.

"Urbino," the man replied. "At the Ducal Palace. I'm a painter."

Diego's heart began to race. It couldn't be. "You're not, perchance, Pedro Berruguete?"

The man beamed, thrust his hand out. "The very same." He put his arm around the shoulders of a young man, about Diego's age, sitting beside him. "And this is my son, Alonso. He is studying sculpting."

Diego was ecstatic. He turned to Varjas. "This man is famous! We studied his *La Virgen de la Leche* at school." Diego's professor had obtained a study of *La Virgen de la Leche*, an artist's sketch that had been discarded at some point in the process of creating the final work. That was how students usually studied the masters if they couldn't sail to Italy or the Netherlands to see paintings in person. He addressed Berruguete again. "The patterns on the woodwork surrounding la Virgen's head, even in one of your earlier versions, were so varied and intricate. I could never achieve that level of variation."

Berruguete was clearly flattered.

"Tell me, did you apprentice with a Flemish artist?" continued Diego. "Because I see some similarities from that school in your work—the details in the faces, the brilliant colors and rich textures of the brocateado . . ."

"You are correct, young man," said Berruguete, delighted. "I studied with van Gent. He taught me the gilding process and the depth it can bring to textiles. Take his famous men series, the one of Ptolemy, for example; the sphere and the jewels on his robe were both painted with his unique process of bringing gold to life. I personally worked on that sphere."

"I can't believe it," said Diego. "Providence brought us to this moment." He listened intently as Berruguete spoke about an upcoming commission for the altar at the Church of Santa Eulalia. It was to be a series depicting several scenes from the life of la Virgen. Diego kept his face neutral, but inside, his heart leapt. He'd give anything to be able to apprentice with this man the way Berruguete had done with van Gent. But that could never be. His father would never abide it. Besides, it was not as if an offer were forthcoming. Berruguete probably had many eager students more qualified than Diego.

As Berruguete described how he planned to bridge the Flemish school of thought with the humanistic techniques coming out of Italy for this new Virgen series, a different thought entered Diego's mind. The reason why Isabel's face was so familiar was because she looked like the Virgin Mary in Berruguete's painting! She had the same auburn hair tumbling down her back, the same wide-set eyes and pale skin. A vision.

He knew he had to see her again. No matter who she may be betrothed to, no matter which type of blood ran through her veins.

The buxom maid came by to refill all of their cups. Berruguete and Alonso turned back to their own table to order olla podrida, a popular dish of pork, chicken, bone marrow, blood sausage, ham, and chickpeas. An older gentleman teetered by, too much drink in his belly. Diego recognized him as Zuniga, duque de Bejar, an old friend of his father's. Well-bred Spaniards did not get drunk and Diego did not relish conversing with the man.

Zuniga spotted him anyway. "Is that you, Master Diego?"

Diego nodded. "Duque." He put on his felt hat. "I'm just on my way out. Sorry I can't tarry and have a drink with you."

"Pity. You must give my best to the count," said Zuniga, accidentally spitting on Diego's cloak.

With annoyance, Diego brushed off his cape. As he went sideways between the two benches, Berruguete spun around again. "You're leaving?"

"I'm afraid so," replied Diego.

"Which count was that man speaking of, if you don't mind my asking?"

"Count Altamirano," piped in Varjas, who had remained silent until now. "Diego's father." Varjas was boasting about his friend, attempting to impress their new acquaintances. Diego did not like it, using names of important people that way. Varjas hadn't labored a day in his life and enjoyed reminding the working class of his status at every opportunity.

Berruguete's eyes twinkled. "You know, I could be persuaded to stay in Trujillo a bit longer," he began. "Instead of going to Madrid, I was also weighing the idea of setting up a studio right here."

"What a coincidence," said Diego, evenly. He knew the reason for the sudden friendliness. Now that Berruguete had heard his father was a count, he saw maravedis in front of his eyes. Competition was fierce for coveted church commissions. Eventually, all artists turned to the private sector to support themselves, servicing wealthy patrons with egos who wanted their own devotionals hanging among their tapestries in the dining room.

"I could use someone like you," continued Berruguete. "A young, eager student, willing to work hard and learn." He paused. "And one who doesn't use his father's position to advance himself."

That was a surprise.

"Unless, of course, you are already committed elsewhere?" asked Berruguete. "It does an older man's soul good to be appreciated. Alonso here wants nothing to do with his old papá. He prefers Donatello. Right, Son?"

Alonso turned red. "I don't prefer him to you, Papá, I just prefer a different medium."

All sons want to break free of the yokes of their fathers, thought Diego.

"So what do you think?" asked the artist.

Berruguete did seem to be a man of integrity. "I'm extremely flattered," Diego began. "I'll need to speak with my father—that is, not for permission." He chuckled. "I mean, he certainly lets me go about my days freely, but to make sure he has no plans for me over the next few months. I only just returned from university." *Stop blabbering, you blaffard.*

Berruguete nodded and Diego bade him farewell.

As Diego rode home that night, he let his heart run free with prospects for the future. One filled with art, and hopefully Isabel. Why shouldn't he have a rebirth in his own life like the one happening in Florence? Diego the apprentice, courting Isabel, in secret of course—with Don Sancho and his newly appointed Familiar father, it was simply too dangerous for them to be seen publicly. And eventually, Diego the painter, married to Isabel the poet.

Of course, there were difficult steps in between. Extricating her from her betrothal and then persuading his father that marrying a New Christian would not taint the Altamirano bloodline.

But first, he must convince the count to allow his precious progeny to become a working man.

One challenge at a time.

15

A banner flew outside the iglesia, adorned with an escudo, or coat of arms. The design was a circle with Latin words from Psalm 73: *Arise, O God and Plead Your Cause.* Inside the circle was a thick wooden cross, surrounded by a leafy tree branch and a sword. It was nearly impossible for Isabel to accept. The Inquisition was actually here, in her little town, waving its flag unabashedly.

The inside of the church was packed to the vaults. Friar Francisco's warning had worked. Isabel's fan did no good. The air stood stagnant no matter how many women's wrists moved back and forth. Before Mass began, she allowed herself one glance around. Maybe Diego was here with his parents. But the crowd was so thick, she couldn't see past the tenth row from the front. She did spot Don Sancho's distinctive shape, sitting in a middle pew. Thankfully, he was packed in there like a sardine. He wasn't going anywhere for the moment.

The members of the Dominican order stood flanking the pulpit in their dramatic white habits and black cloaks, reveling in their positions of power.

"I've never seen this many holy men in our church before," exclaimed Beatriz, giddy with excitement.

One of the friars held the silver cross of the Inquisition firmly in his hand. Little bells dangled from the horizontal bar, while the shiny vertical part of the cross caught the sunlight streaming in from the colored leaded-glass windows above. An altar boy swung a censer, spreading smoke. Normally, Isabel enjoyed the fragrant spice held inside, but today her stomach churned, and the smell made her feel queasy.

As there were no seats available, Papá led Beatriz, Isabel, Mamá, and Abuela to stand together on the right, behind the last pew. Others without seats crowded around them, so that the space quickly became thick with the smell of unwashed bodies.

A hush silenced the crowd. A tall man, gaunt and thin as a wheat stalk, emerged from the smoke and approached the main altar. He had a long, hooked nose and cheekbones so sharp they threatened to slice through his face. Though he was dressed like the other friars in a white robe and black cloak, his face was whiter than theirs, ghostly. "I am Tomás de Torquemada, the First Inquisitor General under His and Her Majesties' Holy Order of the Inquisition Against Heretical Depravity. Pope Sixtus the fourth has given us his blessing for this edict."

The congregation gave a collective gasp. It truly was him, in the flesh. Isabel startled at the volume of his booming voice. It belied the fragility of his body.

"Look around you," said Torquemada. "You think you know your neighbors? I promise you, you do not. You do not!"

The Dominican friar pounded the silver cross on the ground, echoing Torquemada's words.

"There are false Christians among us who are corrupting the Church," continued Torquemada. "They claim to worship our Lord, but they lie.

"We must weed them out, like a poisonous mushroom. These so-called conversos are really just swine. Pigs who are infecting us, soiling our clean, holy way of life. It is time to rid our beloved Spain of their tainted blood. To rid our villages of social anarchy. To rid our families of the disintegration that comes from mixed marriages. To rid our souls of moral dissoluteness."

The entire Perez family focused on Friar Torquemada.

"How do we recognize these Judaizers if they look just like us? If they sit among us?"

No one responded.

"Let me enlighten you. Who among us has witnessed a neighbor, a friend, a family member utter that he is awaiting the Messiah?"

The crowd buzzed with chatter.

"This is blasphemy!" boomed Torquemada. "The Messiah has already come, in the form of Jesús Cristo, the anointed One."

Isabel heard many in the congregation utter, "Eso es," that's it. She tried to remember, had Papá, Mamá, or Abuela ever spoken of the Messiah before?

Torquemada's tirade got louder. "Have you witnessed any father placing his hand on the heads of his children for a blessing without making the sign of the cross? As if he, a mere mortal, had the power of the Almighty?"

Isabel covered her mouth with her hand.

Beatriz looked rebukingly at Papá, as if to say, *See what you've done to us? To me?*

The sermon continued. "I have just come from Seville, where we have discovered a great many of these false Christians hiding among pious Old Christians. One foolish converso even took the oaths of the priesthood. And do you know what he did? Whenever he offered communion, he turned the Host upside down!"

The silver cross of the Inquisition pounded the floor.

The congregants were shocked at this outrage.

"These Marranos do not deserve the protection of the hand of God. They do not deserve our mercy." Torquemada lifted his face, peering all the way to the nave, where the Perez family stood.

Isabel felt her sister come to attention beside her, standing on her toes. She wanted to be noticed by him! As if he were a handsome theatrical player, and they were all gathered around the stage for a show.

"If you would turn to the back of the room, we have a small surprise for the good Christians of Trujillo."

Behind Isabel, the heavy wooden doors opened, creaking under the weight of their hinges. In walked three men and a woman, roped together at the ankles.

Mamá pointed to one of the men. "Is that . . . Señor Franco?"

He was a city governor. He held a long-time position of power. Isabel had seen him just two days earlier when she delivered four bottles of Papá's best brandy to his chambers. Now he stood with the three others, heads uncovered, bent in shame, barefoot and carrying unlit candles.

"How can this be?" asked Isabel.

All four prisoners wore strange yellow tunics, different than the gowns Señor and Señora Cohen wore. On the front was painted a large bloodred X.

"They must have done something terrible," said Beatriz.

"Behold the sanbenito," called Torquemada, "the cloak of the Inquisition. Notice the symbol on the front, the cross of our beloved Saint Andrew, who showed enormous humility before death. He asked not to be crucified on the same-shaped cross as our Lord, because he was not worthy. So he was nailed to a saltire, shaped like an X." The resonance of his voice, emblazoned with passion, echoed off the stone walls. "Let us pray that these penitents show even a modicum of that same humility."

"Tell us their crimes!" shouted a congregant.

"The prisoners are accused of Judaizing," said Torquemada. "Witnesses have come forward, anonymously of course, to denounce them, revealing how they tricked good Christians. Do not be fooled. These conversos were baptized, yet never gave up their Jewish faith. All four have done something different. One sat in a flimsy shelter of green branches in the back of a Jewish house and exchanged gifts of food with others."

"He speaks of a suca!" whispered Isabel.

Beatriz poked her sister with her fan. "Now do you see what I've been talking about?"

"Another did not have smoke coming from his chimney on Saturday, refusing to cook food on his day of rest," intoned Torquemada.

Isabel sweated through her dress. Here was a second transgression her family was guilty of.

"The third man asked a Jew to recite a passage for him in sinagoga, so that his son might recover from an illness. And lastly, the woman you see before you—" He paused, clearly distraught at this particular crime. "She . . . she washed the spot on her baby's head that received the holy baptismal water."

The crowd erupted in shouts of dismay. A woman genuflected in the pew in front of them. Isabel heard her whisper, "At least the baby is safe now with its Christian father."

Isabel took Abuela's hand, which was trembling. This was what it must have been like for Grandpa Crescas, hearing the preacher Martínez incite the crowd into a feverish mob.

Beatriz hissed into Isabel's ear. "We can always say the Cohens forced us to eat outside on their patio. Or that our own hearth was damaged on Friday so it couldn't be used on Saturday. If needed, I'll take a war hammer to the chimney and break it myself." She continued rattling off even more excuses before Isabel shushed her.

Slowly, the four prisoners made their way through the center aisle.

"Shame be upon you!" yelled a congregant.

Someone else cried, "Interlopers! You will take a job from a true Christian no longer!"

Another spat at the prisoners.

"What will happen to them, Fray Torquemada?" called out a male voice.

"We will turn them over to the civil authorities. The Church only captures. It does not punish. The alguacil and his bailiffs will interrogate these poor souls, encouraging them to speak the truth through whatever means necessary. A notary will keep records of the proceedings."

"Did he just say the alguacil?" whispered Isabel.

"All the more reason for you to devote yourself to Don Sancho," said Beatriz.

"Use the pié de amigo on the heretics!" yelled an angry parishioner.

"The toca!"

"The garrucha!"

Isabel suspected those were all devices of torture. What would she do if she were in their place, shut in a small cell and punished with bestial instruments? Would she succumb to the pain of what was being done to her body and name other Judaizers? Or would she be brave and die silent?

Torquemada raised his hand to calm the crowd. "I assure you, if the penitents don't confess and name other Judaizers, they *will* be put to the question. That will be their last chance. If we are satisfied with their answer, then we will reconcile them to the Church. If not, then a worse fate awaits them."

"Put them to the question right now!" a woman called out.

"In good time, friends," replied Torquemada. "In good time." He bowed his head. "Now let us pray." He recited some words in Latin. *"Sicut eciam faciendum est in republica que pro vnum malum hominem, huiusmodi corrumpitur, unde tales circumcidenti sunt per iusticiam et mortem."* Then in Castilian, he repeated, "The mere presence of these heretics will turn our kingdom to decay. We must circumcise them by justice or death." Torquemada opened his arms, encompassing the entire church in his embrace. "Arise, O Lord, and judge thy cause! The fox endangers us!"

The amens reached a crescendo. Beatriz joined the crowd, calling out her amen with passion. Isabel was too stunned to open her mouth. Just as Diego had warned, she now understood she was the fox. They all were.

16

The week was passing slowly for Isabel. It was Thursday and still she had not had a decent night's sleep. Whenever she lay down, Torquemada's skeletal figure loomed behind her eyelids. What had he said Señor Franco was accused of? Sitting in a flimsy shelter of green branches in back of someone's house?

Just days ago, they sat in the Cohens' own suca. But where exactly, Isabel wondered, was the crime in that? Since when did eating honey cake under palm fronds become a transgression against God? Spain was finally united. Only Granada remained under Moorish control, but it would surely fall. With their marriage, Queen Isabella and King Ferdinand had turned Spain into an empire, rivaled only by the Ottomans. Everyone born here was a Spaniard. The Perezes were no less Spanish than their neighbors the Herreras or even the Altamiranos. Must all its citizens be united in faith as well? Did tolerating other religions in one's country make a ruler weak?

Isabel paced the small area of her bedroom. Diego warned her about making mistakes in front of Don Sancho. What if Don Sancho went about opening drawers and cupboards in the cellar and found a silver Kiddush cup? Or the cinnamon-and-clove-filled spice box they passed gingerly from hand to hand on Saturday evenings to signal the end of the Sabbath. Once they were officially betrothed, he had every right to inspect her family's possessions. And what about after they married? What if Isabel murmured a Hebrew prayer in her sleep, lying next to him? Innocent indiscretions could happen at any time.

All her mundane tasks felt frivolous. The vine grafting she was working on with Papá. Who cared about seedless grapes? Her sister's preoccupation with a new dress for the Herrera granddaughter's baptism. (Yuçe did end up delivering the fabric. Mamá and the girls agreed not to mention it to Papá. He probably wouldn't notice their new dresses anyway.) Peeling carrots, de-feathering chicken, setting the table. It all felt pointless.

She recalled a conversation between her and Abuela earlier this week. They were preparing supper and were alone in the kitchen. Ever since her walk with Diego in the Moorish quarter, Isabel had been trying to understand the concept of free will as it applied to life during the Inquisition.

"Abuela, do we truly have free will if we can't live freely?"

Her grandmother had been filling a pot with water for boiling and set down the heavy iron crock. "I think God gave us the ability to apply reason and understanding to the universe so we can make sense of why things happen, both good and bad. If we can become closer to God intellectually, then we can be less troubled by what evil befalls us. We can live freely in our own minds."

At the time, Isabel had been comforted by her grandmother's words. But now, with her thoughts spinning out of control again in the privacy of her bedroom, the momentary balm of Abuela's wisdom had been replaced again with fear. She did not accept that any connection to God would protect her from the evils of Torquemada. Was living in a world such as this, filled with fear at every turn, truly living? Or merely surviving?

"Enough!" she said aloud. She would stop obsessing over the worst possible outcomes. She would go and do what made her happy. A visit with her new friend, Atika, to discuss poetry was just the salve she needed. Isabel tied her long hair in a knot at the back of her neck, securing it with a black cord. Then she dabbed a few drops of rose water and ambergris on her wrists and neck. Though Mamá always insisted the girls bathe in vinegar and water twice a week, they could not visit the mikveh, the Jewish ritual bath, the way observant Jewish women did. The perfume would suffice until she could wash in the wooden tub behind their house on Sunday. She thought of Beatriz demanding that she take more care with her appearance. Well, today she would actually listen to her sister.

She chose an indigo-colored linen gown. Designed in the bliaut style, it belted tight across the bodice and abdomen, with a skirt billowing around her. She felt like a floating cloud. She told herself it was all for Atika. Any handsome green-eyed man she bumped into along the way would simply be a happy accident. With a satisfied nod into the looking glass, Isabel left the room.

Mamá looked up from her needlework, smiling. "Where are you off to looking so pretty?" She and Beatriz were both sitting on floor cushions in the sala.

"For a walk. It's a lovely afternoon," replied Isabel.

"May I join her?" asked Beatriz, putting down her stitching. "Por favor, Mamá. Constanza and Juan Carlos might be out promenading."

"No. You and I are not quite finished with this verdugado." The hoop skirt was the latest fashion coming out of France and England. Stiff reeds were sown into the fabric, circling the wearer, to make the gown hold its shape and swish when walking. "I want you to be able to make farthingales for your own daughter one day."

Beatriz's eyes flashed daggers at Isabel. "*If* I have a daughter, or any child for that matter."

Mamá continued stitching, ignoring the idle threat, which brought great relief to Isabel. Her sister would not be trailing behind her.

"Do you have a maravedi to rent an escort, Isabel?" asked Mamá.

Her mother always worried about Isabel strolling unaccompanied, yet Isabel had been walking alone for a year now. "I'll be fine, Mamá. But I brought a coin just in case."

Isabel left her clogs at home today, walking easily in leather slippers down the uneven dirt road. On the way to the Romani encampment, she would stop by the bookbindery. Perhaps Isaac had more information on the father of her poetess ancestor.

The air was mild for mid-October, kissing her face and neck as she headed into town. On the calle de los cerrajeros, the street of the locksmiths, the prickly smell of hot metal made her eyes water. She paused to look in the windows of the shops on the calle de los manteros, all containing stacks of colorfully striped and fringed blankets. When she crossed the plaza mayor, the smells changed to those of beer and tobacco. Old women sat in cafés, sipping chicory water. Beggars lay on the ground, their hands outstretched. Pages and squires lingered about, clutching pillows for ladies to kneel on and pray. Despite Torquemada's visit, the inexorable rhythm of life continued. On Sunday, the fancy Christian ladies would emerge, like tortoises sticking their heads out of their shells. Once again, Isabel was grateful her mother didn't impose restrictions on her like the Old Christian families did on their daughters.

At the other end of the plaza, Isabel saw a broad-shouldered man standing by a fountain. He wore a green doublet. Her breath caught and she drew closer. But when the man turned, he had a waxed mustache spread across his lip. She sighed. It wasn't him.

"Señorita Perez," said Isaac when she entered his shop. "I was just closing up. My wife is waiting with our midday meal."

"Then it's my lucky day that I caught you. I won't keep you long. I wondered if you had any news from your colleague about the poetess's father. Or perhaps even more information about the girl herself?"

His head bobbed up and down happily. "I do, actually. When Sa'id saw the filigree in the upper corner and examined the phrasing, he said it sounded like the work of Qasmūna, a young poetess born in the twelfth century."

"Qasmūna." The word sounded like a song. "What else do you know about her?"

"Her father was a well-known poet and taught her to finish his verses. This was not uncommon for educated Arab and Jewish women at that time."

Again, Isabel wished she had been born in that century. A young woman, lettered and free to write beautiful poems. No Inquisition lurking around every corner, tearing families apart. Like that rebirth in Italy Diego had spoken about. Diego. Her heart gamboled at the thought of him.

"What was her father's name?"

"Perhaps Ismā'il ibn Bagdālah." He paused. "Or it could have been Shmuel ha-Nagid."

"Your colleague doesn't know for sure?"

"I'm afraid not. It depends on which scholar you ask."

How frustrating. She'd have to ask Abuela if there were any stories of her family that went farther back than 1391. Or maybe there was something written on a gravestone somewhere?

One thing was certain. Abuela had the poem in her possession from her own grandmother. So that meant Isabel was related to a famous poet! All the Perezes were, in Abuela's line. She couldn't wait to tell Atika.

The Moorish quarter was full of activity today. Colorful scarves and block-printed fabric covered rickety stalls. Isabel passed barrels full of aromatic spices and nuts, handwoven baskets stacked precariously, birds perched in cages squawking in protest or in conversation with other birds. Meat sizzled on iron grills. A boy licked sticky pastry off his tiny fingers. She loved the smells inside the souk. Frankincense from the perfume makers; cassia, turmeric, and cardamom from the kitchens. Christian Spaniards never made their food picante, their palates preferring milder tastes. Even their own cooking at home was rendered bland. Mamá and Abuela were reluctant to use too many spices to flavor their dishes, lest a neighbor smell them coming out of their chimney on a Friday night and accuse them of using Jewish flavors.

Isabel stopped in front of the baker's stall, the smell of dough and yeast making her stomach gurgle. She handed the maravedi her mother had given her to the proprietor, an old man covered in a silver beard. She'd much rather spend the coin on a crunchy loaf of bread than hand it to a page.

The Romani camp was located next to the Guadiana River, where it meandered just inside the city walls. As Isabel scanned the dirt courtyard, Atika dropped the multicolored skirt she was hanging out to dry and came running.

"For you," said Isabel, handing her friend the warm loaf of bread.

Atika's mouth erupted in a smile. She bit off a chunk of bread and chewed it with satisfaction. As on the night of the poetry reading, they spoke rapidly in Castilian. Most Romanis didn't learn the native tongue of this country, but Atika had picked it up. Her skill with language probably kept her and her father safe from the police. Those who refused to conform to the Spanish customs were lashed.

"I'm so happy you came," remarked Atika.

"I have some news to share." It dawned on Isabel that the bounce in her step might not be completely about Qasmūna, but rather a mix of thoughts including Diego. Well, if her happiness was due to anything, perhaps both were to blame. "There's a famous poet in my family!"

"En serio?" replied Atika, setting down the last part of the bread and resuming the hanging of laundry.

"She's a distant relative, I'm sure. But my abuela showed me a poem, inked beautifully in Arabic by the hand of a young girl. The parchment was old, maybe three hundred years. Her father was also a poet and they wrote together, finishing each other's verses!"

"How did the poem go?"

Isabel recited the short verse from memory.

Atika stopped what she was doing, holding a wrinkled men's shirt midair. "Was her father Ismā'il ibn Bagdālah?"

"Quite possibly! But how would you know that?" asked Isabel.

"I've heard his poems recited before. He often wrote with his daughter. What was her name?"

"Qasmūna."

Atika faced Isabel, curtsying with a flourish, and spoke.

"I have a friend whose mistress has repaid good with
*   evil. Considering lawful that which is forbidden*
*   to her.*
Just like the sun, from which the moon derives its light
*   always, yet afterward eclipses the sun's body."*

"How ingenious," said Isabel. "The sun generously gives its light to the moon, which cannot otherwise shine. The moon, however, doesn't appreciate the help. It blocks the sun during an eclipse."

"Exactly," said Atika. "The mistress is ungrateful to her lover, receiving his benefits, then somehow doing him harm."

"I could never take a phrase like that, about an affair of the heart," began Isabel, "and turn it into something about astronomy. You could, though."

Atika grinned at her. "Something tells me you can do anything you set your mind to."

"I wish I knew what that was exactly," Isabel demurred. "If I were Qasmūna, I'd be accepted as a poet and not marriage fodder for a boorish, power-hungry Old Christian." She squinted up at the sky. "Sometimes I wonder if there's something more out there, something spiritually greater, that I somehow can't grasp."

"You mean like Allah?"

Isabel nodded. "Perhaps. All I know is that I feel like an outlier. I don't fit in to my family's religion or Spain's." As Isabel tamped the fear of the Inquisition further down in her belly, it dawned on her that she now understood Atika's desire to escape reality. Today she was doing the very same thing. "You figured out the secret, my friend. A simple, nomadic existence where all one needs is a tent and a poem. Maybe I'll move in with you."

Atika finished the last of her bread. "You're always welcome here." She took a sip of water from a jug, then offered it to Isabel. "But there's no armario. You'll have to give away a few dresses before you move in."

Isabel held out the side of her gown. "Believe me, I'm not attached to any of these things." Isabel was not nearly as enthusiastic as her sister about her wardrobe. To Isabel, the dresses were fussy, laborious garments that took too long to put on in the morning and too much time to untie when she was tired and simply wanted to go to sleep.

"So is there a boorish Old Christian in your future?" asked Atika.

Isabel grimaced. "Don Sancho Aguila. I loathe saying his name, let alone the sight of him."

"That sounds dreadful. Has a date been set?"

The water tasted cool in Isabel's mouth. "I think I bought myself some time. I told him I wanted to wait until I was eighteen. By then maybe he'll develop leprosy and have to live in a lazar house."

"You're terrible."

"If only I'd met Di—" Isabel stopped herself.

"Who?"

Oh, all right. She was bursting to tell someone. "Diego Altamirano. Handsome. Educated. Radical. Compassionate. Did I mention handsome?"

Atika giggled. "He sounds like my Abū."

"Abū? I should call you the two As," said Isabel.

"He's a perfume maker and would-be poet."

From the way Atika's eyes glazed over, he was no doubt her lover as well.

"Maybe you need to have one last tryst before marriage ties you up forever," said Atika, eyebrows dancing up and down.

"You read too much poetry."

Forever. Isabel couldn't picture having to carry out her wifely duties with Don Sancho even one time, let alone for the rest of her life. When she imagined showing her nakedness to someone, it was Diego whose face popped into her mind. She flushed and turned away from Atika, not able to look at her friend squarely. These were not thoughts that a proper girl was meant to have in her head.

Isabel's eyes roamed the encampment, catching a small figure making her way through the tents, peering in each one. From this distance, it looked exactly like little Rachel Cohen.

"Rachel?" Isabel called.

The girl crept closer, surprised at hearing her name.

Isabel stared. "What in God's cankers are you doing here?"

"It's Mamá!" Rachel cried.

17

Despite Papá forbidding her from seeing the Cohens, Isabel walked Rachel home. The young girl was overcome with sadness. Her mother had taken ill, and Isabel's heart went out to her.

Yuçe answered the door, surprised to see Isabel.

"I came to help," said Isabel.

Inside, the air felt stale, odorous with something she could not name.

Rachel ducked between them, darting into the house. "I want to see Mamá!"

"Hold on," said Yuçe, holding out his empty palm.

Rachel handed her brother a small calfskin pouch. "The Gypsy woman said Mamá needs to take a tea of the mixture. It's dandelion and nettle and fennel and something else, but I forgot."

"My mother is resting in the other room," Yuçe told Isabel.

When Isabel entered the Cohens' second room, she had to swallow the sound of surprise that almost escaped from her mouth. Señora Cohen was unrecognizable. Gone was the dark-eyed beauty Isabel had known all her life. Her legs were swollen to three times their size. She lay abed, eye slits barely visible in the cushions of her cheeks. She appeared gigantic, probably weighing at least fifteen stones. Señor Cohen sat in a chair by his wife's side, holding her hand.

Señor Cohen smiled wearily. "Isabel. You don't have to be here. Doctor Cetia is coming soon."

Isabel knelt by Señora Cohen's side. "I wouldn't dream of leaving. What does the doctor think it is?"

"Dropsy," said Señor Cohen. "There have been bouts before, though this is the worst we have seen. It came on suddenly, which is why I sent Rachel for the herbs. We are desperate to try anything if it will help her void the extra fluid she is carrying."

"Why don't I go and prepare the tea tincture and make something for the twins to eat?" suggested Isabel.

"That would be nice," said Señor Cohen, watching his wife.

"I'm not hungry," said Yuçe, standing up straighter, trying to look older than his eleven years.

"All the more for me," said Rachel.

Señor Cohen lifted his head. "Oh, and Isabel?"

She turned back at the door. "Yes?"

"Tell your father that I . . ." He stopped.

Isabel waited. Nothing more was forthcoming.

"That you what, Papá?" asked Yuçe.

"That . . . I am sorry for the other night. The way I spoke to him. I am not proud of it."

Isabel nodded and left the room. That could not have been easy for him. But she wondered if relaying his message would do any good at all. Her father was the most obstinate person she knew. And there was the other problem of admitting she'd come here against his orders.

Isabel worked over the hearth, steeping the herbs, boiling eggs. She poured the tea into a glass. Then she set everything on a pewter tray and carried it into the bedroom. Yuçe woke his mother.

"Who's that?" murmured Señora Cohen in a thin voice.

"It's me, Mamá," said Yuçe. "Isabel's here, too."

Isabel held the tea to her lips. "This should make you feel better."

Señora Cohen's fingers were so thick and filled with fluid that she could not hold the cup herself. The herbal mixture dribbled out of her mouth.

"Let me help you sit up straighter, Mamá," said Yuçe, propping her up.

Señora Cohen managed to get down most of the warm liquid before she laid her head back, heavy on the pallet. "Gracias," she said, before drifting off to sleep again.

While Rachel ate, Yuçe eyed the eggs.

"You're sure you're not hungry?" asked Isabel.

He shook his head.

Isabel pointed to a stack of papers, stitched together between leather covers, open on Señor Cohen's lap. "Is her illness so serious that you have to pray for her?" she asked him quietly.

"This is not a prayer book," Señor Cohen answered testily. "It is the Talmud."

An actual Talmud? If only Abuela were here!

Isabel peered closer at the book. "Why are the texts different sizes?" Her voice was quiet, out of respect for Señora Cohen, but she could not help her curiosity.

Señor Cohen said nothing.

"Why won't you answer her, Papá?"

His father shifted in the chair, remaining silent.

"The Talmud is different from the Hebrew Bible," began Yuçe, explaining it to her himself. "It's the oral law, full of rules and opinions. The reason the texts don't match is that different scholars have added their commentary. The main text, or Mishnah, is in the center, but over hundreds of years, other rabbis wrote their own interpretations."

"How is it different from the Torah?" she asked.

Señor Cohen crossed his arms and huffed.

Yuçe paid him no mind. "The Torah is the story of our people, but it does not go into much detail about certain customs. For instance, we know to take four species of trees during Sucot and make a booth, but we do not know which ones. The Talmud tells us specifically how to carry out God's commandments. Is that not right, Papá?"

Señor Cohen closed the book and did not look at them, keeping his eyes on his ailing wife.

"I'm going outside to play escondido," announced Rachel. "Want to come, Yuçe?"

He glanced at Isabel. "I'd rather keep watch over Mamá."

Isabel wanted to know more about the Talmud. "If it's oral, why does it have to be written down at all?"

Yuçe grinned. "You ask smart questions. For hundreds of years, the Talmud wasn't written. Jews passed it down through generations by retelling the stories. But after the second temple was destroyed, with all our people spread through Europe, Africa, and Asia, we needed to have one book guiding us on Jewish life so that traditions wouldn't be lost."

Señor Cohen rose abruptly from his chair. "When the doctor arrives, come find me in the workroom."

After he left, Yuçe called after him. "Papá, you forgot your book."

"I've read enough for today," came Señor Cohen's answer. "Return it to the sinagoga when Isabel leaves." Then he slammed the front door.

"Madre mía," said Isabel when he left. "He still seems angry at my father. At our whole family."

"I think he doesn't like women discussing the Talmud," said Yuçe.

And a baptized woman at that, thought Isabel. It struck her that this was a major difference between Christianity and Judaism—the idea of women scholars. Nuns prayed all day long. Many must be experts in the Bible in order to do their daily devotions. And females had been canonized as saints since the first century. Yet the Jews did not allow a woman to study. "My abuela seems to know a lot about the Talmud and she's a woman. The grand-daughter of a rabbi, though."

"That's unusual," admitted Yuçe. "The women don't come to the sinagoga often. When they do, the men sit apart from them, and they're separated by a curtain. In larger cities with bigger sina-gogas, the women sit up in the balcony, far away from the pulpit."

"So according to Jewish tradition, women are not allowed to study the ancient scroll *and* must be separated from men at sinagoga?"

Yuçe shrugged. "That's how it's always been."

"It's as if they believe that women are somehow less than men." It was the same way she was made to feel as a conversa. That she was somehow not as Spanish as an Old Christian.

"I've never thought of it like that before." Yuçe picked up his father's bound pages. He pointed to a chunk of tiny text on the left, separated from the center by a thin white line of parchment. "See this section?"

Her interest in what was directly in front of her quelled her outrage. She ran her fingertip down the stack of strange words. "The words are aligned so perfectly."

"It's made by a printing press using Rashi script. Have you heard of Rashi?"

Isabel shook her head.

"He was one of the greatest voices of our people. But so as not to confuse his handwriting with the more square-shaped letters in the Torah scroll, the printers made a typeface using slanted letters that looked just like it came from Rashi's own hand."

Isabel's eyes lit up. "This is entirely different than the printed Gutenberg Bible. With Rashi script, you can almost see the man who composed the words."

"You remind me of an old Jewish man, Isabel."

She laughed. "What are you talking about?"

"You question things. That's just what the Talmud is. One giant conversation full of questions and answers that's taken place over hundreds of years."

Isabel gazed longingly at the book in his hand. She touched her finger to the page again. She felt the same sense of awe as when she first saw Qasmūna's poem. The young poetess and Rashi were real people. Who lived full lives. Who feared. Who celebrated. Who loved.

Isabel felt Yuçe's eyes on her.

"What?"

He blushed. "Nothing."

But Isabel could see it plain as day. He gazed at her the same way she was looking at the Talmud. Drinking her in. She must be careful with his feelings. He was still a boy.

"Would you like to borrow it?" asked Yuçe abruptly.

"Oh, I could never," protested Isabel. "It's too dangerous."

"Dangerous?"

Isabel immediately regretted using that word. She didn't want to be the one teaching Yuçe about the Inquisition if he didn't already know. Anti-Jewish laws were one thing. Condemning conversos for Judaizing and burning them at the stake was another thing entirely. He may have flights of fancy toward her, but he was still innocent at heart. Let him think Spain was still safe. "I just mean, it's so sacred. What if something happened to it? What would your rabbi say?"

"I can make my own decisions. I'm almost at the age of majority, thirteen, when I can wrap tefillin. I even fasted until the third hour after noon on Yom Kippur this year." He was practically preening like a peacock, trying to impress her.

She forced her expression to remain as serious as he was, even though she wanted to giggle. "Our family fasts as well. I know how hard it is to go without food for a whole day." It was always around the start of Lent. Sometimes they fasted again, one month later, before Easter Sunday. Isabel never knew why, as the other Old Christian girls she knew didn't do it. Now that Yuçe mentioned it, perhaps fasting at certain festivals was a custom held over from when her great-grandparents were practicing Jews.

They both watched Señora Cohen sleep, her breathing shallow and labored. Then, abruptly, Yuçe handed her the book. "Por favor, Isabel."

"Really?"

He blushed again. "It would be my honor."

With the Talmud actually in her hands, it was hard to refuse. How Abuela would love to see one! "Well, all right. Just for a short while." She looked around the señora's bed. "Do you have something I could wrap it up in?"

He darted out of the room and returned with a kitchen rag. He wrapped up the book in the white cloth. "I know you'll take good care of it." She nodded, picturing the canister where Abuela had hidden Qasmūna's poem.

She placed the wrapped book underneath her mantle, folded at her feet.

For the rest of the afternoon, Isabel sat at Señora Cohen's bedside. When the doctor came, Yuçe fetched Señor Cohen and brought him into the bedroom. After the examination, Doctor Cetia asked Yuçe to bring him a bowl for some bloodletting. He made a small slice in the pale skin, underneath Señora Cohen's forearm. Isabel closed her eyes, but she could hear the blood dripping into the shallow wooden container.

When Isabel finally left before dark, Señora Cohen's condition had not improved.

The graying sky held little light as Isabel knelt by the shed in back of her house. She easily found the spot where Abuela had buried Qasmūna's poem. The dirt was still overturned, like a newly dug grave. She pulled out the now empty tin canister, but Yuçe's Talmud wouldn't fit inside. What had she been thinking? The spine was nearly as wide as her palm. And unlike the rolled parchment of the poem, the Talmud wouldn't bend. It appeared that inside the leather bindings were sewn two hard pasteboard attachments. She'd have to bring it in the house and remove those two bricks in the cellar where she had seen Papá hide his book of blessings.

"What do you have there?"

Isabel jumped. Beatriz was behind her.

18

"Why must you always sneak up on me like that?" said Isabel.

Beatriz looked poised for a fight. "You didn't answer my question."

"You didn't answer mine."

The sisters glared at each other.

"It's none of your concern," said Isabel finally. She held the book to her chest so Beatriz wouldn't notice the Hebrew writing.

"Let me see!" said Beatriz, lunging at Isabel.

Isabel swerved and the Talmud dropped. "Now look what you've done!" Isabel brushed off dirt from its spine. "Have you no decency?"

"Discúlpeme," she said, though Isabel knew she was not sorry at all. "That's a Jewish book, is it not?"

Isabel ground her top and bottom teeth. Not again. She had grown weary of her sister's suspicions. She had no more fans or jewels with which to bribe her. "What if it is? Are you going to turn me in to the Inquisition?"

Beatriz hesitated.

"Are you?"

"Do you think there's some powerful message from God in there?" Beatriz asked instead.

This gave Isabel pause. She wasn't sure what magic it held. But she liked having it in her possession. Knowing Abuela would read it to her if she asked brought her comfort. "Perhaps."

"Which God?" asked Beatriz. "The God of Moses or el Dios?"

Isabel sighed. "I don't know, honestly. I used to think the poets were my Gods. But they can't explain Torquemada. Why he preaches those vile words. They can't explain all this hatefulness."

"According to the gospel of John, 'Whoever says he is in the light and hates his brother is still in darkness.'"

"Then the Inquisition spies are in darkness. They don't think of us as their brethren. They never have."

"You could be an object of their light now that you've received the baptismal waters." Beatriz looked again at the Talmud in Isabel's arms. "I wish you were more curious about our Bible." This was no longer an attack. Beatriz seemed genuinely hurt that her beloved New Testament wasn't the object Isabel was holding.

Why *didn't* Isabel want to learn more about the teachings the Dominicans espoused each Sunday? That Gospel her sister had just quoted was rather lovely. If Isabel were really being honest, it was because Christianity felt too intertwined with the monarchy. The fears that governed their lives as conversos each day were becoming so overpowering she felt like they might squeeze the breath out of her. "I guess it doesn't speak to the freedom I'd like to live by."

Beatriz's face grew hard again. "You mean the rebelliousness you'd like to live by, don't you? Because that's what freedom is to you, permission to rebel against convention. Against the Holy Father. Believe me, Sister. Without the hand of God guiding you, you would be a reckless soul, lost to the devil." Their momentary understanding disappeared as fast as it had come. "You never could see the truth." She turned back to walk to the house, then paused mid-stride. "Allow me to enlighten you now. You've chosen the wrong side."

"Why must there be a right and wrong side?" called Isabel. But her words fell on deaf ears.

With the Talmud safely hidden in a niche in the cellar, Isabel worried over something else. Should she tell her family about Hannah Cohen and the dropsy or not? Mamá would want to know, but Papá would be furious when he learned Isabel defied him and went to visit. Then again, what if something terrible happened to Hannah Cohen? Isabel would never forgive herself. So in the morning, as the Perez family was gathered in the kitchen for their tea and biscuits, Isabel decided to inform everyone. "I have some news."

"Mine first," said Papá, spreading mermelada on a roll. "Don Sancho and I have finally had a chance to speak."

Oh, the ugliness of his name. For a few pleasant hours, she had not thought of him.

"I have given him my acceptance of your hand, Isabel. You two are now officially betrothed."

At least let it be postponed, Isabel prayed.

"To be wed next April," continued Papá.

"But that's so soon!"

"Soon would be next week," said Mamá. "This gives us plenty of time to prepare your wedding chest."

Even though it was still six months away, Isabel felt a dread as heavy as a basket of grapes on her back.

Mamá refilled Papá's cup. "And what was *your* news, Isabel?"

Her head was foggy. She nearly forgot what she had planned

to tell them. "Oh, right. It's . . . it's Señora Cohen. She's very ill with dropsy."

"Poor Rachel and Yuçe," said Abuela. "If the worst happens, what will become of them?"

Papá said nothing. Just sipped his tea. Beatriz dipped her biscuit in honey.

"We should pay our respects with a visit," said Mamá. "It's the least we can do."

"I made a vow," her father thundered. "We will never step foot in that man's house again!"

"Señor Cohen passed along his apologies," said Isabel. "He's not proud of what he said."

"I don't accept his empty words!" said Papá. "And later, we will deal with your punishment for going against my will."

Mamá looked at him, her arms out in supplication. "Can't you forgive this one transgression, Manolo? I'm talking about both Isabel and David. Hannah is my oldest friend. She didn't say those ugly things. He did."

Papá stormed out of the kitchen, biscuit in hand. He yelled back to them from the sala, "And don't even think of going there alone. You are my wife."

Beatriz flashed her eyes at Isabel. "Why must you upset Papá so?"

"You're one to talk. I'm not the daughter who argues with him at every meal," said Isabel.

Mamá touched Abuela on the arm. "Go talk to your son. I beg of you."

"I can try. But you know how willful he is," said Abuela.

As Abuela stood up from her stool, a clarion blared from the street below, steady and insistent. "Oye! Oye!" It was the town crier, with the official trumpeters in tow, making a public announcement. Usually, it was to inform the town of a new rule of law or a birth or death.

The family followed Papá into the sala to get a better view outside.

"What is it, Papá?" asked Beatriz. "What's the messenger saying?"

Papá leaned out the window. "Something about a gathering. I can't hear the details from this distance."

Mamá frowned. "You'd better go find out."

Papá left the house and returned ten minutes later, breathing heavily.

"Sit down," said Mamá. "You look like you've seen a spirit."

Papá sat and began to twiddle his thumbs. "There's an auto de fe tribunal happening today." His normally booming voice was weak.

"But it's Shabbat," said Mamá. "We have too much to prepare."

"I'm afraid this was the sole purpose. To make all the conversos attend."

"Is it the prisoners from church?" asked Beatriz.

Papá nodded. "They've already been condemned. They're marching from the prison right now. The penalties will be announced in the plaza mayor."

"Will . . . will there be burnings?" asked Isabel, thinking of Diego's warning.

He nodded gravely. "The crier told me the quemadero has been prepared with stakes and firewood." Papá stood up. "We'd better get dressed."

"I refuse to go," said Isabel.

"I want to see it!" said Beatriz.

"How you can express excitement for something so dreadful is beyond my ken, sister."

Beatriz appeared nonplussed at Isabel's surprise. "I heard there were autos de fe in Seville and Madrid. Constanza spoke about them. I'm simply looking forward to seeing what everyone has been talking about, that is all."

"This is not a traveling band of performers, entertaining us with their juggling," continued Isabel, irate. "There will be no jester from the Spanish court twirling for our merriment."

"I never described it as such," shot back Beatriz.

Abuela turned to Isabel. "Your absence will be noticeable, I'm afraid. Don Sancho might look for you."

Mamá started to cry, her shoulders shaking in small up and down motions. "First Hannah, and now this." She genuflected, then began to sway back and forth, murmuring words in Judeo-Spanish.

Beatriz genuflected, too, though Isabel knew when Mamá made the sign of the cross, she was just going through the motion out of habit. Chanting in Hebrew was what brought her comfort.

Papá wrapped his arms around Mamá. "Shhh, Benita."

Isabel watched her parents, and tears welled up in her own eyes. Theirs was an arranged marriage when they were young, but their partnership had grown into something genuine. They could argue as they did about Señora Cohen and return to a place of caring and affection. She would never love Don Sancho with even a morsel of what they had.

"Gather your veils, everyone," directed Papá, his voice muffled in Mamá's hair. "We must hurry."

By the time the Perezes arrived, hundreds of villagers had surrounded the plaza mayor, creating a hum of spectators. Every horse and private carriage in the region was there as well. Having ferried their owners, the animals and carts stood waiting on the outer streets. The sun was high, beating down on Isabel's back, and she began perspiring immediately.

A steady drum announced the arrival of the processional. Isabel strained to see where the music came from. Over the tops of heads, she saw two somber drummers sitting on lower scaffolding, banging instruments that rested between their knees. Above them were tiers of seating. The last time she'd seen seats arranged publicly like this was at her first poetry reading. How the world had changed in so short a time. She feared there was no place for poetic words any longer.

The heat was oppressive. She lifted her veil away from her face and thirstily gulped air.

A few city officials were already seated in the tiers. Even from a distance, it was easy to spot Don Sancho. He wore his signature black plumed hat. He was talking animatedly to the man next to him, as if he were attending a social gathering. What was his role here today? She was grateful for the cover of the crowd, for the anonymity it provided. If it were two years from now and she was accompanying him as Doña del Aguila, she would not be able to hide.

She looked back in the direction of where they'd come to watch the processional approach. Leading the pack were the bearers of the green cross of the Inquisition. Behind them came the mounted notaries and Familiars, dressed in black with the white cross of Saint Dominic on their cloaks. Isabel saw Diego's father, Count Altamirano, among them. He managed to look both regal and smug at the same time. Diego was not on a horse, nor walking beside him. Could he be elsewhere? Isabel scanned the crowd, looking for his brown hair and broad shoulders. It was simply too thick with people to see. Perhaps he'd stayed home, like she had wanted to herself.

A priest followed next. Not Friar Francisco, but someone Isabel had never seen before. From the capital, perhaps? He sat triumphantly in a chair under a canopy of scarlet and gold. The whole apparatus was carried by four men. The priest held a gold monstrance in his hand, which looked like a miniature sun with rays. From attending church weekly, Isabel knew all about that vessel and the holiness of its contents, the consecrated Host. When the priest's chair passed by, everyone in the crowd knelt. The Perez family did the same.

Tiny rocks dug into Isabel's knees. She could withstand the discomfort, but poor Abuela winced. She wished she had a pillow for her. It took Abuela half a minute to stand up, even with the help of Isabel and Mamá, which only made Isabel angrier. By kneeling, they were all, in effect, celebrating a man who was ceremoniously leading four people to their likely deaths.

Finally, Isabel saw the prisoners. Except there were only three. Where was the woman? This time, the rope was tied around their necks and trailed down their backs to their wrists. The only thing they could move was their feet as they shuffled along the street. Each prisoner was flanked by a Dominican on either side. The priests were whispering in their ears. What could they possibly be saying to them at this late moment? Giving them their last rites?

Señor Franco had worsened since Isabel saw him being paraded in church. Bruises the color of eggplants blazed on his face, mostly around his mouth. He was a tall man, but now he was hunched over and limping. He seemed ancient. He and a second man still wore the same yellow sanbenito they had worn in church last week, except the yellow had turned brown with dirt and the gown was now spotted with bloodstains. The third man was wearing a black sanbenito, the front painted with the face of a grotesque devil encircled by flames. He also wore a tall, thin, conical hat.

"Are you sure there are no jesters present?" asked Beatriz snidely.

Papá looked grim. "That's a coroza."

"You mean a corona?" asked Beatriz. A crown.

"No, a coroza. They call it that as a joke because it sounds like the same word. I assure you, it's anything but an honor."

After the prisoners came Torquemada and the other Inquisitors, whose servants carried banners of red silk adorned with the papal arms, the seal of the Catholic monarchs, and the escudo of the Inquisition. Torquemada's expression was triumphant, nodding to the spectators on either side of the street.

More villagers brought up the rear of the procession. Like Torquemada, they looked almost gleeful, as if a parade had come to town and they were joining it. To them this was a celebration. Isabel's worst fears were being realized.

The prisoners were led to a lower tier, decorated with black crepe. The friars sat down in between them, continuing the barrage of whispers into their ears.

Isabel smelled incense, and soon a haze covered the participants. When it dissipated, she spotted a triangular shape on the ground level near the platform. Could that be an easel behind the drummers? Indeed, it was. A painter sat on a stool in front of a canvas, a brush in his right hand. Was he actually going to capture these proceedings for posterity? Isabel felt disgusted.

The Inquisitors and their servants sat on a platform that contained an altar with lighted candles and carpet beneath their feet. Next to them stood a servant holding the green cross. The priest, the one from the canopy, began to conduct Mass. Isabel had never seen a Mass held outside the church. It felt unprotected, as if she and the other villagers were suddenly naked. His sermon dealt with the same theme that Torquemada had spoken about. Limpieza de sangre, the cleansing of impure blood. It was a long talk, and Isabel's feet ached from standing in one position.

Beatriz pointed to an empty row of scaffolded seats surrounding the plaza. "Can we take those benches? Please, I am weary of standing."

"I will not dignify these proceedings by taking a seat," glowered Isabel.

"I agree," said Papá. "That shows our intent to stay and listen."

"But we *are* staying and listening," protested Beatriz with a frown.

Then Torquemada rose and recited the oath of allegiance to the Inquisition. Once again, the Perez family fell to their knees and repeated after him. "We swear to defend to the death the Holy Office, against all adversity."

As Isabel straightened her legs, she felt a thump against her.

"Abuela!"

Her grandmother lay on the ground, unconscious. No one around them noticed, too enthralled with the tribunal. In fact, people were stepping forward into the newly created space to get a closer look at the altar. She would be trampled.

"Clear the way!" shouted Papá, waving his arms to push people back.

Isabel knelt down again, putting her ear to Abuela's nose. "She's breathing."

"That's good news. She only fainted," said Papá.

"I'll fetch water," said Mamá.

Isabel shaded her eyes, squinting up at her sister. Beatriz's face was darting every which way. She did not know where to rest her eyes, on Abuela or the altar.

"Your priority is with your family," Isabel barked at her sister.

Beatriz finally knelt. "What's wrong with her?"

"Oh. I don't know. The heat, the incense, the worry, the fear. Pick one."

Isabel gently slapped her grandmother's cheek. "Abuela, can you hear me?"

Abuela's eyelids fluttered.

"Gracias a Dios," muttered Papá. "Let's get her to one of those seats."

Beatriz looked pleased now that they would be sitting.

"Remove your smile, sister," said Isabel.

Isabel and Beatriz took Abuela's feet; Papá gripped her strongly under the arms. Elbowing their way through the throngs of people, they carried her to a bench on the opposite side of the main platform. Once they got her seated, she was alert enough to sit up on her own. When Mamá found them with a tin cup of water, Abuela drank it greedily. Reluctantly, Isabel sat.

Meanwhile, the auto de fe continued. Now a different Inquisitor was standing, reading from a scroll while Don Sancho smirked behind him. "Gonzalo Franco. A converso accused of sitting in a suca. In his defense, he claimed he was collecting the alcabala tax from the Jew, Meir Barchillón, and it was the only way to go into the home since their suca was at the entrance. We found him guilty of Judaizing since he could have collected the tax on a different day.

"Manuel Garcia. Two witnesses saw no smoke escaping from

this converso's chimney on Saturday, the third of September in the year of our Lord Jesús Cristo. In his defense, he claimed he was out of Trujillo on that day. But our records show his horse was in the stall, cleaned by Juan de Torres. The Holy Office has found this converso guilty of Judaizing by refusing to cook food on his day of rest.

"Fernando Lopez, a converso. He stands accused of paying the beadle of the sinagoga to buy oil to light a candle for the health of his sick child. He then asked the beadle to say a prayer for the child. By donating maravedis, it is an act of charity and honor toward those who remain devout Jews. He is found guilty of Judaizing.

"And lastly, we have Maria de Chaues, in absentia. She washed the spot on her baby's head that received the holy baptismal water. Six different citizens bravely came forward to say they witnessed this act in the public baths. She was unable to provide any defense and did not confess when put to the question. Thus, she is found guilty of sins and transgressions against Christianity."

"In absentia?" asked Isabel.

"They are sentencing her, even though she's not here," explained Papá.

"Where is she?" Isabel's voice trembled and she realized she already knew the answer.

"Under this cloth lies her carcass," announced the Inquisitor. "She expired while in prison."

Tortured to death, no doubt. Isabel's eyes blurred. She recalled Señora de Chaues as she walked into church last week, scared beyond words. Only to die alone. Isabel hoped the woman expired while picturing her infant, held safely in her arms. Isabel closed her eyes and imagined the señora kissing the air where the baby's forehead would have been.

Torquemada took over. "We now abandon these condemned souls to justice. Friars, please stand."

The six whispering religious men stood up.

"Were you able to convince these prisoners to confess their sins?"

"We were not," they intoned in unison.

The crowd erupted in shock and then approval. Beatriz was transfixed.

"Then I invite one last speaker to the altar," said Torquemada. "My colleague and fellow Inquisitor Padre Morillo."

He was a red-cheeked man with a ring of hair circling his shaved upper head, in the same tonsure style as the other friars. "I ask that the secular arm of the law show mercy to the guilty." His voice was soft, almost sympathetic. Could he have any influence at all? Would someone listen to him? Isabel held Abuela's hand on her left and Mamá's on her right, praying his words would have some positive effect.

After a few seconds, Don Sancho stood. Isabel's entire body recoiled. So he was participating in this horror after all.

"Look how important he is," said Beatriz.

Isabel wanted to kick her sister.

"Will the prisoners Gonzalo Franco and Manuel Garcia please stand?" said Don Sancho.

Isabel released Abuela's and Mamá's hands. The soft-spoken plea of Padre Morillo turned out to be nothing. Just a formality. No one answered. No one would show mercy. The Inquisitors, with their self-satisfied expressions, could now tell themselves they had done all they could. Isabel forced herself to look at the two prisoners and give them the respect they deserved. She would not look at Don Sancho.

"You two men will be reconciled to the church," came Don Sancho's familiar voice. "For six Fridays, you will walk in procession through Trujillo, unshod, bareheaded, and barebacked. You will discipline your body with hemp cord. You will never again hold public office. You cannot become a money changer, shopkeeper, or grocer. You are forbidden to wear silk or scarlet or colored cloth of any kind. No gold, silver, coral, or pearls will adorn your body. You cannot stand as witness in a court of law. Your sanbenitos will hang on the walls of the church in perpetuity so everyone will know your family name and the shame you brought down upon them. If you fall into the same error again, the penalty will be death by burning at the stake."

The crowd cheered their hurrahs.

"Fernando Lopez, please stand," said Don Sancho.

He was the one in the black gown and the hat. Isabel's heart thumped inside in her chest. What were they going to do to him?

"You are sentenced to death by burning. This is your final chance. Do you wish to be reconciled with God and receive mercy from the fire by strangulation first?"

What sort of bargain was that? It was a devil's choice.

Silence fell over the plaza. A stork squawked from the top of a tower. Someone to the left of her coughed. A woman's skirt rustled nearby.

Isabel kept her eyes on Fernando Lopez. She could tell he had been a handsome man once. Now his gray beard was long and matted. Flies swarmed around him. She hoped his wife was far away from here and his son, who had been sick enough to need a blessing, had recovered, and that they had found happiness as a family for a short while.

Underneath Fernando Lopez's gown, urine pooled on the ground between his legs. He opened his mouth to answer. A whisper came out.

"Please repeat that," said Don Sancho.

"I confess to Judaizing," he said, slightly louder.

Isabel reviled Don Sancho so much she thought she might scream.

"Gloria a Dios," said the six friars.

"Gloria a Dios," echoed the crowd.

"You will die by noose," said Don Sancho. "Then you will be burned."

At this, Isabel gasped and felt faint herself. She slumped against Papá, yet his powerful torso prevented her from falling sideways.

Fernando Lopez was strapped tightly to the back of a mule. He would not be escaping from those ties. Another mule was roped to the first animal, with the corpse of Maria de Chaues strapped to it. Both beasts were led out of the plaza.

The quemadero was located just upriver, outside the city walls. Isabel, Beatriz, and Papá joined the crowd following the procession, but Mamá stayed behind with Abuela. Papá felt that they had done their duty by being seen at the sentencing and that Abuela's collapse would provide ample cover. Isabel walked blindly, in a kind of dazed, superstitious thinking. Perhaps if she didn't get to the burning place, it would not happen. At least the crowd was somber during the fifteen-minute processional. No one gossiped or cried out.

When they arrived, two tall wooden stakes were waiting there, wood chips piled high in a circle around their bases. Some rough-looking men were stringing up the rope where Fernando Lopez would be hanged.

Isabel felt an urge to turn her head, not to avoid watching Lopez die, but because she felt a presence, almost like eyes on her back. She spun around.

And gasped.

Diego stood a few meters away. Her eyes met his. There were at least thirty people between them. An inexplicable longing tightened her throat. She took a step closer. He gave a small movement of his head, nearly imperceptible. No. She could not go to him. Nor he to her. Not with Don Sancho so close and Beatriz and Papá at her side. She stood still. His gaze held hers, keeping her in place. They remained like that until Beatriz shook Isabel's arm. "Look. Your betrothed has the striker."

"Before we commence with the burning, allow me to introduce a special guest," announced Don Sancho.

Don Sancho walked over to an exquisitely dressed woman, resplendent in red velvet, even in this heat. A jeweled crown rested atop her head. "Her Eminency, Princess Joanna of Aragon, House of Trastámara, queen consort of Naples."

"That's King Ferdinand's sister," said Beatriz, impressed.

Don Sancho continued. "As the sole relative of the Spanish crown, you grace us with your presence. Thank you for traveling all the way from Italy." He then handed the princess a thin piece of wood, about one meter long, enveloped in green ribbons.

The combination of Princess Joanna's attire and the beribboned stick put in Isabel's mind a line from a poem she had read once: *In death, there is beauty*. She had not understood its significance until now. The poetess had been lamenting her lover's death and how his face shone like the moon, even in repose. But the way the Christians tried to cover up the blackness of the auto de fe with color, this was the irony the poet was trying to convey.

While the crowd was watching the princess, Fernando Lopez's body was being strung up on the noose. Now one of the men tightened the rope. Lopez twitched wildly. Isabel's belly quivered, threatening to expel her morning biscuit. She closed her eyes. When she opened them, Lopez's body had already been lowered and tied to one of the stakes. Next to him, Maria de Chaues was tied to the other stake. Her head hung down, awkwardly, as they had not strapped it. They were both naked, stripped of their sanbenitos.

Don Sancho used the striker to light the fire. He turned to the princess. "Please add your stick to the blaze."

Princess Joanna threw in the piece of wood. A flash of green, then orange flames. Back in the village, the church bells tolled. Here at the quemadero, the friars chanted and the drummers beat a dirge. The air took on the heavy, sweet, sickly odor of burning flesh. The greasy smoke drifted upward toward Heaven.

Isabel wondered if there even was one.

Diego pushed the haunting memories of the quemadero out of his mind and concentrated on Isabel's face. How he had wanted to reach for her when he saw her in the crowd yesterday, to protect her from the evils of that place. She looked so vulnerable, her beauty accentuated by her fear.

He would paint her portrait so he could always gaze at her, in the morning when he rose, and in the evening when he lay down. Her skin, the color of an unripe peach, must be perfect on the canvas or it would not do her likeness justice. He riffled through his pigments. He had a few bright colors in his supply box from before he left for Lisbon, but none of those would work for rendering flesh. At university, he had learned about the three different sources of color—minerals, plants, and insects. The only materials he was able to bring home with him when he so abruptly left school were the minerals of green earth. Now he removed some prason and stirred in gum arabic, the sap from an acacia tree. All pigments needed a binding medium to make them wet and soft enough to go on a brush and, ultimately, a canvas.

He brushed a stroke of paint onto a paperboard. It wasn't right. Damn. He supposed he could wait until he visited Berruguete's studio, maybe borrow some powders there. Their first meeting was scheduled for four days from now. But Diego was impatient. Inspiration had struck and he wanted to get Isabel's image down now. He couldn't think what to do.

The breakfast bell rang downstairs. Frustrated, he made his way to the dining room. It would just be his mother and him this morning, as his father was at court in Toledo and not due back until tomorrow. He snapped open the napkin on his lap and waited for the countess.

"Sorry to keep you, m'hijo," said his mother, sweeping into the room. "I spent longer than I thought at my morning devotionals." Even this early in the morning, she was dressed formally, in a crimson silk gown and matching veil. She lifted her face covering and regarded him. Her face was covered in heavy powder. Two circles of rouge blotted her cheeks. Her eyebrows were drawn in darkly and her lips were stained red. Diego wondered if Jesús appreciated all the effort his mother put into making up her face for Him.

"Did you have a pleasant sleep?" she inquired.

"Yes," he lied.

"It wouldn't hurt you to join me once in a while for morning prayers," she responded, slicing him a piece of quince pie.

He had never relished spending time in their family chapel. Or doing anything more than what was required of him by his parents on Sundays. At university, they did not mandate worship and Diego went to the campus chapel as little as possible, preferring to spend his free time in the art studio or debating one of his professors.

"It's not as if you have to travel all the way into town," she continued. "You merely have to walk down a flight of stairs."

He ignored her and ate his pie.

His mother wiped her red lips on the white napkin, and he caught a glimpse of the smear. Crimson on white. And he thought, pigments! If he were a gambling man, he would bet his mother had a powder in her cosmetic drawer that he could mix with his green earth. It wasn't out of the ordinary at all. Everyone knew finely ground king's yellow, for example, was used to color a woman's face both on the canvas and in the flesh. He might be able to find a match for Isabel's skin after all.

Diego took a sip of tea. "Mother. Could I take a peek in your cosmetic drawer? I'm looking for a specific pigment for a painting and I don't have the right color in my supplies."

She laughed. "You want to draw with my eyebrow paint?"

He endured her teasing so he could get what he wanted. "It's the powders I'm after, not your eyebrow tools."

"You know your father doesn't like it when I indulge you and your little painting hobby." She put down her napkin. "But seeing as he's not here, I don't see the harm."

The red velvet curtains were still drawn when they entered his mother's bedchamber. A thin opening down the middle let in a ray of sunlight that bisected the four-poster bed. Sumptuous paisley coverings lay across it in a jumble. A thick tapestry of a hunting scene hung on the far wall.

The countess drew open the curtains. "Honestly, I must have a word with Concha about her laziness. She has not yet been in here to do her tasks this morning."

Diego walked to the boudoir, a small room adjacent to the chamber. It held a chair and vanity table, a polished ebony desk with a looking glass attached. Various powders, creams, eyeliners, lip stains, and rouges lay stacked atop the table in shiny silver jars. Two wig stands flanked either side of the glass. One held a curly-styled wig, the other a straighter hairstyle, pulled up on top into a twist. Mantillas and veils poured out of open boxes strewn on the floor.

"You, alone, must be keeping Madrid in business with your weekly orders," said Diego pleasantly. He could dig at her just as easily as she at him.

He opened one of the silver jars, dipping in his pinky finger and brushing a line on the back of his hand to see how the color looked against his own flesh. He was darker than Isabel and his mother, so most powders stood out on his skin. It wasn't right. He tried the next jar and the next jar and the next. Until he had opened everything.

"Is that it, Mother?" he asked testily.

"I suppose so."

He looked at all the open jars, the boxes from Madrid, the excess. "How is it that you have a veil in every color of the rainbow, and I can't even find the right pigment to paint with!" He swept his arm across the vanity, sending the jars flying. Powder flew into the air. Glass broke on the polished stone floor. Silver tops went rolling.

"Diego!" yelled his mother. "What's come over you?"

He said nothing, fuming silently.

"Is this really about a paint color? Or is it something else?" Her mouth parted slyly. "It's a woman, isn't it?"

She saw through him, as always. "You're wrong,"

he told her. "I'm merely frustrated that you and Father do not make it easy for me to pursue my passion. Verrocchio doesn't have to ferret through his mother's powders to find the right colors, I can assure you." He knelt down and began to sweep up the powder with his hand.

"Don't. There's glass down there. Concha will get a broom."

"I can at least pick up the lids." He reached farther across the floor for a few of the silver jar tops. One was facing upward, still rocking on its rounded edge. There appeared to be something etched into the underside. A name? "Reina Benveniste," he read out loud.

"What did you say?" came his mother's voice from across the room.

The door opened and in ran Concha on her short, sturdy legs. "Are you hurt, m'lady? I heard crashing."

"Everything's fine, Concha," said the countess. "You can leave us."

"But you just said she should sweep the glass," said Diego. And before that, you were complaining about her laziness, he thought.

"It's all right. I can wipe it up," his mother insisted, kneeling.

Concha stood still, torn between obeying her mistress and wanting to do her job and clean.

"That will be all, Concha," she said sternly. "Gracias."

When Concha left the room, the countess stood and told Diego to leave as well. "I shouldn't have let you come in here in the first place. Go!"

He left the room, perplexed. His mother was acting strangely. He was also angry at himself for losing his temper. It *was* about Isabel. He was in love with her and his parents would not allow the match. He had to play this carefully.

He spent the day in his room with a charcoal and parchment. If he couldn't paint her, he would sketch her. He disliked charcoal because it smeared too much, but it would do for now. He made a few attempts. They weren't poor likenesses; they just didn't do Isabel's comeliness justice. While he drew, he kept thinking about the name he had seen carved into the silver lid. Reina Benveniste. Had his mother stolen that jar from someone named Reina? If so, then what other items in this house were ill-gotten? Could it be that their fortune wasn't theirs at all? He had to know the truth about his family. Before his father returned home.

He found his mother in the pantry discussing a meat order with the cook.

"Mother, may I speak to you a moment?"

"I'm in the middle of something," she answered.

He waited in the hallway, staring at one of their many doors decorated with the ten circles of the Altamirano family shield. Was their good name all a farce?

His mother came out of the pantry. "I don't appreciate you interrupting me in front of the servants. Especially after your childish display earlier this morning at my vanity table."

He wasted no time. "Mother, is the Altamirano money legitimate?"

She scoffed. "What, pray tell, are you talking about?"

"You stole that cosmetic jar, didn't you?"

"Don't be foolish. I'd never steal anything."

"Then how did you come to have a jar with someone else's name? I demand to know."

Her right cheek gave a twitch.

"Mother?"

She glanced down the hallway in both directions. "Come into the chapel where we can speak freely."

Diego followed her inside. A leaded-glass window with ten circles stood regally above the altar. Small statues of the Virgin Mary and the Lord Jesús perched on pedestals. There were two pews and a velvet cushion for kneeling.

She took a seat in the pew, patting the spot to her left. "Join me."

When he had settled next to her, she inhaled as if to gird herself. "Reina Benveniste is my real name." She paused dramatically. "I was born Jewish, in Hervas."

Diego's mouth fell open. This couldn't be. His mother's name was Graciela. Her surname Guzman before she married the count. The Guzmans were wealthy sheep farmers, part of the Mesta guild for centuries.

"It's a shock, I know."

"I don't understand," he said.

"I was about three years old when we converted," she explained. "My father's silver shop had been looted one too many times. My parents saw their New Christian friends prospering, some in government, some marrying hidalgos and receiving the respect they sought, even if they were the lowest of the aristocracy. A Dominican priest rode through town, rounding up Jews for conversion. He preached that if they took the baptismal waters, their businesses would not be destroyed. I don't know whether my parents debated that evening or not. But the next morning, they gathered with other Jewish families in St. Mary's Parish and were dipped in the font.

"I don't remember any of my life before that time. My religious memories are of going to church every week and celebrating our Savior's rising. Thirteen years later, when my parents died of the pox, I went into a convent."

Diego thought that maybe she was making this entire story up. But her expression was dead serious.

"During the time I took the veil," she continued, "your father came to socialize with the young ladies. Many eligible men did at that time, preferring to choose their own wives rather than succumb to arranged marriages by their families. He became a Galán de Monjas." A courtier of nuns. "One night, he played the lute under my window. It was the most tender melody I'd ever heard, and I confess, that's what made me fall in love with him. When he learned of my bloodline, he had papers drawn up with a different parentage."

"He falsified documents about your lineage?"

She nodded. "The Altamiranos would never allow a converso to taint their bloodline. And you know how obdurate your father is. He was determined to have me. So I became the daughter of a long line of wealthy members of the Mesta guild."

Diego was stunned, momentarily speechless. "Do . . .

do you ever think about it? Your history. Your beliefs. Moses even."

"Never. I loved being a Christian. It was all I ever knew. But at the age of sixteen, I was all alone. I owe your father my life." She lifted her head, her nostrils flaring in pride. "I am Countess Graciela Guzman Altamirano."

"But . . ." Diego began, running his hands through his hair. It was preposterous. This entire conversation. "Never mind."

Her eyes darted to the chapel door, shut firmly. "You have more questions," said his mother. "Please, go on."

He stood up, pacing in the small room. "According to Mosaic Law, every child born from a Jewish mother is . . ."

"Jewish. I'm aware of that. But you, m'hijo, are no more Jewish than our very own King Ferdinand. Our papers are stamped by the Order of Chivalry of King Henry III, grandfather to Queen Isabella. No one has ever questioned it. And no one ever will." She rose, giving him an imperious stare. "Understood? This conversation ends here. And we will not mention this to your father."

He gave her the briefest of nods. A wind was blowing through his mind, clearing the clouds of confusion away. He now knew the reason why he never felt accepted by the other children at court. Why he did not fit in with the young men at grammar school. Why he stayed up until dawn at university debating Maimonides, one of the greatest Jewish philosophers of all time. Why his Hebrew language class was so fascinating to him.

He was Most Illustrious Lord Diego Altamirano, next in line to the countship. And he was a Jew.

19

For the first time Isabel could remember, her family did not have Shabbat dinner in the cellar. After the auto de fe, no one could stomach food, even Beatriz, who offered a ritual sacrifice to el Dios by abstaining from eating for twelve hours.

Isabel wondered if she herself would ever be able to eat again after the horror of yesterday. But when she opened her eyes to the sunlight on Saturday morning, there was a rumbling in her belly, the body belying the mind. Along with her hunger, she remembered the Talmud, hidden in the cellar, forgotten in the rush to get to the auto de fe. She felt certain that showing it to Abuela would lift both their spirits tremendously.

Isabel kicked off the linens and sat up. Beatriz was not abed. The house was silent. Maybe Mamá, Papá, and Abuela were taking their warm milk outdoors? She placed her feet on the cool stone floor and walked to her window to peer down into the courtyard. It was empty. She thought of two of the prisoners yesterday, Maria and Fernando, their last days of life spent hemmed in, sleeping in a cell in the basement of the Holy Office. What were their thoughts? How did they not rip out their fingernails digging in the dirt, trying to escape? In some ways, Maria's premature death by torture was merciful. She did not see it coming. Fernando had to be paraded in front of the entire town and then hear his death sentence pronounced. His last few minutes of life were spent in full awareness of his doom. Isabel breathed in the sweet air from outside and thanked Dios she was safe in her own home.

It was there, stuck atop one of the iron bars of her window, that Isabel found the second note from Diego.

I need to see you. Meet me outside the south gate of the city wall at half past noon.

Her pulse raced. Had he heard talk at the auto de fe? Was there another warning for her family he needed to convey? Or . . . did she dare dream it? Maybe he had been thinking about her as much as she had been missing him?

Isabel wandered into the sala in her floor-length white night-dress. She shivered in the thin cotton fabric and pulled the ribbon tighter at her neck. Silence. Where was everybody? "Mamá, Papá, Abuela?" She opened the front door, looking up at the sky. The sun was not directly overhead but approaching it. It was likely between the tenth and eleventh hour. God's navel, how would she slip out to meet Diego in such a short time?

Beatriz and Abuela entered the house from the rear door in the kitchen, carrying their chamber pots. They were both dressed for the day in street clothes. Abuela looked practical, as always, in a simple green skirt, sleeveless tunic, and chemise. Beatriz stood out in her color-coordinated veil and gown of red satin.

"Where are Mamá and Papá?" asked Isabel.

"Visiting Señora Cohen," said Beatriz with contempt.

"No puedo creerlo!" exclaimed Isabel. "I don't believe it! What made Papá change his mind?"

Abuela smiled. "I convinced your father. Don't ask me to do it again, though. It was a singular success."

"What did you say to him?"

"That we mustn't hold grudges in our hearts. Maimonides commands us that if someone apologizes to us, we must forgive."

Diego had said something to that effect during their walk. Where could he have possibly gotten that idea?

"Besides," added Abuela, "visiting a sick person is performing a mitzvah." A good deed.

And after the auto de fe, we don't know what the future brings, thought Isabel, offering her own silent reason for why her parents should visit Hannah Cohen. We must seize opportunities for forgiveness now so we don't die with regret. "I'm glad," said Isabel. "The Cohens will be home for the Sabbath. It's good timing."

Beatriz yawned, bored with the conversation. She turned to Abuela. "Shall we go?"

"Go where?" asked Isabel.

"Promenading," said Beatriz. "Abuela will be my duenna."

"Is that wise?" asked Isabel. Ever since her grandmother's fainting spell, she had been walking unsteadily. "Are you well enough, Abuela?"

"I'm fine," Abuela assured her. She looked pointedly at Beatriz. "Don't you have something to ask your sister?"

"Whatever do you mean?" said Beatriz innocently.

"Come now," said Abuela.

"I suppose you could join us on our walk." Beatriz shrugged as if she didn't care whether Isabel said yes or no.

Isabel smiled most sincerely. "How lovely of you to offer. But I think I'll stroll by the river and compose my thoughts." The Talmud would have to wait.

"Your thoughts from yesterday out by the shed?" asked Beatriz, her voice going higher at the end in hope.

Isabel could read her sister's mind as easily as the alphabet. Beatriz wished Isabel would amend the errors of her ways, specifically her choice to possess a Jewish book and to choose the wrong side, as Beatriz had accused her of doing. Although Isabel had not yet decided to choose any religion at all.

"I meant, take a walk and compose some poems," said Isabel, correcting herself.

Beatriz stiffened and left the house without saying goodbye.

Qué suerte! What luck! She'd be able to meet Diego today after all. Atika had told her she should have a passionate tryst before she became trapped in an arranged marriage forever. But it was more than that. After witnessing the auto de fe, she knew she would never be completely safe, even as Doña Isabel Aguila. She would always be labeled a converso. She would never *not* be prey to the Inquisition. In case the worst happened and she was captured, she wanted to experience the truest, purest love she could. The kind they rhapsodized about at the poetry readings. The kind where, when you've met your equal, he looks you in the eye with the same ardor that you feel toward him. What if Diego was that person? She would never know if she didn't take the risk.

Once Abuela and Beatriz left the house, Isabel chose one of her prettiest gowns, made of a rose brocade fabric with red fleur-de-lis patterning. It was cut at the elbows so that her white chemise puffed through the opening like a small cloud. Without Mamá's help lacing up the back, it took some time to put each layer on and secure the stays herself. As she painstakingly hooked and tied, she blushed, imagining Diego's hands unhooking and untying all her hard work.

Using the looking glass, Isabel wrapped her hair in a knot at the back. She left a tail of hair hanging down from the knot, then crisscrossed it with a rose ribbon that matched her dress. She then removed some strands from her left temple and braided them, softly draping the braid over the knot so it hung on the right. Inside each intersection of braid, she stuck straight pins, studded at the ends with pearls, pilfered from Mamá's sewing basket. The style was so fancy, she wished Beatriz could see her now and appreciate it. When they were younger, Beatriz used to let Isabel fuss over her hair, coiffing it into elaborate designs. And she in turn would fuss over Isabel. Sadly, those moments almost never happened anymore.

Isabel splashed rose water on her neck and wrists. On her way out of the house, she stopped by the kitchen and took a pinch of cardamom seeds between her fingers. Chewing them would freshen her breath. Just in case.

When she got to the south gate, Diego had not yet arrived. She was relieved, wanting to observe him approach as opposed to him seeing her first. A four-horse carriage passed through the archway heading into town. A glimpse inside the cabin revealed a veiled rich matron, traveling alone. In less than two years' time, that could be Isabel.

She would not be sidetracked with dark thoughts. Diego was coming. They had the whole day ahead of them if they chose to spend it together.

After the carriage passed, it was quiet. Not many people were about in this part of their village, save a vagabond or two. Isabel felt suddenly exposed and wished she had a mantle to pull tightly around her. It appeared as if Diego had chosen this spot purposely, so the two of them would not be seen together in the bright daylight. Isabel did not know whether to be encouraged or frightened by this prospect.

The clip-clop of a single horse's hooves compelled her to look up. Diego was approaching on a steed. He cut a fine figure in his beautifully made clothes. He wore a white jerkin with black edging over a linen chemise trimmed with gold lace at the top, and gray kid gloves. His hose-covered legs disappeared into high boots of soft leather. His attire was a positive sign. He would not have dressed so handsomely if he had bad news to bear.

As he approached, he tipped his felt hat, revealing his untied hair.

"Señorita Perez," he said, dismounting.

"Count Altamirano."

"The count is my father. I'm just Diego." He pulled the reins over the horse's head, using it as a lead. Then with his free arm, he reached for one of her gloved hands and brought it to his lips. "And may I say how beautiful you look today?"

Her toes tingled. All her efforts on her hair and clothes had been worth it. "Gracias." Then she added, "Diego." How could calling someone by their name for the first time make her feel both anxious and exhilarated at the same time?

"I see you received my note," he said.

"Next time, you should write it in sal ammoniac moistened with a little water. It makes the words disappear until heated. My nosy sister can't read, but she would have given me a devilish time with her questions if she'd seen an inked message stuck in my window iron."

He grinned. "Don't tell me I'm in the presence of a sorceress!"

Isabel explained the sal ammoniac. "Practical magic is all. My abuela and I discovered the trick while she was giving me writing lessons, not wanting Papá to find the remnants of our studies and grow cross. He said learning to read and write was a waste of time, that my skills were better put to use with activities like grape-pressing." She sighed. "Messy business, that."

"But that's precisely what's unique about you. That you *are* lettered."

"I never told you I was. What made you presume I could read your note at all?"

"Girls who can't read or write don't visit bookbinderies. Or attend poetry readings, for that matter."

She reddened, flattered and impressed at his attention to detail. Her details.

"Your note sounded urgent," said Isabel, praying he was not a messenger of bad news today, but rather merely wanted to enjoy her company.

His eyes darted around them. "Not here. Let's ride somewhere where we can speak privately."

"On a horse?"

He laughed. "It would take hours to walk anywhere outside the town center. And that would not allow us very much time together."

So he did want to spend the day with her! She smiled, then her expression changed when she eyed the sitting apparatus on the horse. She had not ridden much, save for the occasional rounds in the neighboring vineyard, and was not entirely at ease atop these once-wild beasts.

"Don't fret," he assured her, following her gaze. "I removed the saddle and set the horse for bareback riding. That way it will be more comfortable when you sit sideways." A sheepskin pad lay over the horse's middle section, cinched underneath its belly with a tight belt.

"You thought of everything."

"If I brought you your own horse with a sidesaddle, the whole town would know I was bringing it for a lady. Best not to give the gossips something to wag their tongues about."

Or something to tell Don Sancho. "I appreciate your discretion."

"Allow me to introduce the two of you," said Diego. "This is my horse, Pepe."

Isabel removed her glove and put her hand on the side of Pepe's face. She knew enough from her father's grape deliveries by their own mule that horses needed to establish trust with their rider. Pepe's coat, white with black spots, reminded her of an inked page.

The horse brought his long lashes down over his eyes.

"He likes you," said Diego, putting his own hand on Pepe's face to pet him.

Their hands met briefly. The touch of his gloved hand on her bare one nearly made her gasp. She stopped stroking the horse and quickly put her glove on, lest she throw herself at Diego.

"Have you been to Monfragüe?" asked Diego.

She nodded. It was a wild area of forest, mountains, and streams about five kilometers outside town. "It's beautiful. I played there as a child."

"I thought we'd head over there." Diego put one knee on the ground and propped up his other knee as a ledge. "Easy now, Pepe," he said in a soothing voice. With the reins still in one hand, he reached out his other hand. "Step up, please."

"On your leg?"

"I can withstand it." Though he tried not to smile, she caught a glimpse of his mouth turning upward.

"I'm glad I'm providing amusement for you." She stepped both feet onto his leg, feeling wobbly.

"Now lift yourself atop the horse."

Isabel did this part easily, though she giggled when she found herself lying on her stomach over the moist sheepskin, wet from the sweat of the horse underneath. She did not know quite how to sit up.

"Well done. Now use your hands to right yourself."

By scooting her bottom onto the front of the padding, she was able to get upright. After she was settled, her legs dangled down one side of the horse's body.

"Fit your left knee into this groove created by Pepe's withers." He did not touch her leg, though she wished he would. Instead he pointed to a V shape between her and the horse's neck.

Her leg rested there perfectly. This side-bareback riding might not be not so bad after all.

He brought the reins back over the horse's head and to the left of Isabel. Then he mounted astride the horse, sitting behind her. The nearness of his body startled her. "Hold on to the mane," he told her.

She gripped Pepe's coarse neck hair tightly.

With a cluck of his tongue and a gentle kick to the side of the horse, they were off. He walked the horse quietly for a few minutes, but when they reached the river, Diego cued the horse with a kissing sound and a strong kick. Pepe accelerated into a canter and Isabel squealed in both delight and fear. She concentrated on sitting up straight and not falling. Every few beats of the hooves, she would shift position unwittingly and feel Diego's chest, strong and protective against her shoulder. Soon, her breathing matched his, moving into rhythm with the horse's four-count stride.

She knew from Papá's map that the Tagus River was long, flowing all the way from Trujillo to Lisbon, where it emptied into the Atlantic. They passed patches of farmland with peasants in the fields. Smoke drifted lazily out of the chimneys of mud-bricked homes. Perhaps some of this land even belonged to the Altamiranos. She did not inquire, realizing with a small smile that it didn't matter. She would be just as intrigued by him if she had met him in a taberna and knew nothing of his family.

A stone bridge, made of bricks that formed dramatic arches, stretched over the river. Diego slowed the horse back to a walk as they crossed. He leaned into her ear. "We can thank Juan de Carvajal for this puente. It's sturdy as an ox." His voice vibrated right through her, reaching her chest.

"I'm happy to know we have no risk of falling in the river, then."

"Unfortunately, this bridge has become the preferred route for gold and drug smugglers," he told her. "Do not come here at night. Ever."

"I don't plan to," said Isabel.

Once across the river, they continued inland, the horse picking its way over shrubs and bushes. Presently, they came to a meadow lined with oak trees. "Ho," he told Pepe, scooting back from her and dismounting. She felt the absence of Diego's body behind her, like a sudden rush of cold wind when a door is opened. She wanted him to return to the sheepskin and warm her. He helped her slide down off the horse, then led Pepe to a nearby stream.

"How was that ride?" he asked her.

"I rather enjoyed myself," she said, grinning.

While the horse drank his fill, Diego handed her his bota bag. She hesitated, having never before sipped from one. Her throat was so dry, she quickly tilted the nozzle into her mouth. But she couldn't gulp fast enough to stem the flow. Mortified, she felt a thin line of liquid dripping down her chin.

Diego reached out his thumb to wipe her face but stopped and gave her his kerchief instead. The tiny piece of white linen smelled of him, musky and freshly washed at the same time. She did not want to relinquish it and tucked it under her sleeve at the wrist.

Isabel looked around her. "It's so quiet here."

"I used to come here all the time to paint," said Diego. "This is the first time I've returned since I left for school." His eyes suddenly clouded.

"If you enjoy it here so much, why the concern on your face?"

"How can you see that, having only just met me?"

"Perhaps I'm a keen observer."

"You're much more than that, Isabel Perez," he said, holding her gaze.

Her heart quickened. She was a New Christian girl with an Old Christian man of noble birth, unaccompanied, in the middle of a forest. No one knew she was there. She was breaking every rule.

"You are correct," said Diego, finally breaking his stare to tie the horse to a tree, now that the animal was finished drinking. "I *am* preoccupied about something." He hesitated.

"What is it?"

"A discovery. Something I learned recently . . ."

"Yes?"

His eyebrows moved together. If she wasn't mistaken, he looked in pain.

"I discovered that . . . I am . . ."

"Are you ill?"

"No, no," he assured her. "Nothing of the sort. I discovered . . ." He took a deep breath and exhaled loudly. "A new artist, right here in Trujillo! He would like me to apprentice with him."

"How wonderful!"

Visibly relieved, Diego stood up straighter. "His name is Pedro Berruguete. It's an opportunity I've been waiting for all my life, but I'm afraid to ask my father. He will say—"

"That you're a nobleman with familial obligations," she said, finishing his thought. "I know all about being dutiful." She gave a wan smile. "You should try and figure out a way to do both. You'll regret it if you don't. An experience like that may not come along again."

He nodded. "I've been thinking . . . with Berruguete's studio right here in Trujillo, I can still do the tax collections during the day and paint at night. When Father sees Berruguete's portraits of important scientists, the saints hanging on walls of cathedrals, perhaps he'll realize how prestigious the apprenticeship could be." He paused. "Though I don't have much hope. Sometimes I loathe my birthright."

"There was a painter at the auto de fe yesterday."

"Oh?"

"Surely you saw him."

"I only arrived at the quemadero. I had been collecting taxes outside town in Cáceres the greater part of the day."

"Then you are lucky, I suppose, to have missed most of it."

His eyes narrowed. "That is true. The entire affair was a horror."

She was glad that he felt the same way about the vile tribunal as she did.

"Let's not talk of such things. Why don't you recite me one of your poems?" suggested Diego.

She was too shy to quote the one she had just written about him. She may as well have the town crier declare her feelings in the public square. But on the other hand, why shouldn't she be honest? Life was becoming more tenuous every day. Wasn't this moment, right now, all that mattered? "Very well." She curtsied like Atika did, hoping that would give her the confidence to say the words in front of him.

> *"O brother of the full moon in resplendence and*
>   *glory*
> *May God preserve the time which caused you to rise!*
> *If my nights have grown long after your departure,*
>   *I remain complaining of the shortness of the*
>   *evening with you."*

"When did you compose that?" Diego's voice was low.

Isabel swallowed. "After our walk in the Moorish quarter."

He took a step closer. His head tilted forward, his eyes on her lips.

She held her breath, suspended.

Then he stepped back.

God's fingernails! Why must he behave with such honor?

He extended his crooked arm. "Let's walk. I want to show you the wonders of this place."

She threaded her hand through the opening, the insides of their bent arms resting against each other. That spot beneath her elbow was aflame.

Above them, the blue sky was a vast canvas, with the occasional brushstroke of a cloud. Two eagles painted circles, searching for prey.

They left the meadow and the terrain changed to woodland. Oaks grew closer together—Isabel recognized at least four different types of trees—preventing the sunlight from streaming in. A small spotted creature darted in front of them, pausing to stare at the human intruders. Its ears were upright and alert, its eyes large and shining. Then it disappeared into the thicket.

"What was that?" exclaimed Isabel.

"A genet, I believe," said Diego. "They're harmless." Still, his arm muscle tensed, and he tightened his grip on her.

"Are there snakes here?" asked Isabel.

"Quite possibly. Wildcats, lynx for certain. Once I saw a lion."

"You did not!"

He laughed heartily.

She playfully hit his arm with her free hand. They walked in silence, the only sound a *caw, caw* of storks somewhere nearby.

"Careful," said Diego, gesturing to a muddy patch.

She lifted her hem to clear it, and he withdrew his arm from her elbow so he could better support her. She felt the heat from his hand on the small of her back, all the way through the three layers she wore. He let his hand remain there until they were out of the tree cover.

When they emerged, they found themselves facing a reservoir of sparkling blue water. A quartz outcropping shot straight over them. Isabel shaded her eyes to look up. At the top of the rocks stood some ruins—a few wall fragments along with a circular tower and a cistern.

"Those ruins are what's left of the old Moorish castle," explained Diego. "The legend tells that the castle was the home of Princess Noeima, who fell in love with a Christian. She showed the boy the secret entrance to the castle and he was discovered by her father, the sultan, who killed him upon sight. Now her ghost wanders the mountains in eternal punishment."

"What a terribly sad story," she remarked.

Would her ghost be made to wander these forests if she fell in love with Diego? At this moment, she didn't care. She just wanted to feel his lips on hers.

Yet he did not kiss her but continued to point out different sights. "Beyond those mountains is Portugal. And inside those jagged crevasses are caves with paintings by people who lived over three thousand years before Cristo."

That was older than the Jewish people. Abuela had told her that the history of the Jews began in the year 1300 before Cristo. An image, just a heartbeat's flash, made her shiver. She saw a line drawn between then and now. From cave painters to early Jews who descended from Abraham, to her and Diego in the year 1481. "Who will be the people of the future, the ones walking in this park one thousand years from now?" she murmured aloud.

"Our descendants," said Diego.

Was he referring to a child made from their union? The possibility thrilled her, then she quickly chided herself for getting too far ahead.

"It's interesting to think about what was here before the cave people," said Diego.

Clearly, he was not thinking about creating a child with her at all. Oh, he was maddening! Yet his mind was like nobody's she had ever met. Nor had she read any texts by a writer who thought like he did.

She swept her arm to encompass the whole forest. "I assume what was here before were the same animals and plants that are here now."

"Do you think God made the animals and plants?" he asked.

"Of course. He created them when he made Adam and Eve."

"What if the world, the animals, the plants, the ground we're walking on was always right here?" said Diego. "All the scientific matter that makes up this sphere we call Earth . . . what if it were eternal. Unchanging."

"And God had nothing to do with it?"

"The Bible says that God created the world out of the void. But what if that nothingness was actually ancient material, God's paints and brushes if you will?"

"I sense a philosophy lesson coming."

He grinned. "Who made the heavenly bodies?"

"God."

"Why does our sphere spin the way it does? Why do some stars emit more light than other stars? Why are certain areas of the night sky more crowded than others?"

"I've never thought of these ideas before."

"I ask you now, are all those details in the heavens necessary for the universe to function? Perhaps. Or perhaps not, and it is simply random. We do not know. Scientists are just beginning to study size, speed, and distance of the nine spheres of our universe. So until we know for certain that everything was placed randomly, we must posit that God created the world from nothing and fashioned it in a particular way. Thus making the arrangement of the heavenly bodies necessary."

"But didn't you just say that there was some sort of eternal world that existed before God?"

"I did indeed. I'm saying that there is room for both theories."

"Yet it is written in the Bible that God created the world out of the void," she said. "So that negates the idea of ancient matter."

"The Bible is not meant to be taken literally."

Reflexively, Isabel looked around. They were still alone, gracias a Dios, because if anyone heard them, they'd both be arrested for heresy. "You've not met my sister, obviously."

"I should like to debate her. For when it is written 'Their poison is like the poison of a serpent' or 'And I will be to them as a lioness,' the passages do not refer to actual poison or the figure and shape of a lioness, but to some abstract idea."

"A simile, as in poetry."

"Yes!" He was so excited, he nearly grabbed her arms. She would not have minded.

"What about when the Bible refers to the wrath of God, or the hand of God?" asked Isabel.

"This, too, is impossible. We cannot think of God as having a human body."

"You jest! Jesús was human."

Diego turned away from her.

Curses. Had she offended him? They were having such a stimulating conversation.

He remained quiet.

She wanted to bring him back. Though to his ideals or to her, she wasn't certain.

"How should we describe God, then?"

He turned to look at her, and his face showed such tranquility that great relief flooded over her. "He is an essence," answered Diego. "He is unknowable to us. For only God is the Knower, the Knowledge, and the Act of Knowing."

She was so happy to have his full attention, she did not bother to try to comprehend this strange way of thinking.

They stood gazing at each other. She was overcome with desire for him. Surely, he felt the same way. She had caught him staring at her lips more than once today. Did he fear the wrath of Don Sancho? If so, she wanted to shout to the heavens that she hated that odious man and would fight the betrothal tooth and nail. Or was it her converso blood? Was he simply like everyone else in Trujillo, destined to follow the rules and not the heart?

"Isabel, I was not entirely truthful before," said Diego.

"Oh?" she replied calmly, while inside she was anything but. What if he was not who she thought, after all? Was he going to denounce her to the Inquisition?

"I did discover an artist, but that wasn't what has been occupying my mind."

She watched him, waiting.

"Do you ever wonder about your ancestors, those family members from before you converted?" he asked.

Her heart sped as if she had run a kilometer. Could he know about their cellar? Could he see something in her face, a telltale sign that she was a Crypto-Jew? Was she actually in trouble here, or could she finally reveal the truth after all these years of keeping her family's secret?

She hesitated, then whispered, "Yes."

"Yes?" he repeated.

"I do think of my Jewish relatives."

His eyes shone. "I am one of them. I am a Jew."

"You are a converso?"

"On my mother's side. I only just discovered the truth yesterday," he said.

"My family . . ." she began. "We are Crypto-Jews. We have not lost our tradition."

"You practice in secret?"

She nodded.

"Then that means we are the same," he said in astonishment. "That means I can . . ." His voice, gravelly now, suddenly went quiet.

She swallowed, not daring to look away.

He brushed a lock that had come loose from her braid. She shivered under his fingers. Then under hooded eyes, he leaned down and kissed her. When his lips touched hers, her body arched to him. Her mouth opened and a small sigh escaped. He quieted her with his tongue and pulled her to him, pressing himself against her. She touched his cheek, marveling at the way the skin changed, coarser near his throat. His hands disappeared in her hair.

"Isabel," he whispered.

At last. She finally understood what the poets were talking about. She was hopelessly in love.

With a Jew.

20

They rode home by way of the river. As Pepe loped, his hooves lifted off the ground, so at times she felt as if they were floating.

Behind her, Diego brought his head forward so that their faces were touching. His breath caressed Isabel's cheek. Then he removed one hand from the reins and turned her chin toward him, resting his lips on hers. A few moments later, he did it again. And then again. He could not go one hundred meters without kissing her.

To her right, the river churned, fueling her with blue-gray energy that moved through her veins like blood. To her left, the marshy grass was wet and green, filling her lungs with verdant air.

Her hair, so carefully braided, was completely undone.

She was completely undone.

Reluctantly, they said their goodbyes at the same spot where they had begun. Yet nothing was the same for her. It never would be. Where the south gate archway appeared dull and dirty earlier, it now looked shiny and clean. Even the pigs nosing around in the slop that collected alongside the road endeared themselves to her.

"Buenas tardes," she called happily to an old basket weaver. The woman gave Isabel a toothless grin.

But as she walked home, her felicitous thoughts began to darken. She had always lived a double existence: a Crypto-Jew by birth, a Christian on the outside. Today she faced another duality: betrothed to Don Sancho, her heart with Diego. How could she marry that putrid creature after seeing what life could be like with Diego? Their days would not cease to be stimulating. And their nights . . . She trembled, imagining his body lying next to hers. It would be a world of ideas and beauty, rather than a world of punishment and fear. For Don Sancho was the Inquisition in human form. Tears welled in her eyes. The abject frustration! She finally felt pure joy and she did not know how to keep it.

Once when she was small, she held her breath to see how long she could go without air. Her cheeks turned purple and her eyes burned before she exhaled in a forceful motion, her lungs gasping for life. Her body acted on its own accord. In a way, she had been doing that same thing her entire life. Acting on instinct. For surviving in a Christian country meant perpetrating a lie. Being a good New Christian and never questioning anything.

Until now.

She no longer wanted to merely survive. She wanted to live! She wanted to act of her own volition to secure happiness. To have free will. All free people deserved a choice, in both religion and marriage.

But this was impossible because she needed to survive.

It was a circular argument.

There had to be a way out of the maze.

When Isabel arrived home, Mamá and Papá had not yet returned from visiting Hannah Cohen. Beatriz, laundering clothes in the wooden tub out back, told her Abuela had just retired for a siesta.

"You exhausted her," said Isabel. "You need to find another duenna."

Beatriz wrung out one of their father's shirts. "I guess you'll just have to accompany me next time, then."

"Or perhaps you should not promenade at all," answered Isabel.

Beatriz squinted at her. "Something's different about you this afternoon."

"Por favor," scoffed Isabel. "I'm still the same older sister you've always had."

"Your cheeks are flushed, and your neck is pink."

"You always say that. Must be the rigor of my walk. I took the long way home." Isabel turned toward the kitchen door. "I'll be in the house if you need something."

Once inside, she leaned against the chopping block and exhaled. Nothing got past Beatriz. Isabel would have to start acting less in love and more somber. Given the reality of Don Sancho, that shouldn't be difficult. Isabel quietly opened Abuela's bedroom door to see if her grandmother was asleep.

"Is that you, mi nieta?"

"I'm sorry," whispered Isabel. "I didn't mean to wake you."

"I only just lay down. Come in."

Isabel hesitated, knowing Abuela should rest. But she was desperate to speak to the only person who might comprehend the ideas Diego spoke about. She could not reveal his identity or the secret about his past. Not until he told her it was safe. And she did not know when that day would come. They had not discussed future plans when they kissed goodbye. They simply relished the newness of each other. But at least she could feel closer to him by understanding the way his mind worked. "Maybe I'll come inside just for a short while."

The sun was low, but it passed through her grandmother's

small window opening. Dust mites swirled around in the light beams.

"How goes the poetry writing?" asked Abuela.

"Hmmm?" Then Isabel remembered she had told her grandmother and sister that she would be walking by the river gathering thoughts for a poem. "Fine, gracias." She sat down on the pallet. "Are you terribly tired from the walk?"

"Your sister can socialize, I'll give her that. Some boy named Juan Carlos was there. A rogue, no doubt. We saw him from afar. A convent might be good for her, temporarily."

Isabel recoiled. "You can't mean that."

"Let's be honest. She'll never be a Jew. And she enjoys the company of women. She stopped to talk to all of her friends and their mothers and aunts. I think she'd thrive in a nunnery. It's quite normal, you know, for girls with no dowries to stay for a time. Men even court women behind those walls."

"I've heard. Some of the sisters encourage it. Though I don't think Beatriz is the type of girl to attract a man that way. She's too self-righteous. She would not approve."

"Maybe." Abuela sat up a bit straighter in bed and regarded Isabel. "You have a faraway look in your eye. What are you thinking about?"

"Abuela, do Jews believe that God created the world out of nothing?"

"Moses does, so therefore all Jews do." She tilted her head. "Where is this coming from? First you ask me about free will, and now you talk about creation."

"You sparked my curiosity when you told me about Al-Andalus." She laughed. "I guess my mind has been wandering while my hands have been busy with grapes." Isabel stood up from the pallet, preferring to pace. "But what if there were elements, I don't know, some sort of matter present, *before* God created the world?"

"Well, there is something called the Laws of Nature."

Diego had spoken of that, she remembered.

"Maimonides believed that changes concerning nature and the animal kingdom occurred spontaneously and randomly without direct interference from God. So I suppose these processes could have happened just as easily *before* God created the world."

This answer frustrated Isabel. "No one knows for sure which came first, do they?"

"I'm afraid not. Our knowledge and understanding of creation is less than a drop in the ocean. We do not know the real truth. We may never know. Even the Talmudic sages differ greatly when discussing creation. For instance, the timing. Whether Heaven or Earth was created first or if they were made simultaneously. Whether light was manifested first or whether the entire world was."

"Maybe the Talmud wants us to think for ourselves."

"I would agree with that. The Torah, our Bible, is absolute. It is the word of God. The Talmud is ever changing. It is the word of man."

The Talmud reminded Isabel of Diego's philosophical arguments. One thought led to another, which in turn led to another, and so on. Had Diego actually studied it? No, he couldn't have. He had only just discovered his background. But his ideas were so radical, he must have learned at least some Jewish teachings at university. Suddenly, Isabel could wait no longer. "Abuela, I have a surprise for you. Do you think you can walk downstairs with me?"

"I am getting too old for surprises."

"It will be worth it, I promise. Then I'll let you rest."

Isabel held Abuela's hand as they descended the stairs into the cellar. On the fourth step, the air abruptly changed, as it always did, to something cold and damp. Isabel lit extra oil lamps, hoping to warm up the space faster. "Have a seat, por favor."

Moving aside a stack of empty grape baskets, Isabel removed two loose bricks in the wall.

"Are you getting your papá's book of blessings?"

"Something better." Isabel removed the Talmud and placed it on the table in front of her grandmother. The leather cover had one word embossed on it, which Isabel could not read.

Isabel heard Abuela's intake of breath. "Is this . . . ? No! It cannot be."

"It's true, Abuela. It's a Talmud." She was swollen with pride now that she saw her grandmother's face. It was truly a gift to be able to show it to her.

"Where did you get this?"

"I borrowed it from Yuçe."

"That child knows not what he has done." She quickly covered it up with the white cloth Yuçe had wrapped it in.

"Are you not pleased?"

"We mustn't have this here."

"But we have Papá's book of prayers. No one has ever found that. The hiding place is secure."

"The Talmud is different. More holy. Women aren't supposed to read it. Something bad could happen."

Her grandmother had always been a believer in superstitions. She put salt in the pocket of a new dress before she would wear it. She would not gaze in a looking glass. When Isabel was young and someone remarked on her beauty, Abuela would spit three times onto the ground so as not to arouse jealous spirits. "Abuela, I can always return the book to Yuçe, but it's here now. You may as well examine it."

Abuela shifted in her chair. Then she lifted up the cotton rag and peeked underneath. Immediately, she covered it again.

"You aren't going to turn to dust, Abuela, I promise."

Her grandmother hesitated, then retrieved her spectacles—wire-rimmed with cloudy glass inside—from the pocket of her gown. *"Hashem yishmor."* May God protect. With reverence, she removed the cloth and opened the cover. "I cannot fathom it . . . after so many years of hearing my father talk about this . . . yet it's as I imagined. So beautiful." She continued to turn pages.

Isabel peered over her grandmother's shoulder. "While I was at the Cohens', Yuçe explained Rashi script. I know that printing presses can now make Talmuds available everywhere, but how do you think the first one arrived here in Trujillo?"

"Someone probably hand-carried this. Maybe they rode from Venice or Constantinople, even Levant, stopping at cities where there were Jewish communities. They would of course bring it directly to the sinagoga, after which a local scribe would copy it down. Then the courier would move on to another village."

"Yuçe also said the laws were first passed from one person to another through stories. Then they were finally written down so more people could practice Judaism."

"I guess my father was like our ancient ancestors, because he passed the stories down to me orally."

Isabel pointed to the center of one of the pages, the Hebrew letters as mysterious to her as a man's naked body. "What does this say?"

"*Ketubot*. It means marriage contract." She leaned in closer. "It seems this section is all about guiding a bride in her new role. Though you won't have such a document when you marry Don Sancho, I'm sure there is wisdom in here to help you."

How Isabel wished she could have a marriage contract with Diego—a Jewish one! With disgust, she pictured the life of servitude that lay ahead of her as the wife of Don Sancho del Aguila. What in God's tumors was she going to do? A radical notion popped into her mind. What if she did become Doña del Aguila, but kept Diego as a lover? This was done at court all the time. Grandees had mistresses and their wives looked the other way. Then the notion withered as quickly as it had blossomed. She was fooling no one. She would not be able to live within such an immoral framework. Committing adultery went against all her beliefs. She wanted Diego purely or not at all.

A shout from upstairs interrupted them before Abuela could give her an answer. "Isabel, Abuela, come quickly!" It was Beatriz's voice, shrill and panicked.

21

Isabel took the stone stairs two at a time. When she opened the cellar door into the sala, she was met with a frightening sight. Papá lay on the settee, moaning. Dried blood cut red rivulets through his dusty face, from both ears down to his chin. His left arm was bent in an unnatural position. Mamá sat at the table, her face colorless. She wore no hat, though she had left the house with one. A white area of scalp, as big as a spoon, stood out from the thick black hair on the crown of her head. Had someone pulled out a chunk of her hair? Isabel did not know whom to attend first.

"See to your father," whispered Mamá, giving Isabel her answer.

Abuela finally entered the room, her eyes full of apprehension.

"Something terrible has happened, Abuela." Isabel's voice broke.

Her grandmother went into the kitchen and brought out a damp cloth.

You cannot afford to fall apart, Isabel told herself, taking the rag from Abuela. "I'll clean Papá. Can you go next door and ask Señora Herrera for some willow bark? It will help with the pain."

"What shall I tell her?" asked Abuela. "She is a gossip, that woman."

"That Papá hit his head on the wine press. And, Beatriz, you go fetch Doctor Cetia," said Isabel. "If you hurry, you will return before nightfall."

"But he's a Jew," said Beatriz weakly. She did not speak with her usual force when discussing non-Christians. In fact, her top lip was quivering. The situation frightened her.

"Are you actually putting your intolerant zealotry ahead of Papá's well-being?" said Isabel, beginning to wipe her father's ear.

"I just thought . . . well, couldn't we ask Doctor Andreas?"

"Papá doesn't need a barber surgeon. He needs his arm reset. And Doctor Cetia is the best in Trujillo."

"I can go to the judería if she won't," offered Abuela.

Beatriz's neck turned pink. "No, Abuela. I can walk much faster than you."

Isabel nodded. At least her sister felt properly ashamed that her grandmother showed more love than she did. As Beatriz exited the door, Papá gave a forceful moan.

"I'm sorry, Papá. I'll be gentler," said Isabel.

"Wherrrrrrre isssshe . . ." His voice sounded like there were pebbles in his throat. The sounds he made were not distinguishable.

"What are you saying, Papá?"

Papá didn't respond to Isabel, but looked to the door. He struggled to get out the words, as one slow of tongue might. "She . . . must . . . not."

"She mustn't what? You mean Beatriz?"

He ignored her and slapped his hand on the table. "Inqui. At gates. Judería."

"The Inquisition is at the gates of the judería?" Isabel rushed to open the window and called down to Beatriz.

"There is no danger," Mamá informed her, though her voice

was strangely monotone. "The Inquisition is no longer at the gates. All the officers left with us."

This was a relief. Despite her sister being a scholar of Christendom, able to talk her way out of any interrogation, Isabel had no idea what Beatriz might say when confronted by the Holy Office. She could denounce the whole family for all Isabel knew.

Isabel returned to her father's side. "What did the Inquisitors do to you, Papá?"

He did not answer, but closed his eyes, his head lolling back on his neck.

"He can't hear you," said Mamá.

Isabel's heart beat a warning. "What do you mean?"

"They separated us, but I heard him being hit," continued Mamá, staring into the empty space in front of her. "One of the blows must have landed too close to his ear."

"Oh, Mamá." Isabel went to her mother and embraced her, never wanting to let go. She buried her face into Mamá's frail shoulder. "I'm so sorry. This is my fault. If I had not followed Rachel home . . ."

"It could have been worse. We weren't put to the question." Mamá's voice was affectless, as if she were reciting a recipe for stew.

Isabel held Mamá at arm's distance, wanting to shake her, to make her go back to the way she remembered her always. Her giggling, capable mother.

"We told them the truth, that we were visiting a sick friend," intoned Mamá blankly. "But they wanted to see for themselves. They stormed into the house, and accused the Cohens of coercion."

"What does that mean?" asked Isabel.

"Tempting conversos to observe Jewish rites. They tried to

bring all four of us in, but Hannah was too sick to move. They beat David in front of the children and took your father and me to the Holy Office."

Isabel turned to her father. "Papá, can you hear my words?"

No response.

She clapped in his face. He did not even startle.

"Let's get you both out of these soiled clothes," said Isabel, holding back tears. She put some water on the hearth to boil before leading Mamá and Papá outside to the bath. Mercifully, there were no sounds from their neighbors. No cries from Señora Herrera's granddaughter. No *chink-chink* of Old Señor Tejada hammering an iron shoe for his horse. No gossip floating from the courtyard as the del Castillo sisters hung their laundry while their dog barked and ran in and out of the hanging sheets. Isabel would not have been able to tolerate the sounds of everyday life were this the case. For today was no ordinary day. What had started out as perfect joy would forever be etched in her mind as a tragedy.

Isabel began to fill the tub with well water. On her third trip from the well, Abuela returned, willow bark in hand.

"Did Señora Herrera seem suspicious?" Isabel asked her.

"I don't think so." She handed Papá a piece of the bark for him to chew on.

For a moment, Isabel and Abuela just stood still, listening to Papá's teeth grind the bark. Then Isabel walked inside, fetched the boiling water, and carried the heavy pot back out. She poured the hot water into the bath, mixing it with the cold. The steam rose, obscuring her view of Mamá and Papá. Briefly, she allowed herself to imagine perhaps they weren't there at all. That this nightmare had not truly happened. But then the steam dissolved and there were her broken parents. Abuela helped Mamá undress and began to wash her. Isabel looked at her father. With his head hung, he turned his back to her and slowly removed his clothes.

How could it be that in one afternoon, she had become the parent and they the children?

By the time Beatriz brought the doctor, Mamá and Papá were already resting. Doctor Cetia examined them as they lay on their pallet.

After some time, he lowered his tong-shaped specula and looked at Isabel grimly. "Your father's right ear has suffered complete hearing loss. The nerves may have been severed."

"And the other?" she asked.

"Hearing in the left ear may or may not return. We must wait and see. For now, I'm afraid he is deaf." He removed more tools, some quite frightening. Razor-pointed cutters, a mallet. "Do you have a bottle of brandy?"

Beatriz brought one up from the cellar. Doctor Cetia made Papá drink nearly half the bottle. Then he put another, larger piece of willow bark in Papá's mouth for him to bite down on. When he reset the arm, Papá wailed. Isabel screamed silently, along with her father.

Later, in her own bed, Isabel thought about her family's future. She could take over the wine sales by writing notes for Papá while she verbally spoke the terms to his clients. Her mother's hair would grow back. She supposed they were lucky. Next time they would not be.

While Beatriz slept soundly, Isabel turned over onto her stomach and buried her face in her arms, crying herself to sleep.

Four days after the discovery of his mother's secret, Diego stepped up to number 4, Calle Sillerias, the site of Berruguete's newly rented studio. This past week, he had begun to process all the changes that were happening in his life—his Jewishness, Isabel. His world had turned upside down. He did not have a precise plan for anything. The only thing he knew was that in the short term, he wanted to learn to paint from a master. In some ways, the apprenticeship was a welcome distraction. Diego could follow a prescription, the steps needed to impress Berruguete and secure a position. It was like putting one foot in front of the other. This was much easier than trying to imagine how to live in Spain as a Jew with the woman he loved.

A rusted forge lay in Berruguete's grass, a remnant from the previous tenant, no doubt a smith. The artist and Diego were to have their first meeting today. Not to begin apprenticing, but to share ideas. Berruguete wanted to show Diego what he was working on, and the artist had asked to see samples of Diego's work as well.

Although Diego knew he had drawing talent, he was still nervous. His heart was a cantering horse. On the walk over, he kept tapping his leather folio on the side of his leg in a one-two-one pattern. If he lost syncopation and the tapping became a two-two-one instead, he would start again. It was not just the act of showing his work that agitated him—it was the deeper knowledge of his Jewishness. Diego knew he had not changed a whit on the outside since they first met in the taberna. But inside he was a new man. He felt like he wore the truth on his sleeve and everyone who looked at him could see it.

Thankfully, his father had not noticed anything amiss with Diego at all. He returned from Toledo preoccupied. Their Majesties had just formed the Council of Castile to be the central governing body of the kingdoms of Aragon and Castile. It seemed those of lesser birth who proved their loyalty to the Crown were to be given power in the council. It was rumored that a small cadre of noblemen would be allowed to attend meetings but could not vote. The count was determined not to be pushed out. He needed to show the monarchy his worth.

Given his father's concern for his position at court, Diego did not broach the subject of the apprenticeship at that time. But he knew this meeting with Berruguete was fast approaching. He did not want to go behind his father's back and have him find out through idle gossip. So the entire next day, Diego devised possible scenarios for asking permission. He thought about setting up an easel on the camino, the path where his father took his morning walk, so that it would look as if the count happened upon his son accidentally. Diego planned to place a canvas there and begin to paint the environs, perhaps the castle and river behind it, to use as a conversation starter. Alternatively, Diego considered retiring to the parlor after dinner and replacing the large map his father kept on the wooden stand with a beautifully illuminated manuscript such as *The Miracles of the Blessed Virgin Mary.* He would then lead the count to the map and remark, "How surprising! One of the maids must have dusted it and replaced it with this." What followed would be an organic segue into illuminations, and Diego's scholarly knowledge of the trade would leave his father in awe.

In the end, Diego opted to ask him in their private chapel at home. Diego reasoned that appealing to his father's religious passion was the key to receiving his blessing to pursue a life of art. The idea of sitting and actually praying the Catechism proved more difficult than Diego could have imagined. But after a few minutes, habit kicked in. By the time Mass was over, he had figured out how to live with the hypocrisy. Acting one way on the outside, going through the motions, was only that. Faking Christianity meant nothing. His truth was on the inside. He supposed he had been preparing for this all along, with his growing indeterminacy at school. He always had a vague confusion and could not define who he was. Now he knew—he was a Jew.

His father and he had been alone in the chapel. His mother had retreated to the kitchen to check on the preparation of lunch. He laughed to himself, thinking that all the important discussions in the family were occurring in this sacred space. An open Gutenberg Bible rested in Diego's lap. He had chosen a particularly beautiful spread, adorned with a golden scale, a human hand, and bit of red cloak on its arm holding the scale. An illuminated Bible was still rare, but the Altamirano money was plentiful and it was a sign of prestige to have a private copy in one's home.

"Let us take our leave," said his father, standing. "Our meal is waiting."

Diego pointed to the page in the Bible. "Look at the way the artist painted those tiny lines. It almost looks like an insect."

"Yes, yes, quite skilled."

"If I may, I'd like to speak to you about an issue of great importance to me."

He sighed impatiently. "My stomach is empty, Son. Your mother is waiting in the dining room."

"I will make haste," said Diego.

His father sat back down.

Diego closed the Bible. "When I was at university, my philosophy professor asked us to imagine resting in Heaven. He wanted us to see ourselves as old men who had lived a full life of earthly devotion. To understand that it was time to live out the rest of our spiritual days knowing we had done all we could, whether it be as a commander of an army, an advisor to the king, a devoted husband and father, or even a craftsman. He hoped we had pride in ourselves no matter how we earned a wage."

"A noble endeavor."

Diego took a deep breath. It was now or never. "When I imagined myself in Heaven, it was as a painter."

"A painter?"

"Yes, Father. It was a vision that came to me, the way the archangel Gabriel appeared to the Virgin Mary telling her she was with child."

The count was mute.

Diego had not lied, unless one considered the

embellishment of certain facts lying. It was true that the professor had given them the assignment and Diego had indeed pictured himself satisfied at the end of his life, having completed many paintings, his works becoming known throughout Spain and beyond. As far as an angel or saint descending from Heaven to speak to him, that had not occurred.

"Father? What say you?"

"I must think on it. There is also the matter of managing our estate and holdings. It is an ongoing responsibility. There is no end to tax and rent collection."

"I am confident I can do both, sir."

"I do not like the idea of my son, a lord and count-in-waiting, being known as an artisan."

"It's not as if I would be soldering silver, Father, or milling wood. I would be an artist, receiving commissions from some of the most powerful people in Spain."

His father harrumphed. "One cannot argue with a vision from God. You may try it for a month. Then we shall revisit the matter. And if you shall fall behind in any way, with our tenant farmers or shopkeepers, then you will say goodbye to this passing fancy."

As Diego lifted the iron knocker on Berruguete's brown, wood-slatted door, he knew painting was no passing fancy. Nor was his affection for Isabel. His identity as a Jew was most certainly permanent. He must figure out a way to bring all three of these passions together.

"Young master Diego," said Berruguete, sweeping his arm to usher him in. "How good to see you."

Diego basked in the familiar smells of the studio. To some noses, it would be offensive, but to Diego, it was tantalizing. The sharp odors of copper carbonate, vinegar, and lead for manufacturing pigment. Pine tar and linseed oil for emulsions. Egg tempera and gum arabic for binding. A small tub of gold powder rested casually on a table, as if it did not cost as dear as lapis lazuli. Various props lay around the room: vases with budding hibiscus flowers, bowls of fruit. A green cloth draped over a window, the way a woman would wrap a shawl. On another table sat a spinning globe, a compass, and several palettes covered in colored blotches of paint. A door led to a second room, where Diego could see a folded-up cot leaning against the wall.

This was Diego's idea of Heaven on Earth.

"I trust your father is agreeable to our arrangement?" asked Berruguete with those furry-dog eyes.

"All is well between my father and me."

He slapped him on the back. "Good, good. Now let's see what you've brought in that folio of yours."

Diego removed eleven charcoal sketches and two pen-and-ink studies, for that was all he had in Trujillo. His oil canvases were still at school in his rented room.

Berruguete studied them intently. He lifted a fragile piece of parchment, ripped in the center where Diego had pressed the quill too hard. It was a study with close-ups of eyes, feet, and hands in groupings on the page.

Under the scrutiny, Diego tapped his fingers to the syncopation he had fashioned on the walk over. No working artist, and certainly not one of Berruguete's stature, had ever viewed his work before. The professors at school were multifaceted: doctors, philosophers, theologians. And while some painted as a leisure pursuit, none did for their vocation.

"You can do hands, gracias a Dios. That's the most difficult, always."

Diego relaxed a little. "I have not yet painted an entire figure with live models."

"We can remedy that," said Berruguete, carefully returning the sketches to the folio. "I am having a sitting this week with the alguacil. He commissioned his own portrait. I believe he wants to present it to his betrothed as a matrimonial gift."

Diego swallowed. "Don Sancho?"

Berruguete nodded, standing.

His rival would be here, in this very room. Diego would have to study his brow, his ears, his fingers. Fingers that might touch Isabel one day. Would he be able to paint him without revealing his jealousy? Would he charge at him with a palette knife?

"Diego?" said Berruguete.

"My apologies. I didn't hear you."

"I was telling you about my latest piece." He led Diego into the second room, chuckling. "It's such a large canvas, it needs its own quarters. This is normally where I bed, but I've propped up the pallet so I can view the work unencumbered by anything in my vision."

There was no easel. The canvas had already been pulled tight over wood backing. It reached floor to ceiling and nearly wall to wall.

"Is that . . . ?" Diego's words fell away. He was staring at a familiar scene. The scaffolding where a prisoner had been hung. A platform with a fiery priest. Somber Dominican friars behind him. A royal sibling, dressed in red velvet. Two stakes with nearly naked dead bodies. Jewish bodies. Bodies that in another place and time could have been Diego himself. "You . . . painted the auto de fe?" He thought his voice might fail him again, but it came out strong.

He shrugged. "Normally, I do not do pictorial narration. Too many things can happen that are out of my control. Weather, stubborn beasts, an angry mob. In addition, it's hard to settle on one image when the event keeps unfolding and changing. I prefer the studio and a sitting subject."

Diego moved closer to examine the painting. "I didn't realize the tribunal was so boring that someone fell asleep."

"You like that dozing figure on the bench, eh?" Berruguete laughed, misunderstanding Diego entirely. "I thought it added some realism."

"Oh, I don't think you have anything to worry about there. The whole scene is quite believable."

"As you saw when you came in"—Berruguete gestured to the other part of the studio with the vases, flowers, compass, and globe—"I'm experimenting with figurative objects. Still life is quite radical, you know. The only other painter I've heard about who is doing this type of subject matter is de'Barbari out of Venice." He paused. "Now where was I?"

"The auto de fe," said Diego tightly.

"Yes. It's the first time I've created a work of this scale. The Madonna I did for the church in Paredes de Nava was one quarter this size. But the corregidor in Trujillo is an acquaintance of my parents. And someone in the royal court asked if he knew any painters who might capture the tribunal. The request came about on such short notice, I almost declined." He stared at his own painting. "But the Holy Office pays well."

Diego was enraged.

"I confess I was quite moved by the entire experience." Berruguete's eyes shone brightly.

"Moved?"

"It is amazing, is it not? The way the monarchy can dispatch evil from our midst so handily? It's a brilliant deterrent. Conversos being forced to watch their brethren and sisters burn. I had not seen that before."

Diego felt the urge to scream. He regarded Berruguete. For a painter who studied in Italy, at the vanguard of the rebirth of art, philosophy, and architecture, he was the very opposite of enlightenment. He was pure darkness.

"You were in Italy, studying art at the Italian court, were you not?" asked Diego.

"Indeed. I worked at the Ducal Palace. Truly an architectural masterpiece. They even have a room just for contemplation."

"Ah yes, the classical Greek influence. Surely among the great thinkers who passed through the palace, you heard talk of earthly judgments rather than those handed down from God?"

"You mean prison? Queen Isabella's holy brotherhood has created local policing systems and jails that are quite successful. Or perhaps you speak of an angry mob who takes justice into their own hands? That works as well."

Diego bit down on his lip to control his rage. Plenty of innocent Jews were murdered in killing sprees. It happened all over the country. That hardly sounded like justice. "I am referring to something less punitive, such as, in the case of a transgression between two men, forgiving the one who has committed a crime if they have accepted the error of their ways and repented sincerely."

Berruguete looked aghast. "Even in Giotto's masterpiece, *Kiss of Judas*, with all its figurative realism, Jesúcristo has the final word on forgiveness. Not the man who was wronged."

"The ancient Romans gave power to the people when they overthrew the empire," countered Diego. "This is the essence of a republic. How can the Catholic Church expect the people to accept them when they do not accept the people? The people are autonomous beings who can adjudicate their own sins."

"The people must accept the word of God."

Diego dipped his head slightly. "I mean no disrespect to the Church. Or to you, Señor Berruguete. But surely you agree that when it comes to Judaizing, the punishment does not fit the crime?"

"On the contrary, it is quite apt."

"Torturing and burning people whose only fault is

that they descend from Israelites? We should be embracing them. They were chosen by God for a covenant. His favor and love afforded them special sanctification. The laws of Cristo are merely a continuity of the laws of Moses. Christianity is actually a completion and fulfillment of Judaism."

"You blaspheme." Berruguete walked away, and into the main room of the studio.

This conversation was over. Diego had tried logic and debate, but it was futile.

Berruguete turned back, looking at Diego askance. "The canvas is not a place to reveal your opinions, my dear boy. If you are not up to the task, tell me now."

No, he did not feel up to the task of apprenticing under a man who would paint such vile imagery of Diego's own people, who followed orders like a sheep to a dog, who sold his soul to the highest patron. But he desperately wanted to paint, to learn to use oil, and short of moving to Madrid, which held other artists but no Isabel, Berruguete was the only choice in town.

"I am your humble servant."

22

Isabel watched the parchment curl in the flame of the kitchen hearth until the thin paper was merely bits of black. It was Diego's sixth note in two weeks, since the day they had ridden up to Monfragüe. All had gone unanswered. She wanted to see him desperately, but after Papá's and Mamá's mistreatment at the hands of the Inquisitors, she was afraid of bringing more harm to her family if she and Diego were caught.

As each missive burned, a small piece of her died along with it. If she could cut open her chest, spread her ribs, and peer into her own anatomy, she would not be surprised to find her heart had shriveled to the size of a prune.

Last Thursday, she had ventured out to visit Atika, and even that excursion proved dangerous. She had gone to seek advice about the man she loved and the man she was betrothed to. She needed a friend she could trust, not like her own sister, who couldn't wait for her to fail.

Atika had been in the amphitheater, setting up cushions for another poetry reading.

"Your father told me I'd find you here," said Isabel, panting from climbing so many steps.

Atika turned to her. "Are you coming tonight?"

"My heart isn't in it, if I'm being honest."

She raised one eyebrow. "You have to. I've got a real salty one to recite. There are also going to be dancers doing the zambra, I heard." Atika started swaying her hips to music only she could hear.

Isabel just sighed.

Atika took a seat and patted the space next to her. "What's wrong?"

Isabel lifted up her skirt and joined her. "Diego and I . . ."

"No!" Her mouth spread in a sly grin. "You took my advice and lay together?"

Isabel allowed herself to laugh. "What? No! We shared nothing more than kisses, but . . ." For a girl who loved words, she was having a very hard time expressing herself.

"You will, though, soon?" asked Atika.

"I can't take any more chances with him," she said, sidestepping the question. "Things with my family, our situation, has worsened. Also, Don Sancho and my father reached an agreement for next spring. He's been sending gifts." Though they were beautiful—a hand-painted fan, a pair of pink gloves as pale as the dawn—Isabel loathed them. "This came yesterday." She pulled a silver-filigreed and sapphire ring out of her pouch. "Look inside."

Atika examined it more closely. *"Isabel y Sancho, siempre."* Isabel and Sancho, forever. "There's no backing out now, is there?"

Isabel began to cry. Atika put her arms around her and let her mourn her future. "I'm so sorry, Isabel."

On the way home from the visit, when Isabel turned onto Calle de la Victoria, she had seen a stranger loitering near their house. His back was to her, so he could not see her approach. He did not look like a pícaro in dirty rags and worn shoes, but he was no tradesman either. He wore a clean, well-pressed black doublet over gray hose, yet did not carry himself with the air of a grandee. She had certainly never seen him before in the neighborhood. Isabel thought he might be a spy.

Isabel quickly came up with a ruse. She went back the way she'd come, ducking into a nearby lace shop. Using a spare coin her mother had given her, she bought a cheap veil. She covered her face with it, something she never did, and left one eye peeking out in the way the streetwalkers did when they wanted to proposition a man. Even though it was not yet dark, the hour when the unsavories came out, he was still a man. If he did not respond to her provocations, she would know he was a spy.

"Buenas," she called to him, swaying her hips and pausing directly in front of him.

He did not answer. He was chewing búcaro, the reddish clay used in pottery, which people had recently discovered was enjoyable to put in their mouths. Isabel hated the stuff. It tasted like what came out of a horse's back end.

She lowered her lashes coquettishly. "Feeling lonely? We could have a grand time together, you and I."

He chuckled and his eyes traveled down her body. "I'd like to, señorita. But I'm meeting someone. Move along, now."

"As you wish."

He was a spy; she was sure of it. Was her family the target? She continued along the street for a few meters, when he called out to her.

She turned back, heart pumping. This was good news! He was not a spy after all. But, God's bunions, what debauchery had she gotten herself into? She might actually have to do something untoward with him!

"Do you know who lives in that house?" He pointed to her wooden door.

"No, señor," she said, trying to keep her voice steady.

"I just thought if this street was where you, uh, worked, you might know."

"I'm sorry I can't be of more help, señor." She meandered away from him, swaying her hips. When she turned the corner, she scurried back in the direction of her house on a parallel street. Gathering the folds of her skirt up around her waist, she managed to climb over the back fence, landing with a thump in their yard. The del Castillo dog barked from the front patio, hearing the disturbance, but she paid him no mind.

So they *were* being watched. Now that the Inquisition knew they were friends with the Cohens, the Perez family must be on an official list for suspected Judaizers.

From then on, she would not be leaving the house except for church, wine deliveries, and the market. She told her whole family to do the same.

Staring at the hearth in her kitchen, she took out Don Sancho's ring. She wished she could throw the befouled metal into the fire, too. But she would wear it on her finger. With spies in their midst, Don Sancho was the only assurance for their safety. She could not forsake him. If she and Diego were discovered, the alguacil would be publicly humiliated. He would not hesitate to find evidence against his adulterous heretic whore, and turn her—or worse, those she loved—in to the Inquisition.

Grief overtook her and she sank to the floor in the kitchen. She was also completely exhausted. Her days had been spent accompanying Papá on deliveries in case a customer had a question or a problem and a note needed to be written. In addition to her regular responsibilities of adding up the ledgers, she also helped clean grape skins from filters, checked for sugar content in the wooden vats, ordered empty bottles from Abraham the glass-blower, and transferred red grapes from baskets to press. Because the baskets were so heavy, she enlisted Beatriz to help her. It had to be completed bowl by bowl in small batches, so it took much longer than when Papá and his servant, Pedro, lifted it. Pedro was mostly unavailable now, having to spend all his time at the vineyards, tasting grapes and haggling with the farmer for lower prices, tasks that Papá had always done.

She closed her eyes to stem the tears, but they poured down her cheeks anyway. She missed the strength of Diego's chest support-ing her on the horse. The feel of his hands in her hair when they kissed. She removed his handkerchief from her wrist and covered her face in his scent. An idea for a poem came into her head, about being caught, or stuck, as it were, in a kind of purgatory between Don Sancho and Diego. She had not written anything since that verse she recited in Monfragüe for Diego. She stood up and walked straight to her bedroom to write it down, so as not to lose it.

O you who claim to be supreme in law and order
You bring storms of fear to my nights
Yet he erased the flashing bolts of lightning
And soothed my tumultuous heart.
Why must I languish 'tween fire and water
Hell and Heaven?
I am but a kite
Chinese silk
With no one holding my string
Untethered, never to touch the ground

She supposed she should be grateful for the inspiration. Poems never came this easily. Melancholia was a mixed blessing.

"Isabel," called Mamá from the sala. "Papá needs you in the cellar."

Closing her notebook with a sigh, she made her way downstairs.

One of Papá's best customers, the duque of Alba, was waving around a bottle of wine, his face red as a beet. It was early enough in the day so that if the cellar door was propped open, one could see easily without the need of an oil lamp.

"You cannot expect me to serve this líquido asqueroso, this contemptible drink, to my guests. It's no better than common table vinegar." The duque's ruffled collar shook.

"WAS THE ORDER MISSING SOME BOTTLES? I PACKED IT MYSELF. TWELVE CASES." Papá answered him too loudly, with words that had nothing to do with the situation.

Duque Alba looked perplexed.

The hearing had still not returned to Papá's good ear. In addition, certain sounds had disappeared from his speech over the past weeks, so that when he said doce casos, twelve cases, it sounded like DO-AY CA-OS. Between the volume and the dropped consonants, most Castilian speakers could not understand him. Isabel had been able to intervene in most deliveries, but when a customer stopped by the house, she was not always around. And Papá was stubborn and proud, unwilling to admit he could not conduct business in the same way he used to.

This was the first time, however, that it appeared the quality of the wine had suffered. Isabel thought perhaps some sort of contaminant had gotten into the press and turned the wine.

"Duque Alba," began Isabel. "My apologies. Allow me to serve you some finely aged brandy instead?" She walked farther into the rear of the cellar to open a bottle. "Por favor." She handed him a splash of the sweet liquid in a glass.

He sipped it, nodding. "This will do, thank you. But I expect to be compensated for my investment in your vino."

"Of course. I have ducats here at the house to repay you. Please come upstairs and finish your brandy while I retrieve them." She did not want him to see the hiding place where they kept their gold coins. It was behind the loose bricks, where Papá kept his Jewish prayer book and where Yuçe's Talmud now lay.

She carried the bottle of brandy and led him upstairs with Papá following. Isabel asked Mamá to bring out olives and bread and sit with the duque and Papá while she went back downstairs to get the money.

Isabel removed the two loose bricks in the cellar wall and reached in her hand. She touched the dusty leather cover of the Talmud. She had not looked at it since the day Mamá and Papá had been taken.

The sounds of Mamá's and the duque's voices drifted down to her. Hopefully, her mother was holding up her end of the conversation without sounding too affectless. The hair on Mamá's bare spot had begun to grow back. Fuzzy baby hair filled in the whiteness. Life went on. Though her mother remained a shell of her former self. She had never been an overly joyous person, but she was generous with her smile and ran the household with a steady hand. That had all changed since her encounter with the Inquisitors.

Isabel pulled out the Talmud, frustrated that she could not even read the word embossed on the front. The wisdom within the pages was locked to her and she had no key. What secrets did it hold? Was God inside there? Or was He in Monfragüe with the wind whistling through the leaves of the trees? Wherever He resided, He was the same God for both her and Diego. Yet she couldn't reach either of them.

Her life since Mamá and Papá had been taken by the Inquisition was busier than ever before. Full. Yet unfulfilled. It would continue like this until she married Don Sancho. And then it would be more of the same. With a shock, she realized she had nothing to look forward to any longer. No reason to wake up each morning. Without hope, what did one have?

With a heavy heart, she returned the Talmud to the niche and took out the metal box of money. Two gold coins was worth 750 maravedis. This would set them behind significantly.

It had to be done.

That evening, after supper, when Abuela was retiring, Isabel knocked softly on her bedroom door.

"It seems I'm forever visiting you before you lie down," said Isabel, shutting the door behind her to make sure no one in the family could hear them.

"Everything all right, mi nieta?" said Abuela, removing the pins in her bun.

Isabel wasted no time. "I want you to teach me how to read Hebrew."

"Cómo? What?"

"The aleph-bet. I want to learn it."

"So you can recite the blessings?"

Isabel shook her head. "So I can study the Talmud."

"Do not say such a thing!" Abuela reached for the hand-shaped hamsa charm she kept near her breast to ward off evil spirits.

"But, Abuela, I want to understand God."

"*I* can teach you about God."

"But I have questions that you may not know how to answer. My friend . . ." She stopped. She wanted to tell her grandmother everything. But the less Abuela knew, the safer she would be if she were ever questioned by Don Sancho or the Inquisition.

"Which friend?"

"Forgive me, Abuela. I don't know what I'm saying." Her lip quivered and she tried to compose herself. "I'm just so . . . unhappy. I thought perhaps reading the Talmud would give my days meaning."

Abuela's eyes softened. "What's come over you? Are you still upset about Don Sancho?"

Her grandmother's sympathy touched her deeply and she began to cry. "It's so much more than that, Abuela. I don't understand the point of anything anymore. Why are we even on this earth? To marry someone we don't love? To live in fear every time we walk out our door? To watch a parent lose his hearing or, Heaven forbid, his life? Is this all there is?" She sobbed harder.

Abuela wrapped her in her arms. "Shhh, mi nieta. Shhh. I did not realize you had fallen into an abyss. It pains me to hear you speak like this. Knowing our purpose in life is one of the great gifts of being human." Then she pulled away and held Isabel at arm's distance so she could look into her eyes. "I never thought I'd consider something like this. But we are living under different rules than my father and grandfather had. And perhaps it's time for Judaism to treat its women differently." She took a deep breath. "The Talmud is written mostly in Hebrew, the ancient language of our scholars. But there is some Aramaic in there as well. It's a mix of Arabic and Hebrew, more commonly used by the people." She frowned. "Though both languages use the same letters, learning two different spellings could take months. Surely you must return it to Yuçe?"

Isabel sniffled, letting the sobs subside, allowing herself a glimmer of hope. "We can keep it for a short while. Yuçe gave me no indication that he needed it back right away."

Abuela considered this. "Putting aside the obvious danger of having a book such as this on our property, learning to read it is just the first step. Interpreting the text is another challenge entirely. My father spent his whole life finding new meanings in those laws."

"Then we'll do the best we can with the time we have left."

Abuela gave her a rueful smile. "I always say that your impetuousness will be the death of you, but *you* are going to be the death of me. *Hashem yishmor.*"

23

Isabel sat at the cellar table, an oil lamp beside her. She rested her head atop Papá's ledgers, just for a moment. She was bone-tired. The next moment, she was asleep.

"Mi nieta," whispered Abuela. "Should we forgo the lessons tonight?"

Isabel raised her head, rubbing her neck where it ached from being turned at an awkward angle. "How long was I out?" Her voice came out slow and thick.

"At least three-quarters of an hour."

"I want to study. Por favor." Learning with Abuela had brought a more welcome distraction than Isabel could have imagined. Though the frequency of Diego's notes had not diminished, learning a new language had helped take away the all-consuming sadness over not seeing him. Over the past few weeks, she and Abuela had made much progress. Isabel had memorized all twenty-two Hebrew and Aramaic letters, plus their five final forms. She could now read rudimentary sentences and was anxious to delve into the teachings.

"Very well," said Abuela, pulling out a chair.

Isabel twisted the cap closed on the glass ink pot and cleared space on the table.

"Now, where were we . . . ?" said Abuela, opening the Talmud.

"You were going to begin with some commentary." Isabel knew from Yuçe that Rashi had written his opinions next to the law. Abuela had shown her other handwritten comments as well from descendants of Rashi's school of thought, Maimonides and other commentators.

"We may as well begin with Shabbat, since you already know a pinch about it from our Friday night dinners." She carefully turned the pages. "It's still so strange to see this book in front of me. I used to listen at the door to my father's study as he sang these laws. He said that singing the words helped make them permanent in his mind." She directed Isabel's attention to the parchment. "Here they are talking about the law of refraining from any work on the Sabbath."

"These rules put us Crypto-Jews to shame," admitted Isabel. "We always go about our regular schedule on Saturdays with nary a feeling of guilt." She paused. "Sometimes I wonder if Mamá and Papá took the easy way out."

"The Babylonian Talmud was first scribed in the year 500. This is 1481. The world is vastly different today. You can't apply the same standards."

"You mean Jews weren't afraid back then?"

She shook her head. "We have always been an oppressed people. I just think that now is the worst we have ever seen with these forced conversions. We are not openly Jewish like the Cohens. But our faith is still real. God understands. He doesn't judge your parents, and neither should you."

The Cohens. Isabel was wracked with guilt. She was so busy with Papá's duties and studying that she had not thought about them in over a month. Mamá had not asked about them either, which was understandable. Isabel suspected she had buried the entire episode deep in the recesses of her mind in order to avoid reliving it. If Señor Cohen had been beaten in front of the children, how serious was the damage? Were his hands broken? Could he cut cloth or still travel to the port in Cadiz? How were Yuçe and Rachel handling all of this? With their mother sick, what were they doing for food? God's nose hair, she felt responsible. After all, it was she who convinced her parents to pay Hannah a visit. And here she was using the Cohens' Talmud and she had not even gone to see them. It wasn't right. Yet the fact remained that the Perezes were being watched, which made slipping out for anything other than necessities very challenging.

Isabel slowly sounded out the words before her. "*Katav ot echat* . . . what does that mean?"

"It means *wrote one letter.* The rabbi is saying that if someone wrote a letter from the aleph-bet on the Sabbath as an abbreviation, representing an entire word, he committed a sin."

"Just by writing a single letter?"

"It sounds like a small thing, but it can mean so much more. If he altered a word in any way or completed a sentence, it is considered working on the day of rest and that's a violation of the rules of the Sabbath."

Isabel pointed to a word that looked different for some reason. "Is this Hebrew, too?"

"It's the Aramaic word for *rules.* See how it's just stuck in the middle of all that Hebrew?"

Isabel was awestruck. What a treasure trove. She felt insatiable. She wanted to devour as much as she could before she would either have to return the book to Yuçe or marry Don Sancho, whichever came first.

She had a new enemy now. Time.

*   *   *

The next morning, Mamá stood gazing out the window in the sala.

"What are you looking at?" asked Isabel. She sat on the floor with a bucket of thyme water and soap, trying to scrub the crimson-colored stains from her fingers. Cleaning the filters and handling so many grapes had permanently stained her nails. Beatriz and Abuela were on floor cushions, mending woolen socks. There had been no time lately to knit new ones, but it took little effort to stitch the holes closed on the old ones. Also, it saved money, which was becoming scarcer.

"Nada," said Mamá in her monotone voice. Nothing. She worried a stone in her hand, rubbing it this way and that.

Isabel dropped the soap into the bucket, an idea forming. "When's the last time you visited Ruy's grave?"

"Hmmm?"

"Soli's grave, Mamá. When did you last go?"

Mamá turned from the window, her expression blank. "I'm not certain."

"Come," said Isabel, rising. "Let's you and I take a walk over. You can bring a stone." It was a tradition for Jewish families to lay rocks atop the graves of their loved ones. Isabel looked at her sister. "You too, Beatriz." An Inquisition spy following them on the calle could hardly complain about a grieving mother visiting the grave of her son.

Beatriz continued sewing. "I'm too tired. Also, we are near the hour for the sext prayer."

Isabel shook her head in exasperation. "Sext prayer? What in the world does that even mean?"

"The third of the midday prayers," explained Beatriz.

"How many times do you pray a day?"

"Seven."

"The habit is actually taken from Judaism," interceded Abuela. Beatriz turned sharply to their grandmother. "You lie."

"Abuela never lies," said Isabel.

"The Jewish practice of reciting daily prayers comes from *zmanim*, or specific times of the day in Jewish law," explained Abuela.

Isabel was immediately curious. She wanted to dash downstairs to the hidden Talmud this very instant and look up how the rabbis defined a calendar day. She supposed the words for *sunrise* and *daybreak* meant two very different things. It was incredible the amount of specificity written into the commentary. The way the sages parsed each root and phonetic sound. But she must wait until everyone in the house was asleep before she could indulge herself and study further.

"I'm remaining here no matter where the idea originated," said Beatriz.

"Well, I'd like to go to the cemetery," said Abuela, preparing to stand. Though try as she might, she could not rise from the floor cushion.

"You stay here and rest, Abuela," said Isabel, gently putting her hand on her grandmother's shoulder.

Abuela did not argue, but she looked sad. There was no denying her mobility was now permanently limited.

"We'll take the mule next time, Abuela. And you can ride in the cart." Isabel removed her mother's hat from the wall hook. "Come, Mamá."

The spy was in his usual spot. With nary a glance at him, she led her mother toward the cemetery. Outside on the calle, the world was busy as always, even though life inside the Perez family had constricted. Horses pulled wagons of fresh vegetables or goatskins full of drinking water. A messenger boy hurried past, carrying a parcel. The smell of turrón, the holiday dessert of roasted almond, egg whites, and sugar, drifted in the air.

"They're baking for Navidad earlier and earlier every year," said Isabel. "It's only the beginning of November."

"Are they?" remarked Mamá. "I hadn't noticed."

Isabel could see the alcazarejo, Diego's home, standing out majestically on the hill. Her heart tightened. What was he doing this exact minute? she wondered. Eating a midday meal with his parents? Collecting taxes out of town? Hopefully, he was letting the wax harden on his writing desk, knowing Isabel was correct not to meet him, not to answer his letters. It was better for both of them this way. She drew closer to her mother, seeking comfort in her familiar fragrant scent of lemon oil.

She did not look behind but sensed the spy was following a short distance from them.

Señora Herrera was walking toward them, heading back home, with one of her many grandchildren in tow. "And where are you two ladies off to this fine day?"

"The cemetery," replied Mamá. Then she turned left and began to walk toward the city walls.

"Why, it's down there," said the woman, pointing in the direction Isabel and Mamá had been walking. "You were going the correct way."

Mamá stopped. "I'm confused. I thought the cemetery was outside the gates."

Isabel knew Mamá was thinking of the Jewish cemetery, not the Christian one where Ruy was actually buried. "Mamá hasn't been feeling well, Señora Herrera," said Isabel. She gently placed her hand on Mamá's arm and walked her back to where their neighbor stood.

"My poor Soli," murmured Mamá.

"You mean Ruy," corrected Isabel with a false smile.

"Who's Soli?" said Señora Herrera.

The little boy pulled on his grandmother's hand. "A turrón, you promised!"

He dragged Señora Herrera away, so Isabel did not have to answer. Hopefully, the woman would not remember the exchange.

Both New and Old Christians buried their dead in the churchyard next to the Iglesia de Vera Cruz. Unlike the Jewish cemetery with its tombstones in the dirt, listing left and right like crooked teeth, this was pristine. Isabel thought the fountains and statues, well-pruned trees and oleander bushes that were tended so well by the Dominican friars were more important to them than the people buried here. Flower-lined pathways traversed the interior, which was surrounded by the poorer section, simple white crosses atop raised coffins. Wealthy families rested in crypts and vaults, which stood apart even farther from the center, like casitas, or little houses.

When Ruy died, a few of Papá's influential clients insisted on paying for a tomb in a wall. One of those clients was the duque of Alba. Mamá reacted with such enmity toward Papá that he nearly refused the nobles.

"I don't want a tomb!" she had shouted.

"But we can't afford our own family crypt," said Papá gently. "The entombment wall is quite respectable."

Mamá broke down in tears. "He needs to be belowground, in the Jewish cemetery!"

But practicalities prevailed and of course they adhered to the New Christian custom.

A stork flew over them as Isabel and Mamá reached Ruy's niche in the brick wall. Mamá extended her fingers, touching the wall. "What does it say, Isabel? I've forgotten."

Of course, Mamá did not read, but Isabel knew her mother could never forget the number above his spot, 117, or the words carved into the stone as well. *Rodrigo Perez, con Jesús y los angeles. Se nació 1469, 8 febrero. Se murió 3 diciembre, 1474.* Rodrigo Perez, with Jesús and the angels. Born February 8, 1469. Died December 3, 1474. As far as her eye could see, there were no niches with a body as young as Rodrigo's inside.

"Where does it say his Hebrew name?" asked Mamá in a small voice.

"We weren't allowed to carve that, Mamá, remember? We had to bury him here, among the Christians."

"My poor Soli," mumbled Mamá.

Isabel glanced around her. The churchyard was empty. The spy must be lingering somewhere at the entrance, chewing clay no doubt. There was no reason she should not bring her mother the small pleasure of addressing her dead son in his Hebrew name. Did the Jewish cemetery feel more sacred than this? she wondered. All those who were willing to die for their beliefs, lined up next to each other. She dared not ask her mother, for fear of upsetting her again. But Isabel wanted to walk through the aisles of the Jewish cemetery and experience it for herself.

Isabel used the side of her chopine to clean the ground in front of the wall. Mamá stood stiff as a tree trunk.

"Would you like to put your rock up there?" Isabel asked her. The tombs stretched out for three hundred meters or so, but the wall was only three niches tall, so a person could easily reach the top. The Inquisition most likely knew about the Jewish tradition. A stone at the Christian cemetery would not cause suspicion on the ground, but atop a niche it would. Isabel would discreetly put it back on the ground before they left.

Mamá opened her hand and the stone fell.

"No matter," said Isabel, letting it lie there. "How did you choose the name Solomon?" Perhaps by talking about happier memories, Isabel could find a remnant of the woman her mother used to be.

"It means peace."

"From *shalom*, is it not?" All the time spent reading the Talmud had given Isabel a better understanding of the roots of words. The Perezes always greeted each other with a *"Shabbat shalom"* on Friday nights. It could be used for hello, goodbye, or peace.

Mamá looked at Isabel, surprised. It was the first sign of life Isabel had seen in her mother's dead eyes in weeks. "Yes. Solomon was the king of Israel. Your father and I simply liked the name. It sounded strong."

"What was it like, carrying Soli in your belly?"

Mamá hugged herself, recalling. "He gave me a rough pregnancy. Kicked constantly, whereas you girls glided around in there. His head was larger, as well. I lost two babies before him. That's why he was so much younger than Beatriz."

"And when he came out? Did you scream to the heavens?" Isabel couldn't recall where she was the day the midwife came.

Here Mamá actually smiled. "He slipped out after three pushes. And when the midwife smacked his bottom, he was the one who screamed."

Together they laughed, the sounds echoing off the wall of

drawers. It was a welcome moment, even though Isabel knew her mother would retreat back into her silence when they returned home.

"Do names have a deeper meaning than what's on the surface?" asked Isabel.

She had been thinking about this the entire way home from the cemetery. She could hardly wait to discuss it with Abuela and was finally able to ask the question now that they were alone in the cellar.

Abuela adjusted her spectacles. "Names define us. They capture our essence. The sages believed that our names are the key to our souls."

"But how do people know before a baby is born what their soul will be like?"

"An angel comes to parents and whispers the Jewish name that the new baby will embody." She carefully turned the pages through the Talmud. "Ah, here it is. It says that parents receive one-sixtieth of prophecy when choosing a name."

"How much is one-sixtieth? I thought I was good at numbers, adding up Papá's ledgers all these years, but I don't understand."

"All you need to know is that it's a tiny amount."

"Can you see it?"

"It's too small for the eye, but big enough to be felt. It is a gift. Divine wisdom comes to us when we struggle to find the perfect name for a child. The names of children are the result of a partnership between name-givers and God."

The flame on the wick flickered in the darkness of the cellar.

"Did the angels whisper to Mamá and Papá, telling them to name me Eva?"

"Do you think they did?"

Isabel wasn't sure. "What does my name mean?"

"Eva is the Spanish name for Eve, the first woman in the Bible. In Hebrew, it means life or living one. It can also mean mother of life." She stroked Isabel's hair. "And that is exactly who you are. Even though I am forever warning you about your impetuousness, that is the part of you that makes you alive." She reached for Isabel's quill and, with the little ink that was left on the feather, wrote out the name Eva. "The sages believed that each of the twenty-two letters in the aleph-bet possessed a particular life force and power. They assigned a numerical value to each letter. *Aleph* is one. *Bet* is two. *Gimmel* is three and so on. Take a look at your Hebrew name. It is spelled *aleph, vav, vav, hay. Vav* is equal to six. *Hay* is five. So in your name, you have the numbers one, six, six, five. What does that add up to?"

"One thousand six hundred and sixty-five."

"No. I mean across. One plus six plus six plus five."

"Oh." Isabel calculated in her head. "Eighteen."

"Eighteen is a very special number in Judaism. It is the numerical equivalent of the word *chai*, which means life. *Chai* is spelled with a *chet* and a *yud*. Eight and ten. Making eighteen the symbol for life."

"Like my name!" Isabel touched the parchment. "Numbers. Abbreviations. Deeper meanings of a given name. With all these puzzles and riddles in the Talmud, it reminds me of the game escondido."

"Very wise, mi nieta. You are seeking what's hidden."

"Without having to get dirty outside."

They both giggled.

"Somewhere in this book is a midrash, a teaching about the

importance of a given name. When the children of Israel were held captive as slaves in Egypt, God took note and rewarded them with their freedom. He saw that even though the Jews had assimilated into Egyptian culture, they had not changed their names."

"This pleased Him?"

Abuela nodded. "He knew their names could be a weapon in the battle to maintain their unique identity when they went out into the world. He felt it would help the Jewish people survive."

"Our family has not done such a fine job of that, have we, here in Spain?" asked Isabel. "Taking Christian names at birth?"

"Unfortunately, I don't know of a better solution."

"We could worship out in the open like the Cohens."

"Not after we've been baptized," said Abuela. "You saw what happened at the auto de fe. It is too late, I'm afraid."

"Hidden faith. Like hidden meanings in the Talmud."

Abuela's eyelids drooped. She was tired. "In the end, it is up to each one of us to be worthy of the name we have been given."

As Isabel blew out the candle, she thought about her name. *Mother of life.* She would bear children. That must be what she was meant to do. With Don Sancho? The thought sickened her. She wanted to have Diego's children, but that was impossible now, too. Though admittedly, she had allowed herself to dream about their lives together. Her favorite vision was one of her writing poetry and their children running through the house, making the parchment flutter in their wake, while he painted in his studio. Maybe he would even illuminate the poem she was working on. Her eyes pricked. Those children would never be. Oh, Diego! She could not imagine there was yet another man out in the world who would lie with her and father her babies.

Perhaps that meant her name signified something else entirely?

Misery. Hell and damnation. Fire and brimstone. Demonic beasts eating their prey. Diego shut the book. Though it was an illuminated manuscript, with exquisite details of the Apocalypse, the images landed too close to his heart. For this was how he felt without Isabel in his life. He must find other pictures to study.

She had not met him at any of the suggested rendez-vous points he had requested in his letters. He had waited at the mezquita, at the river, at the well in the Moorish quarter, at a church on the opposite side of town. He had covered the entire village. Why would she not see him? She had not taken ill. He had inquired with the two barber surgeons in town and even the Jewish doctor. She had not been taken by the Inquisition. His father, with the privileges of a Familiar, knew who all the prisoners were. Her rejection was making him desperate. He thought about changing his clothing, posing as a peddler of some kind and knocking on her door brazenly. He imagined a life with her by his side, though he knew not where they could escape to. He would apprentice with someone worthy, not the accursed Berruguete. She would write poems and nurse their babes. He would help her get published. They would invite the greatest thinkers of their time to dine with them, talking deep into the night about the writings of Maimonides and ha-Levi. They would play music in their home, the percussive sounds of the *dabdaba* or the melodic bowed strings of the *rabāb*. If his father followed them, or worse, the Inquisition did, they would board a boat bound for the New World. He had heard stories of native peoples discovered in the

Indies. Explorers were setting sail all the time from Lisbon. Why couldn't he do the same with Isabel?

He tortured himself with these fantastical thoughts, which for their impossibility proved more searing than the beast's tentacles in the book before him. And to add acid to the wound, he must be at Berruguete's studio at half past the hour. Don Sancho del Aguila, the honorable alguacil, was sitting for his portrait today. A holy hell if ever there were one. Diego steeled himself for more conflagration and left the house.

Berruguete was cleaning brushes when he arrived. "Diego, mi buen hombre. Big day today. Big day."

The painting of the auto de fe had been appropriated by the Holy Office. With the money earned, Berruguete had bought himself a golden chalice, a mere frivolity. Diego saw it on a table, half-full of wine from last night's dinner, no doubt. Of course, Berruguete did not think to reward his apprentice with a ducat—not that Diego was in want of funds. But Diego would have appreciated a chance to paint something on his own. A cloud, a feather, even background in the corner of a canvas. Verrocchio had given da Vinci a chance. When would Diego have his?

"Our esteemed guest will be arriving shortly. Help me mix this pigment."

Berruguete handed him a bowl of terre verde, or green earth, and some egg tempera.

"You are going to put paint on canvas today?" asked Diego, stirring a stick. "Might you begin with a sketch or do a few studies first?"

"There is no time to waste," said Berruguete. "A man of his stature does not want to sit idle for more than an afternoon."

"I hardly think being the subject of a portrait is sitting idle. Besides, grandees abhor work. I should know. My father does not begin his day until eleven in the morning. And then takes a siesta a few hours later." Diego despised the nonworking nobility. "Now that I'm collecting his taxes, I declare, there's nothing for him to do all day except worry about his position at court."

"Well, Don Sancho is more than nobility. He is an appointed official who keeps our streets safe. And we are grateful for it."

Diego turned so Berruguete would not catch his sneer. "I will be sure to thank him for his service."

The iron knocker made the alguacil's presence known.

"He's here!" said Berruguete gleefully.

Don Sancho stepped over the threshold. Diego busied himself with mixing the colors, not able to bring himself to look at the man who would wed, and bed, the woman he loved.

"Señores," he said, including Diego in his address.

It was a sign of respect for an apprentice. Diego must answer the greeting. He lifted his gaze. "Don Sancho."

Diego did not think Don Sancho recognized him as the son of Count Altamirano, for he wore a cap on his head, paint-splattered pants, and a tunic, not the doublet and hose he usually donned. Berruguete had no reason to reveal the identity of his apprentice either. He had made it clear that he respected Diego for making his own way in the world.

The one time the count had made the acquaintance of Berruguete, his father behaved perfectly in character as the snob that he was. Diego and his parents had been promenading when they passed Berruguete in the street. His father did not hide his displeasure at the slovenly-dressed painter and, after exchanging a few words, spotted a colleague and made a hasty exit. The countess, on the other hand, was delighted, touching Berruguete on his arm and giggling like a maiden. The chapel in the alcazarejo needed an altarpiece. What better way to show status than a religious painting from a prestigious master hanging in your own home? She would be an unlikely ally for Diego should his father change his mind after the monthlong trial period.

"I have been awaiting this day for over a week," said Don Sancho, removing his matchlock gun and resting it on the table.

Diego eyed it, tempted to brandish the weapon and smite his adversary down right here and now. But would this act have the opposite effect, with Isabel disapproving of a crime of passion? He did not know what she was thinking, and this frustrated him to no end.

"It seems I am to be called to the front," announced Don Sancho.

"Granada?" asked Diego.

"By order of His Royal Highness himself." Don Sancho's chest was as inflated as a full bota bag.

Perhaps he would die in battle, thought Diego. But then poor Isabel would be forced into mourning for a year.

"Well then, we must work quickly," said Berruguete. He directed him to a stool by the window. "Actually, why not wear your gun belt and your cloak? It is more regal that way." Berruguete handed Don Sancho his belongings.

Don Sancho's mouth erupted in a yellow-toothed smile. "You flatter me."

While they waited for Don Sancho to adorn himself, Berruguete said, "How goes the Inquisition? I hope my painting is pleasing to the Holy Office."

"Oh yes. We are getting much delight out of it in our frigid meeting rooms. You captured the flames so well, I almost felt the heat emanating from the frame."

Berruguete inclined his head. "Now you flatter me."

"I only wish my face was more discernable in the crowd."

Berruguete turned white. "I'm . . . I'm sorry—"

Don Sancho burst out in laughter. "That was humor, my good sir."

Berruguete laughed in relief. "Of course."

"You captured the most important part—the friars, the stakes—and rendered the scene swollen with onlookers. Why, we'll show Madrid that Trujillo can turn out a bigger auto de fe crowd than they can!"

"Indeed," agreed Berruguete. "Now, once you've taken position on the stool, my apprentice will arrange your legs so that one leg is propped up on the cross-piece of the stool and one is extended."

Diego had no choice but to lay hands on Don Sancho's person. How easy would it be to reach for his neck instead and squeeze the life out of him? Diego could take him in an instant. Could possibly even take Berruguete, who would surely come to the alguacil's rescue. Or he could stab Don Sancho's eye with the point on the globe. Then he could force lead-white pigment down his throat, where the poison would spread through his veins and kill him within seconds. Diego reached for the globe.

"Diego?" called Berruguete. "Adjust our esteemed guest, por favor."

Diego hastened to the stool, his fingers barely brushing the globe.

"Now then," said Berruguete. "Let us begin."

That evening, Diego told his mother he would sup in his room. Martín delivered a tray of smoked carp, crusty bread, and some sugar-coated berries. When Diego finished eating, he removed a quill and paper once again.

My dearest Isabel. I am begging you. Please meet me
He began again.

My beloved. I was with your Don Sancho today and it made me realize

He crumpled that one as well. He wished he could write her a poem. She would respond to that. But he was not clever with words in that way and she might laugh at his attempt. No, he would send her something that only he could do.

He withdrew his old colored powders from his desk. He moistened a brush with water from his washbasin and painted her a message. For a border rimming the parchment, he took some vermillion and drew ornamental eyes, like those found on peacock feathers; golden suns with rays curling around lapis figs; elegant winged birds of gold drinking nectar from violet flowers; a genet leaping one way (in direct reference to their afternoon in Monfragüe) and a rabbit bounding in the other direction. He drew stars inside whimsical shapes. Then, using a brush of cat hair, he wrote these tiny words in the center:

The Spanish oak in Plaza Santa Ana. When the church bell tolls five.

When Martín retrieved his food tray, Diego asked him to tell the porter to prepare the carriage.

He had a letter to deliver. He would not hide it in the iron grates of her window this time. He would somehow gain entrance to her interior courtyard and throw a pebble through the slats so she would awaken. He wanted to hand-deliver his masterpiece.

If this did not convince her to meet with him, he was out of ideas.

24

"Whatever are you doing?" asked Beatriz. "You never stitch anything."

Isabel looked up from the floor cushion where she was sitting. She quickly covered her needlework with a quilt Mamá kept on the sofa. "I thought you were praying in church, celebrating one of your seven sacred times of day."

"I was. But I've returned." Beatriz fingered her scalp. "Constanza and Juan Carlos weren't there as I had hoped."

"Was our friend the spy out front as usual?" asked Isabel.

"I'm afraid so. He followed me to church and back."

"Surely he must be bored of us by now."

"He seems harmless," said Beatriz. "I may even stop to speak with him next time."

"Don't be a fool," hissed Isabel.

Beatriz eyed Isabel's lap. "You never answered my question about your stitching."

"It's nothing special. Just linen for my trousseau. When Don Sancho and I are married, I should like our bedsheets to have our initials embroidered on the corners."

Beatriz had nothing spiteful to say about this wifely duty. She yawned and stretched her arms upward. "I'm sleepy this morning.

That ruckus outside last night kept me awake between matins and lauds."

"What ruckus?"

"I was just finishing my prayers when I heard what sounded like hail hitting our grating."

"Hail? But it's not yet winter."

"Clearly, it was not hail. The del Castillo sisters' dog began barking in fits of hysteria. By the time I was able to open the grating, the pinging sound had stopped. The dog was running in circles in the courtyard. And you slept through the entire commotion."

"I was up until the wee hours of night doing Papá's ledgers." Obviously, she did not mention studying with Abuela. "When I fell on my pallet, I slept the slumber of the dead."

Beatriz looked around the room. "Where's Mamá?"

"Outside, plucking a chicken for our armico this evening."

"Abuela?"

"Taking a siesta."

"Papá?"

"In the cellar." Isabel stood, sweeping up her stitching materials in the quilt. "I should go to him, lest he injure himself with that press. It's been acting devilish lately, and he can't hear a warning squeal when the screw needs oiling. Not to mention he only has one good arm at the moment."

"I suppose I should help Mamá with the chicken. Santa Madre, I miss Zahra."

Isabel smiled. Her sister sounded almost human.

But when Beatriz went out back, Isabel did not go down to the cellar. Still holding the quilt with the contents wrapped inside, she went into the center courtyard and knocked on Señora Herrera's door.

"Buenas, Señora Herrera," said Isabel. "One of our feed buckets fell over on your side of the yard. Can I slip through your back door to retrieve it?"

The mole on Señora Herrera's cheek quivered. Her eyes scanned the street. "I suppose so."

The arrangement of rooms was the same as the Perez home, so Isabel easily found her way through the sala into the kitchen. The only difference was that the Herrera house had many more crosses on their walls. A miniature nativity scene with tres reyes—the three kings—a manger, sheep, and baby Jesús was displayed on a windowsill. Another grandchild, whom Isabel had never seen before, was playing with it, rearranging the figurines. Isabel heard Señor Herrera cough in another room.

"No need to let me back in. I'll just let myself out of the gate and go around the front," Isabel told her.

There was no feed bucket, of course. Isabel needed to gain access to the back and avoid the spy. There was vertical wood fencing dividing all the houses in the back, so Beatriz and Mamá would not see her, either, if she were in the Herreras' yard.

When Isabel turned the knob on the Herreras' back door, she felt a touch on her shoulder. "Before you go," said the señora.

Isabel's stomach fluttered. "Yes?"

"How is your papá feeling?"

Relieved, Isabel thought quickly. "Better." She shrugged. "I suppose no matter how long you've been working a wine press, it can still get the best of you."

"I understand. I'm glad I could offer you the willow bark. I'm so sorry this happened to him." She paused. "To *them*," she added, emphasizing the word. Then she nodded and patted Isabel on the hand.

Isabel stared at the older woman. Señora Herrera knew about her parents being held by the Inquisition. It was obvious. How wrong Isabel had been about their neighbor. She was not suspicious at all. She was as afraid as they were.

Isabel kissed her on both cheeks. "I am touched by your kindness."

Out on the calle, Isabel scurried over the packed dirt. When she reached the paved road, she ducked under an archway and knelt close to the ground, opening the quilt. She tucked the loose needles and thread into a pocket of her dress and held up a beige sackcloth gown with a red circle on the left breast. This was the actual garment she had been sewing. A required uniform for a Jew. The circular symbol was not a perfect replica, but hopefully, no one would notice.

She pulled the sackcloth over her head and let it fall so that it covered her rose-colored dress underneath completely. Por Dios, it was heavy on her shoulders wearing so many layers. Thankfully, the November air had become crisp and she did not perspire. Her hair was pinned at the neck so that when she wrapped a muslin scarf over her hair and forehead, any recognizable facial feature was almost completely hidden. Two servants carrying baskets of fruit and vegetables passed her under the archway. An emaciated dog followed them, hoping for some scraps. She nodded at the maids, stashed the quilt behind a low wall, and headed to her destination.

The judería.

She knew it was risky, evading the Inquisition spy in the front of her house and entering the Jewish quarter disguised as someone who lived there. She could get discovered on both ends. But she had two strong reasons for taking this daring trip. First, she wanted to see how the Cohens were faring. There had been no news of Hannah Cohen's health or how severe a beating David had sustained. Her own guilt had become too much to bear. Perhaps she could even jar some fruit or cure a bit of meat to help them through the winter. Anything to help the twins. The second reason for this trip was of a more religious nature. Now that she had been studying the Talmud, she wanted to experience everyday life—the cemetery, the butcher, the families walking on the street—through the eyes of a Jew. On her first visit, she had felt removed and preoccupied with dress fabric. Then the fathers had gotten into the fight. Her second visit consisted of sitting at Señora Cohen's bedside. This time would be entirely new.

It was challenging, navigating the tiny alleys of the quarter without knowing where she was going and trying to seem like she had lived here for months. Isabel saw a dirty-faced woman selling geraniums and remembered her from their visit on Sucot. The Cohens' house was close by. But on which street? Everything was windier and narrower than even the Moorish quarter.

She couldn't very well ask someone where the Cohens lived. That would give her away immediately as a stranger. She saw a group of children running with a wooden hoop and a stick. Maybe they were playmates of Yuçe and Rachel's. Though they were young, she would have to tread lightly. Before he lost his hearing, Papá mentioned a little boy who denounced his own parents to the Inquisition.

The children shouted and laughed as she approached. "Hola, chicos. Have Rachel or Yuçe Cohen run down this way?"

The youths exchanged glances. Isabel thought of a cover story. "I'm their cousin and their mother sent me to fetch them."

A boy with crooked teeth and bright brown eyes answered for the group. "They were here earlier. They went home, though."

"Gracias," said Isabel, crossing the street.

"Where are you going?" shouted the boy. "It's that way!" He pointed to a narrow, winding street.

She hit her forehead. "Silly me. I got all turned around."

Once Isabel was on the correct street, she recognized it from before. She easily found the Cohens' house, remembering the way it tilted to the left. But as she approached it, a man stood outside, unmistakable in his blue uniform. His matchlock gun hung on a leather diagonal across his torso. He was from the local police. They reported directly to the alguacil. So the Cohens were being watched, too. What if Don Sancho was behind it all, both this officer and their very own clay-chewing spy? She shuddered at the thought. If her betrothed was spying on her and everyone she knew, what kind of freedom could she ever expect to have once they were married?

She backed up and went another direction. She would go to the butcher and listen for local gossip. She might be able to find out something there about Señor and Señora Cohen and the twins. For everyone knew that no matter in which quarter of Trujillo one found oneself, the butcher shop was a gathering place for busybodies.

Isabel was concentrating so deeply on finding her way that she nearly bumped into two giggling Jewish girls, their hair un-covered and dripping wet.

"Perdóname," muttered Isabel.

"No, it's our fault," said one of the girls, about her age, with a friendly smile and rosy cheeks. "We were hurrying and didn't see you. Jemila forgot her cloak and since the weather turned, it's cold walking with wet hair."

"Were you in the river?" asked Isabel.

The second girl, Jemila, laughed. Her pointed chin made small up and down movements with her merriment. "Surely you jest? We were at the mikveh."

"Of course, how could I be so daft." Isabel wanted to smash her own toes for forgetting about the ritual bath in which Jewish women immersed themselves.

Jemila regarded her curiously. "Did you just move into the judería? I've not seen you before."

"I'm a cousin of the Cohens. We're visiting them from Valladolid," she said quickly, adding to the story she told the children.

The first girl reached out her hand. "I'm Ezter."

"Isa—" She stopped. "Eva." They shook hands.

"Yuçe and Rachel have a cousin in Valladolid?" asked Jemila. "I didn't realize."

Isabel nodded. "We are distant. Cousins, I mean. And we live a distance away, too," she added with a forced laugh. "I'd best be on my way. If I don't get to the butcher, my aunt Hannah will be cross."

Jemila raised her eyebrows. "That means she's feeling better, then? Her appetite has returned? Last time my mother and I called on her, she couldn't eat a morsel and was as big as the pallet she lay on."

Oh dear. Everyone really did know each other in here. This judería trip was proving to be an unwise plan. "When was that?"

"Four days ago, I believe."

"Well, she's turned a corner, as we say," replied Isabel brightly. "Encantada, lovely to make your acquaintance."

Walking away from them, Isabel berated herself for her stupidity. She could only hope that Jemila would not mention to Yuçe that she had met his cousin Eva. He would know immediately that it was Isabel, for he once asked her about her Hebrew name. He would wonder why she was in the quarter at all, after causing the beating of his father, and most likely being the reason an armed policeman was stationed in front of their house. No doubt he hated her. This would just add fuel to the fire. He did not deserve that.

At least she learned a little bit about what was going on in the Cohen house. Señora Cohen's health was not improving. Perhaps she would find out more at the butcher.

As she walked, she imagined herself having a parallel path in life, one where she was not a converso but an openly Jewish young woman. If Abuela's own grandfather had not taken his life and his wife had not converted, Isabel could very well have been returning from the mikveh today. She and Jemila and Ezter would have been companions. She did not have any close friends from her own social class. None who understood her. Her own sister could have filled that role—she did at one point, when they were small. But that door had slammed shut. And Atika lived an entirely different life. As much as she hated to think about it, the whole Romani encampment could fold up at any moment and move to another city.

What was the mikveh like inside? Was the water cold or warm? Did they say a prayer before they submerged, like Mamá did when she blessed the Shabbat candles? What stories did the girls share? Did they shed tears together? Isabel's own tears stung her eyes. God's parasites! How could two wet-haired complete strangers make her feel such gloom?

When she finally found the butcher shop, there was a line out the door. Peering through the entrance, Isabel could see large slabs of meat, whole chickens, and ducks hanging on hooks, as well as smaller portions on the front table: patties and mounds of ground beef. Flies buzzed around the store, happy to be near such appetizing landing spots. Most customers were dressed in beige sackcloth with red badges, but a few wore simple, yet colorful, street clothes. Perhaps those people were not leaving the judería today. Bits of Spanish conversation drifted around her, but she couldn't hear much. Everyone in line was female, except for one man with a long beard and tufted eyebrows. With his skull-capped head and face full of hair, he looked like someone who should be bent over a prayer book in sinagoga. She had once seen men like him lined up like ivory and black piano keys, swaying in solemnity, when she and her parents walked by a sinagoga years ago. He probably knew Señor Cohen well.

When the woman in front of him stepped out of line to speak to a friend, Isabel slipped into her place.

Isabel smiled at the man. "Long line, do you not agree?"

He grunted.

"I thought I'd prepare cordero al horno this evening. It's my husband's favorite."

He ignored her.

"What is your wife planning to make for supper?" asked Isabel.

No response.

The man reached into a leather pouch and removed a quire, a small collection of papers stitched together, and proceeded to read them, turning away from her.

She could not see the writing on the page and had no idea what type of text that was. It could have been Aljamiado, Castilian,

Arabic, Hebrew, anything. She forgot all about Señor Cohen. "Something interesting there?"

For some reason the man looked at her. His eyes were not unkind and his mouth was not frowning beneath the beard. "If I tell you, will you stop asking me questions?"

"Sí."

They moved up a few steps in line. "They are poems by Moses ibn Ezra."

"A Jewish poet?"

He raised a finger. "You said you would stop."

"You are correct." A few seconds passed. "But I am a poet, too. Or at least I try to be. And I was not aware of his work."

His eyes crinkled at the corners. He did not appear angry, but slightly amused. "Moses ibn Ezra is one of the greats. You should read him." Isabel appreciated that unlike other adults, he was not surprised at the fact that she could read.

"Which works do you recommend?" she asked.

"Start with Tarshish. It will take you a while. It has one thousand two hundred ten verses."

"*Tarshish?*"

"Named because the letters in the word *tarshish* have the numerical equivalent of one thousand two hundred ten."

"Numerology! Like in the Talmud!"

The man's eyes widened in fright and he backed away from her as if she were a witch. "How could you possibly know that? The Talmud is for men only!"

She should not have mentioned anything. She had been warned often enough that her impetuousness would be the death of her. "Of course. I merely meant that—"

The patron behind him, a stout woman in a scarf, poked her nose into their conversation. "Jacov, did you ever locate that missing Talmud? Samuel tells me it's been weeks."

The man shook his head. "It's a mystery. I just hope it hasn't fallen into enemy hands."

Isabel felt the color drain from her face. Could they be speaking of the Talmud she borrowed from Yuçe?

"The last one who had it was David Cohen," said the man. "But no one wants to bother him about it. He's in terrible shape, poor soul."

The woman clucked her tongue. "I heard his son is barely managing the studio."

Madre mía, it *was* her missing Talmud. And the situation with the Cohens was worse than she'd thought.

The butcher, a rotund man in a bloodstained apron, yelled, "Pronto. What will it be, señorita?"

She used every maravedi she had to buy some dried beef.

"Where's your cookery?" asked the butcher.

With embarrassment, Isabel looked around her and noticed that all the women carried their own ceramic ware with which to transport meat. She was empty-handed. The butcher rolled his eyes, then wrapped the cured beef in a cloth and handed it to her brusquely. She muttered a thank-you to the butcher, then darted out of the shop before the Jewish man could accuse her of sorcery.

The guard was directly in front of the Cohens' house. She walked right past him and placed the meat, still wrapped in cloth, in front of their door. She even waved to the policeman. For she was just a friendly Jewish neighbor, delivering food to a family in need.

She wished she could have done more to help them.

Though Isabel wanted to explore the cemetery, she decided to go home. She was rattled from her exchanges today. When she walked out of the gates, Isabel took off the sackcloth gown and folded it up into a small bundle she could carry like a parcel. She walked the rest of the way home as a New Christian. It lightened the physical weight, but the heaviness remained inside.

25

Their spy was chatting with a second man, his back facing away from Isabel when she returned home. Unlike the spy, the other man was wearing the military uniform of a bailiff. They were chewing clay and not paying attention to her as she crossed the street and slipped through her gate.

"Where have you been?" admonished Beatriz the minute Isabel stepped into the house. "Papá has injured himself."

Their father sat glumly on a chair, his thumb wrapped in rags, a piece of leftover willow bark in his mouth.

Isabel knelt by him. "That blasted press. It was just as I feared."

"You're wrong," sniped Beatriz. "A barrel, half-full of unfermented wine, rolled over his finger. He didn't hear it totter and when he turned it was too late." She frowned. "He was all alone in there," she added, as if it were Isabel's fault.

Isabel felt terrible about her selfish excursion. "I'm so sorry I wasn't here. You have done a noble job, Sister. I'm proud of you." She gently unwrapped the rag on Papá's hand. "His thumb looks broken." Between this injury on his right hand, and the sling he wore to support the left arm, which the Inquisitors had broken, he would not be able to do any physical work at all. Isabel searched the room. "Where's Mamá?"

"In the cellar," said Beatriz. "She's trying to right the oak barrel."

"Alone?"

"Do you see any able-bodied men here able to help?"

"Mamá!" shouted Isabel from the top of the stone steps. "You'll hurt yourself!"

Her mother stopped, stood from her stooped position, and looked up at her daughter. "Everything is leaking out. I can't stop it." Isabel went down and turned the spigot closed. A simple fix, but clearly Mamá was too overcome to figure it out. "Come, let's get you upstairs. Leave the rest for Pedro."

Abuela had been at the market and had returned just when the accident happened. Now she plucked threads from Isabel's rose dress. "You look as if you walked through a fabric shop. Have you been to the Cohens' studio?"

Isabel glanced at her father. "Heavens no!" she exclaimed. Though there was no need to worry. Of course Papá couldn't hear what Abuela said.

Her grandmother continued to groom her as a baboon mother would, cleaning the fur of her charge. She held out her hand to show Isabel all the thick beige threads in her palm. The sackcloth must have shed.

Beatriz watched them closely.

Isabel whispered into her grandmother's ear. "I'll explain later." Then she turned to the rest of the family. "I'm going to the vineyard to fetch Pedro. Then I'll stop at one of the food stalls in the plaza and pick up some empanadillas for supper."

Mamá looked toward the kitchen, frowning. "The armico . . ."

"Don't worry about that, Mamá," she said. Then she left the house for the second time that day.

Isabel didn't even bother checking if the spy had finished his socializing. This was legitimate business and she didn't care if he trailed her. She ran the half kilometer to the Zuniga farm, their primary grape supplier. The vineyard stretched out for hundreds of hectares in perfect rows. Pedro's distinct straw hat bobbed up and down in the field. She called to him, waving her arms. He looked up, his large brown eyes questioning. He wore typical laborer's clothing, a sleeveless gray tunic made of frieze, a coarse woolen fabric, over loose pants. She wound her way through the grapevines. Knobby branches with tiny green leaves stretched outward on wire like arms.

"Hola, señorita," he said. Though only a couple of years older than Isabel, his face bore many creases from being out in the sun each day.

"We need you in the cellar," said Isabel breathlessly. "Papá's had an accident."

"Right away." Pedro carried his basket over to the donkey.

She followed him down the hill, and when the road diverged, she turned right, into town, to get the empanadillas. The spy turned right as well.

After Papá, Mamá, and Beatriz had gone to sleep, Isabel and Abuela went down to the cellar. Isabel told her grandmother the reason for the beige threads on her dress. Abuela turned white and looked as though her heart might stop.

"Just when I thought you could not do anything riskier than studying Talmud in your own home, you go and do a foolish thing like that," said Abuela.

"I shouldn't have, I know. But oh, Abuela! Being in the judería was frightening and wonderful at the same time! I met two girls coming home from the mikveh."

Hearing this, Abuela turned wistful. "The day my first monthly cycle ended was just a regular day for me. Conversos couldn't go to the mikveh to cleanse. We might be discovered. I've always wanted to dip in the water."

"Then you don't know what it looks like inside either?"

Abuela shook her head. "Ornate mosaic tiles, probably. It's a sacred space, and therefore a mitzvah, a good deed, to beautify it." She gently closed the Talmud. "I'm glad you got to see the outside at least. Did you stop by the Cohens'?"

"I didn't have a chance," Isabel told her. "There was an armed guard watching their house."

"For protection or for spying?" asked Abuela.

Could it have been the aljama, the Jewish Council, watching over the family and not a spy sent by Don Sancho after all? Isabel certainly hoped so.

"Abuela, have you heard of the poet Moses ibn Ezra?"

Her grandmother shook her head, removing the Talmud from the hiding spot.

"A man in the butcher shop told me about him," said Isabel, taking a seat. "But I don't know anything about the Jewish poets, just the Muslim ones. And of course, Qasmūna can't be the only Jewish female poet. Do you think there's any poetry in the Talmud?"

"I honestly have no idea," said Abuela. "I know the Torah contains religious poetry. My father used to sing Solomon's Song of Songs to my mother."

Isabel turned the delicate pages, browned from hundreds of years of oily fingertips. There was so much here, it would take her a lifetime to go through it all.

"Wait," said Abuela, pointing at the bottom of a page. "What's that?"

Isabel gazed at a short paragraph, written with tighter lines and set apart from the rest of the scripture with more space. "Will you translate it?"

Abuela read:

> *"If the cedars have caught fire, what*
> *hope is there for the moss on the wall?*
> *If Leviathan has been hauled in by a fish-hook,*
> *what hope is there for the minnows?*
> *If the mighty river has been struck by drought,*
> *what hope is there for the waterholes?"*

"That certainly sounds poetic!" said Isabel, excitedly. "Is there a title?"

"It just says the Aramaic word for *lament*," said Abuela, "which means a mournful sorrow."

Isabel found a piece of torn parchment and asked Abuela to write down the lines in Castilian. She wasn't sure what the writer was trying to say exactly, but she understood the sadness. Not being with Diego was a mournful sorrow indeed.

26

Two days later, there was a loud knock on the Perez door. Isabel, Beatriz, and Abuela were in the kitchen preparing a simple supper, although it was mostly the sisters who were doing the work. Abuela had been sitting more and more each day and was currently on a stool, supervising. Isabel wished she could sit as well. She was bone-tired, having taken over even more of Papá's duties. Still, money was dwindling. She did not see an end in sight, for even when Papá gained use of his hands, without his hearing Isabel didn't know how they could survive once she left the house to marry Don Sancho. Abuela would have to take over Papá's ledgers and wine sales. The older woman's stamina was diminishing daily, and the important clients would not do business with an aging grandmother. The entire situation was an impossibility. At the moment, Papá rested on the sofa, his unlit pipe in an ashtray while Mamá sat on a floor cushion beside him staring into nothingness. They were both suspended in time, even more so than before.

Now in the kitchen, with the loud knock on the door, Isabel and Abuela exchanged worried glances. Had someone seen her go into the judería?

"Let me," said Beatriz. She removed her apron and went to answer the door.

"Yuçe," Isabel heard her sister say. "What are you doing here?"

The knife Isabel was holding dropped to the floor, clanging on the tile. "Madre mía," she whispered. "He's come for the Talmud." She rinsed her hands with a pitcher of water they kept near a washbasin. "Wish me luck."

"Yuçe!" Isabel smiled broadly. "What a nice surprise."

Yuçe's mouth was a hard, thin line. This did not portend well.

He waited until Beatriz had returned to the kitchen before he spoke. "Mother is dead."

Now Isabel saw that the boy's eyes were red-rimmed, that his face was not full of anger toward her, but grief-stricken. She opened her arms to him. "Oh, Yuçe, I am so deeply sorry." She allowed him to rest his head on her shoulder longer than was necessary, but he was so distraught.

When he finally let go, he said, "Papá wanted your mother to know." He looked inside the house toward Mamá, who did not react. It was as if she didn't even know they had a visitor. "Señora Perez?" called Yuçe. "Did you hear what I said about my mother?"

Finally, Mamá turned her attention to the door. "Yes? May I help you?"

"Mamá, don't be silly. It's Yuçe Cohen," said Isabel.

Mamá looked at him blankly.

"She hasn't been herself, ever since—" Isabel stopped speaking. She did not want to bring up his father's beating at the same moment he was mourning his own mother.

Yuçe shifted his weight. "Papá is in a similar state. I hardly recognize him. His nose is crooked now."

Isabel ventured a smile. "Was his nose not crooked before?"

Yuçe gave her a thin smile in return. "Actually, it was."

"Can he do any work at all?"

Yuçe shook his head. "I've been making dresses and filling orders with the fabric we have, but soon we will run out of material."

"And Rachel?"

"She will continue to do what she's been doing. The laundry and the cooking. But Papá plans to send us upriver to Portugal, soon. We have a cousin there." His eyes turned toward Papá. "Señor Perez?"

"You need to stand directly in front of him," explained Isabel. "He can't hear you."

"I didn't know . . ." He walked over to Papá and waved hello. Then he took a quill and ink from a small table and penned a note. "My mother is dead."

After Papá read the note, he took Yuçe's small hands in his older ones. Papá's eyes were wet with emotion.

"Look at Papá's damaged arm and thumb," said Isabel. "It seems both our fathers are no longer the same vibrant ones they used to be. We are broken and whole at the same time."

Yuçe released his hands from Papá's grip. He stared at her, his mouth agape.

"What are you speaking about?"

"When Moses shattered the ten commandments God gave him, the sages took the broken pieces of stone and stored them in the Holy Ark alongside the second set of tablets. The broken lay next to the whole. Even though there is sweetness, we all experience pain and suffering."

All the color drained from Yuçe's face. "You've . . . you've been studying the Talmud, haven't you?"

God's pustules! She had been so caught up in what she had learned that she forgot to be cautious. "Please don't be angry. It has helped me through some dark moments."

"It's my fault. I'm the one who lent it to you. I didn't realize you would actually—" He put his head in his hands. "I've broken Mosaic Law, Isabel. I could get in trouble with the rabbi."

Isabel turned red.

Papá watched the exchange between Yuçe and Isabel and must have sensed something serious, because he took Mamá's hand. "WE WILL BE IN THE COURTYARD."

When they left the room, Isabel tried to make light of the situation. "It can't be as bad as you say. No one knows." She ignored the memory of the man in the kosher butcher looking at her like she was a witch.

His small lips folded inward. "That might not be true. There's been talk about a missing Talmud."

Isabel feigned surprise. "Really?"

"I need to take it with me now, Isabel."

She was out of options. She nodded reluctantly. "I'll just be a minute."

When she returned from the cellar, she handed the book to him. "I'm so sorry, Yuçe. About everything."

He left without another word.

All at once, Isabel was desperately thirsty, as if she lived in the desert and needed to drink jugs of water because there would be no rain for another seven years. What was that midrash about Avram? What did the lament say about loss? She instantly forgot everything she had learned. She wanted to open the Talmud and check. But it was gone.

Slowly, she made her way back to the kitchen. Within the half hour, another knock came at their door. Yuçe again? Perhaps he changed his mind. He was bringing back her beloved Talmud after all. She and Abuela could continue to read it!

She lunged for the door. "Yuçe?"

But there stood Mamá and Papá. And next to them Don Sancho. Did he see Yuçe leave? Sweet Yuçe in his beige gown with the red badge. Sweet Yuçe who had just lost his mother and wanted to tell his old family friends the bad news in person. Sweet Yuçe who was carrying a sacred Jewish text.

This was it. They would all be arrested. Mamá and Papá would never survive it.

Don Sancho's lips opened, yellow teeth flashing. "Cariña, forgive the intrusion. I have wonderful news to share."

Wonderful news? "Please, please come in." Isabel had never been so relieved to hear words come out of his mouth. "Abuela, Beatriz," she called. "Bring vino. Don Sancho is here."

Everyone settled in the sala, oddly taking the same positions as when he had come to visit them that first Shabbat evening. The only difference was that Papá could not speak in a normal volume and Mamá was not uttering any sounds at all.

Beatriz presented Don Sancho with a glass of wine.

"Gracias," he said, not giving her a glance. It was Isabel on whom he focused all his attention. He was not even pretending to be deferential to her parents like he had been the last time he was in their sala. His squinty eyes zeroed in on Isabel, making her squirm. "I've been called to the front in Granada."

Was this the good news he spoke of? "I didn't realize the war had begun," she replied.

He swallowed a large portion of the wine. "Any day now. I've received a special commission from King Ferdinand to muster a tercio, an infantry unit."

He paused, waiting for praise.

"A great honor indeed," said Isabel.

"Come January, I will be leading three thousand men, one thousand carrying the pike, the remaining wielding the arquebus. Quite a powerful weapon, that."

Papá sat mute, as did Mamá.

Isabel watched her parents, wondering if she should make an excuse to Don Sancho for their silence. Before she could say anything, Don Sancho cleared his throat. "But the true good news, and the reason I am here, is to announce that we will be moving up the marriage date."

"Perdón?" asked Isabel in a small voice.

"I don't want to leave for the front without a wife waiting for me at home. It will give me solace in my challenge in the south. I will be in harm's way, from the Muslim cavalry and their advanced artillery—from Jesús knows what. If I should perish, I will die knowing my wife is carrying my legacy in her belly. For I plan to have you with child as soon as possible."

Isabel looked to her mother, willing her to speak.

After a few moments, Abuela said, "Why don't you write your father a note, Isabel, explaining to him what Don Sancho is proposing?"

Isabel nodded, grateful for the suggestion.

Don Sancho held up his hand. "That won't be necessary, dear Isabel."

"I don't understand."

"I will take charge of you now. I am aware your father has lost his hearing."

Shame, red and hot, filled her. "I did not think it that obvious."

"Come now. Do you think I do not know exactly what goes on in my own municipality? I was there when your parents were questioned in the Holy Office, my dear."

He watched them being beaten? It was all Isabel could do not to charge at him and scratch his eyes out.

"I have been handling Papá's business for weeks now," said Isabel icily. "Quite successfully." While this was not quite the truth—aside from Duque Alba's damaged order, there had been other mistakes as well—she would never admit that to Don Sancho.

Don Sancho smiled indulgently. "That's nice to hear, cariña. But as my wife, you will have other duties. You will stop these pointless tasks of adding up your little figures or stomping on grapes or whatever it is you do down in your cellar." He swept his hand around the sala. "And how do you think your family will remain in this comfort? They will need my patronage. An allowance of six thousand maravedis a month should suffice. We would not want your aging grandmother sleeping on the street, now would we?" He looked at Abuela with pity.

My grandmother is just fifteen years your senior, Isabel seethed silently. "The doctor said Papá may recover hearing in one ear."

"Perhaps," said Don Sancho. "But that could be months from now. Or never. I have scheduled Fray Francisco to perform the ceremony at Iglesia Santiago in eight days' time." He paused to let this sink in. Then he stood. "I should think you might show me more gratitude. Your father's condition could have been much worse. I'm the one who got them released."

At this, Mamá rose from her cushion and threw herself at Don Sancho's feet. She lay prostrate, murmuring Christian incantations. "Our Father, who art in Heaven. Hallowed be thy name. Thy kingdom come. Thy will be done. Gracias, Don Sancho. Gracias a Dios for saving us."

Isabel knew one thing for certain.

There was no way out for her now.

27

Isabel had to get a message to Diego. It was only right. He had been writing her for weeks and deserved to know the truth. Had she been too rash in refusing to see him? At least they would have been able to spend this precious time together. If only Mamá and Papá hadn't been questioned by the Inquisition, if only she hadn't been so fearful. If only they lived in a different time and place.

So the day after Don Sancho's visit, she sat down at her writing desk with a quill and parchment. She would make a stop at the mercado in case the spy followed her, then secretly slip a page a coin to deliver her letter to the alcazarejo.

Outside her window, a bird sang its song to a fellow comrade. The del Castillo sisters gossiped in the courtyard. Isabel heard it all so clearly but could not think with any clarity how to tell the man she loved that the future they hoped for, the Jewish life they longed to share, was over before it began. A poem would express her feelings.

No, a lament.

> Love-sick, she weeps bitterly, tears running down her
>   cheeks.
> She laughs before the company to make them merry,
>   while fire—the flames of marriage to the wrong
>   man—eats away at her flesh.

In seven days' time, it will be done.
But O, do not despair.
She will love only one man, the right one, until the day
wanes and the sun coats its silver with gold and all
night long, until the moon disappears from the

Beatriz threw open the door of their bedroom.

Isabel scribed the final word, *sky*.

"I left my jeweled fan in here," said her sister.

Isabel finally looked up from her desk. "You mean *my* fan."

"Whichever," Beatriz said impatiently. "Now where did I place it?" She proceeded to open and shut drawers loudly. "I would think you'd be more interested in having your wedding dress sewn than writing silly poems. Papá has rented a carriage to ride Mamá and me to a fitting in Caceres. That was the closest studio we could find with a costumer as adept as David Cohen."

Obviously, they could not go to the Cohens' for dresses. Hannah Cohen's burial was today, in the Jewish tradition of waiting no more than twenty-four hours after death. Isabel wished she could be there to pay her respects, but it was impossible. New Christians could not mourn publicly with their Jewish friends. And Yuçe would not welcome her anyway.

"I have plenty of decent dresses to choose from," said Isabel, answering Beatriz's question. "Any of them are suitable for my wedding."

"But none are white," said Beatriz.

"Then I will wear my nightdress."

"An outrage!"

Isabel laughed, the first time in two days. Though her situation was dire, it felt good to smile.

Beatriz brought the parchment up to her face. Isabel was not concerned. It was gibberish to someone who couldn't read. "Is it a masterpiece, then?"

"This poem? Hardly. It's a requiem."

"What does that mean?"

"Something one reads at a funeral."

Her sister put it down, regarding her. "You're truly sad, aren't you?"

Isabel felt her eyes prick.

"I know you don't love him, but hardly anyone does when they get married. You know that."

Isabel reached for Diego's kerchief in her sleeve and breathed in his scent. "You have no idea what true love is."

Beatriz huffed. "I do too."

"The way you pine for Juan Carlos? By harming yourself each time you utter his name? That's not love. That's guilt and sin and some twisted belief in good versus evil." She knew she was hurting Beatriz, but she didn't care. It made her own heart bleed just a little less.

Her sister's neck reddened. "I don't harm myself."

"I live with you each day. I see your red scalp."

Beatriz turned her face away.

Isabel felt so very lonely. She was getting married in just a few days. She would never share a bedroom with her sister again. How she longed for a friend. Atika was at the other end of town, which required running the gauntlet of Inquisition spies to reach her. Those lively Jewish girls at the mikveh had each other. And here was her sister, her own flesh and blood. So close, but unreachable.

"I'm sorry," said Isabel softly. "That was cruel of me."

Beatriz took out her own kerchief and dabbed at her nose.

"I am not myself," Isabel began. "It's just—"

"Just what?" asked Beatriz, still not able to make eye contact.

"I do love another."

At this confession, Beatriz turned to face Isabel. "I knew it! Those times you walked into the house, pink and trembling. Who is it?"

Isabel decided to tell her sister everything. "Diego Altamirano."

"I've heard of that family," said Beatriz. She did not add her judgment, though. She did not accuse Isabel of recklessness, of dishonor, or the many sins she could have enumerated, considering Isabel's illicit behavior these past weeks. For that, Isabel was grateful.

"You'll have to forget him, you know," advised Beatriz.

"Never. Love is the only thing that matters."

"Even if you can't be with him?"

Isabel nodded morosely.

"Ah, here it is," Beatriz proclaimed, holding up the fan. "It was under my pallet."

She turned to go, but paused, her hand on the wooden door-knob. "You were wrong before, Sister. I do love Juan Carlos. But I don't pine for him. I am waiting patiently for him to see the glory of my light."

During the days leading up to the wedding, Isabel went through the motions of daily life without joy. She was right back to where she started before she and Abuela began learning the Talmud. In the absence of happiness, pain took up residence. She had never understood what a devilish opportunist that emotion was until now. Pain gained potency only when there was something joyful one had to give up. In other words, the marriage to Don Sancho would have been bearable had she not met Diego. But now that a future with him had been ripped away from her, a vile emptiness had entered her heart, more powerful than Torquemada's preaching. She truly had become like her mother after their capture, nearly catatonic. Mamá, on the other hand, came out of her shell, succumbing to the excitement of her daughter's upcoming nuptials. She busied herself fitting verdugados into her own and Beatriz's wedding dresses (Isabel refused to wear a hoop skirt, insisting on a straight white bliaut gown) and keeping the house spotless, lest one of Don Sancho's relatives from the north came calling.

Abuela noticed Isabel's melancholia. She tried to help by asking about Qasmūna and her father. Perhaps Isaac had received further information about them? And what about other poets she favored? But Isabel offered nothing and her mood would not lift. One morning, they were working together, using a stone smoother to press a tablecloth for Isabel to use in her new life as Doña del Aguila, when Abuela said, "Have you ever read your father's siddur?" His prayer book.

Isabel shook her head.

"It's quite interesting. It tells us which prayers to say in the morning, and which ones to recite when we go to sleep."

"That routine is for Beatriz, not me. And besides, what's the use of learning the words to a prayer to God? He does not exist."

"Don't say such things, mi nieta!"

It was true that if anyone heard her, she would be accused of heresy. But that was not Abuela's concern. Isabel knew how much it pained her grandmother that Isabel had lost her faith.

"You must find your way back to God. This will give meaning to your marriage," advised Abuela. "Though you and Don Sancho won't have a ketubah, you will both make your vows before the

Lord. And that is sacred. Just whisper *Elohim*, one of the Hebrew words for God, to yourself during the ceremony."

The only contract she would make with anyone would be a silent one, hidden away in her heart, between her and Diego. At least Diego had not answered her poem with another note. He seemed to understand the gravity of the situation and had stayed away. But even the promises they made to each other would eventually fade. For in time, he would marry another. The thought of him loving anyone else made her chest explode with jealousy.

Papá entered the sala, where Abuela and Isabel were leaning over the table working. He watched them press for some time. Eventually, he tapped Isabel on the arm and motioned for her to come with him downstairs. She rested the heavy smoother on its side, wiped her brow with the back of her hand, and followed him into the cellar.

Two glasses and an uncorked bottle rested on the table. Next to the wine were two quills, a pot of ink, and a stack of parchment.

"What's this, a party?" she said, forgetting he could not hear her. She turned to him and smiled, shrugging her shoulders questioningly.

"CAN'T A FATHER SPEND SOME ALONE TIME WITH HIS ELDEST DAUGHTER WITHOUT RAISING *O-PECHA*?" He smiled broadly.

Isabel smiled in return, knowing exactly what he was trying to say, even though the correct pronunciation was sospecha, suspicion. She took a seat.

He poured them both a splash of wine and held up his glass. She held up hers and they clinked them together. "*L'CHAIM*," he said loudly.

"Mmm," said Isabel. This bottle tasted perfect, as dry and

fruity as the famous Perez vino tinto had always been. She picked up a quill and wrote: *No vinegar taste at all.*

He wrote underneath: *We should invite Duque de Alba over.*

She nodded and laughed, forcing the pain away briefly. He laughed, too. He didn't need to hear to feel merriment.

They sat in silence for a while, sipping the wine. Then he took up the quill again. *I am going to miss you.*

She wrote: *Don't make me cry, Papá. I will still see you, just under different circumstances.*

You are a grown woman now, but to me, you will always be my girl. Then he laid his hands upon her head. And in his overly loud voice, he blessed her, asking God to make her more like Sarah, Rebecca, Leah, and Rachel. To guard her and show favor to her. To show her kindness and grant her peace. She did not tell him it was only Wednesday and not yet Shabbat. She did not try to quiet him. She allowed the pressure of his palms to spread warmth all over her.

On Friday afternoon, Mamá asked Isabel to help her set the table in the cellar. Isabel found herself unable to lay down even one fork. This would be the last Shabbat dinner of her life, probably their last as a family. She could not imagine Beatriz allowing this tradition to continue once Isabel had moved to Don Sancho's estate. Two days from now, on Sunday after Mass, at the third hour past noon, she would become Doña Sancho del Aguila.

Isabel watched Mamá briskly fold napkins: left, right, making a triangle. She memorized her mother's hands the way they looked today, the raised blue veins, the brown spot near the left big knuckle, her cracked nail on the ring finger. Abruptly, she went around to Mamá's side of the table and took her hand. The skin was as soft as when Isabel was small and she would grip her mamá's fingers tight as they walked across the plaza. Mamá looked up, catching Isabel's eyes. Isabel grabbed her mother fiercely, embracing her as if this was the last time. She knew this was not the case. The other day in this very cellar she had assured Papá they would dine together as one big family. But now Isabel felt such a desperate yearning that her throat hitched. She smelled her mother's lemon oil fragrance. She never wanted to let go.

On Saturday afternoon, Isabel was folding her gowns into a trunk to take to Don Sancho's house when the del Castillo sisters' dog was at it again. His bark was incessant. Someone needed to calm that animal. She walked downstairs and entered the center courtyard.

The del Castillo pet had shiny golden hair that one of the sisters brushed daily. It bounded up to Isabel, its nose wet against her hand. "Shhh. That's a good boy." Finally, his barking stopped. "Now, must I stand in this courtyard all afternoon just to keep you quiet?"

The animal looked at her, his tongue hanging out of his mouth. A date palm rippled above them. Isabel looked up and something white caught her eye. What was that, stuck in a pointy frond?

"Stay," she told the dog. Then she stood on her toes to retrieve it. It was perched too high and she could not reach. She shook the branch and it eventually dislodged. A rolled-up parchment fell to the ground. Isabel recognized the red wax seal holding it closed. *DAM*. Her heart leapt. How long had this note been stuck there? Was he here, in her courtyard? Was Diego the cause of the ruckus the night that Beatriz was kept awake? Isabel almost asked the dog but tore open the sealed parchment instead.

She stopped breathing. It was the loveliest drawing she had ever seen. The tears she couldn't shed while writing her lament flowed like a river. A drop of salt water landed on a beautifully rendered eye of a peacock feather, making the color bleed. Quickly, she rolled it up before it became water damaged. She would save this forever.

The note had said to meet him at the Spanish oak in Plaza Santa Ana when the church bell tolled five. But who knew how many days ago that was? And now she had gone and sent him that sorrowful poem without so much as an acknowledgment of his art. God's leeches! She had to see him one last time. With her marriage ceremony scheduled for tomorrow, there wasn't a moment to lose.

28

Where would Diego be on a Saturday afternoon? Likely not collecting taxes, as many of his tenants were Jewish and were celebrating the Sabbath. A taberna? If so, then she was out of luck. He could be anywhere, even far outside the city. It was like finding a lost button in a field of grapevines. What did nobles do on a Saturday afternoon? They gathered for their midday meal as a family. This was her only hope. But how to gain entrance to the alcazarejo? She'd figure that out when she got there. First, she had to sneak past that odious spy.

She looked at Señora Herrera's front door. The woman had been sympathetic to her parents being beaten. Perhaps she would be again.

A few minutes later, Isabel exited the front gate, shuffling slowly, bent over Señora Herrera's cane, her face completely obscured by an opaque veil. The spy even called her by name. "Buenas, Doña Herrera," he said respectfully.

Grinning wildly as she turned the corner, Isabel removed the veil, stuck the cane under her arm, and hastened toward the alcazarejo. She had never walked the road leading up to it before, but because the house was visible from every spot in town, it was easy to find.

Standing from this angle, looking up at the fortresslike

structure, she realized what an expansive property it was. In front there was a moat, empty of water, and a bridge. On either side of the house and behind it, bushes, trees, and trails seemed to stretch for kilometers. A crackling of twigs made Isabel jump. She stopped, her eyes scanning across the property. Could her spy have followed her anyway? When a squirrel tore off behind her, she sighed with relief.

Now, how to get inside? Or better yet, how to get a message to him? A carriage house stood apart from the main house, about fifty meters from the bridge. Maybe there was a footman inside who could help.

"Hola!" she called as she approached the square stone structure. "Anyone here?" But there was no one inside. Just an empty carriage. She was walking away when a maid with stocky legs approached the carriage house, carrying two buckets of water, for the horses, presumably. Seeing Isabel, the woman dropped the buckets, spilling all the water onto the dirt.

"I didn't mean to startle you," began Isabel. "My donkey and cart are down the road. One of the wheels broke on my way to deliver wine for the Altamiranos."

"I'll go get help at once," said the maid.

"I just need the son, Lord Diego. My father deals with him, usually. If you can tell him that Señorita Perez is here, I'd be much obliged."

The woman gave a bow and turned to go.

"But make sure he's alone!" warned Isabel.

The maid seemed confused.

"I wouldn't want to inconvenience the count and countess with such a stupid mistake on my part." She looked sheepish. "They may not want to order from us anymore."

In a few minutes, Diego came running toward her. She moved to meet him halfway when he shook his head. "Not here. Follow me."

She followed him about a three-minute walk up a trail into a grove of Spanish oaks.

They fell into each other's arms. He found her lips, her eyelids, the tender part behind her ears. He moaned into the collar of her dress. "Isabel, you can't imagine how I've missed you."

"I'm sorry I didn't meet you before," she breathed out.

"You are here now."

She pulled back slightly to look at his handsome face. "I have been trying not to think of you, which is like trying not to breathe." She gave him a small smile. "But that illuminated note was exquisite. And the dog must have tried to bite your leg. And that dreadful poem I sent you, I can't—"

He put his finger over her lips. "Shhh." He tilted her head back and kissed her again, harder. She felt his urgency and something vibrated deep in her belly. He reached behind her, finding the laces on her dress.

"Let's go back to the house," he said. "I can sneak you inside like Noeima and her lover in that legend."

Though a part of her wanted to lie with him in his bedchamber, it was foolhardy. She pulled her hands away. "We mustn't, Diego."

He stopped, sighing. "Tienes razón. You are right."

He had not yet mentioned the part in her poem about "seven days' time." Maybe he didn't realize the ceremony was tomorrow. She needed to tell him, but she wanted to prolong this bliss for just a little while. So she asked him something trivial. "Tell me about your apprenticeship."

"My hell-ship, you mean."

"What happened? Did he change the rules of your arrangement?"

He shook his head. "Worse. He painted the auto de fe for the Holy Office."

"So it was *him* I saw that day with his easel. How horrifying that he captured it for history when all we want to do is forget."

"He was commissioned to paint another tribunal, this time in Madrid. I'm to travel with him and have my own canvas, so we can combine our different angles and images later in the studio. Turn it into one large work. Though this is what I wished for, to have something of my own to show, I am sick about it."

"Surely, you can say no. Make an excuse. That as the count's son, you can't travel to Madrid for fear of plague or some such thing."

He laughed. "You are clever, my love. But at the moment, there is no plague or pestilence in the city, gracias a Dios." Then he grew somber. "I thought Berruguete was a man of integrity, that he cared only for his craft. But he would sell his soul if he could. For the first time in my life, I am without hope."

She took his hand in hers. "I felt that same way after the auto de fe. Then Mamá and Papá were questioned and beaten and I lost all—"

"Wait. Your parents were beaten? Are they alive?"

"Broken, but alive."

"I'm so sorry, Isabel."

"You can't see Mamá's injuries. It's her spirit that's beyond repair, I'm afraid." She sighed. "But what I'm trying to tell you is that after all that has happened, I found something else to inspire me."

Diego reached for her hair, winding a curl around his finger. He leaned in close to her mouth and whispered, "And who might that be?"

She giggled and kissed him briefly, with her lips closed, lest they both get carried away with passion again. "Not who. What. I was speaking about a Jewish book. The Talmud. But it's so much more than a book. It's a very long discussion spanning thousands of years."

His eyebrows rose in delight. "I have not studied it, but Maimonides quotes from it. The Talmud is different from the Bible, yes?"

She nodded. "It takes passages from the Bible and interprets them with commentary from many wise rabbis. They even contradict each other, just like a spoken argument."

"In school we studied the Socratic method, where asking and answering questions encourages one to think critically. Many times I went into a debate thinking one way, and left convinced of another idea entirely. I guess that's why I try so hard to use reason and logic. I believe that people's minds can change. But unfortunately, that's not the case with the villagers here."

"Well, that's precisely what the Talmud does! It disabuses you of your preconceived notions and makes you question everything. It has hidden poems and symbols, as well."

Diego's eyes smoldered. "I have never known a woman like you." He grabbed her shoulders. "Run away with me, Isabel. Let's leave this place. We should be in Florence, where life is moving forward, not in Trujillo where our feet are mired in mud."

"L-leave?" she sputtered.

"I didn't know the solution until now." His lips grazed hers. "I want to be with you forever. I have never been more certain of anything."

She inhaled his musk, felt his arms around her. She had to tell him. "I'm to be married tomorrow afternoon at Iglesia Santiago."

Diego pulled away and kicked the trunk of a nearby tree so hard that it rained leaves on them. "He's leaving for Granada and wants to make you his wife before he leaves, does he not?"

She blanched. "How do you know that?"

"The scoundrel was in the studio and announced it like a cocksure braggart." His face darkened. "Berruguete is doing his portrait. I'm not supposed to tell you. It's to be your wedding gift."

"I'd burn it before I accepted it." Isabel's shoulders sagged. "What are we going to do?"

"Let me think a minute." He paced back and forth, deep in thought. At one point, he muttered to himself, and waved his arms in the air. She tried not to laugh even though the situation was so dire.

After some minutes, he stood facing her. "We leave for Florence tonight."

It was loco. Yet she knew it was the only way to escape her life with Don Sancho.

They discussed the meeting place and time, the carriage that would take them to Valencia, the boat that he would book passage on, what to bring, which was nothing but the clothes on her back.

There was one thorn in the plan. Mamá and Papá. "I can't abandon my parents, Diego. Poor Father. He is but half a man. Don Sancho was going to provide for them after we were married."

"We can send for them once we arrive in Florence."

"But what if they don't want to leave? This is the only land they've known. And Abuela, she won't be able to make the journey."

"You just said the Inquisition questioned and released them. They won't get a second chance. I think that once you're gone, they'll realize it's the only solution."

"Will they be in danger after I leave? Don Sancho will send an army after me."

"I'll just have to turn around and go back to Trujillo as soon as we dock in Florence. Hopefully, no one will suspect you've actually left town, as all your dresses will still be at home. This will buy us some time."

He was risking everything for her. What about his own family? "What will your father say?"

He sneered. "I don't give a horse's arse what he says. He covered up my mother's history. My own birthright. I am through paying fealty to that man. We will practice the religion we want. There have been Jewish communities living in Italy since the Roman Empire. Lorenzo de' Medici, besides being a patron of artists, protects the Jews of Florence. We'll live under his rule."

She touched his cheek. "Te amo," she whispered. "I love you."

He smiled in surprise at her declaration. "And I, you."

So this was it, then. A choice had been made. A life of risk and happiness over a life of ease and misery. In the deepest recess of her heart, there had never been any choice at all.

29

Isabel retired to her pallet at the usual time. Her sister was already snoring. In just a few hours, Beatriz would wake herself up for midnight prayers and find the bed empty next to her. By then, Isabel should be far away. But the timing was delicate. Isabel had to make sure it was not too close to the hour of matins or Beatriz wouldn't be in a deep enough sleep. Lying under the sheets, fully clothed, Isabel's nerves were stretched tight like a bowstring.

The only regret she had was not sharing a private goodbye with Abuela. With Mamá and Papá thinking she was leaving them to live with Don Sancho, it made sense to have those last moments— it was expected even. They were saying goodbye to their little girl and she to the life she had known in their care. But now, lying in wait, Isabel realized with dismay that it was too late for her and Abuela. She had never lied to Abuela before and couldn't do it now. It was safer this way. If Abuela were questioned by Don Sancho, she could honestly say she knew nothing. The hardest part of this journey wasn't the danger. It was the fact that Isabel was walking away from the one person who understood her, whose roots helped keep Isabel firmly on the ground.

She heard the faint gong of the church bell ring eleven times. With one glance in Beatriz's direction, she carefully slipped out of bed and put on her leather slippers. The loud chopines would be staying here.

Isabel crept to Abuela's room and kissed her on both cheeks. "Usted es mi heroína. I love you," she whispered. Abuela did not stir. Isabel longed to wake her up, but she did not. She knew she would never see her grandmother again. She imagined the discussion her parents would have with Abuela when one of Diego's compatriots contacted them regarding their move to Florence following Isabel's escape. Though her mother would weep a thousand tears, Abuela would tell them she could not make the journey. She would remain in Trujillo, where she grew up. She would tend to Soli's grave. Abuela would release Isabel's parents from her grip.

Beatriz was another story. Whether or not she would follow to Florence was a mystery.

Isabel lingered at her grandmother's pallet as long as she could. She touched her back one last time, feeling the even rise and fall of her breathing. Then she placed a note under the pillow. *Abuela, Hasta vas.* Until you go. In Castilian, it was just an unfinished message. Until you go to the mercado, to the plaza, wherever. But in Hebrew, it was something else. Part of an abbreviation. The first letters of each word were *alef*, *hay*, and *vet*, or the sounds a, ha, and va. *Ahava.* The Hebrew word for love.

Once she was in the courtyard, she picked up as many rocks as she could find and threw them near the del Castillo's dog, sleeping in the corner. He woke up, barking wildly. She heard the spy's heavy footsteps scurry around the back of the house, trying to find entry into the patio.

This was her chance. She opened the front door and retreated into the night.

A quarter moon shone in the inky sky, giving her scant light to see by. She wished it were a fuller moon, as that would help her locate Diego and the carriage more easily if anything went wrong and he wasn't in the agreed-upon location. Coyotes howled in the distance, joining the protest of the del Castillo dog, which she could still hear yelping as she walked briskly down the dirt road. A bat swooped near her, flapping its wings too close for comfort. She let out a small scream. Returning home from poetry readings late at night had never been this frightening. This time was different: She was breaking every law in Spain.

She was supposed to meet Diego at the stone arch, the south gate to Trujillo, where they had started their ride up to Monfragüe. There had been no time to do a run-through today, but she remembered the arch was an eight-minute walk from her house. That is, if she took the shortcut through Plaza Santa Ana. During the day, the plaza was crowded with promenaders, pages, merchants. But at night, it was emptier, save for the pícaros and the ladies of ill-repute. The safer route by the hill avoided the plaza, but would add ten minutes to her journey. She knew it well because she sometimes took the hillside path when composing poetry.

Concerned she'd stayed in Abuela's room too long, Isabel cut through the plaza. She and Diego had a long ride to Valencia ahead of them.

Sure enough, when she reached the open square, small groups of women stood huddled, waiting for customers. Even with the faint moonlight, Isabel could see their eyes peeking through their veils and their petticoats pinned up on one side, exposing pale thighs. She continued past, almost reaching the far end of the plaza, when a trio of pícaros emerged from behind a thick-trunked tree, the whites of their eyes shining in the dark. One beckoned her with crooked fingers.

"I don't see a purse," said another. "Must be hidden."

They surrounded her.

"Maybe it's in her maidenhead?" said a third, making the other two degenerates laugh.

"Spread your legs, lovely lady," said the first man. "Let's have a look."

The whores were within earshot, but they wouldn't help her. They probably thought she was competition. "Leave me be and I won't call for the alcalde," she said to the men. She had no idea if the judge was about, but everyone knew he was not above paying a lady for a quick one.

Undeterred by her threat, they tightened their circle, near enough that she could smell the wine on them. She took baby steps left and right, buying time.

Then the more emboldened of the thieves lunged at her.

Isabel jerked sideways and made a run for it, zigzagging through the three men. Another pícaro reached out, brushing her skirt, but he was drunk and missed. She was too fast. Grateful for her youth and her leather shoes, Isabel did not slow or turn around until she was two streets away. She hid behind a building and held her breath, listening. They had not followed. She allowed her breath to slowly seep out. Just to be safe, she counted from one to sixty, five more times. Only then did she walk on.

The stone arch rose in her sightline, flanked by two watchtowers. There it was, about two hundred meters ahead: the outline of the enclosed Altamirano carriage. A lit oil lamp hung on a curved pole, suspended above the driver. Isabel could see him sitting on a riser in front, holding the reins in one hand, a pipe in the other. The orange glow of its tip floated in the air like a firefly. Below him, leaning against the carriage, stood Diego. In mere minutes, his arms would be around her. She almost called his name. But something made her hesitate. Gracias a Dios that she did, because a man approached him.

She drew closer to hear what they were saying, obscuring herself by a shopkeeper's shuttered stall that jutted out into the street.

". . . about yea high," the man was saying. "Brown hair, fair of skin. Sixteen years of age."

Isabel gasped. He was describing her!

"She sounds like someone I'd like to meet," Diego replied. "But I've seen no one matching that description."

"I was guarding her house and got attacked by a cursed dog. By the time I made chase, she was gone."

It was their clay-chewing spy! She couldn't see around the stall, but she was sure of it. Curse those pícaros. If they hadn't delayed her, she would have beaten the spy here and she and Diego would be on their way by now.

"Guarding her house?" asked Diego. "From whom?"

"Special orders of the alguacil," the man clarified. "She's his betrothed. He wants to keep her safe until the nuptials."

A load of rotten posset, if she ever heard it. He wanted to keep her prisoner.

"Some thieves pointed me in this direction," continued the spy. "There aren't many people about at this time of night. I thought you may have seen or heard something."

Isabel couldn't remember if the man was armed or not. He was always in street clothes, trying to blend in. He was smaller than Diego. If he had no weapon, Diego could probably take him in a fistfight, but she hoped it wouldn't come to that.

"Well, I'd best be on my way," said Diego, making like he was entering the carriage. "Got a long journey ahead of me."

"Of course," said the spy. "Buenas noches."

When he had gone, Isabel stepped out.

"You were here the whole time?" Diego asked, embracing her.

"Luckily, you didn't have to fight him," she said softly.

The sound of crunching boots made them pull apart.

"What did you say your name was?"

Diego and Isabel turned in shock. The spy had returned!

The man lifted something to his lips. Isabel saw a glint of silver in his hand. Something small and shiny. Not a knife, though. Before Diego could stop him, the officer managed to put the silver object to his lips. A high-pitched sound came out. Isabel covered her ears.

Diego lunged at him, throwing a hard punch. The spy was knocked out. "It's a boatswain's pipe," he told her. "Damned man was in the navy."

The pipe clattered to the ground. But it was too late. The warning had been sounded. Footfalls came at them from all sides.

"Isabel, get into the carriage quickly."

She ran around the other side of the transport, where the door opening was, and lowered the folding steps. She threw herself inside. Why wasn't the driver getting them out of here? Isabel stuck her head out and looked to the front of the carriage. Empty. The coward must have abandoned his post when he heard the whistle.

"Take the reins, Diego!" yelled Isabel.

But he was trapped. Four armed men were already upon him, swords drawn, forming a semicircle around Diego. He crouched, holding out his dagger, eyes darting left and right for whomever would strike first.

"This is private business," said Diego forcefully. "Be on your way."

"Our comrade is passed out on the ground. Now it's our business," said the leader.

The men closed in on him.

"I'm on my way out of the city on an urgent errand for my father, Count Altamirano." Diego waved his blade in the air. "The Familiar," he added. "He'll have you all arrested by the Holy Office if you don't let us go."

Two officers conferred privately. She couldn't hear a word. Then one glanced toward the carriage. "It's the Marrano we want."

How did they know who she was?

Isabel watched anxiously through the window. Diego waved his hand behind him, signaling her to stay inside.

She did not.

If she could just get to the driver's seat without being seen, she could commandeer the horses while Diego made a run for it on foot. She could then pick him up at the second location they had talked about, a well near the Romani camp.

Isabel stepped out the door. Using the folding steps as purchase, she glued her upper body to the carriage and reached out until she felt the front edge. She gripped with all the strength in her hand and held it. Her pulse whirred like a hummingbird's wings.

Two horses were tied to a yoke on her left. One whinnied and stomped its foot, shaking the whole carriage. She nearly fell to the ground.

Out of the side of her eye, she could see the corner of the riser. Carefully, she moved her left foot to a hinge on the harness. The iron was narrow and slippery and her foot slid.

Behind the carriage, she could hear sounds of a fight. Metal scraping metal.

She tried again to get a foothold with her left leg. The other horse swished its tail, again rocking the entire harness and yoke. Again, her foot fell. She was at such an awkward angle. Being right-handed, she had better balance on her right side. Her left hand was weakening. It was now or never. Isabel twisted to the left and threw herself toward the hitch. Miraculously, her right foot landed on solid iron and she grabbed one of the horse's tails. She swung her other leg to an iron bar, and held on to a metal fastener with the other hand. Now all she needed to do was climb onto the seat. As she reached out her arm for the leather riser, the other horse bucked, kicking his leg back. The shoe did not hit her, but she lost her balance and fell backward.

"Ah!" she cried out in pain.

"Isabel!" yelled Diego.

"Grab her!"

Boots clomped to her side of the carriage. Rough, calloused hands yanked her neck, then gripped her hair. Another pair of hands took her legs, lifting her up.

"Let her go!" said Diego.

Then she heard the splooshy liquid sound of something moving through soft flesh, followed by deathly silence.

"Diego!" she screamed.

The next thing she knew she was being dragged backward, her heels scraping the cobblestones. Someone's hands were under her arms, pulling her away from the carriage, away from Diego.

"To the cart. Hurry!" said one of the men.

"What about the lord?" said another.

"Leave him."

She was thrown onto a hard wood surface. It smelled of urine and rotten vegetables.

"Ya!" commanded the driver.

With the crack of a whip, the cart moved forward, bumping and tossing her side to side. Her ankle was twisted and her hip bone throbbed. She didn't care. The man she loved could be dead. And God only knew what awaited her on the other end.

30

"Hola?" Isabel yelled. "Anybody here?"

Nothing.

She was in a frigid square-shaped space. The only way out was through a thick door, which had been locked from the outside. Despite hearing the metal slide into position after she was dumped there, Isabel banged on the door anyway. She hammered again and again until her knuckles were raw.

She sank down onto the dirt floor to think. A faint sound came from the left. Was that clanking man-made? She scooted over and put her ear to the wall. Silence. She knocked. Her rapping barely made a sound against the stone. She took off a shoe and hit the wall as hard as she could. If only she had her hard wooden chopines, she thought grimly. At least the rapid movement of her arm warmed her up a little.

The knocking returned in response. She wasn't alone!

"Hello!" she yelled. She put her lips to the cold stone, willing her voice to seep through to the other side, like smoke. "Can you hear me?"

A thin, reedy voice penetrated through the wall.

She strained to hear what they were saying.

". . . ggrzzz am fwwzz Renato."

"What?" she yelled.

"I am Renato," said a male voice, slightly stronger now.

"Isabel," she called back. "How long have you been here?"

"Weeks. Months. I've lost track."

Did she hear correctly? Madre mía, would they keep her here for that long? "What is this place?"

". . . wzrrrjjj Office."

"What?"

"The puta Holy Office."

There was no mistaking that curse word. But it was impossible! Don Sancho would never allow this. There had been a grave mistake. She would explain everything to him and get this straightened out at once.

"Guard!"

Her words bounced off the walls, mocking her.

"GUARD!"

After what seemed like hours, someone slid the lock. The door opened and a sliver of light crept in, giving her a momentary glimpse of the world outside. A bailiff, wearing military breeches and a jerkin, stood before her, smelling like the unwashed. She didn't recognize him as any of the men who had attacked her and Diego by the carriage.

Diego. Was he even alive?

She mustered all the bravado in her slender body. "Let me speak to the alguacil at once!"

"Don Sancho?" The bailiff laughed derisively. "He can't help you now."

"Nonsense."

"Once the local municipality transfers a prisoner over, our jurisdiction overrides anything else. By orders of Her Majesty the queen."

"What am I being charged with?"

"I wouldn't know, señorita."

"Who has accused me?" she demanded.

He retreated and closed the door.

"Who has accused me?" she yelled, desperate. But the lock slid back into place, imprisoning her once again.

Had she been a target all along? Did someone find out about her and Diego and tell Don Sancho? Goose skin pimpled on her arms.

If it were true, then she did not know how she would get out of this alive.

Diego's eyes shot open. His midsection was afire. He touched his belly and inspected his fingers. Even in the waning moon, he could see they were soaked red. He tried sitting up. More blood gushed from the wound. He moaned and lay back down. Poking a finger through an opening in his shirt, he ripped the soft cloth from shoulder to wrist. He nearly fainted from the effort. He then put the material between his teeth and tore it into two strips. He knotted one strip to the other so it was long enough to encircle his torso. He tied it as tight as he could around his ribs. The burning was so intense, he saw sparks before his eyes and passed out.

When he woke again, he immediately felt his wound. The wetness had caked. With the bleeding stanched, he was able to stand.

Slowly, he walked to the carriage. It took some minutes, but finally, he climbed onto the riser and sat. Wincing, he reached down and found the loose reins.

"Ya!" he commanded the horses.

Though he wanted to go after Isabel, he knew he'd be no good to anyone unless he got fixed up. The knife had sliced him deep. Provided it hadn't hit any vital organs, he had little time before infection would set in. He guided the horses back to the alcazarejo.

31

Hands bound tightly behind her, a wooden stick at her back, Isabel was forced to walk down a hallway. There were rooms on both sides of her, but unlike her first cell, all these doors had small openings covered in bars.

A head of matted hair appeared in one opening, his fingers outstretched. "Ayudáme." Help me, he murmured. Could that be Renato? She dared not call his name.

Another pair of bloodshot eyes made a desperate plea in Hebrew.

At one door, a man simply moaned continuously. She kept her eyes on the floor in front of her, praying she wasn't passing her future self.

She was brought into a large room. This time there were windows, though they were covered in black cloth. The only light came from six candles resting on two small tables on either side of a painting. She gazed at the painting, transfixed. Two wooden posts engulfed in flames. Two bodies tied upright. A mouth agape in anguish. The audience rapt, entertained. She recognized the scene. The auto de fe! This must be one of Berruguete's. There was nowhere to place her eyes that didn't terrify her.

Two men, dressed in long, hooded black robes and the tonsured hairstyle of friars sat before her. One towered above the back of his chair; the other was tiny, wizened, and wrinkled, like a dead tree. A third sat at a desk with parchment, a quill, and ink.

She looked left and right, searching for instruments of torture. The room had none. Was it foolish to hope?

"State your name for the record," said the taller friar. His face was obscured in the recess of his hood. Only the bony outline of his knuckles, hooked together beneath an unseen chin, were discernible in the candlelight.

"Isabel Perez."

"You are Eva, the converso, are you not?"

She blinked twice. They knew her Hebrew name?

"Answer the question!" he roared.

She stumbled back. "I was baptized Isabel Perez, Father," she said. Try to be agreeable, she thought. Make them like you. "At Iglesia de Santiago. We've been attending every Sunday for sixteen years."

"You are the daughter of Bitya and Moshe, the granddaughter of Fortuna," continued the friar.

How did they know these facts?

"My parents are Benita and Manolo. My grandmother is Francesca," she said, giving their converso names.

The friar riffled through some papers. "Ah yes. The same pair we questioned last month."

Papá's blood-caked ear and Mamá's bald spot flashed before her, threatening to make her cry. She forced a blank expression on her face and genuflected. "We are good Christians."

His eyes seared through her. "I believe your sister, Beatriz, is the only one who can make that claim."

Isabel's mouth went dry. Could Beatriz be the one who turned her in? No time to think about that now. She had to convince these people she was just as noble as her sister. "I taught my younger sister everything. The sext prayer and matins. Scripture and the Bible stories."

Not a twinge of reaction from him.

"'And many false prophets will arise and lead many astray,'" she said. "Matthew 24." She racked her brain for the Latin her sister used to recite. *"Media nocte surgebam—"*

"I advise you to confess now, for the sake of your immortal soul," interrupted the tall friar. "For the sake of your mortal, Marrano flesh."

"But I know not what I have done," she said.

The friar tapped his white fingers on the side of his black robe. "Are you a Jew?"

"What?"

"Are you a Jew?"

"No!" she cried. She feared God's lightning would strike her down for rejecting Moses. But the room did not shake. The notary kept scratching. The two friars watched her absently, almost bored.

"Do you believe that the Messiah has already arrived?" continued the tall one.

"Of course."

"Do you own or have you ever owned any Jewish books?"

"Never."

"You blasphemous heretic," hissed the friar. "You have already been denounced."

He shifted and his hood opened wider, revealing his face. An ugly scar ran from his eyebrow to his temple.

"By whom?" she asked in a thin voice.

"Never mind. Admit your Judaizing and walk away. You will

wear the sanbenito, but surely it is better than facing the fire." The wizened friar leaned over and whispered something to him. He nodded. "Or you can name other Judaizers. Your choice."

Isabel would not throw anyone she loved to these beasts. Nor could she trust their word if she did. Admitting Judaizing would just make them assume her parents had led her to it. Then they'd go after them again. Abuela, too. She realized she was back at the beginning. She hadn't wanted to marry Don Sancho because she resented bearing the burden of protecting her family. And here she was protecting them anyway.

"Well?" asked the friar.

Isabel cast her eyes down.

The priests rose.

"Bailiff!" called the one with the scar. "Bring her to the place of relaxation."

Isabel stumbled down some stairs and into a much larger space. She was naked, but too terrified to care. A woman was slumped in the corner, her mouth ripped on both sides from cheek to ear. She stared into nothingness, her thumb twitching.

Hideous devices lay everywhere. A wooden-framed rack with movable bars on each end. Hanging loosely from it were white bindings, still bloodied from where the last prisoner had been tied. A flat board stretched lengthwise over a stone basin. Ropes hanging from a pulley attached to the ceiling.

Isabel's teeth wouldn't stop chattering. The bailiff laid her down on the board. The thin wood vibrated from her shivering body.

"No, por favor!" She tried to sit up, but her wrists were still bound behind her. She kicked the air, hoping to land on something, anything.

He pushed her back down and quickly tied her legs to the board with hemp cords. They were wrapped so tight, the rope sliced into her flesh. An iron clamp secured her head. Wooden pegs were stuffed into her nostrils. A linen cloth dropped down, covering her whole face. The fabric moved in and out with her breath. Then water. So much water. Poured over the cloth. Her eyes widened in panic. She tried to turn her head from side to side but the clamp prevented any movement. The linen sank down, down, down into her gullet. She gagged and coughed.

Abruptly, it was yanked out. It felt like her throat came out with it. Someone placed his ear to her mouth. She could not see his face from her prone position. Couldn't smell him, because of the plugs. But she saw the sweat pouring down in rivulets above his tonsure.

"Anything?" called a voice behind her.

The bald, sweaty pate retreated. "No. No confession."

The cloth went back over her face. More water was poured into her. Her air was running out. She thought of that time she had held her breath as a little girl to see how long she could go.

The body acts of its own accord. It's the law of nature.

She swallowed the water and the linen until she could breathe no more.

Diego managed to guide the horses and cart into the family carriage house. Then he toppled over from the high seat and tumbled to the ground. The footman, a skinny boy of fifteen, ran to get the countess.

"Por Dios, m'hijo," his mother exclaimed when she saw him. "What happened?"

Diego couldn't speak.

Kneeling down beside him, she felt his pulse. "You've lost much blood." She raised her head. "Send Martín out for the doctor."

The footman stared at her, his jaw open.

"Now!"

The boy scurried away.

His mother made the sign of the cross, then cradled his head in her lap. "Just hold on, m'hijo. Hold on."

"Mother . . ." he rasped. His tongue felt like parchment.

"Shhh, save your strength."

Diego tried to sit up. "I must go . . ."

His mother gently pressed his chest. "You are not going anywhere. This wound needs suturing and then you will convalesce here until there is no more risk of sepsis."

"But I must . . ."

The footman returned. "If you'll allow me, m'lady. I can dress the wound while we wait."

"How would you know how to do something like that?" she asked haughtily. Even through his haze, Diego knew her attitude was merely a defense against panic.

"My cousin had a similar injury recently. I took care of him."

She hesitated, stroking Diego's forehead. "Very well."

From a flat angle, Diego watched the boy bow. Within minutes he was back, wringing long strips of clean linens from a tub of boiling water.

He had to reach her. He had to save Isabel. Diego lifted his arm. It dropped down again. Everything felt heavy, so heavy.

"How did your cousin get injured?" he heard his mother ask the footman.

"A scuffle at the Holy Office."

"He was imprisoned there?"

"No, m'lady. He's a guard."

Diego knew this was important information he could use somehow, but his eyes would not stay open. He needed to get to someone. Who? If only he could wake up. Then he would know.

32

Isabel coiled herself into a ball on the floor. Her breathing was ragged. Someone had put her clothes back on, yet she still shivered.

"There is no God," cried a hoarse voice.

Who said that? The woman in the corner? Was she even real? Renato? Isabel tried to make her lips form his name. But her throat hurt too much to emit any sound.

Faces floated around her. Abuela. Diego. Then a sinister smile. The friar? No. Beatriz. I hate you, Isabel told the face. I hate you. Then she drifted off.

She had no idea if it was day or night, how long she had lain there. Her hunger was a dull ache in her middle. Her urine had ceased flowing. She had no fluid in her body to make tears, but that was fine. She preferred anger.

Footsteps approached her. Isabel struggled to sit up. The tall friar with the scar loomed there, smelling of wine that had turned. "Are you ready to admit your Judaizing?"

She should just confess something. Then maybe they'd leave her alone. *I lit the Shabbat candles. I sat in a suca. I read Hebrew. I looked longingly at the mikveh.* Her raw throat couldn't form the sounds. Her mouth was that of a hooked fish, moving in vain.

"What was that? I can't hear you?"

She moved her hands, mimicking the act of writing. If she could just have a piece of paper and a quill . . .

The friar tapped his foot, impatient. "The Church condemns taking a life," he said. "It would be unfortunate if you expired before your confession. Then again, if you die, it will be your own doing."

He left as swiftly as he came.

A different bailiff made her stand up. This time they used the ropes and the ceiling pulley.

The pain seared through her. Everything turned to black.

Diego spent the night on the floor of the carriage house—doctor's orders until the sutures had settled. But the next morning, when the physic returned, he was so pleased with Diego's progress, he not only moved him into his own bedchamber, he encouraged him to take a walk.

A walk? Diego didn't need a walk! Clearheaded now, he remembered everything. He had to rescue Isabel. Diego flailed and thrashed at his parents, at the doctor, when they tried to force him into bed, but he was too weak, and they easily held him down.

The count was in a rotten mood, demanding to know what had happened to his son. His mother was left with the job of disabusing her husband of any foul play. Diego heard bits and snatches of their conversation. The countess seemed to be making up a story to appease him. ". . . pícaros . . . attacked in Plaza Santa Ana."

When the physic and his father left the room to confer on his condition, she accused Diego of getting into a knife fight over being Jewish.

"Are you that full of self-loathing that you attacked another Jew as a substitute for your anger toward yourself?" hissed his mother.

"That's preposterous." Now that her secret was out, she was delusional.

"You know I speak the truth."

Diego tried to muster the strength to protest some more. Then stopped. Best to let her think it was true. Knowing the real reason, that he had been about to run to Florence with the converso girl he loved, and live a Jewish life, would be much worse for his mother. "You're right. I did pick a fight. I hate that I have Jewish blood in my veins."

Her lips parted in a satisfied half smile. "Don't let it happen again."

The footman was the one assigned to walk with him. Later that day, the boy supported Diego's elbow as they slowly made their way over the vast grounds of the alcazarejo. The tall winter-brown grasses undulated around them. Impatient, Diego tried to walk faster, but the pain in his side stopped him.

"Why don't we turn back, m'lord," suggested the footman.

Diego shook his head and exhaled through his nose, continuing on despite the burn. The stronger he seemed, the sooner his parents would let him out. "Luis, isn't it?"

The footman nodded.

"You fixed me up nicely last night. I'm grateful."

"I was glad to help, m'lord."

"Where did you learn how to bind and dress a wound like that?"

"My cousin, m'lord."

"He's a doctor?"

"He works at the Holy Office."

From a deep canyon in Diego's mind, a bell rang. He'd heard this before. "He's a guard, is he not?"

"One of many. But he had the misfortune of being stabbed by a prisoner. With my cousin's own knife, no less."

Brave prisoner, thought Diego. But he said instead, "That must have been painful."

"We didn't think my cousin would make it. His parents are dead and I felt right sorry for him."

"And he's still recuperating at home, your cousin?"

"Yes, m'lord."

Diego watched an eagle swoop down and take a mouse in its talons. He and Isabel would be victims no longer. He prayed he wasn't too late.

"I need you to do something for me, Luis."

Diego explained his scheme. The footman would infiltrate the Holy Office wearing his cousin's uniform and bring back the exact location of Isabel's whereabouts. If he told anyone, Luis would be fired, and his family would be out on the street.

To Diego's surprise, it was fear, plain and simple, that made Luis say no.

But the bagful of maravedis made him say yes. Plain and simple.

33

Her right arm moved. Her hand felt a sharp protrusion sticking out beneath the skin of her left shoulder. She could not lift the left arm at all. The parts were all there, but they were damaged. If anyone looked at her, they would think they were viewing her in a broken looking glass. She was rearranged.

"There is no God," cried a hoarse male voice.

Was she dead? Had she arrived in Heaven only to find God didn't exist?

Screaming sounds came from somewhere below her. Was that hell? No, she was above the room of relaxation. In one of those cells with the bars that covered the windows. For the time being, it seemed the Inquisitors were done with her.

Where was everyone? The woman in the corner had disappeared. Mamá and Papá were far away. Beatriz had gone over to the other side. And Diego? Why hadn't he come?

May you be like Sarah, Rebecca, Leah, and Rachel, said Papá.

Where are you off to, looking so pretty? said Mamá.

Your soul can be saved, said Beatriz, *through pain*.

She shifted on the floor and the burning radiating from her shoulder shocked her into an awakened state. Beatriz had wanted Isabel to suffer, but not like this. And yet. Beatriz watched Isabel spurn Don Sancho and give her heart to Diego while she had no future herself, save life in a convent, pining away with an unconsummated love for Juan Carlos, who may or may not ever see Beatriz's "light." That manufactured enough hatred for her to do the unspeakable.

Isabel sucked in air and managed to push herself up using her good arm. But she was dizzy and the floor looked so comfortable. So she lay back down.

It would be easy to just give up. And she supposed there was even a kind of victory in succumbing. For that would mean the Inquisitors would be left with merely a body stripped of its spirit, to transport and tie at the stake. No screaming whatsoever. And where was the fun in that?

Something furry crawled over her foot. She lay there for some moments, letting it make its way up to her ankle. It was now on her calf.

No!

She jerked her leg to fling it off.

She would not let creeping crawling things move freely over her, as if she were a corpse. She was not dead yet. And neither was Diego. She felt the truth of it in her broken bones.

34

She stirred when the cell door opened. A guard Isabel had not seen before entered the small space. His uniform hung on his shoulders, as if it were two sizes too big. He was about her age and seemed even more frightened than she did. His arm reached out. She flinched. A piece of parchment fell from his hand. A message? He nodded ever so slightly. He was not here to hurt her. Wordlessly, he left.

In the dark, she struggled to read it. The parchment was white, that much she could tell, but the words, if there were any, were impossible to see. Then the door opened again, just a crack. Enough for a hand to slip through. A hand holding a lit candle. He was helping her! Giving her light so she could read. But the note was blank. She flipped it over. Also nothing. Drawing the flame closer, Isabel thought she saw some lines forming. In another minute, the words appeared before her.

Stay strong. I am coming to get you out.

—The bookbinder's apprentice

Diego was alive! He remembered what she had told him, about the type of ink that you cannot see unless heated. Hope surged through her.

She returned the candle into the outstretched hand. Gently, the door shut, and the lock slid into place, covering her in darkness again.

She swallowed the tiny piece of paper. It was her first food in days.

Later, a familiar voice called to her through the bars on her door. This time, Isabel knew how many hours had passed because she had watched the subtle shift of faint light through the slatted openings. Why hadn't she noticed this before? Details like these kept her mind off the pain in her body.

"Isabel," he whispered. It was Renato. "Me voy," he said. He was leaving.

To the quemadero? she thought despairingly.

"I am being reconciled to the church," he explained.

Gracias a Dios.

"Is there someone to whom you want a message delivered? Hurry, before they come down the hall," he urged.

She thought quickly. Her parents' house would be watched closely. The alcazarejo was impenetrable. But Atika. She could slip through the city unnoticed. And Renato, in his sanbenito, would be able to travel freely to the Romani encampment without arousing suspicion. Perhaps she could help Diego in some way.

"There is . . ." She paused, struggling to make the proper sounds of elocution. She forced her lips to move inward. Her tongue touched the roof of her mouth. "A girl. Romani. Her name . . . is Atika."

The pain in her throat and shoulder was dissipating. Diego's note, Renato's release. It energized her. "She lives at the camp by the river."

"I will find her," said Renato.

"She is a poet," said Isabel. "Recite her this: My lover cries alone in his castle, while I am imprisoned in my own cold, dark room. He needs succor. Only he holds the key to my heart."

A strange girl was following Diego. He was sure of it. Unlike when Isabel was near, he didn't smell roses. It was frankincense. He paused at the plaza mayor and turned his neck slightly. A few meters back, she paused, too, and shook her tambourine, twirling for passersby. When he resumed his walking, the tinkling music stopped and the smell of her perfume grew strong again.

He was on his way to Berruguete's studio to pick up a painting, a new commission by the Holy Office. His plan was to hand-deliver it. Once inside the dungeon, he would rescue Isabel. Thanks to his footman, Diego knew Isabel was alive. He knew which cell she was in. He knew where the keys were kept: on a hook two hallways to the left of the relaxation room.

Luis's cousin had returned to work. So Diego would not be able to wear the uniform, as his footman did. Berruguete's painting would provide cover. Berruguete was only too happy to have Diego deliver it. The artist was trying to finish Don Sancho's portrait before he left for the war front and, being in the studio day and night, had heard nothing of Isabel's capture. Diego let him think the wedding was still on schedule.

The entire plan was crazy, since Diego wasn't sure how quickly they would both be able to escape, given his wound and Isabel's presumably weakened body. But he must deliver the painting today. His father had brought gossip from a meeting with the Familiars and other members of court. The alguacil's betrothed was being brought to the quemadero tomorrow.

Diego could not walk very fast on the street, for with

each step, the pain in his ribs stabbed him anew. Finally, the smell of frankincense grew tiresome. He turned around to confront the girl, his hand on the hilt of his knife. "Why are you following me?"

She stepped closer. A multicolored scarf covered her head and face. Intelligent blue eyes peered through a narrow slit. "I am Isabel's friend."

Diego's stomach dipped. "You know me?"

The girl nodded. "She sent me a message. A poem."

Diego smiled. That was his Isabel.

"Do you need anything?" she asked him after she recited it. "Clothing to hide her in? A horse perhaps?"

He eyed the musical instrument in her hand.

"I have a better idea."

35

Isabel concentrated on the details. She counted the number of dark spots in the stones from floor to ceiling. She pulled lice from her hair and watched them flit about in the corner before she smashed them. She recited Qasmūna's poetry to herself. She etched Hebrew letters with her right index finger on the dirt floor, then erased the evidence.

Diego was coming for her.

Voices floated from behind her cell door. Two men? Three? None sounded like Diego. Anyway, she was fairly certain he would not just walk right in and take her away. He would act with more stealth.

The lock clanked and her door opened.

Don Sancho towered above her.

Was he her savior and not Diego after all? So be it. At least she would be let out. She slowly got to her knees and then to her feet. She felt faint and leaned against the wall for support.

His eyes went large, surprised at her appearance.

She made no effort to cover herself. Let him see her in her ugliness.

He was quiet for some time, just observing her. "Such a beautiful girl. What a pity."

She stood defiantly.

"And to think you could have had it all."

Was he merely toying with her? Would he not be releasing her?

"I heard they relaxed you, but I needed to see for myself," he said evenly.

She wanted answers and was not about to keep quiet, despite the pain in her throat and her shoulder. "There was a spy. He blew something. And the men came running. How did they know who I was?"

"Alvaro blew the pipe, good man. He was under strict instructions to watch your house and bring you to me if you strayed. All the town officers knew about it."

"Strayed?"

His lower jaw flexed. "I know what I look like." His eyes flicked away from her, landing at the corner of the small cell. "A fair young woman like you. What could you ever see in me?"

So he *was* human after all.

But when he turned back, he was steely-eyed, all trace of humanity gone. "After Alvaro found you running away with the Altamirano traitor, I needed nothing more to denounce you. But I am a man of honor. I needed evidence. You can understand . . . someone in my position. I mustn't seem like I'm playing favorites."

Favorites? By punishing her without evidence?

"Posterity will remember me kindly," he added.

Posterity. Isabel thought of the notary transcribing her every word. For whom? she had wondered. The king and queen? Which future leader would read the questions and answers of what went on down here? None of it presented a true picture, she was sure of that. Maybe no one would ever know the real truth.

Don Sancho dropped the Talmud at her feet. It thudded, dirt puffing up in its wake. "In the end, it was the boy who gave me what I needed. Stupid Jew. Caved the moment his leg was crushed."

A punch to the gut. Her father. David Cohen. And now poor Yuçe. Too many broken bodies.

"One of my bailiffs was watching the house of the Jews since your parents were discovered there," said Don Sancho. "He told me how the boy carried the book home with him after leaving your place."

Then it wasn't Beatriz who denounced her. She had kept Isabel's confidence! They could stand beside each other and not be at war! Isabel thought of the lament she and Abuela had found in the Talmud. How did it go? *If the cedars have caught fire, what hope is there for the moss on the wall?* She finally understood. She and Beatriz were the moss on the wall. All the conversos were. They were the small players, yes, but they were stronger together. This gave them all the hope they needed. Perhaps it was not a sad, mournful poem after all. It didn't matter what happened to the majestic cedar or the giant whale of the mighty river. Or, in the language of today, the majestic monarchy, the great church, the mighty Inquisition. In the end, the individuals would prevail.

Don Sancho arranged his lips into a devilish curl. There would be no help coming from him. And she would not dignify him by begging. She turned away, no longer able to stand the sight of him.

"Before I go, there is one last spectacle for your entertainment," he said.

She was forced to turn back around.

He took a striker and quartz rock out from beneath his cape, then began to hit the rock against the fire steel. She backed away, watching the sparks fly off his hands. Nothing took.

"It seems I'll need a little help," he said, chuckling. At this, he lifted off his plumed hat. Inside the head covering was a piece of char cloth. This time, a spark landed on the cloth and it ignited. Quickly, he dropped the material onto the Talmud.

"No!" she screamed, leaping forward to save the book.

He blocked her hard, his thick torso connecting with her dislocated shoulder. She flew back to the corner of the cell, screaming in agony.

It was futile. The only thing she could do was watch the sacred text burn, alongside him, in some perverted ceremony of a doomed betrothal.

36

Today was the day of her tribunal. Though Don Sancho had said nothing yesterday, Isabel had an uneasy feeling. All was quiet in the dungeon hallway.

Diego had to come today. He must.

And yet.

If for some reason he didn't make it in time . . .

She forced herself to think the unthinkable. Did she have any regrets? She had loved. She had learned. Studying a Jewish text had given her a sense of belonging, of history. Of God. But she knew there would be others in her place, dying senselessly, before the Inquisition was over. She remembered Señora Maria de Chaues, the woman accused of washing the spot on her infant's head where it had been baptized. Now, in her dank cell, Isabel gingerly made the shape of a cradle with her one good arm. She cooed to an imaginary baby, hers and Diego's, one who would carry on the Jewish line.

Bits and snatches of another poem came to her, from the first poetry reading she had gone to. A lady in a hooded robe had recited a personal piece. By the end, she was sobbing. Isabel had paid her no mind, thinking her a foolish woman revealing her emotions in public that way. Isabel didn't respond to the writing, preferring the more sweeping romantic poems instead. How apt it was now.

The poor lady had lost a child. Today, Isabel was losing a what-might-have-been child. For her future with Diego would never happen. Poetry was like that. You never understood it until you lived it.

> Yes, Time—
> ate up my heart, cleft
> it in two and cut it into bits,
> so that it aches with groaning, panic, plunder,
> confiscation, loss, captivity.
> Why do you crush a mother's heart?
> Why do you aim your arrows at my inmost parts?
> I cannot touch my food, for even honey stings,
> and sweets taste venomous to me.
> Miserably I nibble coal-burnt crusts,
> moistening with tears my dried-out bread.
> My only drink is water mixed with salt from my eyes;
> the blood of grapes does not come near my mouth.

She wished she had remembered it when she and Mamá were at the cemetery. It would have given her mother comfort to know she was not alone. Now it eased Isabel. Though she would not be able to give life, as her name Eva promised, she could die having imagined it. That, at least, was something.

Once again, the lock of her cellar door slid open. A bailiff threw her a sanbenito. She couldn't raise her left arm to put it on and the guard had to do it for her. He was a brute. Tears came to her eyes when he forced it over her arm. As the rough fabric fell over her face, covering her own soiled gown, she smelled the fear of a thousand girls.

Her wrists were tied with cord. As were her feet. Another cord went around her neck. All three of these were knotted together, then secured to yet another longer rope. Isabel was surprised to find other prisoners already tied to the long rope in the hallway. Six in all. Five men and an old woman. Was one of them the man with the hoarse voice who cried out, *There is no God*? She wanted to tell him she understood. If there were a good and compassionate God, then how could He allow a place like the Holy Office to exist? How could God create a world where the rulers had absolute power and twisted and perverted His teachings to fit their theology?

She searched the faces of the men, landing on the one who met her own eyes with his. God isn't to blame for this processional, she told him silently. God is not the punisher. He does not sit on high and decide who will live and who will die. Man does. Woman does. God made us in His image, but He gave us autonomy. Only we have the power to determine our fate. Only we have the power to harm our own soul.

This was the true meaning of free will. Diego would be proud of her.

She took the second position in line. She was the youngest of the group by ten years.

Outside, Isabel felt the sun on her face. She squinted, the harsh light searing eyes that had only seen darkness for days. She moved to shade her brow but, of course, could not raise her hand to do it through the restraints. So she just closed her lids and tilted her chin to the sky.

The drums beat a somber dirge. Though the whole town had gathered on both sides of the street for the processional, she did not scan the crowd for familiar faces. As well as she could, she stepped forward blindly, keeping her eyes closed, nose turned upward.

Tinkling. A sound so lovely and sweet emerged from behind her. Or was it to the side of her? She lowered her upturned face, searching about for the source. A flash of a tambourine. Goatskin pulled taut across the front, bronzed jingles around the perimeter. It got louder and louder. Colors whirling, spinning. A scarved figure shaking the timbrel. Was that . . . No, it couldn't be. Yes! It was Atika! She was creating a diversion like her father, Vano, had when he rescued his beautiful wife from enslavement. Isabel's heart beat as loud as the instrument. Atika had received Isabel's message! Perhaps that meant Diego was not far behind.

And then she saw him. He was in the crowd lining the street to her left. He was masked, like at a costume ball. But she would recognize those shoulders anywhere. The cutouts of the eyes were zeroed in on Atika. Here I am, Isabel wanted to yell, to send them both a signal of some kind. She willed him to see her. But he did not. Atika was the bait. Isabel felt certain that he would strike when the timing was right.

Atika deftly wove through the processional, ducking under the long rope of prisoners that tied everyone together. A friar, standing in between Isabel and the lead accused, glared at her, waving her away.

"You don't belong here, Gypsy!" he cried.

She paid him no mind, continuing to undulate and slap the surface of the *bandair* in a syncopated rhythm. A tall bailiff with pants too short walked beside the line of prisoners, keeping watch over his charges. He was unsightly, with pockmarked cheeks. Atika sidled up to him, tinkling her music. She smiled seductively, flashing her white teeth. The man was awestruck, could not take his eyes off her hips. Suddenly, Diego stepped into the street near the bailiff. Isabel saw Atika's hand reach into the bailiff's front pocket. In one swift motion, she handed a key to Diego. No one noticed a thing.

Watching it all, Isabel immediately wondered: What did he need a key for? To unlock her wrist cuffs? They were tied by rope, not locked irons. Isabel met Diego's gaze. His eyes dropped to her wrists, then went wide, and instantly she knew. He had not planned for this. He assumed he could free her with a key. He looked forlornly at the hemp cord, preventing her movement in three places: wrists, neck, and ankles.

Still the procession continued. The window was closing, the opportunity for escape shrinking.

It was Atika who figured out what to do. Thrusting her hips at the bailiff, she removed his knife from its hilt around his waist. He did not feel anything. She spun around and slipped it to Diego. All at once, Diego was next to Isabel, cutting and slicing the rope at her wrist furiously. Isabel tried to move as far left as she possibly could, to make it easier on him, though the weight of the line of prisoners only allowed her to shift a few centimeters.

Atika continued her dance, whipping her hair into the bailiff's face. Isabel plodded on with the other accused as Diego worked the sharp edge behind her. She could feel that the dagger wasn't cutting the hemp. It was too thick, and even if he did free her wrists, there were also her ankles and neck. Isabel stopped short. The four prisoners behind her stopped as well. The one in front of her was oblivious. He kept walking and she stumbled and fell.

"Ándele!" shouted a different bailiff, poking her with a baton. "Move it!"

She forced her face down onto the ground. Dirt flew into her nostrils. But hopefully, Diego could see that rather than cutting all three points of restraint, he only needed to cut the part where it joined the main rope. They would worry about her ankles, wrists, and neck later.

Slowly, she rose to her feet and felt a gentle tug beside her. In seconds, the rope connecting her to the line of prisoners was severed. He had figured it out! He scooped her up in his arms and they ran.

Someone blew a boatswain's pipe. The drums came to a halt. Everyone was shouting. Friars, bailiffs, spectators.

She wrapped her arms around Diego's neck. She felt his labored breathing through his chest. The bailiffs made chase. Diego darted left into an alley. She recognized it as the one that held the bookbinder's shop.

"It's a dead end!" she yelled.

But Diego kept running. Straight into Isaac's bindery. Isaac stood up from a stool where he was stitching a quire.

Diego yanked off his mask.

"Lord Diego? What are you doing?" Then the bookbinder saw Isabel's sanbenito, her dirty hair and crooked arm, and his expression changed to pity.

"The tunnels!" said Diego.

Without another question, Isaac led them down to the basement, into a storeroom carved out of the dirt. He waited on the stairs, then pulled a trapdoor closed at the top before joining them on the lower level. At the back of the space, no more than ten paces all told, hung a tarp. Isaac pulled it down. Isabel saw an opening there.

Diego finally let her out of his arms so she could stand on her own. He used his knife to cut her ankle and wrist ties, and lastly, the rope around her neck. As he fastened a crude arm sling out of some cloth in Isaac's workroom, she asked him how he knew about the tunnel.

"I guessed as much when I was in the storeroom once before." He grinned at Isaac. "The tarp was hung askew. I reasoned that the Jews must have dug escape routes all over Trujillo once the judería order was given. That's what I would have done."

"Good thing the Inquisitors are not as smart as you," said Isaac.

Diego became serious. "This means more to us than you'll ever know."

Isaac nodded once. "Now go!" He pushed them through the opening. "May God protect you."

Isabel ran through the dark passageway after Diego, single file. It was too narrow for them to hold hands or run together. She had to move sideways and hunch her good shoulder so her head wouldn't hit the ceiling. Each time her foot landed on the ground, it reverberated through her shoulder. All she could do was exhale through the pain.

They ran for what seemed like hours, but Isabel was sure it wasn't. They emerged near the river. It appeared quiet. A few Romanis were washing clothes, but other than that, it was empty. Everyone was at the tribunal. Her tribunal.

"This must be how Isaac smuggles the books out, the sneaky fellow," said Diego.

Isabel didn't understand what he was speaking about, but this was not the time. She was gasping for air. "I need water."

At the riverbank, she tried to cup her hands to make a bowl, but her left arm wouldn't comply and she couldn't get enough water in one palm. Diego's face showed as much pain as she was physically feeling. "Does it hurt?" he asked.

"Not as much now."

"Here, let me," he said, cupping his hands and dipping them into the river. She drank eagerly from them.

She stood up, quenched, and gazed at him. He gently brushed her cheek with the back of his hand. "What did those bastards do to you?"

She leaned into his hand, relishing him. "Later, I'll explain everything."

He put his lips to her cheekbone. "I'm so very sorry, Isabel. Even one day in there would have been a day too long."

How she wanted to stay like this forever.

He held her good hand, the right one, in both of his. "I've gone over what happened at the carriage hundreds of times. I feel like I failed you."

"There were four of them, Diego. Five, counting the spy you knocked out. It was an impossible situation. And you were knifed." She gently touched his rib cage.

He shook his head. "I wish I had planned it better, that's all."

"We're together now, and that is the only thing that matters."

Diego scanned their surroundings. "The bailiffs will catch up to us soon. I need to find us a horse."

Isabel pointed downriver. Two rust-colored steeds were drinking.

Diego nodded. "Some hidalgos', most likely, coming to see the spectacle of the tribunal."

She shuddered, imagining what would have lain ahead if Diego had not come.

Diego opened a leather satchel he wore crossed over his torso. He pulled out a colorful patchwork skirt and white blouse. Atika's. "Put these on. You'll be less conspicuous."

Isabel found a hidden spot behind a cedar tree and large boulder. She would be glad to be rid of the shameful sanbenito. But she could not lift it over her head with her dislocated shoulder. She called him to help.

After he removed the sling and ugly sackcloth gown, he began to unbutton the stays on her filthy dress underneath, the one she had worn the night she left her house. How long ago that seemed.

He laughed. "This is not how I imagined undressing you."

"Nor I," she said, yet goose skin pimpled on her back from his touch. She sighed, enjoying the brief pleasure all over her body after so much abuse.

He left on her undermost layer, a chemise, and kissed the back of her neck. "How do you still smell like roses after so many days?"

"Don't be a daft liar!" she giggled.

"Bury these garments," he instructed her. "I'll steal one of the horses."

While Diego quietly approached the two animals, she used a sharp rock with her good hand to loosen the dirt. Then she wedged the clothes in a hollow beneath one of the tree roots. She covered it all up with the soil.

She saw Diego pat the rear of one of the horses, whispering in its ear. Within a few minutes, he was leading him back to the boulder. "It's a regular saddle, I'm afraid," he told her. "You'll be more comfortable if you straddle it." He looked toward the river. "Don't tarry. I'm not sure where the footman is who watches him."

Atika's skirt had no hoops or layers underneath to limit movement. Isabel was easily able to sit atop the saddle, one leg on either side of the horse's girth. Diego came up behind her and they took off at a gallop immediately. He held the reins with only one hand, wrapping his other arm around Isabel to steady her. Though her shoulder throbbed from the horse's gait, she didn't complain. They were finally together.

The route was familiar, for it was the same pathway they had ridden before. When they got to the bridge, Diego slowed the horse to a walk.

"You warned me about this bridge," she said.

"Yes, but it's still daylight," he told her, though the sun was quite low in the sky. It must be nearing five hours after high noon.

They galloped past the area where they had seen the genet. Where he told her he was Jewish. Where they had first kissed. A short while later, they approached the castle ruins.

"This is where we stop," Diego said, slowing down the horse.

Isabel was confused. She realized she had not asked where they were going. She was just enjoying her freedom and being with Diego. She hadn't thought about a destination at all.

"Are we going to wander forever like the ghost of Princess Noeima?" she asked as they dismounted.

He pointed to the west. "You see that far mountain range? That's Portugal. That will be your new home."

Now, with a slow dawning, she faced the truth. She could not return to Spain. Ever.

37

She gazed out over the tangerine-and-aqua horizon. "So you and I will be together in Portugal?"

"That's my plan," said Diego as he tied up the horse. "But not right away. I have a friend from school riding from Lisbon. Paolo will be here before sundown to take you back with him."

"But what about you?"

"I must return to Trujillo immediately to arrange transport for your family to Portugal. They aren't safe now that you've escaped the Holy Office. It's only a matter of a day or two before they'll be taken in and questioned for any information on your where-abouts. My servant, Martín, will go to them."

"But he knows to tell my parents nothing of your plan, correct?"

"Yes, but the torturers don't know they are in the dark."

Isabel felt horrible for putting her family in danger like this. "Why did that blasted spy have to find us that night?"

"We couldn't have anticipated the ambush, Isabel. If our plan had worked and we'd gotten away, your family would have had a little more time. But not much."

She nodded. This was the reality of their situation and they must not dwell in the past.

He smiled. "I have friends in Lisbon. In addition to Paolo, there's my Hebrew professor, Aron ben Cardoza. I've arranged for you to live with him and his wife and children until I can get back there."

"An openly Jewish family," she said excitedly.

"I can't wait to tell him in person about my heritage, too." Diego smiled. "Though he probably won't be surprised, given how I drank up what little bit of Hebrew he had time to impart before I left." He tenderly touched the sling. "And by the time I get there, this will be healed."

"Ojalá," she said. She hoped so. Isabel gathered her hair at her nape, longing for a comb or even scissors to chop off the knots and tangles. "How will I contact you?"

"You mustn't. My father can't see any letters arriving for me in a woman's hand. It will be too suspicious. Paolo will check on you at the ben Cardozas and write to me. My parents know his seal. He's the son of a duque." His eyebrows moved together in concern. "Isabel, please understand that it will be a while until we meet again. I need to get back to my normal life for a time. Paint with Berruguete. Collect taxes. Gather maravedís little by little so my parents don't notice. I don't want either of them to question what I do. I think it should take about three months. Then I will join you in Lisbon."

"And my parents?"

"Martín will smuggle them out the way we just traveled. With a couple more horses and a mule, of course."

"They won't take much with them, you can be assured of that." One thing her mother was *not* was sentimental with her possessions. Beatriz, on the other hand, with her dresses and veils, was unpredictable. Isabel was grateful she wouldn't be there to watch her sister try to choose what to pack. Leaving Juan Carlos would be difficult enough for Beatriz. But Isabel was certain the safety of her own family would rule in the end and Beatriz would do what she was told. Portugal was closer than Florence. Perhaps Abuela could make it after all.

"With any luck, they should be joining you in one week," promised Diego.

"So this is goodbye?" ventured Isabel, her heart already aching with loss.

His eyes told her everything.

She fell against him, crying. "You saved me."

"I would do it over and over."

His arms enclosed her. She cleaved herself to him, listening to the sound of their breathing blend with the din of the forest— birds cawing, cicadas whirring, water rushing. After a time, he gently created some space so he could look at her.

"Don't move. I want to paint you," he whispered.

"But you have no brushes."

"I'll draw you in my mind."

They remained in that position, the artist and his muse, until the sun teetered before its final descent.

38

For nearly three days, Isabel and Paolo made their way across the mountain range to Portugal. Thankfully, Paolo had brought an extra pair of boots, which were much sturdier and warmer than her worn leather slippers. The nights were so cold that even wrapping herself in Diego's green-and-red-striped cloak did little good. Still, she cherished it. He had draped it over her shoulders before he left. It was the only thing she had of his. The illustrated note, the one with the peacock feathers on the border, was tucked away in a drawer at home. She cheered herself with the certainty that there would be many more drawings to come in their future. Perhaps one of her as an old lady, she thought amusedly.

During the daylight rides, Paolo distracted her with talk of his classes at university. She told him about her life in Trujillo, so different from his privileged life in Asturius. But at night when they made camp, her mind spun with horrific images. The beaten-up men of the Cohen family. The hooded masks of her torturers, with only their cruel eyes peeking out. The rack she was raised and lowered from.

She had to sleep sitting up, the way she had done in the prison cell, because if she lay down, her shoulder hurt too much. Any pressure on it was excruciating. So Paolo set up a lean-to with a tarp and a long stick, stacking their supplies behind her back for support.

On the third day, the wind carried the briny smell up the hill before she even caught her first glimpse of the sea. It delighted her.

Paolo explained that Lisbon was actually at the mouth of the Tagus River, which led to the ocean. The Tagus River was the very same river she and Diego had ridden beside. It made her feel like she had something familiar from home in this new country.

Lisbon looked nothing like Trujillo. White town houses lined the streets, which were nearly all paved or cobblestoned. Where Trujillo was flat, Lisbon seemed to be built on one giant hill, with all roads leading to the port below. The city teemed with people and animals, assaulting her sense of smell. Heaps of dung. Carts with the sour odor of the deceased, their bare feet sticking out beyond burlap covers. The acrid fish market.

The ben Cardozas lived on the first floor of a stucco town house in the Alfama barrio. Aron wasn't at home when Isabel and Paolo arrived, but his wife was. She answered the door holding the hand of one child, about four years old, and balancing another on her hip. Her features were lovely, with almond-shaped blue eyes that reminded Isabel of Atika. Inside, a dark wooden ceiling sagged low. The floor was tiled, but the colors were dull. Upon closer look, Isabel noticed the tiles had some sort of sandy covering. Though the house was not fancy, it felt like a home.

The woman lowered the child on her hip, who promptly crawled away on the dusty floor. "I'm Esther," she said, smiling. "This is Judah. And the baby is Ruth."

Judah grabbed Isabel's hand immediately. The one in the sling.

She winced, but took a deep breath and forced a smile, not wanting to hurt the boy's feelings. This was not lost on Esther. She gently pulled her son away from Isabel. "Leave her be, Judah. It's been a long journey." She turned to Isabel. "I'll get a doctor to look at that shoulder, all right?"

Paolo took his leave, promising to come visit when he received word from Diego. Then Esther showed her the room she and Judah would share. There was a pallet and a small cot, a dresser and a washbasin. Other than some carved wooden animals and a wooden boat in the corner, it was spotless.

Isabel pointed to the toys. "Is that Noah's ark?"

Esther nodded. "I'll get Judah to take them out so you'll have more space."

"No, please. I like looking at them." They reminded her of Abuela. Not the toys, exactly, but the biblical story. Abuela said the forty-day flood was a cleansing process for the earth. That the rainwater was like the mikveh bath, washing away all negativity for whomever it touched.

The doctor came, a hunchbacked man who wore a blue skullcap. He gave her something bitter to drink. It made her very sleepy. When he set her arm back in its socket, she only screamed once, the sound blending in with the baby's crying.

Aron ben Cardoza was short and thin and looked more like a bird than a person. He was a man of few words, preferring to read rather than talk. When he discovered Isabel knew the aleph-bet, he showered her with books. Esther doted on her like an older sister, giving her some of her own dresses and rubbing lanolin into her shoulder. Isabel passed the first few days happily, her arm in a more proper sling. And on Friday night, she was overjoyed to have her first Shabbat meal in a sala with moonlight coming in through the window.

On Sunday, she asked Esther for a quill and parchment to pen a letter to Atika. Hopefully, someone in the encampment would read it to her. Though she couldn't write Diego, nor the Cohens, whom she thought about often, at least she could pour out her heart to her dear friend and thank her for her bravery. Isabel had no idea how long it would take to be delivered. Esther told her one needed to find a messenger on horseback, at the dock, most likely. And that there was a cost involved.

"I'm afraid I have nothing to pay him with," said Isabel, embarrassed.

Esther patted her on her good hand. "Never you mind. I'll take care of it."

On the following Thursday, the clip-clop of horses near Isabel's window woke her up. Judah had been long awake and out of the room. Within minutes, someone was knocking on the front door. She waited, but the knocking persisted. It seemed no one from the family was home. Isabel opened the main entrance wearing Esther's nightdress.

There stood her parents and Beatriz, all looking bedraggled, but alive, before her.

They embraced and shed an ocean of tears. Mamá seemed less affectless, perhaps a result of having to be vigilant on their journey over. It must have been so much harder for her parents than for her, leaving the home they knew and coming to a strange land. Mamá kept touching Isabel's face, reassuring herself that her daughter was real.

Isabel looked beyond them to the street. "Where's Abuela?"

Mamá, Papá, and Beatriz fell silent.

"She stayed in Trujillo, preferring to tend to Soli's grave than ride a horse over the mountains, didn't she?" Isabel said.

Mamá shook her head. "Your grandmother is dead."

Isabel stopped breathing. "When?"

"She passed away the morning after you were captured," said Beatriz with more compassion than Isabel thought her capable of.

So Abuela knew about the Holy Office. Isabel had caused her grandmother's death after all. She hated herself. And at the same time, she longed to hear Abuela's voice one last time. Tears fell down Isabel's cheeks.

"It's not your fault," said Mamá. "She was called to God. It was simply her time."

But this gave Isabel no comfort. Nobody would ever know her the way Abuela did. She stared at her family through wet eyes. They shared the same blood, but at this moment, Isabel felt she had little else in common with them.

Beatriz yawned, surveying the interior of the town house. "I need a bath," she declared, punctuating Isabel's very thought.

Despite the ben Cardozas insisting the Perezes all stay in their small flat, Isabel did not want to put them out more than she already had. Ruth had been sleeping with Esther and Aron, and Isabel knew the baby was keeping Esther up at night. So Mamá sold the sapphire ring from Don Sancho to pay an innkeeper one month's rent. How smart Mamá was to bring it with her! And good riddance to that hideous reminder of her past.

The Perez family gradually adjusted to life in Lisbon. Papá's hearing returned in one ear and, with it, his diction. He was able to find work with a local winemaker. Mamá helped a laundress who owned a shop below the inn. Beatriz collected food for the poor with the nuns of the Carmo Convent.

But the best part about Lisbon was that the long arm of Torquemada had not reached the city. There was a community of Portuguese Jews, of which the ben Cardozas were a part. But more Jews were coming in each week, fleeing the Inquisition. The Portuguese king required each Jew to pay a tax of eight *real brancos* for the right to enter Portugal. Though the Perezes had come illegally, by horseback, Papá did not want to take advantage of their welcome and insisted on paying the tax. This meant they could not move out of the inn into their own home for another few months, but it made Papá feel proud.

Seeing the ben Cardozas light candles on Friday evenings gave Mamá and Papá the courage to stop being New Christians. Everyone except Beatriz joined Esther and Aron in attending sinagoga to celebrate Tu BiShvat, the feast of fruits. This holiday marked one of four cycles in the new year, when the sap ran and the trees awakened from their slumber. Sitting in the women's section, Isabel and Mamá recited Kaddish, the mourner's prayer, for Abuela. They held hands as tears streamed down their faces. It was an awakening not just for the trees.

One Shabbat evening, after more than two months in Lisbon, Isabel asked Esther about Paolo. She was trying not to worry, but she had heard nothing. "Has he been by the house? Perhaps he doesn't know where to find me at the inn."

Esther placed a spinach frittata on the table. Even with Isabel's shoulder as good as new, she wouldn't let her lift a finger. Only Mamá and Beatriz were allowed to help in the kitchen, though Beatriz mostly scowled in the corner. "You know I would tell him where to find you. But he hasn't come."

"But maybe he stopped by when you were out with the children, and left a note?"

Esther shook her head.

Isabel was despondent. She could not sleep another night without word of Diego. If Paolo would not come to her, then she would go to him.

"Where are my vestments?" roared Count Altamirano. He stomped through the corridors of the family's private chambers upstairs, sending Concha scurrying like a mouse.

Diego was in his own bedroom, washing his hands in preparation for supper. He had been thinking of Berruguete and the look on the flatterer's face when Diego announced he was leaving. Diego would find a Portuguese artist to work with, one who didn't pander to the Inquisition.

His father stormed into his room. "Did you borrow my armor?"

"Why would I take something that does not even fit me?"

"I wouldn't know. Perhaps your famous Berruguete wanted to paint someone in formal battle attire? Blasted things. How can three large pieces of decorated metal go missing?"

The truth was, Diego had sold them to a grandee passing through town from Saragossa. He was slowly selling off obscure pieces from the house, amassing enough money to start a life for himself and Isabel in Lisbon. He had found buyers for a tea set his mother never used, a ruby necklace (she had three just like it), some swords without the Altamirano crest, and a crucifix carved out of quartz. Now, it seemed, he had gone too far in selling his father's breastplate.

"Did you check the place of arms?" asked Diego, trying to appear helpful.

"Whom do you take me for? A dunce? That was the first place I checked. The various Altamirano Knights' shields are all there, but my gilded breastplate and sleeves are not."

Diego needed to divert his father's attention from the missing uniform. "How goes the work of the Familiars, Father?"

But his father would not be deterred, even with Inquisition talk. "The archbishop of Toledo is coming to the alcazarejo and I must receive him in formal wear. As long as I can show the representative of our beloved queen and king that the Order of Calatrava is alive and well, they will cease this senseless stripping of our power. My fellow nobles are counting on me."

Diego cared not one coin for the religious military order his father belonged to. It was a group in name only, and it did nothing to help Spain's cause. He could not stomach this life much longer. He was nearly ready to leave for Portugal. He just needed to sell one more object of art and he would be on his way.

"Torquemada will also be accompanying the archbishop," his father informed him. "You'll need to be here, too, tomorrow evening. I should have ordered something custom-forged for you. But alas, I did not. So be it. Your fanciest doublet and ruff will have to suffice."

"Torquemada will be in this house?"

His father straightened up even taller. "It is a great honor, indeed. We will have a grand feast."

Diego exhaled through his nose. "I cannot abide this, Father. I'm sorry."

The count blinked, the gray in his mustache glinting in the lamplight. "What are you blathering about?"

"I will not stand next to you if that bastard comes to our home." It was too much, the idea of looking into his eyes, imagining the friars who followed him blindly like sheep and what they did to his Isabel.

His father slapped him across the face. "How dare you insult the Grand Inquisitor. You're lucky no servants heard your insult. Insensitive and dangerous, that's what you are. You will stand next to me, Diego, or I'll . . ."

"You'll what? Turn me in to the Holy Office?"

The count stepped close to Diego, so that their faces nearly touched. "Your mother told me everything. About your little conversation in the chapel and your ensuing scuffle on the street. Do you think she keeps secrets from me? I am the one in charge here! All it takes is one official letter with my seal, and I can turn you from the son of a count right back into a dirty Jew."

"Then what would that make you, Father?"

The count squeezed Diego's upper arm, holding him in place. "Don't tempt me enough to find out."

Spittle flew into Diego's eye. He wriggled out of his father's grasp, shaken.

As the count slammed the heavy wooden door behind him, Diego knew he could not stay one more night in this house. He did not trust his father. The count could very well destroy his mother, too, claiming the Jewish seductress put a spell on him or some such nonsense, and Diego did not want her to suffer.

He would take what money he had and leave for Portugal by nightfall.

39

Beatriz fell ill with the sweating sickness and Isabel could not go to the University of Coimbra to look for Paolo. She and Mamá took turns nursing Beatriz. The illness came on violently with cold shivers, headache, and severe pains in her neck. After two days of this, Beatriz became listless and fell into a dreamless sleep, barely waking to sip water. Isabel knew that if the situation were reversed and she took ill, Beatriz would claim it was divine punishment for her going to sinagoga or some such thing. But unlike her sister, Isabel took no pleasure in seeing anyone suffer.

A week into Beatriz's illness, Isabel went to the village market to buy cork bark for her father. She overheard a troubling conversation between two women, Old Christians most likely, from the sound of it.

"My servant has the sweating sickness," said the shorter one. "I sent her away to her mother's house."

Isabel almost interrupted them, wondering if there was something more she could do to help Beatriz.

The second woman covered her nose with a piece of linen cloth, and stepped back from her friend, not wanting to be close in case the servant had exposed her. "It's the Jews, I tell you. They brought it here."

The short woman nodded, making the sign of the cross. "I still remember the plague from fifty years ago. They can't be trusted. It's their fault we are in a drought, too."

Isabel shook her head. Portugal was no different than Spain.

Perhaps Beatriz dwelt closer to the Lord after all, because she did not die. Isabel had been sitting with her, giving Mamá a needed break, when her sister opened her eyes and asked for some soup. Isabel was so overcome with relief, she kissed her on the cheek.

"How many days have I been sick?" asked Beatriz.

"Thirteen," replied Isabel.

Her sister gazed at her in surprise, her long nose crinkling. "And you stayed with me the entire time?"

"Me and Mamá, yes."

Beatriz reached for Isabel and hugged her. They stayed like that, Isabel's stronger arms encompassing the thinness of her sister's shoulders. It felt strange, this sisterly reconciliation. But she welcomed it.

Beatriz laid her head back down, exhausted from the mere effort of waking up. "I don't think anyone will ever care for me the way you both have."

"Nonsense," said Isabel. "One day, your husband will sit by your side like we—" She stopped. This was not her sister's future. Beatriz wanted to serve her Lord and Savior, not a spouse.

Beatriz closed her eyes. "It's all right, Sister. No need to hold your tongue."

It was just that with Diego in her life now, it made Isabel wish Beatriz could find the same earthly love as she had. "Do you ever think about Juan Carlos?"

Beatriz turned on her side, away from the conversation.

Isabel stood, remorse flooding her for bringing up the subject. "Forgive me. I'll go get you that soup."

When Isabel came back to the room, she held the spoon out to Beatriz. Her sister's eyes were still shut. She didn't seem to want the soup anymore.

"Juan Carlos did not choose me."

Isabel startled at the unexpected statement.

"He wanted someone else. Someone fairer of face. With thicker hair and a nose that won't poke him in the eye. He found that in Señorita Magdalena de Espina."

"Oh, Beatriz. I'm so sorry."

Beatriz lifted a weak hand and touched her scalp.

Only then did Isabel finally figure it out. Beatriz drew blood from her own skin not because of the zealotry of doing penance for her sins, but because of something much simpler than that. Love. Which, unrequited, turned to hate. Hatred of herself. Poor Beatriz. It felt better to hurt on the outside than on the inside. What was it that Don Sancho had said when he came into Isabel's prison cell to taunt her? *I know what I look like. What could you ever see in me?*

"I knew a man once," began Isabel, "who thought his countenance would never please a woman. He was right. But not because of his looks. It was because of his spirit. He was evil down deep. You are the opposite, Beatriz. Your soul is good. And therefore, you are beautiful to me."

Beatriz rolled onto her back and took Isabel's hand. "I saw death, Sister, and I am no longer afraid of the truth. I am what I am. But I've made a decision. I don't want to join the Carma Order after all. There are those who need me more than God does. Since I won't be having children of my own, I'm going to devote myself to your children."

"I would be honored," Isabel murmured. They were more alike than she thought, her sister and she. They both wanted to choose their own destiny, to act with free will. Isabel, to marry a man she loved, and Beatriz, to live a life of service outside the Church. They were each rebelling against tradition in their own way.

It was a crisp winter morning when Isabel finally slipped away to search for Paolo. She paid a runny-nosed page a half *dinheiro* to cart her to the university.

"But that's in Coimbra," he insisted, wiping his nose with the back of his hand. "A day's journey from here."

One whole day? Diego had said his school was in Lisbon. She was sure of it. "Can you ask someone else? Maybe you're mistaken."

He laughed at her. "I was born in this city." Nevertheless, he obliged her and walked down the block to a well-dressed squire standing in front of a gilded carriage.

When the page returned, he was sheepish. "You're in luck. There are two locations for the school. One here, the other in Coimbra. I never would have guessed it." She prayed luck was indeed with her and that Paolo would be at this campus.

The school was situated in the Alfama neighborhood, just up the hill from the ben Cardoza house. When the page dropped her off, she was enchanted, imagining Diego walking among the thick stone columns or under the scalloped archways. Other than their church in Trujillo, she had never seen buildings this grandiose before. In the center of the red roofs and almost blinding white buildings lay an expanse of grass with a tree planted in the middle. It had the thickest trunk Isabel had ever seen. Its leaves fluttered in the sea breeze, revealing silver on the underside and bright green on top. How lucky Diego was to be able to walk these grounds and receive an education at the same time!

All the students looked alike, in black robes that reached their knees and black square caps upon their heads. She had to start somewhere, so she stopped a pair of young men passing through the archway near her.

"No women allowed," said the blond one, scowling at her.

The red-haired student grinned flirtatiously and stepped closer to her. "But we won't tell."

She took a step back and asked about Paolo. She realized she had no idea what his surname was. Just that he was a son of a duque. That seemed to be enough. They knew him all right. But they hadn't seen him today. Had she tried his house off campus? The flirtatious one said he would walk her there. Then his friend reminded him that a professor wanted to meet with them. It would be impossible.

Isabel was in low spirits. She hadn't told the page to wait for her. Now she'd have to walk down the hill to a main street and order another cart to take her to Paolo's house. As she headed back toward the school entrance, the blond student came running back to her, his cap askew. He pointed in the direction of a large round building, next to the clock tower. "Before you leave, you might try the library. If Paolo is on campus, he can usually be found there." Then he darted away.

Isabel entered the rotunda. A double stairway was before her, bordered on both sides by tiles of blue, yellow, and white flowers. Above her, a gold ceiling held paintings of cherubs, some shooting arrows and some flying through crystal-blue sky. Did Diego stare at this artist's work and wish he had painted it? To her left was a rectangular room with desks and partitions. Many students were seated inside, bent over books. She wandered through the rows, trying to peer underneath the caps. No one looked up, their concentration admirable. She wanted to yell, "Paolo!" but knew from the absolute silence that this would not be appropriate.

At the end of one of the rows, she spotted a familiar neckline, long hair tied back in the style Diego wore. Paolo. She rushed over, tapping him on the shoulder.

He looked up, his cheeks pinkening at the sight of her. "Isabel," he whisper-spoke. "You shouldn't be here."

"I don't mean to make you uncomfortable," she told him. "But I'm worried about Diego."

Standing, he motioned for her to follow him.

Once outside, he took off his cap and fidgeted with the collar of his gown.

She waited for him to speak, becoming more and more impatient by the second.

He stared at the ground. "I'm sorry I haven't come before now. I didn't know how to tell you."

"Tell me what?" she asked, her heart hammering.

"Diego was ambushed on the Puente de Juan de Carvajal."

"Ambushed?"

"By smugglers."

No! Dark images came to her. She wouldn't think it.

"It seems he didn't make it."

"Wh . . . what do you mean? Where is he?"

"His horse came back to Trujillo, found its way to the alcazarejo somehow. But there was no rider." He paused. "I'm sorry, Isabel. More than likely, Diego is dead."

She fell to her knees. Paolo wasn't quick enough to catch her. And she wouldn't have let him anyway. She wanted to sink into the earth, through the grass and into the darkest soil. Let her body rot with the worms. Let her go back to the dust she was made of.

Diego reached the foot of the bridge and gazed up at the inky sky. The sun had long set. He should probably make camp here for the night, but once his father discovered him gone, the count would send out a search party. He needed to get as far away from Trujillo as possible. In fact, at some point, he should have tied up his horse and backtracked over his route, brushing over the hoof marks. Damn. He hadn't thought of that.

He squirted some wine from his bota bag into his mouth. If he rode all night, he would be in his Isabel's arms by tomorrow evening, or the morning after that at the latest.

Kicking the sides of his horse, Diego urged the animal over the bridge. He was traveling light. Just one change of clothes and the money from selling his parents' things—all buried in a pack, tied behind the saddle.

He didn't hear them approach.

The horse did, though, rearing up in fright, nearly knocking Diego off.

"Tranquilo," said Diego, patting the horse on his neck.

Diego counted three men, about 150 meters away. Smugglers. In the dusky light, he could make out a handcannon in one of their arms. How did these pícaros get hold of artillery? His pulse quickened.

"Take my pack," Diego called out to them. "There's over seventy-five hundred maravedis inside." Diego held up his hands. "I'm just going to reach behind me and untie it for you." His sword lay strapped to his right hip. He would draw his weapon and charge at them on the horse.

"Párate!" said one of the men. "Stop!"

Maybe Diego didn't stop his hand fast enough or he thought the verbal threat was simply that, just a warning. Or he thought he was invincible.

Did a shot ring out? Were the smugglers lucky with their iron ball catapulting from a gun at close range? Or did the hand-cannon backfire and the person igniting it get killed instead, allowing Diego time to escape?

40

Isabel awoke into silence. The room she shared with Beatriz at the inn was quiet. It was the unknowing that hit her so hard each morning, more acute than any torture she had endured at the hands of the Inquisitors. Was Diego alive or dead? Her life for the past month had not been a life at all. Abuela once mentioned a rabbi in the Talmud who created something called a golem. It was a creature with the semblance of a man but without a soul or the ability to speak. Isabel was like that golem. Her body was functioning, but her mind was inactive. She could not write a line of poetry, much less read a book or carry on a conversation. Mamá and Papá could not figure out what was ailing her.

She had to do something to shake herself out of her stupor. For existing in this in-between state was not acceptable. It was as if all that free will she had exercised in Trujillo—to meet Diego in secret, to study Talmud, to defy the Inquisitors—had disappeared. She forced herself to place one foot in front of the other, go through her morning hygiene routine, and get dressed.

The mikveh was three streets away, directly across from Aron's sinagoga. She had not yet stepped inside nor, frankly, thought much about it since she had visited the judería and met those girls. It was time.

It was her first day out on the street in weeks. Through a

haze, details slowly came into focus for her. The staircases and alleyways. Awnings protruding from shopwindows. Peasants, merchants, waifs, and maids weaving in and out of one another in a crowded dance.

Entering the mikveh, she saw the glazed black-and-white tiles laid in pinwheels on the floor. She smelled the humidity and heard the *plink-plink* of the moisture dripping from the ceiling. She tasted her own lips, dry from nerves.

"Your name?" asked a woman with round cheeks, her blue robe floating behind her.

Isabel stared at her, unblinking.

The woman waited patiently for Isabel's answer. Suddenly, her vision blurred again, and the woman's features rearranged themselves, shape-shifting into Abuela's forehead, eyes, nose, and lips. Her grandmother was here.

"Your name, *senhorita*?" the woman repeated. "I'll need it for the blessing."

She would be cleansed. Like the floodwaters did to Noah's land. Like Qasmūna and all the Jewish women in her family before they converted. She would be pure. She would no longer be tainted.

"Eva."

She stepped down seven steps into a pool fed by an underground spring. Shivering from the tepid water, she slowly lowered her whole body in, up to her neck. She held her breath and let the water cover her chin, her eyes, the top of her head. As Eva, she could start anew. As Eva, she would wait for Diego. For as long as it took.

41

One Friday night, some months later, Aron ben Cardoza ran into the house in the Alfama. Eva was pulling oranges and herbs out of the hollow of a roasted chicken that Esther had prepared. Mamá and Beatriz were setting the table and Papá was reading a book by the window. The two families had become quite close and enjoyed Shabbat dinners together every week.

"Quick, get to the cellar," shouted Aron, scooping up the baby from the floor. "Everyone!"

Esther stopped pouring wine from the decanter. "Has something happened?"

"In Rossio Square," said Aron, his lips pressed tightly together.

"Not an auto de fe?" asked Papá, glancing at Mamá, no doubt remembering the day he ran into the house in Trujillo with the same fearful expression.

"Worse," said Aron.

Beatriz took little Judah's hand and they all descended the stairs into the cellar. The ben Cardozas' lowest floor was tinier than the Perez's former one. They were not wine producers. It was used to store grains and vegetables. The eight of them squeezed in, knees touching, as they sat cross-legged on the floor. Baby Ruth cried and Esther shushed her with her breast milk.

"I'll light an oil lamp," said Eva.

Esther nodded. "Thank you, Isabel."

"You mean, Eva," corrected Papá.

Esther smiled sheepishly. It was hard for everyone to get used to using the name Eva, even new friends who hadn't called Isabel that her entire life. For some reason, Papá found it the easiest. It was as if his own mother, Abuela, was in his head all the time now.

"I know only what I heard relayed at the sinagoga," replied Aron.

"When was this?" asked Beatriz.

"Shhh. Let him speak," Mamá said.

"Yesterday. Holy Thursday."

Eva recalled hearing the bells beckoning everyone to Mass. Beatriz had wanted to go, but instead decided to watch the children of an Old Christian family who wished to worship unencumbered.

"The whole town was in church," Aron recounted. "The sunlight streamed in through the leaded glass windows and someone swore they could see the illuminated face of *Jesus Cristo* on the altar. The faithful were greatly moved by this vision on such an auspicious day. *Jesus* was there! He had risen!"

"That does sounds miraculous," agreed Beatriz. Since her illness, she had softened her religious fervor. Her tenets had become just a set of beliefs, without judgment.

Aron frowned. "Until a New Christian in another pew chuckled and whispered to the person next to him that it was no miracle at all. Just a reflection of an altar candle on the crucifix."

Mamá gasped.

"Others heard this blasphemy and dragged the New Christian, a man named João Silveira, outside, where he was beaten to death by the crowd. Then they burned his body in Rossio Square."

The small room fell silent.

"I'm afraid that's not the end of it." Aron wiped his forehead with his shirt, not daring to dirty his prayer shawl. "Today, a Dominican friar preached absolution to the ones who killed the New Christian. With no fear of repercussions, foreign sailors from the docks are joining angry townspeople and grabbing *convertos* from their homes accusing them of deicide and heresy. They are running through the streets as I speak."

Faint shouting could be heard coming from above, though it was likely streets away from theirs.

"Deicide?" asked Eva.

"The killing of a God," answered Papá. "Or in this case, *Jesus Cristo.*"

"Where's King Manuel?" asked Beatriz. "Surely he will protect his subjects." Eva noted how her sister did not attempt to debate the veracity of the deicide accusation, but instead showed her concern for the Jews.

"He's gone to his summer residence in Abrantes," said Aron. "There is talk that he's afraid of another plague in the city."

"I believe it," said Eva, remembering the conversation she overheard at the mercado.

Aron put his arm around Esther. "Everyone at the sinagoga is afraid. Today it's the *convertos* caught up in the bloodbath. Tomorrow it will be us. The only thing to do is leave."

Esther seemed bewildered. "Leave Lisbon?"

"On the first ship where we can book passage," said Aron grimly. "It's not safe here anymore. We'll go to Venice, where my uncle lives." He turned to Papá. "I know you'll be welcome in his home as well."

Papá sighed. "I am weary from running."

Mamá turned to him. "Aron is right. Portugal will go the way of Spain."

"No!" shouted Eva.

Frightened, the baby started crying again.

"We can't leave here," Eva blurted out. "Not yet." If they left for Italy, Diego might never find her again.

All eyes were on her. They wanted an explanation. She hadn't yet told her family about her relationship with Diego. Esther and Aron had kept her confidence until she was ready to share it. All her parents knew was that a benefactor helped pay their way out of Spain and into Portugal. They had never questioned it, most likely out of fear of the Holy Office. A gift was being given to them; theirs was not to ask why. Eva planned to tell them eventually. Here in Lisbon, the idea of marrying a grandee who was once a Jew seemed more plausible than in Spain, but with her broken shoulder and Mamá and Papá trying to save for a place of their own and Beatriz's sickness and her own fugue-like state when Diego never came back, the time had not been right to reveal him to her family.

Eva felt frantic, desperate for a way out. "Why don't you go ahead. Someone has to stay and close up the house." She looked at Esther. "Safeguard your belongings for when you return? I will arrange everything."

Aron's and Esther's eyes met briefly. Eva caught it. They were never coming back to Lisbon.

"And then you'll travel to Venice after that?" asked Mamá, believing her scheme.

Eva hesitated.

Papá shook his head. "Out of the question. We are not separating." He took Eva's hand. "I won't risk losing you again."

"Papá's right," said Beatriz, agreeing with their father for the first time ever.

"I can't guarantee your safety, Eva," said Aron. "Nor would we sleep peacefully, knowing you were here all alone."

Eva looked at each and every one of them. The family that raised her and the family that saved her. She owed them. What a selfish girl, thinking only of herself when the world was crumbling around them. Even Abuela would not have approved.

She turned her face into the cold stone wall so no one could see her tears.

So it was settled. Aron pooled all their money and bought passage for eight on the merchant vessel, *São Michael*, bound for Venice the following week. In between packing what precious items they could carry and selling the rest, the ben Cardozas mourned their community. When the week was through, over two thousand Portuguese *converto* Jews had been dragged from their homes and burned.

On their last day in Lisbon, Eva went to the University of Coimbra and handed Paolo a note, instructing him to give it to Diego when he came back.

Paolo's eyes were full of pity. "Surely, you don't believe—"

"I didn't ask for your opinion," interrupted Eva. She had no patience for him since he had not bothered to find her and tell her himself when Diego's horse returned riderless. He was a coward, but he was all she had. "Guard it with your life."

The note explained they were sailing for Venice and that she could be found at the house of Aron's uncle, Daniel the loan-banker.

She did not bother to say goodbye.

*   *   *

Seven members of the Perez and ben Cardoza families carried one suitcase each, and Esther wore a sling for the baby. Even Judah gripped a travel bag in his small hand as they walked to the docks on the morning of April 15. It was still dark, the early hour chosen by Aron, since their neighbor had even accused an Old Christian of heresy two days prior. Everyone was turning on each other in an effort to deflect the attention away from themselves. No one was safe.

A man ran by Eva, his arms full of silver chalices and serving pieces. He accidentally bumped her bad shoulder and knocked her to the ground, shouting angrily in German as if it were her fault.

Papá helped her up.

Aron's eyes darted up and down the street. "They are looting the empty homes of *convertos*. Don't get between them and their plunder." Thankfully, after that, there were no more incidents.

The sun was a sliver of light peeking above the horizon when they boarded the four-masted, square-sailed ship.

"Seems sturdy enough," said Mamá, dropping her heavy suitcase on the wooden deck.

Aron explained to them it was a carrack or long-range cargo vessel, the only thing he could get at such short notice. Not that any of the Portuguese ships were built for passengers. There were only two types: naval and cargo.

"At least this one doesn't contain any arms," said Papá. "The voyage will be dangerous enough as it is."

Eva didn't care about rough seas or warfare. She kept looking toward the Alfama neighborhood, hoping to see Diego limping down the hill.

"Where do we sleep?" asked Beatriz.

A purser took them below deck to the mid-cabin, filled with sleeping berths three bodies high. The air was stuffy and smelled repulsive. Eva felt her stomach give way, acid coating her tongue. She swallowed it down, trying to make the best of the poor conditions.

"We're bedding next to the sailors?!" exclaimed a shocked Beatriz.

A crewman nearby leered at her by way of an answer. She huffed and crossed her arms over her chest.

When eventually the *São Michael* was towed out of dock, Eva stayed on deck, watching the shore until it was a distant line, then a dot, and then, finally, the place of Diego's university was no more.

42

Within two days, everyone in the Perez and ben Cardoza families became seasick. No one had been on a ship before. The sailors laughed at their weak stomachs and didn't bother removing ropes from their pathway when they tried to stroll on the main deck. Eva survived the ordeal by sitting in a corner on the upper deck and penning poems. These weren't love poems, though. They were filled with dark details from her past. Flickers of flames under stakes. Boatswains' pipes. Skeletal cheekbones of Inquisitors. Wet cloths in throats. Cracked shoulders. Scorched Talmuds. Hebrew letters—*mem*, *vav*, *chet*—spelling out death. She was cleansing her mind, like the mikveh did to her body, leaving memories on the parchment. With each word written, she felt stronger. More hopeful. Diego wasn't dead. She felt him whisper to her every night when she fell asleep, the ocean lapping against the hull beneath her.

Thankfully, the weather cooperated and other than a torn sail that took a day to repair, there were no other delays.

Beatriz successfully fended off unwanted advances from sailors who'd been at sea too long. She even held a daily Bible study group for the men. Papá befriended someone who ran the galley and told the man everything he ever wanted to know about turning grapes into wine. Mamá helped Esther with the children and

Aron watched the horizon for potential storms or enemy ships. Judah charmed a crusty former sea captain from Holland who played cards with the boy.

The crew and passengers ate biscuits, sardines, and lentils mostly, but twice a week were given beef or pork. The two Jewish families could hardly refuse the pork, as the rations were so small. So they ate what they were given. Aron said the Torah gave them permission not to starve. They drank water and wine, the grapes helping to prevent scurvy. One night they feasted on fresh bass caught en route. There was a large vat of rice to go with it.

Washing was also rationed, as there were only enough basins and water for sponge baths once a week. Since the only women on board were Esther, Mamá, Beatriz, and Eva, they were able to wash in their own basin inside a supply closet.

When a crew member climbed a mast and announced, "*Terra ho*," everyone cheered with great gusto. Land was here.

Judah pointed at the coastline. "It's a castle, Mamá!"

"That's the Doge's Palace," said Esther. "Where the ruler of Venice makes the laws."

"And what are those skinny boats?" asked the boy.

"Gondolas," she answered. "People ride them around town, instead of horses and carriages."

Beatriz joined them at the railing. "You mean there's even more water than meets the eye?"

"Canals," answered Aron. "A whole system of them."

It did look magical. Shiny tiled domes, imposing clock towers, matching red rooftops. Like a floating city. But when Eva stepped foot on her first patch of solid ground in twenty-five days, she was wistful. She should have been entering Italy with Diego. He was the one who first told her about the wonders of this country.

43

"Today's my eighth birthday," said Mauricio. He was an odd boy, serious like his nobleman father, Signore Correr.

"You had just turned seven when we started working together," said Eva. Had it really been almost a year since she'd arrived in Venice? Her seventeenth birthday had come and gone. But Eva had chosen that day to finally tell Mamá and Papá about Diego. It felt like a present to herself. At least now they had stopped trying to find suitable Jewish husbands for her. For the time being.

Mauricio closed his booklet. "Soon I won't need a tutor."

"Well, for now, we'll stick to our regular schedule. I'll see you tomorrow bright and early. And enjoy your pastel de cumple, your birthday cake." Besides working on reading and writing in Italian, Eva was also teaching him Spanish.

Eva made her way upstairs to her attic room in the Correr mansion. Aron's brother, Daniel, had arranged her employment with Signore Correr when he learned she was lettered. The Corrers needed a tutor and Daniel needed an infusion of ducats to float a loan for an important merchant. Gregorio Correr was more obliged to give Daniel the funds when he saw how nicely Eva got along with his son. Daniel had a good reputation in the Veneto region, having established small loan-banks in numerous cities. Of course, he could never be as rich as the non-Jewish bankers, who lent great sums of money to the Church, but he was quite comfortable. He helped her parents and Beatriz move into a small flat in the Lido district, where Papá was now working for a Jewish cheesemaker. Papá's knowledge of grapes was helping to bring a new idea to cheese eaters: the right wine pairing. Mamá spent her days gathering with other Jewish women to share stories and sew. There weren't nearly as many Jewish souls here as there had been in Portugal, but there were enough for Mamá to feel a sense of camaraderie. Beatriz still prayed in church every day, mostly for Eva to get married and bear children sooner rather than later. Aron and Esther, Judah, and baby Ruth, whom the Perezes still saw regularly, remained living at Daniel's house.

Eva liked to wander the Correr hallways, crowded with devotional paintings. There were works by da Messina and Bellini. The names meant nothing to her, but she knew Diego would have been thrilled to see them. Diego once mentioned a wealthy family in Florence who were good to the Jews and patrons of artists. But she couldn't remember the name. The details of their conversations were getting harder and harder to recall. Every night she scoured her mind before she fell asleep, for any gesture, any expression, any spoken word of his she could conjure.

Signora Correr poked her head out of her bedroom. "Eva? Is that you? Can you come down here, please?"

Eva descended the stairs once more, careful not to trip. Her dresses were plainer than they had been in Trujillo, though still long. Because all Jews of the city were required to sew a distinguishing yellow circle, the size of a small round of bread, onto their clothing, Mamá felt it best not to draw too much attention to themselves with colorful fabric beneath it.

Eva's normally elegant employer leaned against the doorjamb, still in her sleeping gown, her hair uncombed. "I've just received word of my mother's passing. I must go immediately to Ferrara. Please take Mauricio to my husband's place of work and inform him. You can leave the boy with his father for the afternoon. Then hurry home. I know this isn't normally your duty, but the *bambinaia* has gone to buy food and I'm short two staff at the moment."

The *bambinaia* was the nanny, Antonella. She and Eva were friends, though no one could take the place of Atika.

"Death has terrible timing, I'm afraid," added the woman.

Indeed it did, thought Eva.

Even after nearly a year, Eva had not gotten used to the city. One could hardly call it a city, actually, but more a maze of islands connected by bridges and canals. She was forever getting lost. Alleys cut through buildings, then ended abruptly. And always there was the smell of fish penetrating her clothes even when she sprinkled her dresses with rose water.

Eva gripped Mauricio's hand as they walked through the Piazza San Marco. A spice peddler called out to them in Italian, *spezie, spezie*. Eva had picked up the language fairly easily, since it was so similar to Spanish. But when they had first arrived, Daniel spoke to them in Portuguese and even a bit of Hebrew. Out on the streets, in addition to Italian, one could hear German, French, Greek, Dalmatian, Albanian, and Arabic. Everyone seemed to be fleeing from something. Venice felt like those soups Mamá used to make when she threw in everything that was in the larder.

Despite her difficulty in navigating through town, Eva never tired of seeing the grand Palazzo Ducale, or Doge's Palace. The way the sunlight reflected off the white limestone and pink marble was nearly blinding, as if God were right there with her. But those moments were the only time she felt the presence of something greater. The Perezes did sometimes accompany Daniel to one of the *scuolas*, or sinagogas, but her heart was not in it. Without Diego in her life, Eva felt like she was merely going through the motions.

The Doge's Palace was where Signore Correr could be found most afternoons. As a member of the Great Council, he was one of four hundred wealthy Venetian families who advised the chief magistrate.

Eva and Mauricio approached the building. Wrought-iron loggias and a series of balconies dotted the imposing facade. The whole palazzo reminded Eva of a giant cake.

Mauricio made a growling sound. "Guess who I am."

"The monstrous beast that's carved into the colonnade behind you?"

"How'd you know?" he said, stomping his foot.

Eva giggled. The front entrance was locked, so they went around the side by a lagoon.

"Over there." Mauricio pointed. A door was ajar. They stepped through it and found themselves in an enormous courtyard.

A black-robed gentleman, on his way to something in a hurry, stopped abruptly. "Who let you in?" He craned his neck for anyone who might have made the grievous error of allowing them to pass.

"*Mi scusi*," began Eva. "There was no one by the *arco*."

"This is the back entrance," said the man. "I must speak to the guard, lazy man."

Mauricio spoke up. "I've come to see my father. Signore Gregorio Correr."

The boy had already acquired the imperiousness of the wealthy. No amount of tutoring could make him unlearn it.

The robed gentleman masked his surprise with an insincere smile. "Well, in that case, follow me."

Signore Correr met them outside the Senate Chamber. Once Eva had conveyed the Signora's news and dispatched Mauricio to his father, the robed man pointed her down the hallway. "Please go this direction to exit."

"Of course," mumbled Eva. The whole place was very intimidating, and she was anxious to be gone from there. But before she had walked fifty meters, a painting to her left caught her eye. She paused to admire it.

"*Fretta, signorina*. Hurry!" said the robed man behind her. "I don't have all day."

Despite his impatience, she continued to stare at the work of art. The painting was striking because it was the first time Eva had ever seen something on canvas that was not religious in nature. It showed two ladies in profile, gazing out at an unknown subject. They were surrounded by various animals and a servant boy. The pearls around the tops of the women's gowns appeared wet, as if the work had been completed yesterday. Though she knew the paint was dry, Eva had to stop herself from reaching out to touch it. One woman, in rich red velvet, perhaps the mother, was playing with two dogs. While the other younger woman, in a dress with green trim, held a white kerchief—

Eva suddenly felt weak. Could it be? That second woman. The one with auburn hair escaping the small hat she wore on her head. Her face. It was unmistakable.

It was Eva's.

44

She could hardly form words. "Wh . . . who . . . who is the artist of this painting?"

The black-robed man bore a disdainful expression. "How should I know such a thing? I do not procure the art here. I am the secretary for the Great Council."

There was no signature on the canvas, nor a plaque on the bottom of the frame. "Is there anyone else who might be able to help us?" She felt parched. Marooned on an island. Desperate for water. Like when Yuçe took back his Talmud.

He took out a watch from the pocket of his robe. "I really must get back."

She grabbed his arm. "But surely a colleague of yours will know?"

As he jerked away from her grasp, a uniformed guard appeared at the end of the corridor. "Everything all right, Signore Antonio?"

"Escort this impertinent woman out immediately. Then get back to your post." With that, the secretary returned to the chamber in a huff.

The guard gripped Eva tightly beneath her elbow and led her to the front door.

"Wait," Eva pleaded. "You don't know who painted that picture, do you?"

He continued walking. "The one with the two ladies? It arrived a few months ago."

"From where?"

He stopped. "Why, the studio of Carpaccio." He seemed proud to know the answer, prove himself worthy of his post, at least in her eyes if not the secretary general's.

"Here in Venice?" she asked.

He nodded. "Hand-delivered by the artist himself."

Eva stood befuddled in the middle of the piazza. The square was teeming with people, yet there was no one to help her. The only person she knew in Venice who might have reason to know the artist Carpaccio was Signore Correr, and she certainly could not go back inside the building and ask him for an introduction.

She began to run, not knowing her destination. Abuela's old admonition—your impulsivity will be the death of you—made her laugh. It was the only way she knew how to live. Her legs carried her across bridges and down alleyways, pausing only so she could ask strangers if they knew where Carpaccio's workroom might be. After nearly thirty minutes of what felt like going in circles, a dapper gentleman directed her to a *sotoportego*, or underpass. She emerged, panting, in front of a tall building with brick on the bottom half and ochre-colored stucco on the top. Two Moorish-shaped windows with pointed arches flanked an open door. She pushed aside the iron grating. Linseed oil and varnish assaulted her nose. To her left was a room with half a dozen men in various states of sketching or painting. Eva didn't bother to look at what was on the canvases. She scanned the faces of the painters. No one there she recognized.

She hurried to the room on the right.

A tall, broad-shouldered man, brown hair tied in a cord, stood at an easel. He held a palette in the crook of his left arm and a brush in his right hand. His back was to her.

Her breathing ceased.

There was no sound save for the pulsing in her temples.

He must have smelled roses. Because he turned around before his name even fell from her lips.

Epilogue

1530
Constantinople

A small child, dark curls falling over his eyes, runs through the sitting room where Eva works at her writing desk. At sixty-five, she is two years younger than Abuela was when she passed away. One shoulder is slightly higher than the other, but other than the wrinkles of time and her white bun, she looks much the same as she did when she was sixteen. Her Turkish friends may be content to sit in the square, drinking kahve, *but there is far too much writing to be done.*

A paper flutters down to the floor in the boy's wake. Suppler than the parchment Eva used in Trujillo, the pages bear a watermark of the Italian paper mill Fabriano. She liked the feel of it so much, she carried a ream with her when she sailed from Venice to Constantinople. Leaving Italy and migrating a third time was not her choice, but anyone listening could hear the drumbeat of the Inquisition approaching Rome. She is finished fleeing. Besides being too old to travel, she finally lives in a country where Jews are welcome.

But oh, how she misses Spain. Especially when she visits Beatriz's grave. It has been many years since her sister passed, even longer since Mamá and Papá died in Venice. Beatriz remained devoted to Eva's children until her fever returned, a remnant of the sweating sickness she contracted as a child. Though her sister is buried in a church cemetery in Constantinople, Eva always puts a rock on her headstone, the way Mamá did for Ruy in the Jewish tradition. There is no one to clean his grave now, for there are no more Jews in Spain. King Ferdinand and Queen Isabella took care of that when they expelled every last one of them in 1492.

Across from Eva, near the window of the sitting room, stands her husband, Diego. He is painting the minarets outside. They share a smile at the way their grandson, Soli, never sits still.

The boy darts outside, passing through a gate, absent-mindedly touching a tile mounted on their front post. The tile reads Benveniste, their family surname, taken from Diego's mother, Reina, before she converted.

When the nuns from the convent near the Juan de Carvajal bridge asked Diego his name, he told them Benveniste. During the two months he languished there, recovering from the cannon shot, they never knew the man they cared for was once an Altamirano. When he was strong enough to ride a horse, he went to Lisbon to look for Isabel. The couple living in the ben Cardoza house did not know where she was or where the Perez family had fled. His friend Paolo had volunteered to serve the Reconquista and died on the battlefield in Granada. Diego never received Eva's note.

He decided to sail to Florence, the city where they had planned to run away together. Perhaps she might think to look for him there. But he met the artist Vittore Carpaccio on the cargo ship. The painter had hand-delivered an altarpiece to a Portuguese church and was returning home to Venice.

Diego was out of funds. He could not refuse the apprentice-ship offer.

He watches his wife as she writes. The day she appeared at his workroom under the sotoportego *felt like divine intervention. Not free will at all. Perhaps the Christians had been right about God all along.*

1671
Amsterdam

A publisher pulls down the pressure bar on his new Dutch press. He is on the final page of this particular manuscript. The printing process has been slower than usual because he keeps stopping to read the pages. It is a stunning tale of the Spanish Inquisition. A Turkish merchant trader by the name of Nissim Benveniste brought it to his attention. The publisher knew at once it must be spread all over the world.

1739
Mexico City

A *nine-year-old girl stands with her grandfather watching the night sky. "Mira," she says—look—pointing to a particular pretty arrangement of stars. He swats her hand down. "Don't do that. Ever."*

She glances around. They are in a field. There are no people for miles. "Why not?" she asks.

He shrugs. "My mother always told me never to point at stars. She learned it from her mother, I guess."

"That doesn't make any sense," says the girl, kicking a tumbleweed. Lots of things her abuelo does are strange. Like sticking rocks on the graves of their dead horses. And refusing to eat jamón at the Christmas table. He also uses funny words like te rogo *instead of por favor. And sometimes he will tell her she was born* kon mazal i ventura, *with good luck. She knows* ventura *means fortune, but she has never heard anyone in school use the word* mazal. *She takes her grandfather's hand. It doesn't matter how funny his habits are. He is her favorite person in the world.*

MAY 1, 1863
London

A *masterpiece of Renaissance art can now be viewed at the Dulwich Picture Gallery.* Feast of the Gods, *by Giovanni Bellini. The large canvas is one of the few mythological subjects painted in Venice in the early 1500s. Rich color emphasizes the tension and eroticism of this gathering of Jupiter, Mercury, and others, based on a story by the Roman poet Ovid. The Duke of Ferrara, who commissioned the painting, asked for two of the gods to be clothed differently and Bellini refused. Art historians have identified an area that has been reworked by, they believe, one or more artists in Bellini's school, possibly either Dosso Dossi or the Jew, Diego Benveniste. See if you can spot it. Exhibition runs through June 2.*

—*Art critic Sir Malcolm Fitzgerald,* Times of London

1920
Los Angeles

On a chilly day in February, a small group of men gather in an auditorium on Grand Avenue in downtown Los Angeles to worship. They call themselves Comunidad Sefardi. Among them are immigrants from Turkey, Algeria, Greece, and Egypt. So that everyone understands one another, they speak in Ladino, or judizmo, a mixture of Hebrew and Spanish.

The president of the group asks everyone to take their seat.

The rabbi, Abraham Caraco, clears his throat. "Te rogo," he says. "If you please. Let us begin."

2020
New York City

An auburn-haired teacher in her midthirties wears stylish glasses over bright, wide-set eyes. She stands in front of twenty-eight students of AP History at Stuyvesant High School. She is mostly fun-loving, except when it comes to history. Then she likes to say she's as serious as a cavalry attack.

"Will everyone please turn to chapter twelve in your books?"

An opening of backpacks, scuffing of chair legs, and rustling of paper as the students get on the same page.

The book is an epic poem. Like Homer's Odyssey, *told in verse, but in the author's own words. Consisting of 130 pages, it tells the story of a young woman of sixteen on the eve of the Spanish Inquisition. Though official records of prisoner confessions transcribed by the Inquisitors themselves do exist in the town halls of many pueblos of Spain, this book is one of only a few firsthand accounts and is considered to be the definitive primary source of what happened to the Jews of Spain.*

The author is Eva Perez Benveniste. The epic poem is the history teacher's favorite part of the curriculum because the book happens to have been written by her great-great-great-great—she has lost count of how many greats—grandmother.

One of the more talkative students, a girl in the back, blurts out a question. "Why did she title her book Call Me Eva?*"*

By way of an answer, the teacher adjusts her glasses and reads aloud from her favorite passage.

Born Isabel, daughter of Benita,
Now, a daughter of Qasmūna.
My Hebrew name means mother of life.
I have borne four children, which is strife
enough
for those who know the pain of childbirth.
But perhaps, I have given breath
to something more lasting.
May the words inked on these pages
make you never forget, dear Reader.
For history is bound to repeat itself
unless we learn from our mistakes.
You can begin by calling me Eva.

Author's Note

In 2016, my husband and I, along with our youngest son, moved to Madrid for a year. Ever since I was a little girl, Madrid has held a special place in my heart. When I was five years old, my grandfather, Sam White, produced a "Paella Western" movie in Madrid, entitled *White Comanche*. It starred William Shatner, who played twin brothers, one a peyote-loving warring outlaw, and the other, the good guy Comanche, who must fight his own brother to save the town. I can't say this movie was a hit—in fact it's listed in *The Official Razzie Movie Guide* as one of the one hundred most enjoyably bad movies ever made—but it did spark my family's lifelong passion for Spain. After nine months of shooting, my grandfather disembarked from the plane in Los Angeles and I didn't recognize him. He'd grown a mustache, wore a debonair hat, and carried gifts for my sister and me—namely polka-dotted flamenco dresses with matching shoes, peinetas, and castanets. The other fascination with Spain came from my mother's first cousin, Anthony Brand, who was a bullfighter. I listened to enchanting stories from my grandparents about their time in Madrid, along with tales of cousin Tony in the ring. So it was only natural that when my husband and I were looking for an adventure, coupled with a desire to immerse our son in a foreign language, we chose Madrid. In the first few months of living there, we traveled to Toledo and Segovia. Upon seeing the Sepharad plaques marking certain streets as parts of the Jewish quarters, I became curious. What happened to all the Jews of Spain? Where were their descendants now? I didn't know much about the Inquisition and devoured as many books as I could. I dragged my family to every Jewish quarter we could find. I listened eagerly to the stories of our friend Daniel Mazin, whose father founded the Orthodox Synagogue in Madrid in 1968. I began looking at the history of the Spanish Jews in the context of my own family. Though I was born Ashkenazi (my ancestors came from Romania, Hungary, and Russia), I was raised for most of my life by a Sephardic man who married my mother and adopted my sister and me after our biological father passed away. His grandmother, Fortuna Gormezano, was from Istanbul. I remember her singing Ladino songs with gusto and peppering her conversation with sayings like *"vaya con miel,"* go with honey, and *"horas buenas,"* literally good hours, but more like a wish for good health, like "God bless you" when someone sneezes. Her daughter, my Grandma Corene, née Columbia, cooked the most delectable *biscochos,* Spanish rice, spinach frittata, and bourekas.

Living in Spain helped me come full circle—to the stories from my Ashkenazi side and the culture of my Sephardic side. When I returned home to Los Angeles after our sabbatical, I asked myself this question: What if I had been a sixteen-year-old girl living in Spain on the eve of the Inquisition and fell in love with the wrong man? I decided to set my story in Trujillo because it is a microcosm of what was going on in Spain at the time—a midsize town in a vital region of Castile, populated by Jews, Christians, and Moors who became involved in the schemes and politics of the Crown.

The Spanish Inquisition began in 1481 and lasted until 1834. Autos de fe occurred in Spain, Portugal, and Spain's colonies, Peru and Mexico, into the mid-eighteenth century.

Two hundred years later, Spain has made amends for this

dark part of her history. In 1992, King Juan Carlos prayed with the Jewish community of Madrid on the five hundredth anniversary of the Alhambra Decree, when King Ferdinand and Queen Isabella forced the Jews of Spain to leave. "May hatred and intolerance never again provoke expulsion or exile," he said. "On the contrary, let us be capable of building a prosperous Spain in peace among ourselves on the basis of concord and mutual respect . . . That is my most fervent wish. Peace for all. Shalom." And recently, Spain passed a law giving Spanish nationality to any Jew of Sephardic descent who can prove a family connection to medieval Spain. My adoptive father's brother actually went through the process and now has dual citizenship.

Tragically, there are still places in the world where religious tolerance is not practiced. According to the Pew Research Center, today, citizens of fifty-two countries experience very high levels of government restrictions on religion. As I write this, over one million Chinese Uighurs are being held in internment camps because they believe in Islam. Religious minorities in fifty-six other countries suffer from hostilities originating from social groups or individuals calling for their elimination.

Until we accept the "other" in our midst, we will never truly be free.

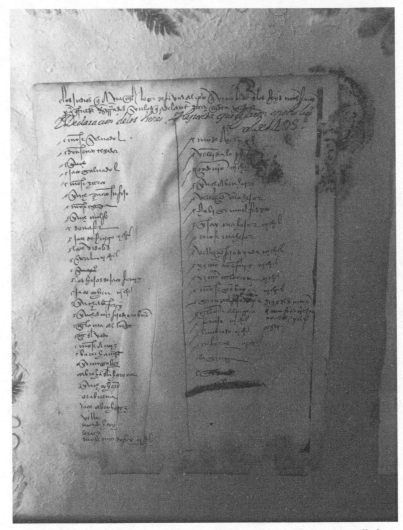

A copy (in the original handwriting) of the list of Jews who were expelled from Trujillo, dated 1493. The translation of old Spanish at the top reads: *The following list of Jews who were still in Hervas, at the time of the coming of the mercy of the Kings our Lords, were banished. (photo courtesy of Cambria Gordon)*

Hebrew letters over the original doorway of a former synagogue in Trujillo, which is now a pharmacy. The inscription reads: *This is the gate of the Lord. The just will enter through it. (photo courtesy of Cambria Gordon)*

The author's feet next to one of many plaques marking the spots where Jewish-owned homes were located in Hervas. *(photo courtesy of Cambria Gordon)*

The author's great-grandmother Fortuna Gormezano (center), with her parents, David and Esther, in Çanakkale, Turkey, around 1905. *(photo courtesy of the collection of Neil Cohen)*

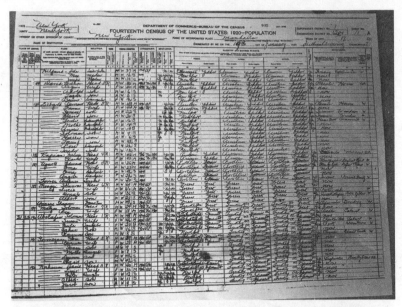

New York census form from 1920, indicating Sam Gormezano, Fortuna's brother, as head of the household. It lists place of birth as Turkey and Spanish as the language spoken in the home. *(photo courtesy of the collection of Neil Cohen)*

Movie poster from the author's grandfather's 1968 movie, filmed outside of Madrid. *(Producciones Cinematográficas A.B.)*

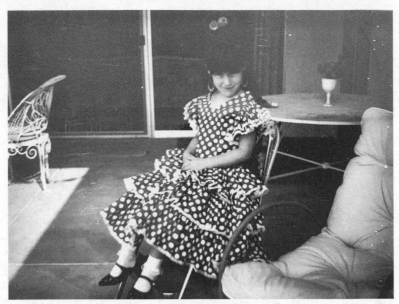

The author, age five, at home in Encino in her flamenco dress, shoes, and peineta from Madrid. *(photo courtesy of Sharleen Cooper Cohen)*

RESEARCH NOTES

I relied heavily on a wonderful book, *Trujillo: A Jewish Community in Extremadura on the Eve of the Expulsion from Spain*, by Haim Beinart. I owe a debt of gratitude to Beinart's painstaking document research from the Trujillo archives. In addition, Erna Paris's book *The End of Days: A Story of Tolerance, Tyranny and the Expulsion of the Jews from Spain* proved invaluable to me.

I first came across the poetess Qasmūna from the Jewish Women's Archive (JWA), a national organization dedicated to collecting and promoting the extraordinary stories of Jewish women. I knew immediately that I wanted to incorporate her into Isabel's family somehow. Further research on Qasmūna's life and poetry came from the *International Journal of Middle East Studies*, published by Cambridge University Press. I discovered other female poets in an academic paper by Asma Afsaruddin entitled *Poetry and Love: The Feminine Contribution in Muslim Spain*.

The JWA website was also where I learned about the Cairo Genizah. Because it is forbidden to throw away anything with God's name written on it, ancient Jews had a custom of burying their books and manuscripts. The Cairo Genizah was discovered in a synagogue storeroom in Egypt in 1792. Inside were fragments of documents and texts describing all aspects of religious, cultural, and economic Jewish life in North Africa and Europe from the year 950 to 1250. Some of the evidence found in the Genizah is letters from Spanish women who wrote home after they left Spain. This helped build a case for Isabel being lettered.

Though the artist Pedro Berruguete lived in Spain during this time period and indeed painted an auto de fe, all his dialogue is imagined.

All New Testament passages are from the Latin Vulgate Bible, which was what the Spanish Church used at the time.

The actual date of the Easter Massacre of Rossio Square in Lisbon was 1506. I moved it up to 1482 for purposes of the story. Though King John II ruled Portugal in 1482 and did allow hundreds of Spanish Jews to take refuge there, I placed King Manuel on the throne in the book, as he was the one who returned from his summer residence after the massacre.

Juan Carlos, Beatriz's love interest, chooses another girl, Magdalena de Espina. I named her after Alphonso de Espina, Franciscan author of *Fortalitium Fidei*. The popular Latin tractate is considered one of the most significant works of anti-Semitism and a key factor in the development of the converso controversy. Author Rosa Doval says it was a true medieval best seller.

Carpaccio's painting *Two Venetian Ladies* sits in the Correr Museum in St. Mark's Square. It was completed in 1495, slightly later than I have it in the book. Though art experts have confirmed it was part of a domestic diptych panel depicting a hunting scene above it, no one has been able to determine definitively who the women were.

The Correr family arrived in Venice in the ninth century. Besides being members of the Great Council who helped elect the Doges, Corrers served as cardinals, popes, diplomats, and art collectors.

In the epilogue, the article in the *Times of London* is fictional, but the painting is not. *Feast of the Gods* by Giovanni

Bellini came out of the Venetian School, a style of painting widely credited with contributing to the Renaissance movement's groundbreaking use of color. It is believed that either Dosso Dossi or Titian painted over some of Bellini's figures because the Duke of Ferrara, who commissioned the work, asked for the change. Because the duke and his wife wore jewelry forged by a well-known Jewish goldsmith, Salomone, I posited that he, the duke, would welcome having someone Jewish work on his painting.

The Sephardic Community of Los Angeles, led by Rabbi Caraco, did gather downtown in February of 1920, and years later formed Synagogue Tifereth Israel. Though I imagine many words were said that day, *te rogo* may or may not have been two of them.

POETRY CITATIONS

P. 2: *A lifetime without love* . . . excerpted from Shams of Tabriz, Persian Muslim poet who lived from 1185 to 1248.

P. 91: *O gazelle, you who graze* . . . Qasmūna Bint Ismail ibn Bagdalah, twelfth-century Jewish poetess.

Pp. 95–96: *By God, I am suited to great things* . . . excerpted from Wallādah bint al-Mustakfi billāh, poetess of Córdoba who died in 1087.

P. 107: *The wind has made a coat* . . . Al-I'timad, wife of the ruler of Seville in the eleventh century.

P. 185: *O brother of the full moon* . . . Wallādah bint al-Mustakfi billāh, poetess of Córdoba who died in 1087.

P. 261: *If the cedars have caught fire* . . . The Babylonian Talmud, third to fifth centuries.

Pp. 270–71: *until the day wanes and the sun coats its silver* . . . line excerpted from Moses ibn Ezra, "Wine Song for Spring."

P. 323: *Yes, Time—ate up my heart* . . . excerpted and edited from Judah Abravanel, Jewish physician, poet, and philosopher, 1503.

SUGGESTIONS FOR FURTHER READING

Nonfiction

Daily Life During the Spanish Inquisition, James M. Anderson, Greenwood Press, 2002

The End of Days: A Story of Tolerance, Tyranny and the Expulsion of the Jews from Spain, Erna Paris, Prometheus Books, 1995

History of the Jews in Venice, Cecil Roth, The Jewish Publication Society of America, 1930

A Medieval Home Companion: Housekeeping in the Fourteenth Century, translated and edited by Tania Bayard, Harper Perennial, 1992

Misera Hispania: *Jews and* Conversos *in Alonso de Espina's* Fortalitium Fidei, Rosa Vidal Doval, Society for the Study of Medieval Languages and Literature, Oxford, 2013

Trujillo: A Jewish Community in Extremadura on the Eve of the Expulsion from Spain, Haim Beinart, Magnes Press, Hebrew University, 1980

Fiction

The Ghost of Hannah Mendes, Naomi Ragen, St. Martin's Press, 1998

Incantation, Alice Hoffman, Little, Brown, 2006

The Last Jew, Noah Gordon, St. Martin's Press, 2000

The Last Kabbalist of Lisbon, Richard Zimler, Overlook Press, 1998

The Mapmaker's Daughter, Laurel Corona, Sourcebooks, 2014

The People of the Book, Geraldine Brooks, Viking, 2008

Acknowledgments

This book would never have been conceived were it not for our friends Daniel Mazin and Gitty Daneshvari. They took us to the Extremadura region of Spain and arranged a converso guide to show us the Jewish quarters of Hervas, Trujillo, and Cáceres.

Thank you to the talented writers and illustrators of Barbara Bottner's table: Antoinette, Barbara, Beth, Denise, Gail, Hillary, Jim, and Michael. You added depth to my words and kicked my butt.

Julie Krone explained the intricacies of horse riding in the fifteenth century.

Dr. Peter Weller, a true Renaissance man, guided me to the Correr family and all things Venice.

Rabbi Morley Feinstein pored through the entire manuscript and imparted his Talmudic expertise.

Karen Friedman read early pages and kept me honest with my Spanish.

Ken Blady gave a wonderful class on the Crypto-Jews of Spain and answered my pestering emails.

The ucLADINO organization at UCLA taught me how to translate Aljamiado.

Neil Cohen generously shared his photos and years of research on the Gormezano family.

Noa Bannick related the story of her Sephardic grandmother, who never let her point to the stars, a remnant from when the Inquisition was spying on conversos.

Fonda Snyder, gentle yet tough agent extraordinaire, sold this book with aplomb.

Lisa Sandell, ridiculously talented editor and beautiful human, saw the importance in this story.

My parents, Marty and Sharleen, have never stopped encouraging me.

And finally, thank you to the fabulous foursome—Howard, Micah, Arlo, and Capp. You give me reason to wake up each morning. Os amo.

ABOUT THE AUTHOR

Cambria Gordon is the coauthor of *The Down-to-Earth Guide to Global Warming*, winner of the national Green Earth Book Award. She has written for *Los Angeles Times Magazine, Boys' Life, Parent Guide News*, and the *Jewish Journal* of Los Angeles. She lived in Spain for a year but spends most of her time in LA with her husband and youngest son while being as near as possible to her two adult children without annoying them.

31901066875743